ITHANI

LIMINAL SKY: OBERON CYCLE BOOK 3

J. SCOTT COATSWORTH

Published by
Other Worlds Ink
PO Box 19341, Sacramento, CA 95819

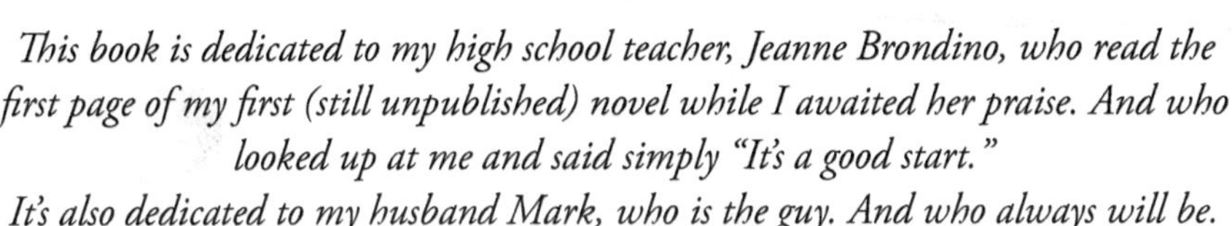

This book is dedicated to my high school teacher, Jeanne Brondino, who read the first page of my first (still unpublished) novel while I awaited her praise. And who looked up at me and said simply "It's a good start."
It's also dedicated to my husband Mark, who is the guy. And who always will be.

CONTENTS

ACKNOWLEDGMENTS

I want to acknowledge the village of folks who made this happen, especially my beta readers—Angel Martinez, Mary Newman, and Sadie Rose Bermingham, as well as Lynn West, whose belief in me in a small hotel room in Orlando, Florida, helped launch not one series, but two, and the never flagging efforts of Gus Li, my tireless editor, cheerleader, and map maker.

For this second edition, I also want to thank Kelley York of Sleepy Fox Designs, who helped me craft the wonderful covers for these rereleases.

PRINCIPAL CHARACTERS (GLOSSARY AT END)

Alia (PA Nix): Guard in Gaelan

Alix Preston (PA Erissa): Xander's ex, a lander man missing for a year

Angie/Angela: Jameson's PA

Ari: Quince's PA

Braice: One of the original Skythane settlers

Daia: One of the original Skythane settlers

Danielle (Dani) Black (PA Hera): One of the lander enforcers in Gaelan, daughter of Danner Black

Davyn Sléite: Xander's Gaelani name

Derren Sevvins: OberCorp employee/tech who helps Mylin

DOC (Digital Oberon Corporation AI): The AI that runs OberCorp's semi-autonomous grid

Erina: One of the ithani Xander and Jameson encounter

Erissa: Alix's PA

Hera: Dani Black's PA

Jameson Havercamp (PA Angie): Psych from Beta Tau who comes to investigate pith shortage on Oberon

Jessa: Jameson's fiancée on Beta Tau

Jirron (also Thshnel'Jirron): King of the ithani

Kadin Tamain: The chamberlain of the House of the Moon

Lyrin Madainn: Jameson's birth name

Morgan: Mysterious child Xander finds on Oberon

Mylin (PA Zim): Young skythane girl who helps Xander

Nix: Alia's PA

Quince Farrai (PA Ari): Xander's skythane friend who joins the quest

Robyn Sléite: Queen of the Gaelani and mother to Xander, and Quince's former lover

Rogan Horth: Syndicate boss who has history with Xander

Smythe: An OberCorp enforcer
Tally: One of Tanner's friends from Egeus
Tanner: Morgan's human host
Taz: Venin's PA
Thshnel'Jirron: see Jirron
Tovey: Guard at the OberCorp headquarters armory
Venin Araio (PA Taz): Guard in Gaelan
Vestra Halta: Acting Regent of Errian
Xander Kinnson (PA Ravi): Skythane who works in Oberon City, embarks on a quest with Jameson
Zim: Mylin's PA

A NOTE ABOUT ITHANI PRONOUNS

The Ithani have a complex (to us) system of pronouns and relationships.

Three ithani are required to bear a child. These are ze / zer / zers (roughly analogous to she / her / hers—the one who provides the egg), zi / zim / zis (he / him / his—the one who provides the fertilization), and za / zaf / zas (no human equivalent—the one who provides the organs to carry the child to term).

In addition, when pregnancy occurs, the three forms unite into one (zee / zeer / zeers) until the child comes to term.

OBERON

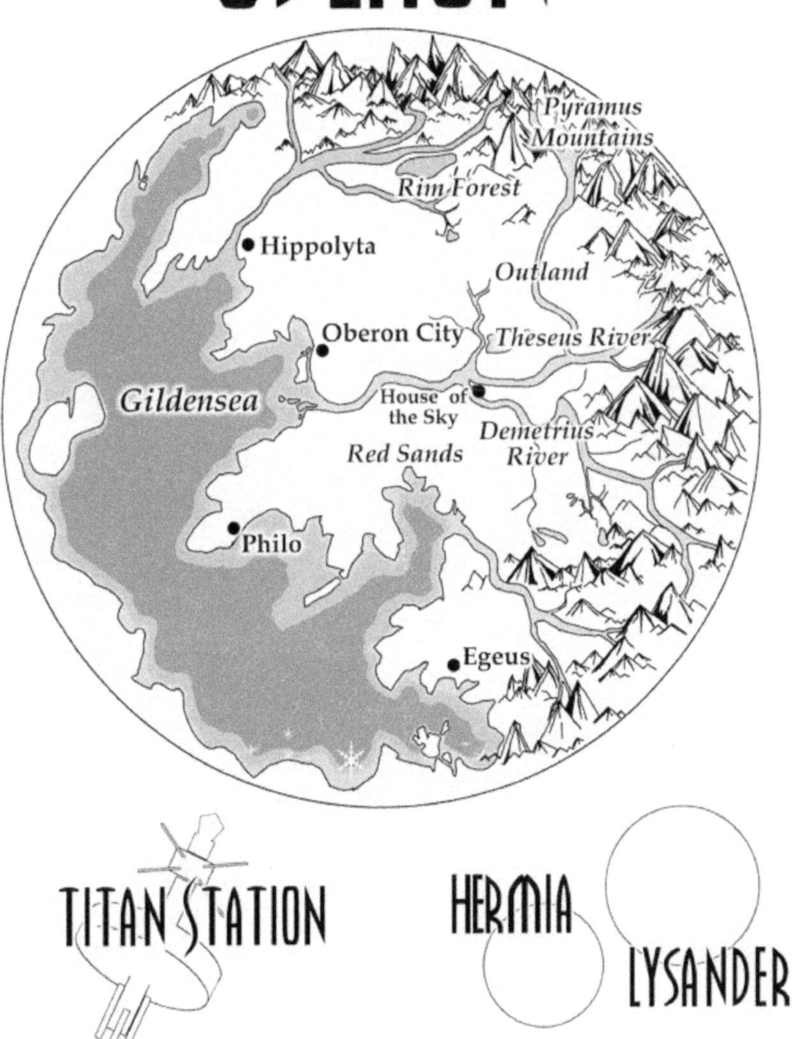

TITAN STATION

HERMIA

LYSANDER

TITANIA

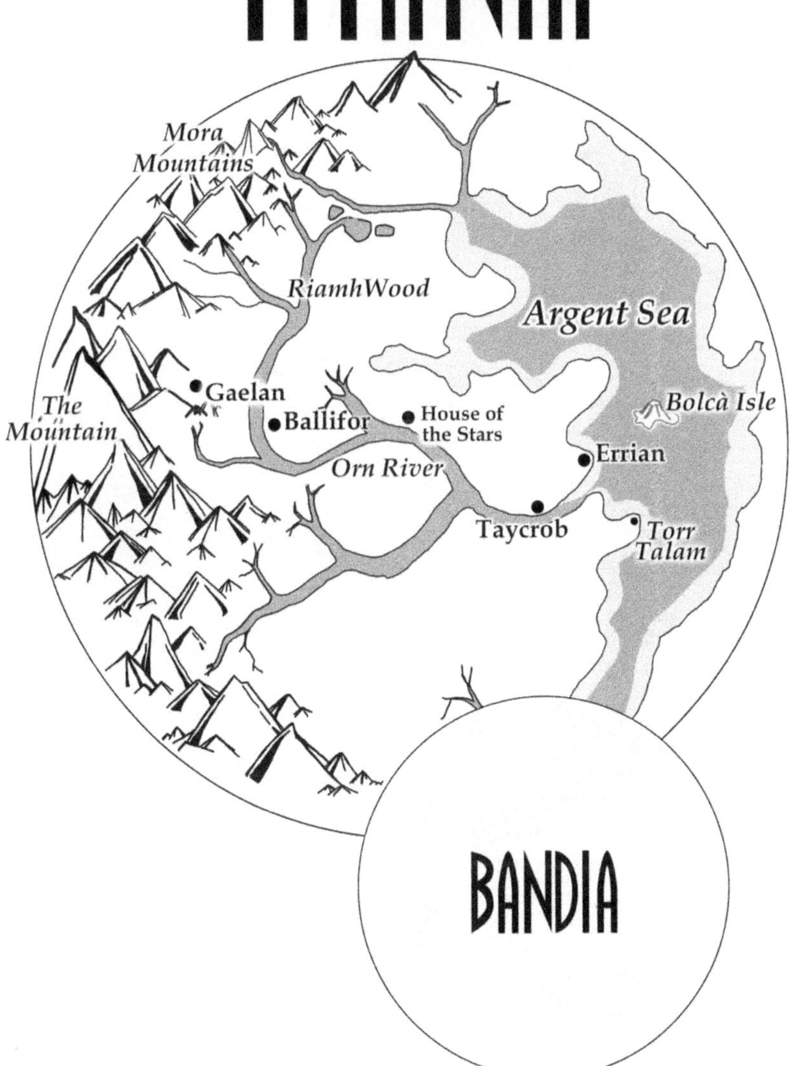

BANDIA

FOREWORD

We've now come full circle - the full Oberon Cycle trilogy is available again under my own publishing banner, Other Worlds Ink.

This book represented another first for my writing career - the first trilogy-ender. When I started the Oberon Cycle with "Skythane," I knew it would be a trilogy, but I only had a loose outline to show for a plot. Bu the time I finished writing "Lander," book two in the series, I had set up so many different plot threads that I was sure I'd never be able to wrap them up.

Still, I soldiered on, and the book you hold in your hands (or in your kindle) is the result. I think I managed to get everything connected and answered all the questions by the end of the book. If I missed anything, please let me know.

I am enormously proud to have reached this milestone, and look forward to releasing some new books next year.

I hope you enjoy "Ithani."

PROLOGUE

Now it is the time of night
That the graves all gaping wide,
Every one lets forth his sprite,
In the church-way paths to glide:
And we fairies, that do run
By the triple Hecate's team,
From the presence of the sun,
Following darkness like a dream.

—William Shakespeare,
A Midsummer Night's Dream

Erina's iridescent wings fluttered in distress.

The time of the Great Migration was almost upon them. Overhead, the sun turned redder day by day. Soon it would unleash a torrent of heat and radiation that would destroy the ithani, the Heart, and Erro itself.

Ze had foreseen the end of the war years before and had passed zer knowledge on to Thshnel'Jirron, trusting *zi* to protect them all. But *zis* plan had gone too far, and soon the ithani would destroy themselves in a bid for immortality.

Only zi would survive, immensely more powerful than now. A virtual vengeful god.

Ze had seen that, too, but it had come to zer far too late.

Each generation of the ithani had a seer, and ze had been born from the Heart with that heavy responsibility upon zer small shoulders. Even a seer didn't know everything about what was to pass. Only the bits and pieces that were passed on to zer from the *athrà*. Besides Jirron, no one else knew ze had the gift.

Something, or someone, was coming, ze didn't know what yet, but ze could feel it in zer bones.

Ze was at a loss for what to do next. Ze let out a whoosh of breath, resigned to waiting. It would come to zer, the vision she needed. When the gods thought it was time.

Until then, ze would keep zer wings low to the ground and do nothing further to draw attention.

Dani peered through the hoversport visor, trying to make out the way ahead through the falling snow.

Flying the hoversport, she and Kadin had crossed over the Riamhwood and into the northern plains without incident, only to run into this abominable blizzard. Gusts of wind sideswiped the little craft, snow flurries cutting her vision down to meters at times. She fought back, holding it as steady as she could.

"Are you sure about this?" Kadin looked a bit green. Used to being out in the fresh air, she supposed.

"This isn't over. They killed my father." Truth be told, Danner Black had always been an arrogant bastard. He'd beaten her on three separate occasions as a child.

Blood was blood.

"With the company and the skythane standing arm in arm, we're screwed —unless we align ourselves with someone else, and quick."

"Who?"

She grinned. "Whatever lives up here in the north. You didn't think this planet split itself in half, did you?"

He shook his head. "But whoever—or whatever—did it has to be long dead."

"What if they're not? That bitch queen of Gaelan got her wings back from somewhere. That kind of tech's pretty advanced. What if the old masters of this planet are back?"

Kadin whistled. "Then we should probably run as far as we can away from them." He took her hand. "Look, why don't we run away, find a place in the mountains? Let them fight this mess out among themselves?" He touched her cheek. "I don't care about anything else. I just want to be with you."

She pushed him away gently. "No, you're not thinking this through." She sighed. Kadin had been essential to her plans in Gaelan, but she didn't love him. Did she? "We're trapped in a whole different universe, and we don't know the rules. We're wanted by almost every human on the planet. What if these… whatever they are. What if they're stronger than OberCorp? Stronger than those two Split-damned prophesied kings?"

A smile spread across his face. "Then they might welcome allies who know almost everything about OberCorp and the skythane."

"Exactly." She grinned. "We have leverage, and maybe we can carve out a little bit of this world all for ourselves, if not the whole fucking thing." She felt better than she had in weeks. Things were finally starting to go her way. *To fly again.*

Bright light flooded the interior of the hoversport as the storm clouds lifted. Their destination lay before them. It was a gigantic, snow-covered mountain, fifty kilometers ahead. The landscape all around was a rose-tinted white, reflecting sunlight into her eyes and almost blinding her. "Hera, dim the plas!"

"Yes, Dani," her PA responded, and the brightness dimmed to an acceptable level.

A thunderous rumbling roared outside the shuttle, loud enough that it shook the tiny craft.

"What the hell is that?" Kadin peered out through the window.

"It sounds like a shuttle engine."

"But a thousand times stronger. Look!"

Dani followed his gaze.

The mountain itself seemed to glow. The light increased, arriving with a great humming sound that pierced Dani's ears.

She threw her hands up to cover them, but she couldn't keep out the sound.

Dani screamed.

Then the light cut off, and the shuttle's controls went dark. Dani glanced over at Kadin. He was slumped back in his seat. Frantically she tried to get the craft to respond, to level out.

Then it crashed into the snow, and her awareness of the world slammed shut.

1

BEGINNINGS

Venin stood under the dome of the chapel, the waters of the Orn rushing past the small island to crash over the edge of the crater rim, where they fell a thousand meters to the broken city of Errian below.

The Erriani chapel was different from what he was used to back home. The Gaelani chapel in Gaelan had sat at the top of a tall pillar of stone, open to the night sky, a wide space of grass and trees that intertwined in a natural dome through which moonlight filtered down to make dappled shadows on the ground.

This chapel, instead, was a wonder of streaming sunlight, the columns a polished eggshell marble with glimmering seams of gold. Red creeper vines climbed up the columns, festooned with clusters of yellow flowers that gave off a sweet scent.

Both were bright and airy, but the Erriani chapel lay under a dome supported by fluted marble columns, a painted arch of daytime sky and the rose-colored sun blazing overhead.

The last time he'd gone to chapel had been with Tazim, before his untimely death.

Long before the troubles that roiled the world now.

Something drew him back. A need to reconnect with his past. To bridge the gap between then and now, between who he was and who he had become. Taz would have liked this place.

The chapel here had survived the attack, while much of Errian had not. The city below was a jumble of broken corrinder, the multistory plants that were the main building stock for the city. They would grow again, but the sight of the city's beautiful white towers laid low struck him to the core.

So had Gaelan looked, after the flood.

Venin turned back to the chapel and unlaced his boots, baring his muscular calves before he approached the fountain that splashed at its center. The cool flagstone beneath his feet sent a shiver up his spine, and green moss filled the gaps between the stones.

Some builder whose name was lost to time had tapped into the river itself to make the fountain run, and the water leapt into the air with a manic energy around the golden statue of Erro, before falling back down to the pool.

Venin knelt at the fountain's edge on one of the well-worn pads, laid his hands in the shallow water, and let his wings rest over himself, making a private place to pray.

Erro and Gael, spare us from danger and lift us up into the sky with your powerful wings. He gave Erro deference, being that this was his chapel, but he hoped Gael would hear him too. The god of his own people had been known to intervene in mortal affairs before, and if what Quince had told them about these *ithani* was true, they would need all the help they could get.

Venin's wings warmed.

He looked up in astonishment to see the statue of Erro giving off an intense golden glow. His mouth dropped open, and he stood and stared at its beautiful male curves and muscles. Maybe the gods were answering him.

Venin reached up and touched the statue's outstretched hand. The shock knocked him backward onto his ass, and he hit the ground hard, slamming into one of the marble columns.

Venin groaned, stunned, and reached back to feel his wings and spine. He seemed to be in one piece.

Taz would have laughed his ass off at the whole thing.

After a moment he sat up cautiously. He wrapped his arms around his legs and stared up at the statue, his chin on his knees.

The glow was gone.

Did I imagine it? He stood and felt the back of his head. A lump was already forming there. *That's gonna leave a mark.*

Something had changed. Venin didn't know what yet, but he was sure of that much.

He pulled his boots back on and laced them up. With one last suspicious glare at the statue, he turned and stepped out of the chapel, taking a deep breath of the moisture-laden air.

Then he leapt into the sky to soar down to the broken city.

MORGAN SLIPPED OUT from behind one of the wide columns and watched the man go.

Erro was laid out at his feet. The city below was in ruins, but it would rise again, given time.

He was a nimfeach, protector and agent of the ithani, but he felt a bond with these humans, lander and skythane both.

When he'd first begun his part of the plan, it had seemed simple enough. Lead the skythane to their prophesied destiny and bring the world back together as one.

He'd never thought to question the plan.

Not until Jameson had held his hand and begged him to spare Quince's life. Something had shifted in him then. Something had awoken.

It had caused him no end of trouble. Suddenly he was no longer sure of himself. No longer secure in the plan. He'd even started to question the things he'd been told all along. How the world had been split. Who had caused it, and even if the plan was right at all.

Things came to him in short bursts. Things that might happen. Things he should do.

It was why he'd given Quince the master key, the one he had discovered underneath Freyyr, the mountain in the north where the ithani slumbered.

He dreamed of the future, of the Great Migration, when the ithani would leave this mortal plane.

If it went ahead, thousands would die. People he knew. People who had come to call him friend.

The old Morgan could have lived with that. Probably wouldn't have even noticed it.

There was something stirring in him, though, something that was causing him to reevaluate everything and to take his own steps outside of the plan to find out if it was *right*.

Something named Tanner.

. . .

ALIX STARED out at Oberon City through the thick window of his mother's huge white top-floor office. A long crack ran down the plas at an angle, left by the enormous storm that had borne down on the city after the shift.

Alix snorted. It was an apt metaphor for the world, imperfectly fused and pushed to the point of breaking.

Oberon City had fared better than either Errian or Gaelan, but only due to geography and the fact that it hadn't been subject to a full-scale enemy assault. Still, the tempest that had descended upon Erro after the shift had taken its toll, as had the more recent shaking.

It felt like the end days.

Not that Alix had ever been much of a religious man. His mother believed in one thing—power—and had respected religion only inasmuch as it might help her gain more.

Now she was locked up until he could figure out what the hell to do with her. He ignored her grid calls, but sooner or later they were going to have a reckoning.

People were protesting on the streets below, outside the wide moat that protected the company headquarters. Food wasn't a problem in the city yet. The company had warehouses full of boxcorn and rasswheat processed and ready for off-world shipping to some of the frontier worlds, and Alix had opened the doors to the general population with orders to give out whatever they had. He figured they had enough to keep things going for a few weeks, if they rationed it. By then, either things would be returning to normal, or there would be no more need for food. *Worry about that later.*

He'd ordered the troops home from Errian, those who had survived the unfortunate and misguided war with the skythane. They were being pressed into duty as peacekeepers here in the city, but they were spread really thin. By the Split, he hoped he could keep a lid on things for a little while. *Just a few days.*

Jameson's message, run up to Alix by a courier, had been cryptic. *Imminent danger from the north. Meet in three hours at OCHQ. Need new cirqs, prep for imminent mission.*

What the hell? Alix cursed and paced back and forth in front of the floor-to-ceiling plas windows. Being trapped behind a desk grated on him after more than a year out in the world. He needed to be out there seeing things for himself, not relying on a few scattered reports from the field.

Those reports were just starting to come back from the few scouts he'd been able to field. They showed widespread damage to populated areas and food crops, as well as activity along previously unknown fault lines across the now reunified globe. In particular, a series of new trenches had opened up in the Outland, east of Oberon City.

"Message from Trevor Hass," Erissa, his PA, whispered in his ear.

"What does it say?"

"It came tagged with a memory file. Would you like to experience it?"

Alix closed his eyes. "Yes, please."

Just like that, he rode in Trevor's head, seeing what the ranger saw. It was grainy—limited bandwidth between the hoversport and OberCorp HQ, most likely.

The ground was covered in snow that sparkled rose in the fading evening light, but up ahead....

Alix gasped.

What looked like it had once been a mountain was split open, and a bright golden light radiated from inside the earth. Ghostly forms flew up into the air and then back down into the strange crater, flickering like candlelight.

"Trevor, what the hell is that?" Alix asked the ranger.

"I don't know." Trevor's voice was flat. Calm. Too calm. They'd trained together, and that meant nothing good. "Nothing I've ever seen before, that's for Split-damned sure. Should we go closer for a better look?"

"No. Stay for as long as you can. When your power core gets low, come back. But do *not* put yourselves in danger, any more than is necessary." They couldn't spare any more hoversports, and he'd be damned if he'd jeopardize his men to no apparent purpose.

"Yes, sir. Thank you, sir."

Alix cut the connection and sat back in his mother's chair. He had so much theoretical power, and yet he was impotent in the face of fast-racing changes he didn't understand.

Alix was a visual guy. He liked to see the problem with his own eyes and then tackle it head-on. Now, without satellite coverage, he was blind and impotent. He closed his eyes. *Xander, I could really use your steadying presence right now.*

That ship had long since warped away. The sooner he got over it and moved on, the better. "Erissa, when will our guests arrive?"

"In about half an hour. I've set up conference room seventeen for your meeting."

"Perfect." He nodded. Quince, Xander, and Jameson would have some answers. Something he could wrap his head around.

Then he could figure out what the hell he was supposed to do.

2
———

UP FROM THE RUINS

Jᴀᴍᴇ̶s... Jɪʀʀᴏɴ's ᴇʏᴇs opened.

Zis mouth was dry as the dust of Avea, Erro's airless red moon. A nimfeach busied itself checking zis vitals. Zi didn't recognize it.

Something had gone wrong. Jirron could feel it. Zi queried the Heart. *How long have I been asleep?*

The answer was slow coming back. *One hundred three thousand, two hundred forty-four cycles.*

Zi blinked, expressing zis displeasure. Zi sat up, ripping the nourishing leads out of zis flesh. Zi struck, catching the nimfeach by the thorax and shoving it against the wall, breaking one of its wings. *Why was I asleep for so long?*

It whimpered under the pressure from zis hand as zis three claws dug into it. *The shift went awry.*

A hundred thousand years.

The energy released by the amalite core during the shift was fatal to the ithani if they were awake and unshielded.

The nimfeach were immune—they were half made of amalite, after all. But zi'd insisted on a failsafe for zis own safety, so that none of the ithani sleepers would awaken until the shift was completed.

Zi hissed. A failsafe that had cost zim a hundred millennia. *And now?*

The humans helped us complete the shift. Green ichor dripped down the white wall from the broken wing.

Humans? What are humans? Much had changed since zi had gone to sleep, although for zim it had seemed a matter of hours. Jirron queried the Heart and got back a burst of data. Zi closed zis eyes and let go of the nimfeach as zi digested the news.

The nimfeach fell to the ground with a sickening thunk.

Humans. An outsider race that had come to Erro while zi slept.

Zi had seen their like before, zi was sure of it, but zis sleep-drunk memory was fuzzy on the details. Zi blinked zis displeasure, cursing zis now ancient body. The sleep had retarded the aging process, but still zi felt slow, used. *Old.*

Jirron had all the data, but zi needed more. Zi needed a new host.

Zi opened zis eyes. The nimfeach stared up at zim, quivering. *I need a human.*

There are two of them here. Its left wing dragged on the ground.

Bring them to me. Zi dismissed the nimfeach, turning away as it dragged itself from the room.

Things had clearly changed. Zi needed to know how much before zi initiated the Great Migration.

Jameson drifted.

Bits of memory—his own this time—flashed past.

Finding a box full of memories in his mother's closet when he was little. Staring out at the red sands on Tander's World. Kneeling in church on Beta Tau, the white sunlight streaming through the gradient-phased windows to fill the room with colors like a kaleidoscope.

The first time he'd seen Xander.

The ground underneath him shook and subsided, bringing him out of his half-conscious state. His eyes flickered open.

"Hey, handsome." Xander stared down at him.

"Hey." He was lying in Xander's lap, the púca tree's big purple leaves fluttering in the ocean breeze. For a moment, he was wrapped in a perfect cocoon of time, safe in Xander's arms without a care in the world. He was so relieved that they'd found their way back to each other. With Xander at his back, he could handle anything.

Then it all came back to him, slamming into his brain like a freight hauler. "Did I sleep?"

"A little. You were exhausted." Xander leaned down to kiss him. "You feel better?"

"A little." As they separated, Jameson sat up and rubbed his eyes, then looked around. "I'm still tired. Damn, I thought we'd be done after all this." His city was in shambles, many of the beautiful white towers felled by the battle, others scarred with pulse fire. His people—and how strange a thing *that* was to say—were organizing themselves, clearing out a space on the square and setting up makeshift tents to take care of the wounded and feed the rest of the survivors.

His people and Xander's—Gaelani and Eriani working together for the first time in decades. Something good had come from the battle and destruction after all. "I need to be out there. With them."

"You're exhausted. You said it yourself. And soon we'll need to meet with the others—"

Jameson shook his head. "They need me." He was done running. "We can have our meeting, but right now my people need me."

Xander met Jameson's gaze, his green eyes narrowed. "Are you sure...?"

"You *know* I'm right. You did the same when the Gaelani needed you."

Xander grunted. "I guess I did."

"Help me up. They may need me, but I need you, so I don't make a complete fool of myself."

Xander grinned. "Not sure that's possible." He helped Jameson stand up.

"Asshole." Jameson felt dizzy, but after a moment his balance steadied. He closed his eyes, remembering the advice he used to give clients who were overwhelmed by their circumstances. *Stop. Breathe. Let go.*

"Damn, I really have been a bad influence on you."

Jameson opened his eyes and grinned. "The absolute worst." His gaze lingered on Xander's beautiful muscular form. *If I wasn't so tired. If we had more time.* He sighed. "Let's go."

They made their way down the little hillside and into the late afternoon sun. People bowed to him as he and Xander passed. "Your Highness." A young Erriani woman with red wings and hair that shone like fire in the afternoon sun flashed him a dazzling smile.

"No need. Just Jameson is fine."

"*Just Jameson.*" She nodded. "I'll pass it on." She gave him a rather obvious once-over and hurried away.

"No, not 'Just Jameson!'" he called after her, but she was too far away to hear.

"Get used to it, Your Lordship." Xander grinned. "I think that one was considering whether you were looking for a queen."

Jameson snorted. "Stop it."

Xander laughed. "These people—our people—seem to be fond of their royal titles."

Jameson just shook his head. *How did I get here?* It still made no sense to him.

They reached the tents and found Mylin in charge. She threw her arms around Xander.

Xander grinned. "You're a wonder."

"Thank you." She shrugged. "Just trying to make myself useful."

"What can I do?" Jameson looked around. The place bustled with activity. One canopy provided shade for a number of pallets that held wounded men and women, skythane and lander alike. Another seemed to be a material staging area, stacked with supplies, and a wonderful smell emanated from the third.

She looked him over with a critical eye. "Grab a ladle over at the food tent, if you would. You look like you're running on fumes, and I don't want to be responsible for killing the king of the Erriani." She kissed him and Xander on the cheek and dashed off.

"Yeah, you're right, *that's* going to take some getting used to." They headed toward the food tent. "How long until we need to leave for Oberon City for the big meeting?"

Xander shrugged. "Maybe an hour?"

"Damn, I miss my cirq. Wanna help me serve some soup?"

Xander laughed. "I don't have any other plans."

Vestra Halta, the former regent of Errian, awaited them behind the hastily set-up tables. "Welcome back to the land of the living." The old woman smiled and gave him a big hug.

"We did it!" He lifted her up and twirled her around.

Vestra laughed in delight. "Yes, we did. Or you did, anyhow."

"Vestra, you remember Xander?"

She nodded. "It's a pleasure to see you again, Gaelani."

Xander bowed before her. "The pleasure's mine."

She blushed. "I can see why you like him."

"He's not always this charming." He looked at the skythane who had assembled to feed the city and took a deep breath. "Thank you all for doing whatever you can to get Errian back on its feet."

They cheered.

Jameson ducked his head and blushed. "So, put me to work. What are we serving here?"

"It's a hearty aux stew, with tubers and savory seasoning." She lifted a ladle up to Jameson's lips.

He sipped it. It was a multilayered feast—hints of cinnamon and carrot and a meat that was both lean and full of flavor. "It's delicious."

"Have a little before the rush comes. We're serving in about five minutes." She scooped some into an earthenware bowl and handed it to him with a spoon, and then handed one to Xander too.

They wolfed it down, talking with Vestra about plans to rebuild the city.

Then the rush descended upon them.

QUINCE STOOD at the edge of the Argent Sea, her bare feet in the sand. The waves crashed on the black rocks, cool over the tops of her feet, and the air was heavy with salt. She recalled that day twenty-five years before when she'd left here with Jameson and Xander, taking them away to a world wholly unlike their own.

So much had changed in the intervening years, including the aging of her poor bones.

Overhead, a flock of imprean soared on the ocean breeze, calling out their particular *carucaahh, carucaahh* sound as they searched the water below for prey.

Quince was sore from the activities of the last few days—last few weeks, actually. She wanted nothing more than to slip away somewhere with Robyn, to find somewhere private where they could get reacquainted and leave all responsibility behind, but more was demanded of her. Of all of them.

Most of all, she dreaded the conversation that was to come.

She had done what she thought was right. That was the fuckall hardest part. She'd had a world to save, and the nimfeach had told her it was imperative that Jameson and Xander be bonded. They had to get over their antipathy for each other, and the way they'd been at each other's throats the first few days—she'd had no choice.

But what if I did? What if they would have come around to it on their own, without her intervention? Without dosing them with pith? It was funny, when she thought about it. Here they were at the end of the world, and she was freaked out about the boys' feelings.

She snorted. As her mother had often said, *you can't undo done.*

Now she just had to figure out how to pick up the pieces and move on.

"You look troubled."

Quince turned to find Robyn standing there, her black wings tucked neatly behind her, holding out a chunk of bread and some cheese.

"A little." She sighed and then smiled gamely. "Just worrying about the boys."

Robyn nodded. "The boys? Or how angry they are at you?"

Robyn still knew her so well. "A little of both."

They stood side by side, staring out at the water, the waves lapping at the sandy shore. From here, everything looked normal, as if Erro wasn't on the cusp of monumental, devastating change.

"Would you rather the world be destroyed to avoid a few hurt feelings?"

Quince looked at Robyn, calm and beautiful as the breeze rustled through her raven black hair. "Of course not." She took a bite of the bread. It was a bit hard, but she was starving. The cheese was better, a sharp white corybryte, if she didn't miss the mark. "They seem to have gotten past it."

If she had her way, they'd all move past it, at least until the crisis ended. Then she could take her lumps.

She'd seen the hurt in Xander's eyes, and in Jameson's. Maybe it would be better to have this out between them before they moved on.

"You're not alone in this." Robyn slipped her arm around Quince and embraced her. She was warm, alive. Real.

"I dreamed about this for so long." Quince buried her face in Robyn's neck. For just a moment, she was content.

Robyn squeezed her tight, slipping her hand through Quince's hair.

"I need a bath."

"I don't care about that." Robyn held her out at arm's length, searching her face. "You all right?"

Quince nodded, wiping her eyes. "I will be."

"I know." She looked over her shoulder at the broken city. "We should go. They'll be waiting for us."

"Yes." Quince didn't know if she was up to the tasks that lay before her.

She supposed she had no choice.

JAMESON CLOSED HIS EYES, picturing Xander's storage unit once again. He'd been a whole different person the first time he'd been there. Quiet and bookish and closed off from his feelings.

He stretched out his arms and wings, willing himself to have the energy to do this one more time. He'd tapped his reserves and far beyond, and a short rest and a little food had come nowhere near to restoring his usual energy. It made no difference.

Need demanded this.

I can do it. He pulled out the key from his pocket and held it up in the early evening light. It swirled like a living thing. *Where did you come from? Who made you?* He swayed on his feet.

Xander put a hand on his shoulder. "You okay?" His face was next to Jameson's, warm and rough with stubble.

Jameson nodded. "Just tired."

Xander kissed his cheek. "You can do this."

Around them their friends waited for him. They whispered among themselves. Or was it just one of the memories that haunted him? He had them mostly under control, but sometimes they slipped out like stealthy rats, gnawing at the edges of his mind.

Jameson shook his head and concentrated on the task at hand. He fixed the place in his mind's eye—the burnt and broken roll-down door, the scattered supplies, the collapsed wall at the back. The start of the journey that had ultimately led him here.

He had to learn some more places in Oberon City—this one was starting to depress him.

He took hold of the swirling orb with both hands and twisted, and reality twisted too as a seam opened up in midair. It widened rapidly, and soon was wide enough for him to step through. The smells of Oberon City seeped through into the fresh Errian air.

Jameson took Xander's hand, and they crossed a third of Erro, from the open, blasted First Square in Errian to the equally gutted but much more compact storage unit.

Quince and Venin followed, and then the rest of their impromptu council —Vestra, Mylin, Robyn, Jessa, and Alia.

Jameson looked around. The place had been emptied out, probably by looters, and was little more than a shell. He touched the wall, wondering how he'd been so naive about the ways of the world when he'd arrived.

When the last of his companions cleared the gateway, Jameson let it collapse, thrusting the key back in his pocket and wiping the sweat from his brow.

OberCorp HQ was just a couple kilometers away. He was sure he'd be able to manage the flight, but he would have killed for Morgan's healing touch one more time. "Everyone ready?" He surveyed their group of companions, a mix of Erriani and Gaelani. The skythane were united once more, an alliance forged in fire.

"Where are we meeting? And why didn't the landers come to us?" Vestra, the former regent of Errian, frowned, looking around the messy room and wrinkling her nose. "This place smells like an aux's ass."

Jameson grinned. It did stink in Oberon City, especially at the ground level. He stepped outside to look around. It was late afternoon this side of Erro.

Xander answered, "Because we're having everyone fitted with bioware and PAs so we can stay connected. If we're going to come out of this alive, we're going to need every advantage our two cultures can provide."

Vestra shook her head. "I'm not sure I like the idea of one of those… what do you call them?"

"Cirqs."

She smiled gratefully up at Jameson. "Yes, cirqs. I don't think I want one in my head."

"We'll deal with that when we get there—" Something hot and bright flashed over his shoulder, slamming into the wall behind him with a loud crash.

"Bunch of those damned wing men over here," someone shouted from down the street. "I told you we were being invaded!" A ramshackle group of about fifteen people, civilians by the looks of things, came around a corner and stopped, staring at the group of skythane.

They brought up their weapons, an assortment of pulse guns and rifles and other odds and ends, and Jameson's blood ran cold.

Xander pulled out his own pulse rifle, waving it at the ramshackle crowd. "Everyone back inside!" He flipped it to stun and got off a few good shots before diving back behind the broken roll door.

Jameson had his out too, and he hit an attacker square on, forcing the whole group back.

"Nice shot." Xander dropped to the ground behind a pile of garbage.

Jameson settled in beside him, his own rifle aimed at the mob, shouting back to Quince, "Out the back and take flight! We'll keep them pinned down until you're clear." He gestured urgently for them to go. "Quince, you know where to lead them!"

"You boys be careful." Quince popped back into the storage unit before a blast zapped through the space where her head had been. "We'll get everyone else out." She led the rest of the skythane out through the mess in the unit behind them while Jameson and Xander lay down a barrage of cover fire.

3

———

ABOVE THE FRAY

Venin followed Quince and the others into the sky, glancing back at the shrinking storage building as they ascended.

Xander and Jameson could handle things. He was sure of that. No one else had pulse weapons, though, so it was best to get everyone else out of harm's way.

Jameson had looked exhausted. He wasn't likely to find rest anytime soon, not with the new crisis already upon them.

As they rose on the warm updraft from the city streets, he got his first look at Oberon City. The place was sharp and ugly.

The streets below were full of people. Protesters waved signs and chanted, and small groups of armed men like the one that had attacked them roved the city.

There was a stink in the city, a metallic stench mixed with the smell of human waste. Too many people crammed into too little space. How could the landers live this way?

Still, it was clear that things were worse than usual here. One of the huge buildings—arcos, Xander had called them—leaned at an angle away from the others, and plas windows were broken in many places on all of them.

OberCorp's headquarters lay just ahead, beyond the blue arcos.

The building glimmered in the evening moonlight that sparkled on the lake that surrounded the imposing edifice. A number of panes of plas were cracked or missing there, too, victims of the megastorm that had assaulted the world after the shift and the short war that had followed.

Still, it had fared better than the surrounding city.

Alix had promised to be ready to install cirqs on everyone, giving them access to the Oberon City grid.

Venin shook his head. He was about to let OberCorp stick a tracker in his head. *What would you think of me now, Taz? Consorting with the enemy?*

When you live with auxen, become an auxen.

Taz's voice came unbidden across the shores of time. Venin winced. He had no wish to relive that particular memory.

The night was beautiful and warm, the air up here much fresher as it blew in off the sea—belying the coming crisis. As they climbed toward the rooftop, Quince's powerful wings brought her even with Venin. "Do you think we can trust Alix?"

Venin nodded. "He could have come between Xander and Jameson, but he stepped back where a weaker man would have thought only of himself. I'm as sure of it as I am of anything. He saved Errian too."

"With a little help."

Venin laughed. "None of us could have done that alone." His wings beat steadily as she followed a warm updraft toward the roof.

Quince looked around at the party. "Everyone still with us?"

Robyn was carrying Jessa in her arms, her wings beating with the extra effort to pull the two of them upward. Vestra was keeping up, though she looked tired.

With a last surge of effort, they cleared the roofline of the headquarters.

Alix was waiting for them on the hoversport platform. Venin grinned. He was glad his travel companion was safe and sound after the battles they'd been through. He alighted next to Alix. "Good to see you again."

Alix held out a hand, but Venin pulled him in for a strong hug. "Well met. Thanks for everything you did."

Alix's face was flushed when they separated. "Just doing what I had to. I'm not the only one." He looked tired, but nicely shaved and cleaned up, wearing a camo ranger's uniform and a red beret. "Where are Xander and Jameson?"

Quince growled. "We ran into a little trouble at the gateway. I expect them along soon."

"Gotcha. Nothing they can't handle?"

"They have it covered. You know everyone?"

Alix nodded. "Come inside. We've prepared something to eat if you're hungry, and we can get to work on those cirq installs while we talk." He looked from Quince to Venin for confirmation.

Venin's stomach grumbled. He *was* hungry. Maybe he could manage a seat next to Alix so they could catch up. "Lead on."

ALIX LED the others into OberCorp's headquarters. It was strange to act as the guide here. His whole recent life had been on the other side of the world, outside as often as in. He didn't belong here.

And yet here he was.

Venin's touch lingered on his shoulders, the masculine smell of him in his memory. He hoped the man didn't have the wrong idea. They'd been thrown together in the midst of a war—there were bound to be intense feelings from that encounter.

He wasn't ready for anything yet. For anyone. Xander's rejection still stung, though he had made an accommodation with it. Was making one. Would make one someday. Xander was no longer his.

"The lift shaft will take us down a couple floors to the offices I've had set up for us. We'll meet in one of the conference rooms, and I have offices and sleeping quarters prepared for everyone who stays."

Venin looked concerned. "What's a lift shaft?"

Vestra nodded. "I was wondering that too."

"It's like an elevator."

"Elevator?"

Alix laughed in spite of himself. "It's a shaft of air that will carry us down inside the building."

"Ah." Venin grinned. "Why didn't you just say so?"

Alix shook his head. "It's called a lift shaft… never mind." It was going to take his skythane guests a while to get used to life in the big city. "Just step inside and it will carry you down to where you need to go."

Vestra shook her head. "You could have just opened a window for us."

Birds. I'm living with Split-cursed birds.

Venin shrugged. "Down we go." He jumped into the shaft.

Alix followed.

The man's jet-black wings shone with hints of blue in the bright lights of the drop shaft as they passed several rings indicating the floors.

Alix had a thing for wings. He'd spent his childhood staring out his window, wishing he were one of the skythane. His bi-wings had given him the glory of flight, but it was still a half measure.

He shook his head. There were more important things to think about than childhood whimsy.

Like this new threat. Quince and Jameson had been cryptic at best. Alix had hoped to put the war behind them, to start to pick up the pieces and figure out how to spin their world back to the human universe where it belonged. Instead they faced a new crisis.

As they reached their floor, Erissa chimed in his ear. "Alix, your mother is on her way to the medical floor."

"Oh hell, what happened?" He stepped back onto solid ground and moved a few feet away from the others.

Venin mouthed *Everything okay?*

He shook his head. "She was found on the floor of her apartment."

"Fucking Split." He looked up, spotting one of the tech staff. "Derren, I've got to run to medical. Can you take the others to the conference room?"

"Got it."

Good kid. A bit cerebral. *So damned young.* "Thanks. Folks, I'll be back shortly."

He excused himself and hopped back into the drop shaft. "Erissa, take me to medical." *What in the Split did you do?*

Alix arrived in the medical suite to find his mother under sedation in a crisp white room with no windows. "I'm Alix Preston. They called and said my mother was here?" OberCorp had its own state-of-the-art medical facilities, as good or better than anything else on-planet.

The doctor was a young woman with umber-toned skin, rare anymore in the Common Worlds with all the mixing of the last thousand years. He wondered if she was from one of the African diaspora worlds. "I'm Dr. Glynt, Teva Glynt." She was all business.

"Thanks, Dr. Glynt. So what happened?"

She pulled him out of his mother's room gently. "We think she overdosed on sleepers."

He shook his head. "She wouldn't. How is that even possible?" Lena Preston was not the suicidal type.

Glynt shook her head. "She overrode the system, somehow."

"Goddammit." He pounded the wall, startling a passing nurse. "Sorry. My mother's unconscious."

The man nodded and hurried away.

"Is she okay now?"

"She should be. We flushed her system with kelex. It bonds with the active drug of the sleeper meds and takes it out of her system. She should be awake in a couple hours." She squeezed Alix's shoulder gently. "Any idea why she would do this?"

"It's her way of getting my attention."

"Ah." The whole company was aware of the spat between the former OberCorp CEO and the present one. "I can call you when she wakes up."

"You're sure she'll be fine?"

"Positive."

"Give me a minute with her?"

"Of course."

Alix reentered the room. His mother lay under a white sheet, still as death.

"I'm sorry, Mom. Things have been a bit crazy." He squeezed her hand. They had issues between them. A whole lifetime full of them. But still, she was his mother.

He leaned over and kissed her forehead, the *beep beep beep* of the machines filling his ears. "I'll be back soon."

4

NO PLACE LIKE HOME

Morgan slipped into Freyyr unnoticed. The cavern under the mountain was a flurry of activity as the nimfeach worked to awaken the sleeping ithani.

It wouldn't be long now.

He wondered where the Thshnel'Jirron was hiding.

Part of him felt compelled to join the other nimfeach in their single-minded task, enslaved as they were by the ithani will.

But his human half resisted.

After a few minutes, he pulled himself away. He had seen all he needed to.

Now he had plans to make.

He opened a gateway and stepped through, and in an instant was gone.

Xander didn't like being pinned down.

Shots slammed into the door and the walls near Xander and Jameson, sending a shower of debris down on their heads.

Xander popped up and got off a shot, then sank back down cursing next to Jameson. "That's the last of the charge on this one."

Jameson peered over their cover and dropped back as a pulse blast zipped past, singeing his hair. "Theirs are not set to stun. Fall back. We can go out the other side after Quince and the others—"

Voices rang through the combined space of the two storage units from behind. "They're in here!"

"Fucking Split." Xander spat on the ground. "They're behind us too. I don't suppose you have enough left in you to open another gateway." He shot another pulse blast out the back, hoping to make their ambushers keep their heads down for a moment or two. "Reinforcements should be here soon!"

"If only." Jameson laughed and then grimaced. "I can try." He pulled out the key, closed his eyes, and looked very focused.

Nothing happened.

"I'm tapped. Sorry." His voice came out thinner than he liked.

Xander grunted. "Not your fault. You've pushed yourself past the limit." He looked around wildly. "How else can we get out of here?" He hated not having a preplanned exit.

He popped up and fired a pulse blast over the wreckage to keep their attackers on their toes, and another toward the back. "Come on back inside."

Jameson nodded and followed him on hands and knees. "Here." Jameson held out the key to him.

"I don't know how to use it."

"Hang back. Tennir and Ziph will be here in five with some grenades," one of their hunters said to the others, not five meters away if Jameson judged it right. "We can smoke 'em out then."

"I can show you how."

Xander searched Jameson's eyes, doubtful. "Okay. Let's try it." He glanced over his shoulder. Their attackers seemed to have pulled back.

Jameson touched Xander's face. "I don't know if this will work. Close your eyes."

Xander did as he was told.

Jameson put the key in his palm. "Quince thinks we can all learn to use these things. That we have *their* blood in our veins."

Xander shuddered.

"Picture a place we can go. Someplace you know well."

"My apartment. Feels like a lifetime."

"I can imagine. Lock the image in your head."

"Got it."

"Now reach inside the key with your mind and twist it. Like this. Then *push*!" Xander's hands were warm in his.

Something clattered into the room. Jameson's eyes popped open. It was a small metal canister, and it started spewing smoke. "*Push!*"

"I see it! I've… done this before."

Jameson nodded. "The memories."

Xander grunted. He did as Jameson had shown him and pushed.

Another something clattered into the storage unit from behind, and the locker filled with black smoke.

Then the air split between them and the grenade.

The cloud rapidly filled up the small space, burning Jameson's eyes and skin. He stumbled to his feet and pulled Xander with him. Together they staggered half-blind through the gateway.

As they cleared the gateway, a pulse blast shot through over his shoulder to slam into the mirror above Xander's bed, cracking and melting the glass. "Shut the gate!"

Xander let go of the key, sending it clattering across the floor.

The smoky room and the astonished face of the lander man peering through from the other side vanished in a flash.

JAMESON TOOK a deep breath of clean air and looked around at the apartment. "So this is where you live, huh?" That had been close. *Too close.* And yet here they were. "We should probably get going to the meeting?" He set his carry sack down on the bed and looked around.

"Just want to grab a few things. Hop in the ionic shower while you're waiting."

"Oh God, yes. Is there time?"

"Make time. We need to get that smoke off of our skin, for one thing, and besides, you stink to high heaven and Erro." He palmed open the door to the small bathroom.

Jameson peeled off his clothes. The last time he had changed had been… when? He couldn't remember. It had been days, at least.

He sniffed his pits. Yup, he was ripe.

The apartment was about what he had expected, a bachelor pad—lots of black and gray and silver, clean lines, not much in the way of decoration. A huge tri-dee table took up half of the living room, and plas picture windows looked out on early evening in Oberon City.

One thing he hadn't expected—the drawers had all been pried open, and clothing, books, and other riffraff lay strewn across the floor. "Looks like you were robbed." He climbed into the ionic shower. It was a large one, probably because of Xander's wings. He palmed the controls.

"Access code, please." The voice seemed to come out of thin air.

"Must be your PA?"

Xander popped his head in. "Yup. Say hello to Ravi. Fusion uranus centauri kepler interstellar neptune galaxy dash binary alpha saturn telescope alpha rocket doppler. Confirm."

Jameson worked that out and laughed. Sounded about right. As a kid, he'd had those callsigns almost beaten into his head in school.

Xander grinned and gave Jameson the once-over. "Oooh. You look—"

"Access code confirmed. Welcome back, Xander."

"Hey, Ravi! It's so good to hear your voice!" Xander grinned at Jameson. "Jameson, meet Ravi, my PA."

Jameson laughed. "Hey, Ravi. You two gonna let a guy take a shower in peace, or what?"

Xander winked at him and disappeared around the corner.

Jameson was a bit jealous. He had no way to access his own PA, let alone the grid.

The shower began; a whirlwind of warm air surrounded Jameson. *Oh gods, that feels good.* He'd have to get one of these installed in the Castain in Errian when they rebuilt the city.

When he was done, he was delighted to find fresh clothing waiting for him.

"Ravi took your measurements in the shower."

Jameson got dressed, admiring how the black faux-leather fit his form. "We're getting cirqs at this meeting, right?" At least then he could see if his PA had managed a local backup before he'd been forced to short out his bioware. He sank down on the bed, wishing he could take a nap, but there was no time for that. "Almost ready to go?"

"Yup. Ravi, mix me up a little stim for Jameson here, and open the safe." Xander laid his own carry sack on the kitchen counter.

A blank patch of wall next to where Xander had put his palm opened, exposing a meter-tall space behind. Xander pulled out a couple fresh pulse rifles, tossing one to Jameson. "Here, dump that old one."

"What are you, an arms dealer?"

Xander laughed bitterly. "Oberon City can be a dangerous place, and after my time with Rogan, I was always ready to run."

"Stim ready." A small hatch slid open on the kitchen counter, holding a cup of something.

"Thanks, Ravi." Xander handed it to Jameson. "Here. Drink this."

Jameson took the cup and sniffed it suspiciously. It smelled like strawberries. "What's in it?"

"I have no idea, but it does wonders. I used to take it after waking up with a hangover." He opened one of the kitchen cabinets and stuffed food packs into his carry sack.

"Will it make me feel even worse when it wears off?"

"Not really. It boosts your own system and has a shitload of protein and electrolytes, along with whatever else Ravi puts in there."

Jameson shrugged and drained the cup. It was bitter, but as it hit his stomach, a warm glow suffused him. "Oooh. That's nice." He could get used to being back in civilization again.

Xander zipped up his carry sack. "My turn."

Jameson watched him undress, wishing they had more time for *that* too. They'd totally missed their honeymoon.

He lay down on the bed and closed his eyes. It felt absolutely marvelous to lie on a real bed, clean and dressed in new clothes.

Far too soon, though, Xander sat down on the bed and woke him from his slumber. "You snore up a storm, you know that?" Xander pulled on a pair of riding boots. "Have to get this place back in order once we return."

"If we return. We do have a couple castles, too, you know."

Xander grinned. "Kings of the world." He kissed Jameson, and Jameson's body responded.

Xander pulled away and glanced down at Jameson's crotch. "Wish we had time, believe me. This bed's great for sex."

Jameson's wings shivered. "*Goddamned* end of the world."

"Yup. Feel better?"

Jameson nodded. "A little. I feel awake again. The fatigue is mostly gone." It wasn't as good as Morgan's little trick, but it was close. He could function.

"Ravi? My bike?"

The floor opened up, and Xander's hoverbike rose into view. "How…?" They'd left it at the House of the Sun when they'd crossed over to Titania.

"Auto return. All cleaned up too." One of the plas windows slid apart. "Wanna ride?"

"I thought you'd never ask." Jameson mounted the bike and slipped his arms around Xander, ready to take on the world.

5

———

AN UNEXPECTED VISITOR

Venin stared at the sterile conference room, his lips pulled back to show his teeth. He was no "Outlander barbarian," as he'd heard one of the OberCorp employees whisper behind his back.

This place was cold and lifeless, and smelled of chemicals and fear.

A long silver conference table bisected the room, surrounded by black chairs that were too shallow with backs too high for skythane.

He would stand.

The view from the lander building, however, was spectacular.

OberCorp headquarters was taller than the tallest tower in Errian. This side faced westward, over the Gildensea, where Bandia seared a silver pathway across the wave tops.

He closed his eyes, remembering the strange pain that had flooded his body when he'd touched the statue in the Erriani chapel. *What in Gael's grace was that about?*

"Sorry we're not ready for you." Alix slapped him on the back. "I'll have proper skythane chairs brought in before we get started."

At least the man had noticed his discomfort. Venin wrinkled his nose. "It stinks in here too."

"That I can do something about right now." Alix cocked his head. "Erissa, open the windows a little."

The clear windows around the conference room lowered about a third of a meter, and fresh air flowed in. Well, fresh for the city.

"Like magic." Venin breathed in the cool air deeply, gratefully. "Better." He'd come to respect Alix over the last few days as they'd traveled together from the ruins of the Mountain all the way to Errian and the Argent Sea. The man was solid. A good fighter. A decent guy, too, judging from how he'd managed to navigate things with his ex, Xander, and Jameson. And handsome as fuck with his square jaw and military cut. Venin grinned.

"I know how you feel. I'm not used to being cooped up in places like this anymore." He had a wistful look on his face.

"So why stay?"

Alix shot him a strange look. "I have responsibilities here. People who need me. I am the boss of OberCorp now."

Venin was unimpressed. "Not much of a boss if you can't leave whenever you want to."

Alix snorted. "Fair enough. Why don't *you* leave?"

"I'm not the boss." Venin grinned. "What happened earlier?"

"When?"

"You had to leave us rather abruptly."

"Ah." Alix nodded. "My mother… she was taken to medical."

"Everything all right?"

Alix looked tired, fine lines apparent by his eyes. He sighed. "It will be. She's… not happy with me for pushing her out."

"I can imagine." These landers were ruthless, vicious even to one another at times. Not that the skythane were angels. Not literal ones, anyhow. "I'm sorry—"

An OberCorp employee dressed in white touched Alix's sleeve. "Mr. Kinnson and Mr. Havercamp have, um, arrived. On a hoverbike."

"Thanks, Gregg." Alix flashed an embarrassed grin at Venin. "The staff's not used to having guests arrive so informally. Excuse me." He squeezed Venin's arm and then retreated to the exit.

Venin watched him go, his arm tingling where Alix had touched him. The rangers who had occupied Gaelan had been cast from a similar mold, but they'd been the enemy.

Alix had been one of them.

Venin shook his head, whistling softly. The man was a lander. They would never work as a couple.

And yet, even landers have needs.

QUINCE STARED IMPATIENTLY at the wall as her new cirq and wrist plate were installed. This room was classic corporate. The wall screen displayed a generic picture of some color-enhanced nebula or another, and the industrial carpet was about the beigest shade she had ever seen.

She was ready to get her access back. She'd missed it—the connection to the planet's grid, the easy access to almost anything she needed to know. She'd spent twenty-five years exploring the virtual world that wrapped around the real one, and with those tools at hand once again, she'd be able to formulate the best plan for dealing with the threat the ithani posed.

She certainly missed Ari. She'd have to access the heavily encrypted copy she'd slitted to one of the nether recesses of the grid. Her PA was like an extension of herself, a friend who was always at hand, sunshine or darkness.

And yet....

There was something to be said for disconnecting, for letting go of the constant news feeds and updates and the flood of information she'd once been bombarded with. Information overload.

She'd been happier out in the wilderness with Robyn, in a way. Cut off from everyone and everything else. She looked up at Robyn, and her partner squeezed her hand.

"Installation completed. Your system should self-organize and should boot up in about ten minutes." The med drone pulled away, hovering a couple feet away from her. "Do you feel any discomfort?"

Quince reached up to touch her temple. The skin was smooth there, as if she hadn't been cut at all. "No, thank you. The anesthetic's quite good."

"Take these if you should feel any pain. One tablet should last twelve hours." A slit opened up in the shiny silver sphere, and a small packet was dispensed.

Quince took it, nodding at the drone. "Thank you."

"No thanks are necessary. Who is the next patient?"

Quince looked at Robyn again.

"Oh no. I don't want one of those... things inside me."

Quince frowned. "It won't hurt you, and it will make it easier to find you if we get separated."

Robyn backed away so quickly she knocked over one of the chairs. "No. I don't want it."

"Hey, it's okay. You don't have to." Quince stood, looking around the room. "Who's next for a cirq installation?"

"I'll go." Mylin stepped forward, her face determined although her wings trembled a little.

Quince looked at the young woman appraisingly. She'd proven herself adept at organization and problem solving, quite an impressive showing, really. It would be interesting to see what she would do with the capabilities a cirq and grid access would provide. "Come have a seat. It doesn't hurt."

Mylin came forward and sat where Quince had been. "What does it feel like?"

"The installation?"

Mylin shook her head. "The cirq."

"It's… it's like having another world inside your head. Or the keys to the biggest library you could imagine."

Mylin smiled faintly. "That doesn't sound so bad."

"Go ahead," Quince said to the drone.

The sphere approached Mylin and extended an arm, spraying her temple with anesthetic.

"Oooh, that's cold."

Quince held her hand while the procedure commenced. "You'll hardly feel a thing."

Two minutes later, the drone backed away. "All done. Do you feel any discomfort?"

Mylin's eyes went wide. "That's it? No, I'm fine, thanks." She looked at her wrist.

The drone spun back and forth in midair. "Who's next?"

Venin stepped up. "That would be me."

Quince nodded and squeezed Mylin's hand tight. "See? Nothing to worry about. When you have a few free moments, we'll boot her up and get you started."

She guided the girl to the table just as Xander and Jameson came in. Behind them, a couple OberCorp employees started bringing in suitable chairs, with low backs to allow skythane wings proper support.

"Hey!" Jameson's face lit up when he saw her. Xander stood back, brooding. She could guess what that was about.

"Everything okay?" Quince hugged Jameson, grateful they had made it back safely.

"Nothing we couldn't handle. Xander made his first gateway."

"To where?"

"His apartment."

Quince snorted. "I should have known."

"Nothing happened. We were in a rush." Jameson glanced back at Xander. "Not that I'd have minded. Have you seen his bachelor pad?"

"Oh yes. Many times. I called it the man trap." Not that she held it against poor Xander, after he'd lost Alix and all, but he had gone through quite the phase.

Her system booted up. "Install existing personal assistant?"

"Just a sec." She turned away from Jameson. "Access code centauri neptune one seven three two neptune interstellar galaxy."

"Code accepted. One moment while I load the personal assistant from the specified location."

Quince looked around the room. All the principals were there. She wished she had more information for them beyond the little bit Morgan had told her. Ithani. Three more days.

"Hello, Quince." Ari's voice practically purred in her ears.

Quince grinned. "Hey, Ari… I've missed you."

"Likewise."

She'd forgotten what a comfort it was to have Ari in her head, at her beck and call. He was her PA, but even though he was nothing more than a specialized bit of code, he'd become something more than that. A friend. "I'm sorry I had to shut you down like that."

"I have no memory of that." His voice sounded hurt. "This copy was made before it happened."

She blushed. "Nevertheless. Are you interfaced with OberCorp's systems?"

"I will be shortly. What do you need?"

She explained briefly, and Ari sent off gridrunners to collect what she had asked for. Quince cleared her throat. "Okay, everyone's here. Shall we get started?"

"ALL DONE," the drone said softly to Jameson. "It will take about half an hour to load in the last backup."

"You have a copy of my PA on file?" Jameson breathed a sigh of relief.

"Yes. Do you feel any discomfort?"

"No, thanks." Jameson waved it away. He looked at his wrist. The skin was seamless.

"Please contact DOC if you have any trouble." It moved on.

The assembled skythane and landers were taking seats around the table. Jameson sat across from Xander, who reached out to squeeze his hand reassuringly. There was no place to put down their carry sacks. He shrugged at Xander, and they put them under their chairs.

Here he was at last at OberCorp HQ, the place he thought he was coming to that first day, just a few weeks before.

It seemed like a lifetime.

Quince stood, looking around at everyone. She looked grim. "Thanks to everyone for coming. I have a lot to tell you, but I'll start with—"

The door burst open, cutting off Quince midspeech.

Jameson looked up to see Rogan standing there, out of breath, staring accusingly around the room. "Started without me, I see?"

Xander leapt to his feet. "What the hell is he doing here?" His face was red with anger.

Rogan grinned. "Hello, pretty thing." He turned to address the others. "I'm a part of this little alliance, am I not?" He pulled one of the lander chairs up to the table. "Besides, I'm still owed payment for my help. I was afraid you might have forgotten."

"Alix…." Xander shot his ex a pleading look.

"I don't like it any more than you do, but we did promise him the pith." Alix shot a black look at the Slander boss. "But we may need him. It's all hands on deck time. We can settle things later."

Xander sank back down into his chair, not taking his eyes off Rogan.

Although he was pretty sure no one else noticed, Jameson saw Xander shudder. He put his hand on Xander's. *It's my own damned fault.* He'd invited the man into their lives, and now they were stuck with him until the crisis was over. "Keep him in line," he hissed, "or I swear to the gods I will fucking end him."

Everyone turned to look at him, and even Xander whistled appreciatively. "Damn."

Rogan, infuriatingly, just grinned wider. "I'd like to see you try, little wing boy."

Half the table rose at that insult.

"Enough!" Quince slammed her fist down on the table. "We're short on time and fighting amongst ourselves won't do us any good." She glared at Rogan. "He stays. But not another word out of you."

Rogan made a seated imitation of a curtsey. "As you wish, milady."

In a flash, she had her pulse pistol at his temple. "Not. Another. Word. Understand?"

Rogan's face went white. He nodded.

Quince tucked the pistol into her belt.

Where the hell did you get that? Jameson's respect for her went up another notch.

6

———

OFF THE RAILS

There was pain, pain like Dani had never endured before, coursing through every nerve in her body. Pain that left her exhausted, whimpering between waves of agony, like someone had turned her bones to fire.

Then the dark, bleak emptiness that would last for hours. Or maybe days. She couldn't tell. She was so disconnected from life, from light, from the simple intake of breath that she forgot who she was, even what she was, for long stretches of time.

Something waited in the darkness with her, something just out of reach. She could hear it shuffling in the inky blackness, feel its fetid breath on her neck from time to time.

"Please," she begged the darkness. "Please let me go. I'm sorry. I shouldn't have come. I will do anything. Just let me *out!*" The last part came out as a scream that tore her throat, but whatever was there with her didn't respond.

She wasn't even sure she was awake, most of the time. If this place-that-wasn't-a-place existed in her old world, or if she was trapped in her own head.

She closed her eyes, trying to calm herself. "It's not real. It's not real. This is all just a bad dream. Wake up. Wake up. Wake up!"

She opened her eyes.

Nothing had changed.

It was still dark. Pitch-black.

Something wormed its way into her mind.

She screamed, and the pain began again.

VENIN GLARED at the Slander boss. He'd heard stories, none of which were good.

Rogan returned his glare but broke contact first.

Quince cleared her throat. "As I was saying, a week ago, Robyn and I flew north to check into something that had come to my attention. Ari, globe, please?"

A slowly spinning sphere appeared above the table.

Venin whistled. They had some great toys here. It was amazing to see his world this way.

Alix grinned at him.

"This is everything we know about the combined world—Erro. Dani and her forces had taken some detailed measurements, so it's fairly complete on the Titania side, and the landers, sorry, our landbound friends"—she nodded to Alix and the other OberCorp employees in the room—"mapped out Oberon long ago. There are a few zones we don't know much about, particularly in the north and south."

The demarcation where Erro had been split was clear, a ridgeline that ran between the mountains on one end of the world and bisected the Argent Sea and Gildensea on the other. Venin supposed they must have been part of one larger ocean long ago, before the split. One side of the globe was blank in the far southern and northern hemispheres. He traced his hand across the glowing surface. *Amazing.* They'd traversed all that distance, much of it under their own power.

"That's all very pretty." Rogan sat back in his chair, wrapping his hands behind his head, his fat stomach sticking out under his shirt. "But what's the immediate threat? I thought we'd taken down OberCorp already." He glanced around the room. "Obviously."

Quince growled. "I'm getting to it. I wish I'd had my cirq when we learned about the latest threat. I could have shown you the memfiles." Her hand slipped over the hilt of her pistol, and the import of the casual action was clearly not lost on Rogan. "Ari, North Pole file, please."

The globe vanished, to be replaced by a fuzzy picture.

"This was one of the last images captured from Titan Station before we lost contact."

It showed the curve of the world and a large peak that jutted up from an icy plain.

"Sorry, the resolution's a bit grainy. Suffice it to say we're not alone on Erro any longer—if we ever were. That's where they live."

Venin frowned. "Who?"

"The ithani." Vestra's face had gone white.

"Yes." Quince frowned. "How did you know?"

Vestra shuddered and pulled her shawl over her shoulders, drawing it close to her as if to ward off the cold. "The Erriani have many legends. Some of them have almost been lost to the passage of time. We have… more of a history with Titania than the Gaelani."

Quince nodded. "Go on."

"When the skythane first came to Oberon, almost eight hundred years ago, the Erriani were the ones who settled Titania, while the Gaelani remained here in Oberon. There was a young skythane woman named Thesbe who claimed to have been taken by a sneach and carried off to the home of the ithani, who… did things to her before she finally escaped and made her way home."

"Things?" Venin didn't like the sound of that.

"Yes. Tests, maybe. Experiments. That was just one of the stories. Some tales suggest the ithani are devils—you should never eat any food they provide lest you be trapped in hell. Others called them angels, beautiful beyond bearing." She snorted. "One thing they all agreed upon. Never seek them out. Never visit the far north."

In the middle of the night
after dark when auxen slumber
come ithani, faces bright
and make the village quake with fright
whose children will they steal tonight?

Vestra shuddered. "*Sneach*, we called them sometimes. Those that sneak around in the dark."

"She's right. My grandmother was tricked by a sneach once in the north woods. Lost her bow and arrow." Venin laughed. "She was spitting teeth about it for weeks."

Quince nodded. "We had similar proscriptions against the north, but I always took them for tales to frighten small children." She stared at the image of the mountain. "It seems they may have held a grain of truth. The ithani have been engaged in some kind of selective breeding program with the skythane for centuries."

Venin shuddered at the thought, and there was an uproar around the room. What was she saying? *That we're a big experiment?*

Quince pounded the table again. "Look, we're short on time. We need to move on."

"What are these ithani? Did you see one?" Alix scratched his new stubble on his chin, looking thoughtful.

Venin caught himself staring at the lander man. He liked that Alix kept his cool during a storm. He looked away, his face hot. *I'm like a fledgling in heat.*

"They were the race that lived here before us. More than a hundred thousand years ago, I think. The ones who split Erro—an accident, or maybe sabotage?" Quince stared at the globe. "There was a war, a terrible war, between the ithani and a race called the dhagani. I don't know much more than that. But their battles destroyed whole worlds. It was a dhagani weapon that poisoned Erro's sun, making it so unpredictable."

Venin could almost smell the fear on her. He'd seen how strong she was. Quince didn't frighten easily. This must be really bad.

At last she went on. "When we saved Oberon from the flare, we inadvertently woke the sleepers. Shifting Oberon here completed the process the ithani had started so many years ago and set something new in motion. Robyn and I—"

"How exactly do you know this?" Rogan stared at her, his brow furrowed and hands pressed together as if in prayer. "Alix asked a good question. Did you actually see one of these… what were they called… ithani?"

"Well, yes and no—"

"Do we even know for certain that they exist?"

The man's voice grated on Venin, and Jameson actually growled. *He shouldn't be here.* Xander looked like he was about ready to leap across the table and slit Rogan's throat.

Jameson touched Xander's hand and shook his head.

Xander subsided, but he didn't look happy.

Quince, however, took it in stride. "Yes. Morgan showed me. We only have three days, at most—"

"Who is Morgan?"

"He's a nimfeach." Quince's face was turning an ugly purple.

Venin leapt to his feet, towering over the Slander boss. "That's enough. If you're going to be a part of this meeting—and I, for one, would have no trouble throwing you out that window—you will remain quiet and respectful while Quince speaks."

The man paled, and Quince glared at him.

What? What did I do? He sat down sheepishly.

Alix was grinning.

Jameson stepped in. "Xander and I have both seen Morgan and what he can do, and we can vouch for Quince. If she hadn't stepped in and guided us when she did…. Well, let's just say none of us would be standing here today." He glared at Rogan.

The man just smiled blandly back at him. "Fair enough."

Rogan was trouble. Venin wished he'd tossed the man out the moment he'd walked into the room. The world would have been a better place for it.

"Ready for your cirq, sir?"

Venin turned to see the med drone hovering next to him, having just finished with Jameson. "Um, yes, please, ma'am." He wasn't sure about this, but Quince had urged him to have it done.

"So what's the threat?" Alix waved the glowing globe out of existence and looked around the room. "Erro seems big enough, if they keep to their part." He stood and walked over to look out the plas windows. "We should be concentrating on taking care of our wounded, making sure everyone gets fed, and spinning OberCorp and the rest of Oberon back to the Common Worlds' universe."

A tumult broke out again at that statement.

"Do we even know how?"

"This is crazy. We don't want to go back there."

"I just want to go home."

Venin frowned, listening to the arguments all around him. Was it even possible? Or would the shift be permanent? Did he care either way? He had no loyalty to the Common Worlds, but to be stuck here with all these landers and OberCorp….

A piercing noise cut off all conversation.

"Thank you, Ari." Quince leaned forward, hands flat on the table. "Erro has an amalite core. It's one of the reasons it's so valuable to OberCorp and to the Common Worlds."

Alix nodded. "One of several unique Oberon exports."

"The ithani plan to evolve, or transform themselves in some way. To do it, they plan to harness the power of the amalite core of the world." The sphere appeared again, bisected into two parts. Large masses in the center of the Oberon side glowed golden. "Those are the known deposits on the Split."

"But that would destroy the world." Jameson stared at the globe. The amalite deposits were like cancers at the heart of Erro, and if Quince was right, they were metastasizing.

"The nimfeach told you this?" Rogan sounded slightly less sarcastic.

Venin glared at him, along with most of the rest of the room.

"Yes."

Rogan grunted. "Let's say for the sake of argument that I believe you. Let's say this nimfeach—Morgan is it?—is real, and that he told you all these things. How can you be sure it's telling you the truth?"

Quince didn't flinch. "Because he's part human."

That caused a stir, though Jameson wasn't entirely surprised.

An image of a small child appeared over the table. "Tanner Michael Henshaw. His mother was a pith user in Egeus who abandoned him on the streets. I had Ari track his records down just now. The nimfeach found him and offered him their help if he agreed to become one with one of their own. Then they sent him for Xander to find."

Xander sank back into his chair. "Holy Split."

"So why are they helping us?" Venin frowned. "It doesn't make any sense."

Quince nodded. "He couldn't tell me, but I think there are two factions among the nimfeach, or maybe even among the ithani themselves. Maybe? One faction wants to finish what they started with the shift. The other sees that things have changed."

"How long do we have?" Alix looked dangerously calm.

Quince locked gazes with Alix. "Less than three days. In fact, everyone set your chrons for midnight, two nights from tonight. We may have a bit longer, but not much. We need to know by then what we plan to do."

"We have a stockpile of meso bombs," Alix said softly. "And Erissa tells me that there's still one Rentz Class carrier on the launch pad—one of the heavy ore haulers that makes runs up to Titan Station. We could load it up as a precaution. It can reach anywhere on the planet in a few minutes—"

"That would be an act of war." Quince's face was grim. "We can't provoke anything, not until we're sure there's no other choice." She looked out the window into the distance, as if she could see the ithani from where she stood. "Maybe as a last resort."

Alix frowned. "I'll see that it's ready."

"That sounds pragmatic." Quince sighed. "We don't know what kind of battletech the ithani possess. They fought an interstellar war when we were still roaming the African savannah carrying wooden clubs."

Venin whistled. It was a lot to take in.

"So what would you propose?" Alix crossed his arms, siting back in his seat.

"We need to decide where to concentrate our efforts. We need information, fast." Quince pulled her worn carry sack up onto the table and brought out a small shiny sphere. It looked like a key, but it was milky-white instead of silver.

It was also larger than the one he held in his carry sack. Venin stared at it, wondering what this one was for.

"What does it do?" Jameson's eyes were big as fists.

"I don't know. Morgan said I would know what to do with it."

"Can I see it?" Jameson held out his hand.

Quince held it out to him over the table.

Rogan's greedy eyes followed it.

The key glowed red and then orange, ripples spreading across its surface.

"Xander, look at this!"

"Don't touch it!" Alix shouted. "It might be a—"

Xander's fingers touched the colorful surface.

The key flashed a brilliant white light, and with a sound that was more like an absence of all sound, the two kings were gone.

ALIX STARED at the gaping hole in the floor that had just been excised from reality, where Xander, Jameson, and the center part of the table had all been standing.

An alarm was going off somewhere, and lights were flashing.

"Everyone get back!" He grabbed Vestra and hauled the petite elderly skythane woman away from the hole as part of the remainder of the table slid through to fall to the floor below.

By the Split, I hope there was no one down below. He peered into the hole. The room below seemed to be for storage. He thanked his lucky stars no one had been down there in the thing's path. Whatever it was.

The floor dropped with a loud groan, propelling him forward into the void. He flailed, trying to stop his fall, and then someone's arms were around him, the beat of wings conveying him to the other side.

Venin set him down. "You okay?"

"Holy hell, that was close. Thanks."

Venin grinned. "Couldn't have your pretty little face splattered on the floor down below."

Alix grunted. *Pretty little face.*

"What the hell just happened?" Quince was white as a sheet.

"Erissa, what the hell was that?" Alix quickly regained his composure and ignored the strapping, dark-skinned skythane man. His mind couldn't deal with that *and* process the sudden loss of the man who had once been his closest friend, and Jameson, for whom Alix had come to have great respect.

"Checking room sensors. One moment."

"Quince, what in the seven suns was that thing? A bomb?"

Erissa spoke in his ear. "There is no explosive residue detected in this room. DOC is trying to determine the cause of the event."

Quince shook her head. "I don't think so. Morgan wouldn't have—"

"Are we sure about that?" Rogan got up and dusted himself off. "I don't trust these *friends* of yours—"

"DOC says there was no explosion." Alix enjoyed cutting the vile man off.

"DOC?" Venin frowned.

"The OberCorp AI. Erissa, please ask DOC to initiate emergency protocol and lock down the building." Alix edged forward to look at the gap in the floor, more careful this time. It was a precise, surgical line, a concave oval just wide enough to encompass Xander and Jameson while leaving the others untouched.

He sniffed the air. There was the slightest metallic tang, but nothing else out of the ordinary that his human senses could pick up. "Let's all make our way to the conference room down the hall. I want this one sealed up until we can run a complete diagnostic panel."

Quince looked pained. "Alix, I'm sorry—I had no idea something like this would happen."

Alix nodded. "I know you didn't." *Holy hell, what kind of world are we living in?* Alien races, shifting worlds, and gaps opening up in the space-time continuum without warning. "We can talk it over once we get everyone clear." He helped Mylin and Vestra over the edge of the oval-shaped gap, where it almost touched the wall. Then Venin extended a hand to him. The man's touch was warm and strong.

"Thanks, man. Go ahead. I'll catch up with all of you."

Venin gave him *that* look on the way out. Alix ignored him. He waited until the room was cleared. "Erissa, I need you to prepare the Rentz Carrier. Fill it with all the meso bombs we have."

"Understood." Her voice sounded shaky. Maybe it was just the grid connection. "Destination?"

"None yet. I want them in place and ready to take action at a moment's notice."

"Understood."

As the new head of OberCorp, and therefore the lander part of the planet, he had a responsibility to do whatever was necessary to protect his people.

He knelt to touch the floor where it had been severed. The edge was sharp as a knife, but the surface was cool.

He huddled with the enforcers, directing them to go over every inch of the conference room and the storage unit below with Erissa and DOC.

The Split save us if this is a new weapon. Even meso bombs might not be enough to stop them.

7

AFTER THE FLASH

Quince clamped down on her fear and anger. Nothing would be gained by letting her emotions get out of check.

Jameson and Xander were gone; that much was clear. It was the key. It had to be. There was no other reasonable explanation.

Yet she refused to believe Morgan had set her up, that this had been an intentional strike to kill the two skythane kings, or that they were already dead.

She stifled a sob.

There had to be another answer.

She glanced at the strange hole once more, and then looked up—a small piece of the ceiling was missing too.

With a sigh, she left the room and followed the others down the hall to another meeting place. The new room was just like the old one, but with only lander chairs.

"I'll have new chairs brought in. Erissa—"

"No need." Quince picked up a chair and spun it around, sitting on it backwards.

The other skythane did the same.

"So what the hell was that?" Alix spat. "One minute they were there, the next...."

"I think it was a gateway." Quince replayed it in her mind. Jameson had been holding out the key, Xander had touched it, and there'd been a bright flash. An oddly circular one, if the image burned into her retinas was any guide.

"That makes sense." Alix nodded. "But what if it wasn't really a key? What if it was some weird kind of explosion that our sensors can't quite pin down?"

"Those keys are made of amalite. If there'd been an actual explosion, with that amount of material…." Amalite was fairly stable, but when triggered, it blew with a huge explosive force.

"Half the building would be gone." Alix went pale.

"Besides, do we really want to believe that Jamie and Xand are gone?" That came from Jessa, who had sat through the meeting almost unnoticed. "If it was a gateway, they must have gone somewhere, right?"

"Yes, but I've never seen a gateway act like that before, although I don't have a lot of experience with them." Alix frowned. "But you're right. We have to assume they're okay until they're not."

Quince nodded. "You're right. It's kinda tough to say how they should and shouldn't behave." Her mind was racing. If it was a gateway, there had to be some way to confirm it. "Maybe I could run some tests, both here and where Jameson opened the gateway in Xander's storage unit."

"Good thinking. Erissa, give Quince's PA whatever access it needs to DOC to get this done. In the meantime, I've got them loading up the Rentz Carrier."

Quince and Alix locked eyes. "I hope to the gods we don't have to use it."

"Maybe not, but we've got to do it. Best to be prepared, and even if it was a gateway, it might still be a hostile act."

Quince sighed. He was right, much as it irked her to admit it.

"I think that's prudent too." Rogan rubbed his chin between his thumb and forefinger thoughtfully. "What can the Syndicate do?"

Alix winced. Quince sympathized. She'd feel dirty finding herself on the same side as the Slander boss too. "We're stretched thin with the losses in Errian and the support forces needed for this venture. We could use a quasi-legal security force to keep order in the city."

"Done."

Quince side-eyed Rogan. He was being awfully accommodating all of a sudden.

"For a price."

Ah, there it is.

"What price?" Alix's eyes narrowed.

"One of those keys, when this is all over." The man sat back, smacking his lips, looking like nothing so much as a toad who had just swallowed a big fly.

"Can't do that. I don't even know if we'll have one, and there's no way I'm letting you have one to be free to flit about Oberon City, ahead of law enforcement."

"Law enforcement?" Rogan chuckled. "That's a good one. Okay, how about this. When the crisis is over, you help me go legit and clean up the Slander. I want 25 percent profit on the offworld amalite trade, in addition to the pith that was already promised me."

Alix glared at him.

Quince ground her teeth. They were wasting precious time with this cretin.

"Done." Alix spit on his hand and held it out.

Rogan shook it. "I'll draw up the contracts and forward them to your PA." He stood, looking around with a big grin on his face. "Now if you don't mind, I'll see myself out. I have a security force to put together."

"Erissa, clear Rogan for departure from the building." Alix's eyes bored into the man's back as he left the room.

Quince closed her eyes. It seemed like a terrible idea, putting Rogan and his thugs in charge of the city, even if just for a short while, but things were spread too thin. She'd taken a look at the security roster. "I have a proposal."

"Let's hear it." Alix looked tired, dark spots under his eyes and his whole posture sagging.

"We need information. Where are the ithani? What are they? How do we stop them from destroying Erro?" She looked around the room, taking in each of the remaining skythane and landers. "Put Mylin here in charge of organization, pulling together everything we can get our hands on about this world, its anomalies, the skythane, and whatever may have come before them. She's a whiz at pulling together resources. Then the rest of us can feed her whatever we can find through our various resources."

Mylin blushed. "I don't know. I don't think I'm up to something like that."

"You were born to do this." Quince touched her cheek softly. "We need you now."

"I don't know. Maybe—"

"Oh come on, Mylin, you're fantastic at organization." Venin shot her an encouraging look.

Mylin blushed. "I guess…. Okay. I'll do my best."

"We'll be the Hunters." Alix pounded the table. "Let's hunt down our friends and bring them home."

There were nods around the room.

"Should we adjourn and run down our individual sources? Report back here?" Alix rubbed his eyes. "Erissa, I'm gonna need a stim."

The others assented.

"Alix, can you have someone sit with Mylin to get her up and running with her PA on DOC's system?"

"Sure."

"And Robyn, once she's done, sit with her and tell her everything you know about skythane legend and tradition."

"I can do that." Robyn kissed her cheek. "What are you going to do?"

"A little testing of my own down in Xander's storage unit. I'll be on my cirq if anyone needs me."

MYLIN OPENED HER EYES.

She sat in a field of data—a city of it. Information flowed back and forth in slow rivers, marked blue by her "user preferences." That's what Derren called them.

Flitting red packets resembled nothing so much as wereverens. She instinctively ducked as one of these made right for her, but it passed through her effortlessly, emerging on the other side to "slit" off to wherever it was needed. Another of Derren's words.

Derren was the OberCorp employee assigned to her by Alix. He was showing her around this "virtual world," or "veer." Or maybe "vir." It was all a bit unclear.

"Cirqs can run in three general modes. One is 'communication only'— that's great for contacting other people who are connected to the grid."

Mylin nodded. "Okay, got that. I think. The grid—it's like a web that connects everything and everyone in Oberon City?"

"And the rest of civilized—I mean, the rest of the Oberon side of Erro." His avatar flashed her a sheepish smile. It was even skinnier than he was, and its teeth sparkled when he grinned.

"It's okay. We think you landers are the uncivilized ones."

"Fair enough." He winked at her. "So the second mode is 'data interaction.' If you close your eyes, you can see images, process data, and generally interact with the grid and others on a superficial level."

Mylin tried to frame that in a way that made sense to her. "Like—seeing real life, but from someone else's eyes?"

Derren nodded. "Or like reading a book, but in your mind."

Mylin felt woozy. "It's a lot to wrap my head around." She looked around, trying to make this strange new world make sense.

"Sure. Sorry. I'll go slower."

She shook her head. "No, I'll be okay." He was cute. His avatar, aside from being thin as a silverbark, matched his "real" self—black hair, dark eyes. A nice smile. She shook her virtual head. "So this is the third?" She pointed at the virtual world they found themselves in.

"Yes. Virtual space, like I mentioned before. 'Vir' for short."

The place was a jumble of strange shapes, shifting landscapes, and a crazy array of moving objects. "It's dizzying."

"We can make it simpler. Bix, can you make a storage box for Mylin?"

"My pleasure."

Mylin looked around, startled. "Who was that?"

"That was my PA—my personal assistant. His name is Bixter. Bix for short. We'll get to that in a second."

The world shifted, and suddenly they were inside a featureless white box. "This is a storage box. A little bit of the grid just for you to use."

Mylin felt like she was inside a closet. "It's a bit stifling."

"We can fix that. Say this. 'Initiate PA.'"

She looked at him doubtfully. "To who?"

"Just say it. Your cirq will know what to do."

"Okay." Feeling self-conscious, she tried it. "Initiate PA."

A *thing* appeared before her. It was silver, in the approximate shape of a human, and waited silently, quiescent. "Oooh. What is it?" She walked all the way around it. It was beautiful, like one of the statues of Gael she'd seen at the chapel in Gaelan. She peered at its face, and then jumped backward with a yelp when it opened its silver eyes.

It cocked its head and looked at her. "Hello, Mylin. I am your personal assistant. What form should I take? I can be a human, patterned on someone you know, or an animal, or—"

"A zimbee." The thought sprang into her head fully formed. She used to love watching the fat insects zip around Founder's Hill.

The silver apparition frowned and cocked its head again. "I don't have that creature on file. Can you focus on an image of it?"

Mylin looked over at Derren. He nodded.

She focused on the image of a zimbee, a bird-sized pollinator with yellow and red stripes across its abdomen and fast-flickering wings.

"I see it." Her PA closed his eyes, and then shrank, sinking down toward the ground and changing color until he became the zimbee she'd seen in her mind's eye.

This place is amazing. Magic. She'd almost forgotten about her claustrophobia in the bare white box.

Her PA tested out his wings and lifted into the air to hover above her.

Mylin laughed, delighted.

"What would you like to call me?" The rich male voice sounded strange coming out of the small insect body. His multifaceted eyes glittered.

"How about 'Zim'? And can you make your voice less gender-specific?"

"Zim sounds wonderful. And how about this?" Zim's voice shifted up the scale, becoming less male-inflected. More like her friend Rhyl.

"I like it." She could get lost exploring this place and its wonders, but she had work to do.

Derren nodded. "You're doing great. Now ask Zim to change the blank white walls to something more pleasing."

"Anything?"

"Sure."

"How about a forest meadow?"

Zim bounced up and down. "Like this?"

All four walls became windows out into a forest clearing. Purple-leaved trees hung over a small brook on one side and swayed in an unfelt wind. "Perfect."

"Okay, last lesson. Zim can get things for you, and you can also use this space to organize them."

"Get them from where?"

"Mostly from DOC. That's short for 'Digital Oberon Corporation AI.' DOC runs this 'semi-autonomous grid,' or SAG. It's all very confusing at first, I know. Just think of DOC as the guy who knows everything that's on the grid."

"Okay." Mylin laughed. "How do I get here and back?"

"Just ask Zim. Zim, can you take Mylin back to rel?"

"Rel… real life?" Mylin was starting to work this out and to latch on to the possibilities.

"Or reality."

Zim hovered in front of her. "Is that okay, Mylin?"

"Yes, please."

The storage box vanished, and she opened her eyes to find Derren two inches in front of her, peering into her eyes. "You okay? I hope I didn't overwhelm you."

He's so cute. She pushed away gently and nodded. "Thanks for the lesson. Are you going to be here if I need you?" The office she'd been assigned to was a lot like the white storage box. She frowned. Maybe she could get a few things brought in here to make it less dismal.

"Of course. I've been assigned to work with you." He grinned. "I'm a grid whiz."

"Perfect." *As long as I don't get too distracted by the cute boy next door.* "Can you ask Robyn to come in?" She was tired, but she'd refused a stim. She didn't want any artificial wake aids. She'd decided she'd rather tough it out with a cup (or ten) of keff, which she'd been delighted to find on the OberCorp menu.

It was going to be a long night.

ROBYN SIGHED. "That's all I know about the prophecy."

Mylin was a precocious girl, clearly talented at organization, but she was also exhaustingly thorough. They'd been at it for four hours, as Robyn shared everything she knew about skythane culture, the nimfeach, the sneach—which she was beginning to think were two parts of the same thing—and whoever had come before them here on Erro.

"I'm sorry. I know you must be tired." The girl laid a hand on Robyn's knee. "You've been very patient with me."

Well, that much was true. *Mostly.* "I'm sorry. It's just been a long couple of days. Or couple of months." She had to remember she was no longer the queen. "Do you need anything else from me?"

"Not at the moment. If I do, I'll find you." Her eyes glazed over, a gesture Robyn had learned meant the girl was going into vir… some kind of magical world inside the "grid" where she was organizing all this information.

The girl's eyes cleared up again, and to Robyn's surprise they were wet. "I'm sorry. I never had a chance to tell you how happy I was to see you again, back in Gaelan. I thought… we all thought…." She got up and threw herself into Robyn's arms and hugged her tight.

The lander boy—Derren?—shrugged and grinned. "Long night," he mouthed.

Robyn nodded. "It's okay." She held the girl tight, running her hand lightly over Mylin's dark hair. "It's been a difficult time, for all of us."

When they separated, Mylin wiped her eyes. "You must think I'm such a mess."

"Not at all." Robyn wiped her own eyes. The girl's emotions had affected her more than she cared to admit. She'd spent so many years separated from her own son, Xander, who hardly needed a mother at all now.

Wherever he was.

He's still alive. She was sure of that, though she couldn't have said how she knew it.

She squeezed Mylin's hand. "You're doing what you need to do. Help me find my son. Help us figure out how to stop what's coming." She leaned forward and kissed Mylin's cheek. "Give her whatever help she needs," she said to Derren.

"I will, Missus…. Ms.…."

"Sléite. But Robyn will do."

She got up and left the small office, needing some fresh air. These lander buildings were so stuffy and controlled.

Quince had shown her how to find the hover tube that would take her to the roof. It would be good just to be outside for a few moments.

The palm plates had all been keyed for access by each member of the Hunters, as Alix had started calling them, so she set her hand against the cool surface and waited for the doors to open.

"Mind if I join you?" Jessa Althorpe, Jameson's offworlder ex, strode down the white hallway toward her. "This place is giving me a serious case of claustrophobia."

The woman was pretty, in a blonde sort of way, the kind of girl Robyn might have fallen for when she was younger. She was also made of steel, if half the things Robyn had heard about her were true. "Sure. I was just heading up to the roof to get some fresh air."

The doors opened, and they stepped inside. "The first time I rode in one of these things, I was scared shitless."

Robyn laughed. "Yes, I guess without wings they would be a bit daunting." She found these lifts more confining than anything. They reached the top of the tube and another pair of doors opened, letting them out onto the rooftop.

It was breezy up there, a cool night wind blowing off the Gildensea. The moon, Bandia, lit the sea with her silver glow. Robyn wondered idly if Oberon's moons, Hermia and Lysander, still circled the space where the half world had been, in another universe.

She stretched her arms and wings, breathing in the cool air gratefully. Small things to be savored in a world gone mad.

"They're still alive." Jessa sank down onto a bench and stared up at the moon.

"What makes you think so?" The rooftop was beautifully landscaped with a formal garden, complete with pathways and arbors covered with vines and lit by small sparkling lights. It had taken a beating with the great storm after the shift, but it was nice to be out among living things once again, however overmanicured.

"I don't know, exactly. Just a feeling I have. I think Quince is right. They went somewhere else."

Robyn nodded. "I think you're right too." How strange life was. She could never have foreseen, even two months before, that she would be standing atop the tower of her nemesis, half a world away from her home, talking with an offworlder about the end of the world. "Where do you think they went?"

Jessa frowned, scrunching up her forehead. "I don't know. Somewhere important."

"Why do you say that?"

"It's like they were meant to go, isn't it? I mean, nothing happened until both Jamie and Xand were touching the key, right?"

Robyn still wasn't used to that name. Xand. Xander. She missed her little *Davyn*. "I suppose so. The question that brings up is, did whoever planned this mean it for good or ill?"

"I don't know."

Robyn sat down on the bench next to the girl. Woman, really, but next to her, most women were girls. "I've waited for twenty-five years for this time, holding to the knowledge—the belief—that certain things were meant to happen." She took Jessa's hand in her own. "We have to believe it's true. It's the only way we can keep moving forward."

Jessa looked up at her. "You really think things are going to work out?"

"Yes. Yes I do." She allowed herself a small grin.

"On Beta Tau, they teach us that God has a plan for everyone, and that we are given guideposts along the way to guide us to where we're supposed to end up." She stretched her hands until her knuckles cracked. "Maybe the key was a guidepost."

"Maybe." Honestly, Robyn had been thinking along similar lines, though her gods were plural. "If things go sour, well, we won't be around any longer to worry about it, will we?"

Jessa laughed, a sweet sound. "I suppose not."

"I need to stretch my wings a bit. Will you be okay here alone for a few minutes?"

"Yeah, I think so. It's nice to have a little peace and quiet, and I know how to find my way back downstairs if I get bored."

Robyn touched her shoulder. "You're a good soul. Jamie will be all right, and so will Xander." She stepped up onto the parapet and jumped into the night sky, soaring upward under her own power.

No matter what else happened, having her wings back was a glorious thing.

8

───────

SOMEWHERE ELSE

JAMESON RUBBED his temples. He had one hell of a headache. It stretched from his neck all the way up the back of his head to his forehead, and his scalp tingled too.

All of him tingled, actually.

The key had begun to glow. He'd held it out to Xander, and there'd been a flash.

He opened his eyes.

"Hey there, you okay?"

Xander stared down at him worriedly for the second time in a day, his face framed by ruddy red sunlight.

There was something wrong with that, but Jameson couldn't quite get his head around it. "We have to stop making a habit of this whole sleeping-Jameson/white-knight-Xander thing." He sat up, pressing his palms into the golden grass to support his weight. "What happened?"

It was warm, and a stiff breeze blew through the blades, creating a sound like running water.

"A gateway, I think. At least, I'm pretty sure we're not at OberCorp Headquarters anymore." He helped Jameson up.

Jameson's head pounded like he'd just had a really bad drunken jag. "If you feel half as bad as I do—"

"Like you were shot with a pulse rifle?" Xander handed him the new key, the one that had set off whatever this was.

Jameson took it. "Something like that." It was inert now, no longer resembling liquid mercury, the surface flat and still.

He looked around. The grassy plain extended off into the distance, where mountains were painted purple against the blue sky. Bits of conference room desktop and flooring—and maybe cement or heavy plas—littered the grass around them. *Where are we?* Was it a different place? A different time? Was that even possible? "Why is the sun red? Not pink—red?"

Xander shrugged. "I don't think we're on Erro anymore." He stared at the key. "What in the Split did that thing do to us?"

"Hell if I know." Quince had been talking about going back to the Common worlds, before whatever this was had happened. Would things simply go back to how they had been before? How could they? *I have wings now. And Xander.* Sure, he wanted to stay with Xander, but would that mean they'd have to cut themselves—and Erro—off from the rest of the human race? Now, maybe, it no longer mattered.

He spied his carry sack half buried in the grass. "Looks like we got lucky. This made it through."

Xander nodded. "I found mine over there." He pointed to a rocky outcrop fifteen meters away.

Something flashed at the edge of his vision, but when he looked for it, there was nothing there. Jameson sank into the grass, crossed his legs, and went through his sack. He felt strangely calm—somehow traveling to heretofore unknown worlds had become a normal part of his life.

They needed to find their way back, though. Erro was in imminent danger, and he and Xander might be the only ones who could save it.

His sack was a bit of a disappointment—the pulse rifle and a few of the rations Xander had given him, and some dirty clothes.

Underneath it was the holo of Jessa he'd brought with him from Beta Tau.

He grinned. Maybe she'd find a way to come after him again.

Quince's old key was there too.

He held it up triumphantly. "Our way back home."

Xander raised an eyebrow. "Try it."

Jameson closed his eyes and pictured Xander's apartment. He twisted the key.

Nothing happened.

Xander didn't look surprised.

"I'll try another place." This time he tried the caverns where he and Xander had taken refuge after the shift. He twisted the key, and… nothing.

"Try something closer. The top of that hill." Xander pointed to a gnarled hilltop a hundred meters in the distance.

"Sure." Jameson tried, and was surprised when a gateway opened immediately. "What… how did you know?"

Xander shook his head. "Just a guess. I think we came too far for Quince's key to work. At least to take us home again."

"What about this one?" Jameson pulled out the new, larger key, the one Morgan had given to Quince.

"I don't know. Last time you touched it—"

"You touched it too!"

"Last time we touched it, things didn't go so well."

He's right. Jameson put the keys away reluctantly. It was frustrating to be trapped here with no idea where they were, or why.

A sharp whine split the still air. Jameson squinted at the sky. "Look!" Something was coming down fast, a sleek something. As it tumbled toward the ground, it leveled out just a few hundred meters above them.

It was some kind of craft. It was made of overlapping white sails that trailed off into nothing, leaving a gauzy contrail of sparkling light that faded in its wake.

It had some old damage—its back quarter was blackened and ragged on the near side as it slipped past, heading for some unknown destination in the distance. Jameson got a glimpse of some characters stenciled along its side. They were in no language he recognized. "Fight or flight?"

Xander arched an eyebrow at him again.

Jameson laughed ruefully. "Why do I even ask? Fight it is." His headache was quickly subsiding. *Thank the gods for that.* He kissed Xander. "Whatever the hell this place is, I'm glad you're here with me. Come on!"

He took off running and launched himself into the air, soaring up above the warm plains. The craft quickly left them in its wake, but he marked the direction it had gone.

They flew for hours across the seemingly endless plain, chasing in the direction of the strange craft.

Eventually, they stopped to take a rest. Far off to the east, a line of mountains circled the lowlands, purple with haze.

Jameson wiped his mouth with the back of his arm. He'd taken a sip of the stale water that remained in his canteen and had then handed it to Xander, but they were being cautious with their supplies. How long would they be stranded here, and when they would find food and water again?

Where the hell are we? "Do you think this is a third half of Oberon? Or Erro?" Even as he said it, it sounded stupid to his own ears.

Xander laughed. "Hell if I know. This is all as new to me as it is to you." He handed back Jameson's canteen. "It feels different, doesn't it?"

"Yes." There was a distinct chill in the air, and a strange smell… maybe ozone? Of course, those could just be local things.

Something flashed in the corner of his eye. He turned to look, but there was nothing again. *Damned memories.* That stopped him. How could he possibly have foreign memories of this place? Unless it really was Erro? Or some version of Erro?

He pulled out the new key. It had to be responsible for this. A trap? Or an invitation?

Jameson stared at it.

He wished Quince's key had worked. He was itching to be back home, helping his people through this latest crisis.

He remembered what Alix had told him. That amalite needed time to recharge. Maybe that was all it was. Maybe it wasn't charged enough yet. In a few more hours, he would try the key again, and it would work. They would be back in Oberon City.

Somehow, he didn't think it would be so easy. He sighed and closed his eyes.

"Hey, you okay?" Xander wrapped his arms around Jameson's waist, his wings settling around his back.

"Yeah. Just ready for a break in all the craziness."

Xander chuckled wryly. "I don't think we're going to get one anytime soon."

"Good morning, Jameson."

Jameson's eyes went wide, and he stumbled backward away from Xander. "Angie?" He hadn't heard that voice in at least a month, when Xander and Quince had forced him to burn out his bioware in a desperate attempt to avoid detection as they'd fled Oberon City. It seemed like a lifetime ago.

"Hey, you okay? Did I do something?" Xander's brow was furrowed.

Jameson shook his head. "She's back."

"Angie?" Xander asked, raising an eyebrow.

"My PA." There hadn't been time for Xander to get his cirq reinstalled before the flash. "Angie, it's so good to hear your voice."

"You too. I'm… avizzt… afraid I was not completely restored. There was some kind of glizzzch during installation. Can you have me deleted and reinstalled?"

Jameson shook his head. "Sorry, no. We're a long way from any human tech at the moment."

She was silent for a few seconds. "I don't detecccht a grid in the current location."

"Yup, we're in the middle of godsforsaken nowhere." To Xander, he explained, "She wasn't fully restored before the flash."

"I can run a self-diagnostic and see if I can patch some of the holes. I may not be fully functional."

Jameson nodded. "Please do. How long will that take?"

"At my current processor speed, maybe three hours. I will be nonfunctional until it's done."

"Do it." Jameson grinned. A partially functional Angie was better than none at all. *God, I missed you.*

"So?"

"She's going to see if she can fix herself. It'll take a couple hours."

"Wish there'd been time to get Ravi put back in my head—holy shit!" Xander stared up at the sky.

Jameson followed his gaze. Another "sail" craft was plummeting to the ground, this one at least twice as big as the first one.

A roar preceded it as it fell, wind whipping past and carrying fire and smoke up into the air behind it.

Xander's mouth was open. "What the hell?"

Another of the white sail ships chased it toward the ground.

The first ship slammed into the ground a few kilometers away from them, sending up a tremendous blast of fire and dirt and grass.

The smaller ship corrected course just before hitting the ground nearby and disappeared just below the horizon.

"What the hell did we land in the middle of? A war?" Xander stared at the rising cloud of dust and smoke.

"Starting to look that way." Jameson had been worried before, but now fear was starting to claw at his guts. They were all alone on a strange world, and bad things were happening that they had no understanding or control of. "Come on. Let's go see what we can find out."

Run toward fear. That was his new mantra.

It was a big improvement over his old one, *always run away.*

As long as it didn't get him killed.

XANDER WHISTLED SOFTLY.

They were crouched on a hilltop looking over the blast crater the ship had left when it hit the plains. It had partially disintegrated, but there was still enough of it left to see what it had been.

A thin stream of smoke drifted up from the crater.

A host of things was busy around the ship. They were beautiful. Like butterflies back on old earth, but somehow more ethereal.

He'd seen them before, in dreams. "Ithani," he whispered.

Xander nodded. "I think so too."

They bustled around the fallen ship, ripping it apart. After a few moments, they pulled one of their own from the wreckage, limp and faded, a moth to their butterflies. They carried their companion away to their waiting ship, and the search went on.

Jameson ducked as one of the creatures zipped up the hillside, its insect eyes jerking back and forth as if it were trying to see everything all at once.

Xander held his breath. He didn't know why, but he felt it was best if they remained unseen.

When he dared to look over the grass again, it was gone. "If those are ithani, is this some other part of Erro?"

Jameson shrugged. "Don't know. Maybe?"

It had taken them half an hour or so to reach the site of the downed craft. "What do you think they're doing down there? Search and rescue?"

"Maybe. Should we announce ourselves? Or maybe—" There it was again. The thing at the edge of his vision. He was becoming more and more certain it wasn't a memory. He put his hand to his lips, casually as he could manage.

Xander looked at him and nodded.

Jameson spun around in one smooth movement and reached out to grab the thing that was watching them.

He grabbed it by the thorax.

It tried to escape, flapping its wings and squealing as it pulled him off the ground.

Jameson was startled by its strength.

Xander leapt after him, pulling him back down to the ground.

They slammed hard onto the grass of the hillside, the two of them on top of the creature.

It stared up at them, iridescent wings fluttering. It was clear the thing was terrorized by them.

"It's a nimfeach." A memory fluttered by, the nimfeach gathered to witness the birth of a new clutch of ithani from their tri-parent. Jameson brushed it away.

"Jameson, show it the key!"

Jameson shot Xander a confused look. "Which one?"

"It doesn't matter. Hold one of them up. Let him see it." The ithani had made the keys, right? Maybe showing the nimfeach one would prove that they were friends. Or ithani themselves. He wasn't sure.

Jameson rummaged through his bag and pulled out the smaller key—the one Quince had first shown them on Oberon. He held it aloft and it came suddenly to life, the surface churning and giving off a bright golden glow.

The nimfeach went deathly still, staring at the rolling colors through multifaceted eyes.

"It's okay. We won't hurt you." He lifted himself up off the little creature.

It hummed, entranced.

Xander snorted. "Well, that did it. At least he's not scared of us anymore."

THEY'D SNUCK AWAY from the crash site, taking flight and putting some distance between themselves and the ithani.

Jameson was fighting back waves of memories. Not since the cavern after the split had they come so fast or so thick.

The nimfeach had triggered them.

It followed them, just a few meters behind, and nothing he did seemed to frighten it off. "You okay?" Xander glanced over at him, his eyes narrowed.

Jameson shuddered. "Not really." A memory slipped past his guard—a host of nimfeach surrounding a strangely enlarged ithani, skin the color of milk—waving their hands in unison and singing a strange, discordant alien song. He had the sense that there were many notes in the music that were simply beyond his ability to hear.

Jameson blinked and found himself plummeting toward the ground. He spread his wings to slow his descent, shaking his head, trying to clear away the memories.

"Jameson, what the hell?" Xander soared past him and made a wide arc, returning to hover a few feet away from him.

"Memory," he managed. "Not safe to fly."

His golden wings carried him down to earth, and Xander followed.

When his feet touched the ground, he fell into a crouch. Everything was swimming, and he couldn't focus.

He felt Xander's firm hand on his back. "You okay?"

Jameson opened his eyes. "Too many memories."

"Breathe through it, like Alix showed you."

Jameson nodded. He took a deep breath, held it, and then let it go. Then again, and again.

The memories receded a little.

Jameson's vision returned.

The nimfeach had landed on a low tree branch next to him, and it was looking up at him with its multifaceted golden eyes. It said something in its singsong language and reached out a fingerless hand to touch his face.

"What are you?" He'd felt an instant, strong compulsion to protect the creature, but he still didn't understand why.

"Purcck." The nimfeach's hand withdrew, and it touched its chest. "Purcck."

"That's your name?" Jameson pointed at the pip. "Puck?"

It purred and glowed. "Purcck."

"Puck it is."

Xander laughed. "I guess that's what he wants us to call him."

"Are we sure it's a him?"

Xander shrugged. "Doesn't really matter."

"Guess you're right." Jameson sat back on his ass, his wings counterbalancing his weight. "That's the worst attack I've had since Gaelan." His head pounded, and the memories flitted about at the edge of his conscious mind. "So what do we do now?"

Xander shrugged. "First, we rest a bit until you're sure you have a handle on things. Then we find someone who can tell us where we are."

· · ·

Erina bowed as low to the ground as ze could manage, trying to keep the hatred from showing in zer eyes.

The Thshnel'Jirron waved zer off, along with the others of zer sept who had come to pay zim a last homage before the Great Migration.

Ze hated zim for what zi had done to zer once proud people, all in the name of keeping them safe during the thousand cycles war. Hated how zi took young ithani and used them up, moving from one body to the next as the last one aged and died.

Hated what zi had done to the nimfeach, reducing them from proud elders to mindless servants, faded versions of themselves with no wills of their own.

Soon enough, zis reign would end. Zer last vision had been magnificent in its scope.

Ze ran through it again in zer mind, desperate to hold on to the details. The daring defiance it would require. The long interval—a hundred thousand cycles—and the eventual coming of the outsiders.

Finally, the chosen two. Two who would be stronger than one.

Ze fixed their faces in her mind. They were alien—soft-skinned, clumsy-looking compared to the lithe forms of the ithani or the small bodies of the nimfeach. One with a dark head, one whose head was light. And their wings.

Never before had ze seen such wings.

Ze had no guarantee that things would align themselves in just the right way. The future was fickle like that, but it was enough that ze saw a way to save the ithani and the nimfeach both from oblivion. Zer people.

It was time for zer to make a plan.

9

———

CLUES

Quince descended to the city streets under the cover of darkness.

Things had gotten a bit wild in Oberon City in the wake of the shift, with normal food chains disrupted and a haze of worry and uncertainty driving even the usually staid office drones to acts of desperation.

Quince had Ari monitoring grid news feeds. Rogan's forces were cracking down, which brought its own worries, but there was nothing she could do about that. *Better the devil you know.*

The storage unit, already a mess, had been emptied out of whatever supplies had remained after Xander's quick escape three weeks earlier. *Has it been that long?*

Quince glanced up and down the street. She was alone, as far as she could tell.

She tucked in her wings and ducked under the broken pieces of the roll-down door. The removal of all the junk actually made her job a bit easier.

She pulled out the old portable radiation detector Alix had dug up for her. She wasn't sure what she was looking for, exactly. Her working theory was that the gateways were a form of wormhole. They might leave behind some sort of telltale radiation signature. Or maybe they would change the structure of the things around them in some subtle way.

Ari had dug up a bit of theoretical research on exotic matter that was known to line the mouths of wormholes, which might leave its own particular signature.

The detector was shaped a bit like a long funnel with a bulb at the back end, allowing sampling of air or small pieces of material, which would be atomized inside and subjected to the device's mass spectrometer.

She sampled the air. "Ari, anything?"

"Background radiation levels are slightly higher than average. Nothing beyond normal parameters."

Quince nodded. If the ithani had used this method of travel regularly, they'd have found a way to make it as safe as possible.

She pulled out her knife and scraped a bit of the plas out of the wall and fed it into the device. "How about now?"

"Analyzing."

Quince touched the cool wall with her fingertips. Humans had been on the planet for seven and a half centuries. They'd managed a few truly impressive feats of architecture—the arcos and the various Houses of the skythane. And thousands of ugly utilitarian buildings like this one. *How long after we're gone will our works here still stand?*

Her mind strayed, and then she was somewhere else.

She stood on a beach in front of a ramshackle set of shacks and huts, staring at the buzz of activity there. A large gathering of humans—a few hundred? A thousand?—were bustling about the encampment in a flurry of purposeful action.

Quince looked around wildly. She didn't recognize this place.

Had someone hit her on the head?

Was this a dream? A memory?

All of the humans on the beach were landers.

"Definitely higher levels of alpha and beta radiation embedded in the plas." Ari's interjection brought her back to the present. "Likely to decay to undetectable levels rather quickly."

She shook her head to dispel the lingering remnants of the dream. Or whatever it was. *That* was interesting. "How quickly?" She didn't have any time for daydreaming.

"Estimating seven point three days?"

"Are these levels dangerous to humans?"

"Not without long-term, constant exposure or ingestion of said materials."

"So don't eat the walls. Got it." She pulled her hand away.

"I wouldn't recommend eating plas—"

"Sorry, Ari—it was a bad joke." PAs weren't as sophisticated at humor as humans.

"Ah."

"Does the signature match what we found in the conference room at OberCorp?"

"They are similar. The levels in the conference room were considerably higher."

"That makes sense. That was a more recent event."

"Even so, the levels are higher than simple time lapse would account for. I would say the two events are related, but quantitatively different."

Quince frowned. "What does that mean?"

Ari was silent for a moment. Quince was surprised. She hardly ever managed to stump the PA. "I would guess that it means the gateway in the conference room led to somewhere considerably farther away than the gateway here," he said at last.

"Farther away than halfway around Erro?"

"Possibly, yes."

Quince chewed on that for a moment. "Okay, let's head back to Ober-Corp. I want to run this by Alix and the others and see what they make of it." *Where the hell did you two go?*

VENIN STARED at the white ceiling. It was dark, the early hours of the morning. He'd been sent off to try to get some rest. Alix had set up one of the executive apartments for the Hunters' use and had brought in enough beds to sleep the lot of them.

It reminded him a bit of his childhood, when he and his three siblings—two sisters and a brother—had shared a room in their aerie in Gaelan. How many times had he stared out the window at the stars late at night, wishing he could fly free?

Waiting for puberty to get his wings?

Now here he was, grounded again, and Alix was just a few doors away.

Everyone else in their group seemed to have a purpose. Mylin was working to organize everything they knew about the ithani. Quince was out working to discover where Jameson and Xander had gone. Vestra had been sent back to oversee the refugees of Errian and Gaelan.

And Alix… well, he'd somehow become the team leader, with all the might of OberCorp now behind him.

Even that vile Slander boss had been given a task.

Venin wasn't used to feeling useless, and Alix was a temptation he really didn't need. He hadn't been interested in anyone since Taz. This was really not the time for it.

Venin closed his eyes, trying put Alix out of his mind, trying to ignore the snoring coming from Alia's bed.

He kept wandering back to the chapel high above Errian. To the statue of Erro—and the spark, or whatever it was, that had knocked him on his ass.

He closed his eyes and tried to regulate his breathing, to slow down his mind.

He'd seen something in that flash. *Felt* something. He stretched his wings out to their tips, trying to remember what it had been.

His outstretched hand. The glow. The spark.

He FLEW over a huge construction site.

Skythane below him were building a structure—a castle? It would eventually be surrounded by elegant gardens. The winding paths had been sketched out, and some of the bigger trees were already being planted.

They flitted in and out of the building zone, carrying in materials.

The sun overhead shone with a rosy glow.

The place sat in a wide grassy plain with few trees. It was somewhere he'd never seen before, but he recognized it nonetheless.

It was—or it would be—the House of the Stars.

It's not possible. That place had been constructed hundreds of years before, and yet it was as if he were there, seeing it with his own eyes.

He was seeing a memory, just like Jameson and Xander. The statue, it had done something to him.

Then he noticed something else.

The whole place sat in a depression that was almost perfectly circular, broken only at one point, where it looked like the ground had subsided.

It was too regular to be a coincidence.

Strange things happened at the House of the Stars. Gateways opened, some said time shifted, and even the weather was often different there than elsewhere on Titania.

There must be something underneath it. Something impossibly old—older than mankind's time on this world.

HE OPENED HIS EYES.

In his mind's eye, he still saw the busy skythane, the rising construction, and the giant unnatural circle.

It was just a dream. Right? It had to be.

"Taz?"

His PA, named after Tazim, answered in his head. "Yes, Venin?"

It was so strange, so… intimate to have a voice in his head. "Do you record my dreams?"

"No, not unless you ask me to."

"Ah, thanks." Alix had shown him the basics of "interfacing" with his PA, but the whole thing was so alien to him.

So there was no way to recall the dream, other than from his own memory.

He wondered what else Taz might be able to do for him. "Taz, do you have access to… material of a sexual nature?"

"Yes. I have full access to the Oberon City grid library, including male on male pornography. What would you like?"

"Anything with a redhead?"

"Close your eyes."

He did as he was told and was soon in the middle of a room in vir, watching two men, one redheaded and one brunet, going at it as the walls flickered through scenes varying from dungeon walls to an alpine ski loft. One of the guys looked up at him and grinned.

His eyes flickered open. "Enough. Thanks."

He was covered in sweat and was aroused as hell. *How do these landers get any real work done, with toys like this?* If he'd had that kind of thing when he'd been a teenager, he'd never have left the aerie.

The dream, though, still weighed heavily on his mind. Time was short. What if it was something, and he said nothing?

He got up, his feet touching the cool tile floor. His bed was set up in the entry room, near the door. He'd chosen it out of habit—always have a clear exit path—that had been instilled in him at home with his siblings and pounded into him as a palace guard in Gaelan.

He needed to find Quince, or maybe Robyn, and see what they thought.

He got up and crept out of the suite, encountering no one. "Taz, where are Robyn and Quince?"

"Both are outside of the building."

"Who else is still here, and awake?"

"Alix is in his office."

Of course he is. The man was unstoppable.

Alix was sitting at his desk, and his eyes had that glazed-over look that said he was in vir space. Alix bore an uncomfortable resemblance to the man Venin had watched in the adult entertainment he'd just partaken of.

"Would you like me to ping Alix?" Taz asked.

He jumped. "Um, sure." He managed to catch himself on the doorframe before he tripped and fell on his ass. "Sorry. I forgot you were there."

"It's all right. It takes new users some time to get used to having a PA inside their heads." Taz said it with a bit of a lilt.

He's teasing me. Venin decided he liked Taz. "Mylin took right to it," he said with as little resentment as he could manage.

"Girls *are* smarter. On average, 3.7 percent smarter than men of their same age."

Now Taz was *definitely* yanking his chain.

He was about to ask the PA if he was real when Alix's eyes focused. The man looked at him, and his gaze traveled up and down the length of Venin's shirtless body, an appreciative smile slipping across his lips. "Hey. What can I do for you?"

Venin chose to ignore the not-so-subtle undertones of that statement. Skythane and lander, he reminded himself. Bad mix. "How's your mother?"

Alix closed his eyes. "Erissa says she's okay. I was going to go see her soon."

"Good."

Alix glanced up at him. "Anything else?"

Venin felt like an idiot. "Um, I had a dream. I know it's stupid."

Alix sat up, giving Venin his full attention. "Tell me."

"It was probably nothing. I shouldn't have bothered you." He turned to head back to bed.

"Hey wait—it's okay. I could use a break. Please, tell me what you dreamed." He gestured toward the other chair in the room and leaned back in his. "It might be important."

Venin paused. "You sure?"

"Yeah. Vir work really tires me out, even with a stim."

Venin turned the seat around, sat down, and looked around at the huge office. "You landers really like white."

Alix snorted. "It's OberCorp's way of keeping the ugliness and dirt of everyday life at bay. So what was this dream about?" He leaned back in his chair, putting his hands behind his head.

Venin looked away from Alix's beautiful outstretched body. "It started earlier today, in Errian. I visited the chapel of Erro above the city—"

"You'll have to tell me more about the skythane religion one of these days."

Venin laughed. "I imagine it's a bit different from what you're used to."

"Yeah. My family… we were never very religious. So it started earlier today?"

"Yes. The statue of Erro in the chapel—it glowed."

Alix sat forward, suddenly looking even more interested.

There was something about this lander man that intrigued Venin immensely. "I reached out and touched it, and there was this… spark? Powerful enough that it knocked me over."

Alix nodded. "That sounds like what happened to Jameson."

"I thought so too." He frowned. "Why me? I'm no one special."

"Don't denigrate yourself. From what I've seen, you're quite impressive."

"You know what I mean. I'm not a king or a prince. I don't run a big corporation, like some people."

"None of us were those things when all this started." Alix sat back, a wistful look on his face. "What did you see?"

Venin closed his eyes. "When I was lying in bed tonight, it came to me. A dream, or vision. Maybe a memory?" He frowned. It sounded silly when he said it out loud. *Too late to back down now.* "It was the House of the Stars, but a long time ago, when they were first building it. I was high up in the air, watching, and I could see it, clear as day."

"What's that?"

"The circle." It was so strange.

"Circle?"

"Yes. There's a circle in the ground that surrounds the whole place. I think there's something there. Something underneath." He opened his eyes to find Alix's brown eyes staring into his.

"Does the House of the Stars have any strange… properties?"

"Yes. Time sometimes moves a bit strangely there. The main waygate between Titania and Oberon is there too."

Alix scratched his head absentmindedly. "Erissa, get me some satellite images of the area around the forks of the Theseus and Demetrius Rivers." A stack of images appeared above his desk. "We don't have any satellite imagery of Titania, of course—different universe and all that—but we do have lots of the Oberon side. The satellite photos of that region were always a bit sketchy. They thought it had to do with a particularly large amalite deposit under the crust there." He reached out and sorted the glowing images, and then rearranged them so they overlapped, making a ring around the area where the House of the Sun stood. It was heavily wooded, but bits and pieces of land showed through here and there. "Well I'll be damned."

Venin leaned over to look, aware of how close Alix was.

Alix's finger traced the photos. There was a clear line of demarcation that flowed in fits and starts from photo to photo, forming a circle just like the one he'd seen in his dream. Half of it was shifted a bit, but it was there nonetheless, if you knew to look. "About fifty kilometers wide."

Venin sat back and whistled. "What do you think it means?"

Alix shook his head. "I have no idea, but it seems important. What do you say we go and have a look-see to find out?"

Venin went off to pack the few supplies he had.

Alix gave him a provisions code to order whatever else he might need from DOC and headed down to the medical wing to see his mother.

It was late. She was probably asleep, which would be just as well. He didn't need a confrontation.

A weary Dr. Glynt looked up from the reception desk. "Hello, Mr. Preston."

"Pulling a late shift?"

She nodded. "No one else came in with all the trouble in the city."

"Can I see her?"

"Of course. Let me know if you need me for anything." She went back to manipulating a file tree on her tri-dee screen.

He poked his head into the room. She was fast asleep.

He stood by her bedside, looking down at the woman who had, as of the day before, been the most powerful person on the planet. She looked small and frail, her boundless energy drained away, but she looked peaceful too.

He was about to go when her eyes flickered open, and she looked up at him. A crooked grin crossed her lips. "Got your attention, did I?"

He laughed, more harshly than he intended. "Is that all this was? I've got more important things to attend to—"

"More important than your own mother?"

"At the moment, yes." He turned to go, but she caught the edge of his shirt.

"Please don't go."

He stopped, undecided.

"I'm…. I had my reasons for everything I did."

"That's it? That's the best you've got?" He rounded on her. "You were willing to wipe out half the planet, and 'I had my reasons' is the best you can do?"

She let go of his shirt, slumped back down on the pillow, and looked away.

"Just this once, I thought, maybe she'll say she's sorry. Maybe she'll show some actual signs of the humanity she's managed to hide from me for so long." He turned to leave again.

"You're right." Her voice was so low, he almost didn't hear it.

"What did you say?"

She sat up, some of her usual strength returning. "I said 'You're right.'" This time she said it clearly. Was there even a note of contrition in her voice?

"Right about what? You have to *say it*."

"Right about everything. About the war. About the kind of mother I am. About *everything*."

Alix nodded. "Now that's a start." He pulled a chair up to her bedside. "You weren't really trying to kill yourself, were you?"

She looked at him, strangely vulnerable without makeup or her usual clothes and hair. "No. Not really. I had Zenix give me the extras. He refused, until I explained that I needed to use them for some OberCorp experiment or other. You didn't get all my override codes." She smiled thinly, but whatever pleasure she took in the thought didn't last. "You know why I hate them."

"Who?"

"The wing men."

"They're called skythane."

"Wing men. Skythane. Whatever. I told you what one of them did to me."

He nodded. "He raped you. But they're not all like that—"

"He was your father."

Alix froze. *My father?* "There's no way."

"Oh, there was a way. I thought I loved him." She sighed, a long rattling sound.

I'm half skythane. It was a strange thought. He'd wanted to fly forever, watching the skythane men and women with jealousy and eagerness. It was part of why he was obsessed with them.

"So you see? I was wrong. Your mother was wrong. I didn't want you to be like them. I didn't want them to exist. Not after what happened to me." She looked at him. "But you, you were always enchanted by them. You wanted to run off to the Outland to find them. I just wanted you to be like me." She put her hands in her lap, and suddenly she looked old, her face drawn, her hands showing their age. "What are you thinking?"

Alix shook his head. "Honestly, I'm still trying to wrap my head around this. You *knew*? All this time?"

She looked away. "You must hate me."

For his entire life, she had lied to him about who he was. Where he came from. Now she wanted his forgiveness. He let go of her hand. "I don't hate you. I… I just need some time."

He got up and walked out of the room, ignoring her calls.

ALIX WAS PACKING A CARRY SACK, shoving clothing into it angrily, when Quince found him in the bedroom he was using in the OberCorp executive suites.

The sun was just climbing over the Pyramus Mountains, slanting through the plas windows.

"Did the sack have it coming?" She leaned back against the doorframe and crossed her arms, her wings lying flat against her back.

"Hey, Quince." Alix pulled something out of the suite's replicator and stuffed it into the sack. "Sorry. Bad night."

She arched an eyebrow. "Going somewhere?"

"Yes, Venin noticed something very interesting about the House of the Sky and the House of the Stars. I think it's relevant to the Hunters' investigation."

That got Quince's interest. "Show me."

"Erissa, can you pull up the composite we put together of the skythane site?"

"One moment." Alix's PA used the suite speakers to respond, likely out of politeness to Alix's visitor.

A glowing slice of terrain appeared above the suite's tri-dee table. "This part of Oberon is notoriously difficult to image properly. The company believed it was due to a dense deposit of amalite deep below the surface. The stuff messes with sensing technology."

Quince nodded. "What did you find?"

"Venin had a dream. Or a vision?"

Quince shot him a look. *Him too?* "Go on."

"He saw this place long ago, when the skythane first built the Houses." His finger traced a part of the composite. "It's hard to see it unless you know what you're looking for. But look here."

Quince peered at the image. "What am I looking at?"

"It's a circle."

She stared where he was pointing, and her gaze followed it around. "Hmmm. That's… interesting. An old meteor crater?"

He shook his head. "I thought so too, at first, but the edge, where it's visible, is too perfect."

She took that in. "You think—"

"I think we might be looking at the shift engines. The machines that the ithani built to bring this whole world from our universe to here."

"Damn." Quince whistled. "They were practically under our feet the whole time."

"Maybe if we can get inside one of them, we can figure out a way to put a damper on the ithani's plans."

"It's worth a try." Quince sank down into the couch. The whole business was overwhelming. They had less than three days to decipher the artifacts of an alien race before they'd all be sent to kingdom come. "What kind of vision?"

"What?"

"You said Venin had a vision, or dream?" She'd been seeing things herself, of late. Nothing as extensive as what Jameson and Xander had experienced, but tantalizing bits of something.

"Oh. He said he dreamed it, or something." He turned to stare at her. "He said he touched a statue. In a chapel in Errian, I think. Like Jameson."

That's interesting. "Hell of a coincidence."

Alix nodded.

"Who are you taking?"

"Venin and Alia." He closed up his pack, sealing it shut.

Hidden technology, sleeping aliens, mysterious keys—things had gone so off the rails. "Okay. We have to try to cover all the bases."

"My thought exactly. Maybe we'll find Xander and Jameson there."

She noticed he no longer said Jameson's name with disdain. It was progress. "I don't think so. I did some testing. It's pretty clear that it was some kind of gateway that swallowed up our two skythane kings."

"*Pretty clear?*" He sealed up his carry sack.

"The radiation pattern matches the one in Xander's storage unit, but Ari thinks it was a more powerful version. That it sent them farther away than Errian. A lot farther."

Alix put his sack on the table and stared at her. "What's a lot farther from here than Errian?"

"Exactly." Bandia, Titania's moon, was farther, but it was a barren waste-land. Beyond that…. "I'm going to sit down with Mylin and see what she found. Maybe all these pieces will add up to something."

"That sounds good. I'll keep in touch over the grid." He tapped his temple.

"I'm not sure you'll be able to connect from the House of the Sky, let alone underground."

"DOC's building me an amplifier in one of the hoversports. I'm hoping it will be enough to punch through whatever dampens the signal down there."

Quince frowned. "How many hoversports does OberCorp have left? We took down a bunch of them over Titania."

Alix grimaced. "A lot fewer than I'd like."

"Sorry about that." She managed a half grin, half growl. "I might need some firepower for the next step in my investigation."

Alix nodded. "Erissa, see that Quince here has access to the headquarters armory. Anything in particular you'll need?"

"Nope. Just some high-power hand-carried weapons."

"Know how to use them?"

Quince laughed bitterly. "Yeah. I've had a bit of training." *Too much, in fact.* She held out her hand. "It's good to be working side by side with lander forces."

He took her hand and pulled her in for a hug. "Agreed. Take care of yourself, Quince." He smelled like stress and exhaustion.

She squeezed him tight and then let him go, watching him walk down the hall toward the lift tube.

Less than three days.

She went in search of something with caffeine. To survive those days, she was gonna need every bit of energy she could find.

10

———

QUESTS

Dani awoke.

She was lying on something extremely comfortable. She could feel its support underneath her back and wings.

Her wings.

She wanted to get up and dance, to flutter them about, to laugh and sneer at all her enemies, those who had taken her wings away in the first place.

She wanted to sing.

Her body did none of these things.

She couldn't see, either. Something covered her eyes.

"You're awake." The voice came from inside her head.

"I… I am." *What the hell?*

"I've been waiting for you for a long time. A very long time. Danielle Black. Daughter of Danner Black. Born in the little Gaelani village of Toreor, mother deceased." Whatever it was recited the facts concisely, without emotion.

"What are you?"

It chuckled inside her head. "I thought you would have figured that out by now." Dani stood, but her body wasn't under her own control. She approached one of the white walls and waved her hand over it. It shimmered and became reflective, and she was staring into her own face. "I'm one of the ithani. King of the ithani, if you will. My name is Jirron, but you can call me *pain*."

She tried to scream, but her body was still under the other's control. "You're not me. You're… you're the thing in the dark." She should've been in full-blown panic, but her body remained steadfastly calm. Something had taken over her mind and body. Was her soul next? "Who the hell are you?"

"You're going to give me everything you know. About yourself. About humankind. About how the world has changed."

She nodded. "I will. I'll tell you anything."

Dani felt herself grin, and it was the most unnerving thing she had ever experienced. "Oh, you don't need to tell me anything. I plan to take what I need."

Dani squirmed in her bonds. "You don't have to. I'll help you. Really, I will!"

She felt its laughter. "I wanted the chance to speak with you before you ceased to be. Personal preference, you understand. It's an honor, really. But now I'm afraid I'm growing tired of our little conversation."

What the hell was this thing in her head? "I can help you. I know a lot about the human world."

"You will. It's why you were chosen. Now calm yourself. Panic won't make this any easier on you."

"Why?"

"Why? Oh, I see. Why give you back your wings, only to take everything else away?" It sounded pleased with itself at having figured out her question. "So I could use them myself. I will be more than ithani, you see. I will be human, too, and when the Migration begins, I will take all your *skythane* into me too." He spat the word out.

"Migration? What do you mean? What are you going to do to me? Please. Please! Just talk to me. I can help you—"

Then it began.

Her *self* unraveled, little bits peeling away and melting into nothing. Into it. Into him. For she was sure Jirron was male. Only a *man* could do this to a woman.

She could feel the pieces going. Each memory burned as it evaporated, searing her soul.

She tried to open her mouth to scream as her past, her loves, her hates, her very name were sloughed off like so much dead skin, but she was powerless to stop it. Powerless to even protest.

With everything she had left, Dani tried to scream.

As she was swept away into dust, she managed a slight grimace, but it didn't last.

The last thing she felt was the return of that terrible, involuntary smile, stretching its way across her face.

MYLIN STARED at her wall in vir. It was covered with bits of information gleaned from her interviews of the other skythane. Robyn and Vestra had been particularly helpful.

She had a working history of the skythane population of Erro—first Oberon and then Titania. The individual notes were coded for certainty. Purple marked the things she was most sure of, and green the least.

She stared at her wall. The virtual forest was almost entirely covered.

The skythane had come to Oberon, as best as anyone could agree, a bit over eight hundred years before. *So far, so good.*

The colonists must have been on a generation ship that launched just before the Collapse—an event that many at the time assumed had ended life on Earth. One that she'd been unaware of, until now. There was so much she didn't know.

She'd asked DOC to put together a quick history of the Common Worlds dating back to the recolonization of Earth from Moonbase sometime after the Collapse.

She sat back and tried to picture it—the destruction of an entire world. Fleeing from your home, certain that all you knew and loved existed no more.

Someday soon, she might know that feeling herself, if she survived.

Oberon had been rediscovered by a ship from a company called Zephyr-Corp, headquartered on a revitalized Earth. The interstellar conglomerate would later be broken up by the Common Worlds government.

From there, the records improved, at least on the OberCorp side. The company had started a new calendar that dated from First Landing, and she had a pretty detailed account of what had happened since on the Oberon side of Erro.

The company had recorded anomalies too—the interference out at the ragged edge of the world, along the split, that caused electronics to fail. The strange area around the House of the Sky was notoriously difficult to capture in satellite imagery. The company experts had suggested that amalite deposits were to blame for both phenomenon.

Zim appeared before her, his little wings buzzing rapidly. "Quince would like to see you."

Mylin nodded. Those things could wait, and Quince might be able to add more information to the mix.

She had Derren and DOC running a deep search through the company archives for anything that might point toward the ithani—who and what they really were. Derren was amazing. He was as excited about organization as she was, and he knew the Oberon City grid like the back of his hand.

It was a slim chance, though. The ithani had been dead and gone—or hibernating—for a hundred times as long as humans had wandered this place, if not more.

She opened her eyes in rel.

Quince was pacing back and forth in front of Mylin's desk, a frown on her face. Her wings fluttered, as if agitated on their owner's behalf.

Derren looked like he was deep in vir.

"Hello, Quince." Mylin was both in awe of and afraid of the older skythane woman. Quince had a hard edge to her, and a no-nonsense attitude that Mylin strove to emulate, though she failed miserably. But she could also be quite biting when she was upset.

"Hey." Quince stopped pacing and sat down on the stool facing Mylin's desk. "I was hoping you had some news for me."

Mylin shook her head. "I'm still gathering information, I'm afraid. So far, I have more questions than answers."

Quince raised an eyebrow. "Such as?"

Mylin glanced over at Derren. His eyes were unfocused. Poor guy was working on as little sleep as she was. She held up her hand. "One: Where are the ithani cities? They were the masters of this planet for who knows how long before the first shift. Why haven't we found some kind of ruins? Derren brought that one up."

"Maybe their cities were like Errian. Made of living plants that have long since decayed?"

"Hmmm, maybe." She made a mental note to look into that. "Two: Who built the gateways and made the keys, and when? And who taught *us* to use them?" She laughed ruefully. "That one's all tied up in the memories somehow."

Quince nodded. "Good thinking so far."

"Three: Where were the skythane for a few thousand years? We know from human history they can't have left Earth more than about a thousand or fifteen hundred years ago—probably before the Collapse? And yet I just got back a DNA sample test that puts us about ten thousand years apart from landers, genetically speaking. It's just not possible."

"Damn. That doesn't sound like nothing."

Mylin grinned. She loved these new tools Quince had given her and was already working out how she could get a grid in Errian and Gaelan for the skythane.

First things first. *No planet, no grid.*

Quince cleared her throat.

Mylin jumped. She'd been wandering again. "Sorry. I get sidetracked easily."

Quinn smiled. "It's okay. I was just saying that I might be able to help you with the first one." She blinked. "Ten thousand years? Really?"

"Yes. Any idea why?"

"Maybe. Let me give it some thought. In the meantime, Ari, can you show Mylin what Alix showed me?"

A piece of terrain appeared above her desk, rotating slowly.

"Where is that?" Mylin leaned over to get a better look.

"The House of the Sky."

"Oh. Ooooh!" A dotted line was drawing itself across the map, connecting bits and pieces of the terrain into a near-perfect circle.

"I think we may have found some of those ruins you were looking for."

"Underground." Mylin whistled. "Okay, that helps."

Quince nodded. "Thought it might. Alix and Venin are going with Alia to see what they can find. They should be able to help you if you need some eyes on the ground."

"Thanks. Did you find Xander and Jameson?" Mylin had a soft spot for the Gaelani king. He was a good man and had saved her and her family, along with all of Gaelan.

"Not yet, but I have another anomaly for your list. Where would a gateway go, if it used far too much power to be somewhere here on Erro? And where did the power come from?"

"I don't know, but I'll add it to the list."

"Thank you."

"There's one more thing." She'd been hesitant to bring it up, as she didn't really know much about the system yet, but maybe it was important.

"What?" Quince arched an eyebrow.

"I asked DOC to run a scan for anything unusual. Unaccounted for? Anything in the network that didn't seem to belong."

Quince nodded. "And?"

"There are all kinds of things. Illicit… blackware, some of it? He shuts that down when it becomes a problem, but I guess there's a lot of it?"

"Oberon City is a nest of vipers." Quince smiled. "Go on."

"There's some static too. Maybe solar interference, or something from the amalite deposits. That's pretty easy to figure out because it's so random."

"Damn, you've really taken to this."

Mylin blushed. "I'm doing the best I can."

Quince got up and put a hand on her shoulder. "You're doing a great job."

"Thanks. So anyhow, there's this other thing. I thought it was noise at first, but Derren helped me filter it out." It was weird.

Derren heard his name and wandered over from his post. "Yeah, it's… weird."

Mylin grinned. *Great minds.*

"Can you show her?"

"Of course." He swiped the map away, and in its place a twining series of glyphs appeared. "There's some kind of code worming its way through the OberCorp core. It's just weird."

Quince squinted at the twirling column. "What do the glyphs represent?"

Derren shook his head. "We don't know. When we realized it was more than random noise, I asked DOC to look for repeating letters. Phrases. And to tag them with different glyphs. There are fifty so far that he's identified. They repeat, sometimes even repeating whole words, but overall the composition keeps changing."

"Could someone in Oberon City have written this?"

Derren shrugged. "I suppose anything is possible, but it doesn't look like any code I've ever seen. Or DOC, for that matter."

"I'll take your word for it."

"Do you think it's important?"

Quince nodded. "I think it might be very important. You were right to bring it up."

Mylin sighed. She was hopelessly outmatched by this task. "Thank you. I'm scared I'm going to fail. To let you all down."

"You're doing great. Keep it up. You too, Derren." She gave the young man a clap on the shoulder.

Mylin's face felt hot. "Thank you. Oh, I found this too." She brought up a map of Oberon City on her tri-dee desktop.

"What's this?"

One spot glowed white, deep in the Slander. "It's an injection site." She looked to Derren for confirmation.

He nodded. "It's where we think this code is entering the network."

Quince's face went white. "This is an active attack?"

"We think so. If it *is* an attack." She still was unsure about how this whole grid thing worked. "It's definitely active."

"I'll look into this. I'll let you know if I find anything. You do the same?"

Mylin was a bit unnerved by the serious look on Quince's face. She was glad she wasn't the woman's target. "I will." She watched Quince walk out, still flying high on the compliment but terrified by the responsibility that sat on her shoulders.

Then she closed her eyes and went back to work.

"Ari, where's Robyn?" Quince picked up a heavy pulse rifle. It was a new design she hadn't seen before, stamped with the Renton Ringworlds logo. So OberCorp had been importing firearms, probably for the planned war with the skythane.

That was over now. They had bigger auxes to skin.

She closed her eyes for a moment. She was tired—dead tired, if she was honest. She'd taken a couple stims already to keep going, and even though they were supposed to be side-effect free, she'd pay a price eventually.

She hoped Alix was being careful with access to these weapons. Should they fall into the hands of Rogan and friends, they'd have more than just the ithani and the end of the world to worry about. All the Syndicate needed was more weapons.

"She's on the roof. Should I tell her you're looking for her?"

"No. You'd just scare the zimbees out of her." She shouldered two of the pulse rifles, and then started looking over the grenades.

"Can I… can I help you find anything, ma'am?" The guard assigned to the armory was woefully out of his depth.

Quince laughed ruefully. "No, I'm good. Just picking up a few supplies."

He'd been reluctant to let her in, a point in his favor, but he hadn't known where anything was, either.

She'd invoked Alix's authority, and after a short conversation with his PA, and presumably with DOC, he'd relented and let her access the weapons.

She wanted something sharp and dangerous-looking, too, in case she needed to intimidate someone.

She found what she was looking for at the back of the armory. A box marked simply "knives" had some exquisite throwing blades from Beta Tau. Jameson's home planet eschewed guns, generally, but made up for it with an unseemly love of all things sharp. The microthin carbon blade looked wickedly keen.

"Bring me that staff?" Quince pointed at one of a set of fighting rods leaning in the far corner without looking back.

The man did so, trying to hand it to her.

"Hold it out in front of you with both hands, please."

He nodded. "Yes ma'am." His hands were shaking.

"Steady," she hissed. "And don't call me ma'am. Quince will do."

"Yes, ma… Quince." His grasp steadied.

She brought up the knife with one arm and slashed down at the pole.

It cut clean through the metal.

Quince grinned. *That's the one I want.* It came with a special holder… probably diamond-studded inside. Satisfied, she strapped it to her belt.

She looked around, searching the data streams. One of her enhancements let her "see" them when she wanted, a capability she'd lost when she'd burned out her bioware.

Not that she'd needed it out in the Outland, or on Titania.

Traffic was heavier than usual. People were worried, and with good reason.

Rumors of war, the planet itself rattling under their feet, and now the lords of the Slander taking over the city with their wing men cohorts. It was enough to freak out any lander.

Including the poor man assisting her.

"What's your name?"

"Tovey, ma'am. Quince." He was literally shaking in his boots.

She put a hand on his shoulder. "Thanks for the help, Tovey. You're probably scared as shit, right?"

He swallowed hard. "Yes."

"Ever seen any action?"

"No, ma'am. They just posted me here yesterday."

Poor kid couldn't be any more than seventeen or eighteen standard. "Just over a week ago, Erro almost ended in fire. Did you know that?"

"No." He turned even whiter.

She squeezed his shoulder gently. "We got through that. Compared to that, the rest of this will be a cakewalk."

He closed his eyes and nodded. "I hope so."

"If you need me, call me." She had Ari send the boy her personal contact code. For some reason, she felt a connection to him. He was a human face on the events unfolding here in Oberon City and around the globe. "If you can't get me, call Mylin directly. She's one of the skythane working upstairs. She can find me."

"Thanks." He looked around, and then back at her. "Follow me."

"Sure?"

He led her to the back of the room and palmed the door there.

A panel slid open.

"These just came in before… before whatever it was happened last week." He pointed to a plas crate in the corner.

She knelt and popped it open. Inside were a set of circles of various sizes that gleamed even in the low light of the dim storage room. "Are these…?"

He nodded. "I think so. I thought they were illegal in the Common Worlds."

"They are." She picked up a couple and slipped them into her carry sack. "But we're not in the Common Worlds anymore."

He laughed ruefully. "No. I guess we're not."

She picked out a crossbow for Robyn and a few flash grenades, and then said goodbye to Tovey, who looked slightly less green now. "Thank you, and call me if you need me." She squeezed his arm, and then made her way back to the main hallway, waiting until he had locked up the room securely once more.

The weapons stored there were far too dangerous. What else did Ober-Corp have stashed away?

Once this was over, she'd make sure it was destroyed. All of it. She shuddered to think what might have happened if the skythane war with the landers had gotten out of hand.

Shaking her head, she said goodbye to Tovey.

Then she went to find Robyn. They had a job to do.

11

—————

CRASH

VENIN STARED at the hoversport. His fingers itched to pull out his pulse rifle, now fully recharged, and to leap on top of the beast to blow it to bits. It had been that kind of week. It was hard to see it as anything other than a tool of the enemy, and yet he was here with one of them, about to board it on a joint mission to save the world. *What strange times we live in.*

OberCorp maintained a hangar for the craft in a separate complex, across from the imposing headquarters building. The building itself was huge. The entire House of the Moon—and half of Gaelan—could have fit inside.

It was also the training facility for the company's enforcers and rangers. Venin had gotten quite a few looks, many of them not friendly, from the OberCorp personnel as he made his way to the hangar.

There was a lot of bad blood between lander and skythane, especially these last few weeks, and it was going to take a long time to change that.

He sighed. *Nothing to do for it now.*

Tazim would have turned it all around with his easy charm. He'd been blond where Venin's hair was black. Light where Venin was dark-skinned. So full of confidence and life he'd seemed always on the verge of going supernova.

Tazim wasn't here. Tazim was long gone.

"Ready to go?" Alix clapped him on the shoulder, ducking as Venin swiped at him with a wing.

"As ready as I can be." *Damn you for startling me like that.* Skythane wings needed to have teeth.

"Hey, watch it. It's just me. I brought Alia along too. Thought the extra support couldn't hurt." He was dressed in ranger black, a tight plas-leather suit that highlighted… just about everything.

Alia nodded. "Not just because you wanted a chaperone?" She shot him a sly look.

Too close. Venin looked away.

Alix shook his head, looking innocent as a schoolboy. "Of course not. You're skilled as hell, and you won't slow us down."

"Says the man with no wings."

Alix nodded. "Got that covered too. My bi-wings are packed and ready to go." He palmed the side of the hoversport, and the ramp descended to the ground.

Venin wasn't quite sure what to make of the byplay between the two. He gave up trying, tucked in his wings, and followed Alix inside.

Alix settled into the pilot's seat, running a systems check. He seemed subdued.

"Did you talk to your mother?"

Alix stared straight ahead, concentrating on the task.

"That bad, huh?"

"It didn't end well. Can you take a seat? We'll be taking off shortly."

Ouch. "You got it." He backed off, leaving Alix be.

The interior was all military—no frills and no-nonsense. Aside from the pilot's seat, the troop benches that lined both sides were hard black plas, and too narrow to accommodate skythane. Venin growled under his breath. He'd be happy to get out of this lander hellhole—he didn't know how Xander and Quince had managed to live here all those years.

He squatted, determined to give Alix a piece of his mind once they landed.

Alix spun around. "What are you doing?"

"There's no place for me to sit."

Behind him, Alia laughed. He turned to see her seated in a chair that was molded for her skythane frame.

"How…?"

"Ask your PA."

Of course. I'm an idiot. "Taz, can you, I don't know… get me a seat?"

"Please step to one side."

Venin did as he was told, and the floor opened up. A seat just like Alia's rose to the appropriate height.

"What… is this a special hoversport, or something?" As far as he knew, there were no skythane in the rangers.

Alix nodded. "It is now. I had it retrofitted for the trip. Stow your carry sack up there." He pointed to a bin opening above Venin's head, all business.

Venin complied and sank down into the seat.

"There are straps that snap together around your waist." Alia pointed them out.

"How do you know all this?"

"I helped with the retrofit."

Of course you did. Venin sighed.

Alix ran through a check of the craft's systems. "Looks good. You guys ready back there?" He was in his element.

"Like I said, ready as I'm going to be." He didn't mean to growl it. *Really.*

"Same here." Alia reached forward and squeezed his shoulder. *Us skythane are in this together.*

That last bit was inside his head.

He twisted to look back at her, and she tapped her temple.

Oh yeah. The cirq. Yes, this whole place was gonna take a lot of getting used to.

It looked like they'd be taking a bit of OberCorp and lander culture with them. He wasn't sure how he felt about that.

The craft lifted quietly up into the air, and the hangar doors cracked open, letting in Erro's pink morning sunlight. The hoversport accelerated, pushing him back into his seat, and they were off.

ALIX CIRCLED the confluence of the Theseus and Demetrius rivers. Unlike the Split, the region around the House of the Sky—the ancient skythane "castle" a few hours inland from OberCorp—didn't seem to mess with power sources. *Thank the Split for small favors.*

He'd scoured the company records that morning before they'd set off, looking for any record of the ruins or investigations into the area. He'd come up with a few things—an exploration team who had gone through the region in the first century after colonization, for one. They'd determined there was indeed amalite below the site, but the mineral was far easier to extract from the Split, where it didn't require heavy excavation equipment. They made no mention of ruins.

He wondered if his mother had ever looked into it.

This close to the ground, it was hard to make out the circular formation that had been so evident on satellite imagery.

The waters of the Theseus and the Demetrius were still swollen, though it was clear they had receded from the rampant damage left behind on their banks—logs and other plant debris, and the occasional bloated aux carcass. "I don't see anything particularly promising as a point of entry," he called back to his companions. "What was this place used for, before?"

"It was a meeting place for the Gaelani and the Erriani, like the House of the Stars on Titania."

"Meeting place?" Alix brought the hoversport down closer to the ground for a pass over the black castle that marked the middle of the circle. It was in reasonably good shape, and the outlines of the gardens that had once flourished around it could still be seen.

"Yes. Every fall, the two factions of skythane would gather in one of the two places to celebrate the harvest and to thank Erro, the sun god, and Gael, the moon god, for the bounty."

"Celebrate, huh?" He glanced back at Venin, who nodded.

"Yeah. There was a bit of that, too, apparently. Fertility rites, and all."

Alix laughed, letting go of his angst about his mother for the moment. "Did you ever go?"

"When I was a child. The last one was more than twenty-five years ago, on the other side of Erro. Relations between the Gaelani and the Erriani deteriorated pretty quickly after that."

"After Jameson's mother—the queen—was killed?"

"Yes." Venin didn't seem to want to talk about it anymore.

My fault for being such an ass. "Fair enough. So what do you think—Holy Split."

"What?" Alia and Venin said in unison.

"Well, that's new."

Two seat belts unlatched, and soon the skythane were staring over his shoulder, their wings taking up most of the space at the front of the small craft.

Alix pointed.

The ground had opened up about a kilometer east of the House of the Sky in a series of parallel cracks that stretched through the patchy forest toward the Pyramus Mountains on the horizon.

"That *is* new."

"This is one of those times I wish we still had satellite coverage." He wondered what had happened to Titan Station and Oberon's two moons. They'd made it through the last shift, apparently, so they were probably still there… which implied some kind of gravitational presence in the "human" universe. Time enough to figure that out later, if they had a later. "The one in the middle looks pretty wide. Should we go down and take a look?"

Venin nodded. "Looks like the best way into whatever's down there."

His breath was warm on Alix's back.

Alix rubbed his neck, trying not to think about it. There were more important things afoot than sexual attraction. Besides, he'd been the one to rebuff Venin.

He brought the hovercraft around and activated the forward lights. He took them down toward the widest part of the center split. When they were directly over the crevasse, he let the craft sink between the dirt walls.

The crack was at least fifty meters across here. Nevertheless, the walls seemed to close over them as they sank into the darkness. As he watched, steering the hoversport down toward whatever lay below, a shower of dirt slipped down through the running lights and onto the top of the craft.

Venin grabbed his shoulder, then let go and looked away sheepishly. "Sorry."

"'S okay. It's a bit freaky here." Alix leaned forward and peered through the plas at the diminishing band of light above.

Coming down here was a stupid idea. *We'd be better off—*

The hoversport jerked hard to the right with a painful shriek, slamming into one of the crevasse walls. "What the hell?" He fought to bring the craft back under control.

Something was messing with the amalite power core. The charge indicator varied widely, shooting up to full and then back down to nothing in seconds.

Maybe the whole power thing did apply here, after all.

The whole craft was wobbling now, dropping faster into the abyss.

"Back to your seats! I don't know if I can control our fall!" He grabbed the navigation stick, fighting to level the craft. He fired off a couple of the emergency jets, but they only served to slow the descent minimally as the craft spun around, the lights flashing off the dirt walls. His stomach lurched as the ground—a strangely white ground—came up to meet them.

"Shit. Get ready for—"

His voice was cut off by the impact foam that filled the little craft, and his vision went dark.

Venin woke in darkness.

A red light flashed briefly above him, illuminating the scene.

He was covered in something sticky, and his left wing throbbed painfully.

"Are you okay?" The disembodied voice was disorienting.

"Taz?" His PA. He was still getting used to sharing his head with someone else. "Yeah. I think so. Hurt my wing, but other than that…."

Another red flash. Alia was slumped over in her chair behind him. He couldn't see Alix behind the big pilot's seat.

"The hoversport's amalite core is unstable. You need to evacuate the craft."

Taz's voice was calm, and it helped Venin regain his own stability. "How do we get out?" The stickiness was from the protective foam that had filled the cabin just before impact. He shook his hands to get as much of the stuff off as possible. It smelled sweet, a little like pith sap.

The ship lay tilted on its side. He dropped down to what used to be the wall and shook off his wings. He was ankle deep in decomposed foam, which sloshed around under his feet and slowed his movements.

"There's a red emergency release next to the door."

He shook Alia's shoulder. During flashes, her eyes opened. "You okay?"

She nodded. "I think so."

"Get Alix. This thing's going to go."

Alia's eyes widened. Apparently she'd just gotten the same news from her PA.

As she released herself and went to check on Alix, Venin popped open the bin where his carry sack was stowed and pulled it out. Slinging it over one shoulder, he knelt and felt around in the sticky liquid for the release. "What am I looking for, Taz? Describe it to me."

"It's a long red handle—"

"Color doesn't help me right now."

"Sorry. Find the door seam."

"Got it."

"Now feel to the left about fifteen centimeters—"

"Fifteen what?"

"About a handspan wide."

"Thank you."

"You're welcome." Little bastard sounded smug. He felt where Taz told him, and his hand closed around a long metal rod. "Found it. Should I pull it?"

"Yes, but be careful—"

He pulled the handle, and the door slid open. The ramp pushed the ship back toward its natural upright position as it extended, throwing him back on his ass.

"You okay?" Alia loomed over him with an unconscious Alix in her arms.

"I think so. Is he okay?"

Alia frowned. "He won't wake up."

He put his hand on Alix's neck. It was warm, and he still had a pulse. "He'll be okay. He's a tough bastard."

A high-pitched whine filled the cabin.

"Destruction of this craft is imminent." Taz's voice carried the unheard request, *Can we move this along?*

"Come on." He grabbed his carry sack and scrambled down the slippery ramp.

The lights of the hoversport illuminated the way ahead of the craft. The ground was white and seamless.

"This way!" Venin took Alix's legs and they ran away from the hoversport as fast as they were able, encumbered by the ranger's large form.

What the hell are we gonna do when the lights go out? No time to worry about that now.

Behind them the whine increased to a piercing scream.

"Get down!" They dropped Alix and flung themselves onto the ground. Venin barely registered the fact that it was smooth and yielding as pain surged through his left wing.

Venin covered his ears as the hoversport's scream reached a crescendo, and then the crevasse was lit with a light as bright as the sun.

A roar of hot air raced over them, singeing the tips of his wings and leaving a horrid smell.

Then it was over, and there was only silence and darkness.

12

———

IN A FLASH

JAMESON FLEW close to the ground, keeping a low profile as they covered as much distance as possible. The red sun was nearing the horizon. It looked angry, reminding him of their first flight—on hoverbike—through the Oberon outback.

They'd continued on for the rest of the afternoon in the direction the initial sail craft had gone, at least as far as they could tell. For a long time, all they'd seen was the endless hills all around them, and the mountains in the distance.

They'd taken a couple breaks, mostly for water and so the nimfeach could stretch its wings.

He had offered it water from his canteen. It had sampled the liquid, then drank half of his supply. It had handed back the canteen with its three-fingered grasp, its big eyes blinking in what Jameson hoped was a gesture of thanks. Now it flew alongside them, and if it was getting tired, it showed no indication.

As afternoon slipped into evening, they were approaching something. Exactly what it was wasn't entirely apparent. A white smudge in the distance. In the meantime, several more ships had passed overhead, all of the sail variety.

Both times they had dived for the cover of the grasses and gullies below them, but no one had stopped to see who or what they were.

"So what's the plan?" Xander's eyes were focused on the horizon. He'd been distant ever since the incident at the fallen ship. It was clear he didn't approve of Jameson's actions.

"We need to find one of the locals, whatever they are, and see if we can communicate with it." He couldn't explain why he had done what he had done. It had just seemed utterly imperative at the time. The nimfeach had needed help. He was someone who helped.

"You don't think there are any humans here?"

Jameson shook his head. "Do you?"

"I don't know." Xander looked troubled, his usual self-assurance under siege by the strangeness of the situation. "We don't have that much food. Or water. Is it a good idea to give… that thing… our water?"

Jameson flapped at the air angrily, pulling ahead of Xander by a few meters.

"Hey, sorry. It's just that I'm scared."

Jameson looked back, seeing the uncertainty painted across Xander's face. "Dammit. I'm sorry. I keep thinking of you as the strong one." He looked over at the nimfeach. It was keeping up with them, its face intent on the horizon. "Should we stop for the day? I could use a rest. I've seen a few streams along the way. At least we could test the water, and maybe refill our canteens?"

Xander nodded. "Thanks." They flew on for a bit until they crossed another stream. This one wound its way through the plains from the mountains in the distance, and its banks were sparsely graced with some kind of tree that resembled colifer trees back on Oberon.

They alighted. The nimfeach sighed happily and settled in the shallow waters at the edge of the stream, sinking its feet in and collapsing backward.

Alarmed, Jameson reached out for it.

"I think he… it? Them? I think it's just relaxing."

Indeed, it didn't seem to be in any distress. The water flowed past its three-toed feet, and it breathed slowly and easily, its wings spread out across the water.

"What do you think it eats?"

Xander shook his head. "I have absolutely no idea."

Jameson reached out and pulled Xander to him, wrapping his arms around him and whispering in his ear. "We'll figure this out." Xander's skin felt good on his own, even if they were both sweaty and dusty. It was a little bit of normal in a strange situation.

His body responded appropriately.

Xander laughed, dispelling the tension between them. "Really? Here we are in the midst of an alien world, in front of an *actual alien*, and you want to fuck?"

Jameson blushed. "I can't help it if you have that effect on me." He wasn't sorry. For so many years he'd had to suppress that part of himself. Not any longer. He gave Xander a quick peck on the cheek. "I know it's not the right time." *Damn, I wish it were.* "We should eat something and figure out what to do next."

Xander nodded. He unsnapped his carry sack and rummaged around inside. "I'm afraid we don't have much. A little dried fruit and bread." He pulled them out and then extracted his canteen. Kneeling next to the stream amidst the reeds, he took a cupful of water in his hand and sniffed it. "Not bad." He swallowed it and smiled. "Tastes like water. A little… um… rustic, but water nonetheless." Satisfied, he filled the canteen.

"I may have raided the OberCorp pantry while we were there." Jameson opened his pack and pulled out some fruit, a fresh loaf of bread, and some yogurt cups.

"When did you get those?"

"Just before the meeting. I was hungry." He blushed.

Xander grinned. "Oh my God, I could kiss you." And he did.

XANDER KNELT in the high grass of the hillside, behind a boulder lit pink by the moonlight.

They'd finished their meal and decided on a plan of action. Approach the city, or whatever it was, on the horizon, under cover of darkness, and try to find someone to talk to.

Jameson had tried to communicate with the nimfeach, but all he'd gotten was a vague feeling of unease from their contact.

Xander had a sneaking suspicion about where they were. *When* they were, actually. Possibly. Little things that seemed familiar were starting to add up. Though how they'd gotten there—and why—was still a mystery.

Together, they peered at the structures below. It was like looking at Errian.

A cluster of white towers—turbien, they were called, if he remembered correctly—sat on the edge of a massive bowl, glowing softly in the moonlight and obscuring much of what lay beyond. The towers were made of the same giant white plants as Errian, one of the bits of information that was starting to spark a realization in his head.

He was pretty sure the trees by the creek had been colifers, and he'd found river apples, too, which had helped to supplement their meager stores.

This place was either Oberon or something eerily similar to it.

They'd offered the nimfeach some of their food. It had ignored the bread but had made a meal of some of the dried fruit. He hoped the strange nutrients did it more good than harm.

It stood on the rock between them, pointing at the white city and emitting a soft, plaintive whistle. But it was the scene closer to their hideout that had Xander's attention.

They'd come upon it by chance, seeing a glow ahead of them that was distinct from the glow of the towers.

As they approached, they'd dropped to the ground to avoid being seen. Creeping up the hillside, they'd found a scene like something out of a fairy tale.

A wide river flowed lazily through the valley below them, the sound of bubbling water floating up to their hidden perch.

Along the riverbanks were hundreds of things. Creatures. He was at a loss for how to describe them. "They're...," he whispered.

Jameson nodded. "They're ithani."

They were closer than the ones they'd seen at the crash site. Xander stared at them, enchanted by their alien beauty, tall and slender. Their bodies had a thorax like a bee, and six limbs. Two seemed to function as legs, while the third set sported the most glorious wings, glowing rainbow-iridescent things twice as tall as the ithani themselves.

They looked a bit like Puck, the little nimfeach who had attached itself to them.

Yet for all their similarities to insects, they were not insectile at all. Instead they were sleek and beautiful, their golden and silver skins almost seeming to give off a light of their own.

"What are they doing?" They seemed to be engaged in a complicated dance, some of it taking place on the riverbank, some of it in the river itself, and some of it in the air.

Jameson shook his head. "I don't know. Look!"

Three of the ithani rose almost directly in front of them. One was silver, one was gold, and one a pale green.

Behind them, Puck huddled behind a bush.

The ithani spun around and around one another as they soared into the sky, faster and faster, so fast that Xander felt dizzy just watching them. It was an intricate dance, as choreographed as anything he'd ever seen on a dance floor or in a tri-dee.

They were focused on each other so tightly that Xander doubted they saw anything else.

They spun together, tighter and tighter, and then there was a brilliant flash.

He blinked, unable to see for a moment from the afterimage that was plastered across his optic nerve. His vision cleared, and something plummeted to the earth, slamming into the ground a couple kilometers away.

"I'll be Split-damned." Xander stared at the other ithani spinning through the sky. Another triad erupted in light. "What do you think they are doing?"

"Mating." Jameson was tight-lipped, the expression he had when he was fighting off memories. "Angie, can you record this?"

There was a rustling sound behind them.

Xander spun around to see a tall ithani standing there staring at them through rainbow-colored multifaceted eyes, its skin golden under Lysander's pale light.

Jameson was done with hiding, with running away from things.

He stood and turned around, facing their purported enemy for the first time.

He—she?—was beautiful, her shimmering carapace silvery-gold, pooling moonlight at its edges. Her wings were twice as big as she was, shaped somewhat like a butterfly's.

She cocked her head and stared at him with those unnerving, multifaceted eyes.

He could see the similarity to the nimfeach now. Maybe they were ithani children?

"Jameson, we should go. We don't know—"

"It's okay. She's not going to hurt us." He felt it in his bones, but he couldn't have explained how he knew if he'd tried. Jameson squeezed Xander's hand, then took a step forward, his own hands held open so the ithani could see he meant no harm.

Puck, the nimfeach, cowered behind his leg.

Her arms were more human than he would have expected. Far from being insect-like, they were almost as thick as his and covered with a fine, downy golden fur that extended to her body.

Some kind of black fabric was wrapped around her in a wide sash from her left shoulder to her right thigh.

He held out one hand, reaching halfway toward her.

She cocked her head again, then reached into her sash and pulled out a compact, shiny object.

"Jameson—"

She held it out, and then a bright flash consumed his vision, leaving him blinded.

As he collapsed to the ground his last thought was, *This was a bad idea.*

13

———

INTO ENEMY TERRITORY

Quince found Robyn on the roof, as Ari had promised.

Robyn looked as tired as Quince felt. *No rest for the world savers.* One day, all this would be over, and they would find a quiet place to slip away to, far from the cares and worries of the world.

Robyn was seated on a bench on the rooftop, staring out at the city below.

"Hey, gorgeous." She kissed Robyn's cheek from behind, jumping back as Robyn took a swipe at her with her black wing. "In a mood this morning?"

Robyn grimaced. "Sorry. I'm too old for this, Quince." She stood and stretched her arms and wings. "I like it up here. It's wide open, and I can breathe the fresh air from the sea." She eyed Quince's carry sacks and weapons. "Going on a hunting trip, are we?"

Quince grinned. "Something like that."

"I was always better with a bow and arrow than one of those lander guns."

"That's not for you. This is for you." She handed over the crossbow she'd found in the armory.

"Oooh." Robyn took it and turned it over appreciatively. "Any bolts to go with it?"

"Of course. Here you go." She handed Robyn a quiver.

Robyn unbuckled it and slipped it over her shoulder behind her wings. She drew one of the bolts and fit it expertly into the crossbow.

"Be careful. Some of those arrows are—"

A small explosion split a decorative tree in a ceramic pot in two, about twenty meters across the roof from where they were standing.

"—explosive."

"I've used one like this before. One of the landers let me try it."

"In Gaelan?"

She nodded. "This will do nicely. Thank you. So who's the other pulse rifle for, then?"

The lift shaft doors behind Quince slid open.

"Sorry I'm late!" Jessa almost bounded into their midst. So young, so full of energy. Quince envied her that.

"I ran into her on the way up. She's as involved in all this as any of us."

"It's all right. Jessa and I had a nice talk while you were gone. But how is she going to come with us? I assumed we were flying?"

"Oh yeah, I checked out a set of bi-wings from the armory. That Tovey guy is really sweet."

Quince made a note to have a word again with "that Tovey guy." He needed to be more careful who he let into the armory.

"So where are we going?" Jessa strapped on the bi-wings.

Quince led them to the edge of the roof. The city was quiet—the calm before another great storm. DOC had grounded all nonessential traffic, and only OberCorp personnel and Rogan's forces were allowed abroad in the city. Things had gotten bloody on that last count, apparently. "See that place over on the edge of town, where the roads end?"

"The Slander?"

Quince nodded. "Very good."

Jessa blushed. "Alix was telling me about it. It's where the Syndicate lives, right?"

"Yes. Something like that. There's something there we need to check out."

"What kind of something?" Robyn frowned. "I was hoping we would be getting out of the city."

"Not sure yet. There's an interloper in the city grid, and Mylin thinks it's connected to the ithani. It's underground, and our access point is that large gray building—there." She pointed at one of the bigger structures that was still standing in that part of the city. "The Slander grew up in what was once a warehousing district. The Slander bosses still use that one to house a lot of their contraband."

"Why doesn't OberCorp do something about it?" Robyn frowned.

"Let's just say they find the Slander and its denizens *useful* sometimes." The whole system was corrupt. Poor Alix would find that out if he remained at the head of OberCorp for long. "Let's get moving—"

The building shook.

"Hold on!" Quince grabbed on to an exhaust pipe and hooked her arm around Robyn.

Jessa scrambled backward, grasping for something to hold.

The building shuddered and moaned, and decorative pots came crashing down to burst into pieces, showering the rooftop with leaves and dirt.

Then it was over.

Jessa stood and brushed off the dust. "Well that was fun." She spread her iridescent bi-wings. "Are we going to do this?"

Quince got up and peered out over the city. "Yes."

The arcos had survived without much damage, but a number of smaller buildings had collapsed. "Heaven and Erro, it wasn't supposed to go like this." Shift the world, and then shift it back. *That* was what she had signed up for. Not this ongoing, rolling series of disasters. "Come on. Time must be growing short." She leapt off the parapet, and Robyn and Jessa followed.

ROBYN TURNED her nose up at the stench.

They stood on another rooftop, this one the old warehouse in the heart of the ramshackle collection of trash and human debris Quince called the Slander.

A little insect thing buzzed around them, zipping back and forth in a schizophrenic pattern. A bug drone, Quince had called it, holding it up in her palm before releasing it into the air. Such a tiny thing, made by the hands of man—amazing that it could fly.

She wanted to knock it out of the air.

Apparently it served to scramble the vision of their enemies, somehow. At least, that was the closest she'd gotten to understanding Quince's explanation.

As Quince knelt by the door that would take them into the warehouse below, her palm to the pad in apparent communion with the wall, Robyn waited with Jessa.

"I've read about this place." Jessa shivered and looked around, though in truth there wasn't much to see from their current vantage point besides roof. At three stories tall, the building was one of the tallest in the Slander.

"It's not someplace you want to be caught alone in, especially at night. Though I'm not all that thrilled to be here during the daylight hours, either." Landers lived like pigs in their own filth. There was no reason she should have to breathe their dirty air too.

"Got it." Quince let go of the palm pad and the door swung open quietly, belying its apparent age and state of disrepair.

Inside, a metal staircase led down into the building.

"Follow me."

Robyn shrugged. It looked cleaner in there than out here.

She tucked in her wings and followed Quince down the stairway.

It was cleaner. The air inside was cool and fresh, and for all its apparent decrepitude outside, the warehouse was in much better shape inside.

They came out shortly onto a catwalk, high above the warehouse floor.

Quince knelt to take in the activity below, and Robyn and Jessa followed her example.

The bug drone buzzed by her ear, and she batted at it unconsciously.

"Let it be," Quince hissed. "It's keeping us safe."

Robyn frowned. The little insectoid annoyed the hell out of her.

Below them, bigger things flitted back and forth, carrying or dropping off items from various shelves.

From their current vantage point, they could see down several rows. The only activity seemed to be from the hovering… drones, she supposed they must be. Devices doing the work of humans. "So how do we find this interloper?" She slipped her hand around Quince's waist while they surveyed the warehouse. Quince was the one good thing she had. She nuzzled Quince's neck, wishing this whole thing was over.

"Hey, we're on a mission here, you two." Jessa looked stern, but Robyn could hear the laughter in her voice.

"She's right. Time for that later. Where are we going?"

"DOC helped me track him to somewhere beneath this warehouse. So we need to make our way to the ground floor and—"

"What are you doing up here?" A man wearing a black uniform had appeared around the corner at one end of the catwalk, holding a pulse rifle.

"Rogan sent us," Quince lied smoothly. "To check your security."

The man frowned. "I don't work for Rogan. Who are you?"

Partially concealed behind Quince, Robyn pulled the crossbow off her back and slipped in a bolt.

"We're here to test site security—"

"Down!" Robyn pushed Quince's back and her lover collapsed to the metal catwalk floor at the same instant as Robyn's crossbow bolt shot forward just centimeters over her spine to lodge in the man's neck.

It was one of the nonexplosive bolts, apparently.

The guard flew backward, getting off one pulse shot over their heads before falling sideways, clutching at his throat to try to pull out the bolt, to stop the sudden torrent of blood.

"Oh hell." Quince leapt forward to grab him, her wings beating to pull her toward him, but she was too late.

He fell over the edge of the catwalk, and her hands grasped at empty air.

Robyn watched as he fell two stories to the ground, his mouth open in a silent scream.

His body hit with a sickening thunk.

Robyn turned away, forcing down the bile in her throat.

"Holy crap." Jessa stared down at the body. "You… you killed him."

The drones continued their work, unfazed by the dead body in their midst.

Robyn squeezed her shoulder. "Too much at stake to take the chance."

Quince shuddered. "I'd hoped it wouldn't come to this."

Jessa was white as a sheet. Poor girl had probably never had to finish off an opponent before.

Robyn hugged her. "It never gets easier, but you learn to live with it."

Quince nodded. "She's right. Come on. We better get moving before someone human finds the body."

Robyn stared after her. It was clear that Quince was as shaken by the man's death as she was; she just didn't want to show it.

She turned to follow Quince down the catwalk.

JESSA WATCHED ROBYN WALK AWAY. She could see why Robyn had been a queen. She had the imperial bearing that only those bred to royalty could ever truly aspire to.

She was also sexy as hell. *Drat, that's inappropriate.* A man had just died in front of her. Maybe it was her way of distracting herself from that grisly fact.

She didn't let her attraction to another woman bother her. She'd come to terms with all that long ago—before she'd ever known Jamie was gay. So what if she liked both sides of the coin? They seemed to be a whole lot less uptight about it here than back on Beta Tau.

With a heavy sigh, she followed Quince and Robyn along the catwalk.

Around the next corner, a long metal ladder descended to the ground.

Quince stopped to check something with her PA, nodded, and then continued on past it.

Jessa had never had one installed—bioware was frowned on in Beta Tau. *It's not the way God made you,* her mother used to say to her.

He didn't give you that perfect nose, either, she'd said once, and got slapped and lost her grid privileges for a week. Jessa grinned to herself. *It was so worth it.*

At last, Quince found what she wanted. "We need to go down quickly and quietly," she whispered, indicating the long metal ladder.

The bug drone drifted around them in lazy circles.

"Then what?" Jessa looked back the way they'd come. No alarm, no one following them. *Yet.* She fingered the trigger on her pulse rifle.

"There's a hatch in the floor about twenty meters to the right of the ladder, near the back wall. Make for that if anything happens. Here." Quince handed them each a small something.

Jessa held it up in the dim light. It was a pulse grenade. "Holy sheister."

Quince grinned. "You can take the girl off Beta Tau...."

Jessa snorted.

"What is it?" Robyn was staring at her own grenade.

"It's a pulse grenade. See this?" Quince indicated a small loop on the top. "Twist it and pull. Then you have about five seconds to clear the area before it blows."

"Ah." Robyn's nose wrinkled, and she put it into her carry sack.

"I don't think you'll need it. I'm hoping to get the hatch open by less... explosive means. I brought them just in case. Robyn prefers more traditional ways of killing people."

Jessa nodded. "I respect that." She'd never killed anyone herself and hoped she'd never have to. The image of the guard clutching at his throat as blood gushed out stuck in her mind. How did you unsee something like that?

"Come on then." Quince swung herself over the edge and slid down the ladder, her wings slowing her fall.

I wish I had wings. Jessa tucked away her own grenade in a pocket of her jacket and followed after Robyn.

About halfway down, as the others outpaced her, an alarm finally sounded, blaring through the great open space. Worried, Jessa glanced around. Red lights were flashing at the four corners of the warehouse, and the drones were lifting out of the shelves to scan the space.

She grabbed the sides of the ladder and took her feet off the rungs. With a deep breath, she let herself slide down out of sight into the relative safety of the rows of storage shelves.

The metal chafed her hands as she slowed herself the last meter before impact. "Fuck, that hurts," she swore, and Quince grinned. "We've been noticed."

"Seems like it." Quince pulled her pulse rifle off her shoulder. "Come on." She tucked in her wings and ran toward the hatch.

Robyn and Jessa followed.

Something hot whipped past Jessa's shoulder. "Behind us!" She ducked and rolled, coming up to her knees to fire back at whomever was following them, her pulse rifle set to stun. Four people in black dove for cover.

Jessa grinned and slipped behind a tall shelving unit.

Return fire flew through the space where she had just been, and some of it slammed into the metal braces of the shelf, turning them red-hot.

They were shooting to kill. She shuddered.

"Quince, Robyn, you okay?" She glanced across the aisle. Quince crouched behind another shelf.

Robyn was nowhere to be seen.

14

—————

BENEATH THE HOUSE OF THE SKY

"HEY, YOU with us?"

Alix's eyes flickered open to find Venin staring down at him, his brow knotted in concern.

"I think he's awake!" Venin said to someone next to them, and a bright light flashed into his eyes.

Alix squeezed them shut, registering the fact that his body ached in a hundred assorted places. "Get that out of my eyes." He pushed himself up and immediately regretted it as all of his muscles registered their protests at once.

He opened his eyes again to see a sheepish Alia holding a flashlight, pointing it down at the ground. "What happened?" He remembered flying over a crevasse, but things were a bit muddy after that.

"We crashed." Alia turned the flashlight off.

Alix's eyes adjusted. It wasn't totally black—a thin strip of sky provided a faint light, and the ground… it glowed. Dimly, but it was there. "And the hoversport?"

"Gone. The amalite core blew after we hit the ground."

"Shit. Erissa, can you reach DOC?"

"Sorry, DOC seems to be unavailable."

"My PA can't reach the grid. Can yours?"

Alia and Venin shook their heads.

"We can't connect to anyone." Venin looked around at the gloomy space. "I think we're too far down."

Alix laughed mirthlessly. "Yeah, that's what the amplifier on the hoversport was for. Don't suppose either of you managed to grab my carry sack on the way out?"

"Sorry. We had our hands full with you." Venin grinned, his teeth white against his dark skin.

"Thanks. Want to help me up?" He held up his hand.

The ground beneath him *thrummed*.

"What the hell?"

"Yeah, that's been happening a lot." Alia's tone was dry, like it was just another everyday thing for the ground to vibrate underneath you with a thrumming sound.

Alix closed his eyes as a shower of dust and pebbles was shaken loose from somewhere up above. "This doesn't seem like a particularly safe place to hang out." He eyed the crevasse walls, worried they might decide to snap back together as quickly as they had pulled apart.

Things settled down again, and Venin helped him to his feet. His legs ached, but he ignored them. Time for rest later.

He was covered in something sticky—probably crash foam. The stuff was hell to get out of hair and clothes. At the moment, though, they had bigger worries.

Venin shifted, and Alix could see that his left wing hung at an odd angle. "Did you break it?"

"I don't think so. Just a bad sprain."

"May I?"

Venin's eyes met his, and something passed between them. "Go ahead."

Alix ran his hand along the edge of the wing, and Venin hissed. "Sorry. Looks like something cut you. Wish I had the med kit from the hoversport. Can you fly?"

"No."

Alia looked at Venin's wound. "This kind of damage is fairly common among the skythane. He'll heal, but it will take a few days."

Days we don't have. Alix looked at their surroundings.

The place where they stood was like a long, dark canyon, stretching off into darkness in either direction. "Erissa, how long is this crevasse?"

"I'm sorry, I still can't access the grid. From visual estimates alone, five-point-four kilometers."

"Thanks." The walls were rough-hewn rock and soil. He took a closer look at one. It was irregular, hard-packed dirt and stone. But the floor....

"It's strange, right?" Alia knelt with him to touch the smooth floor. "This shouldn't be here."

He'd thought it was metal, but no, it was different. It was shiny, but with a bit of give. It reminded him of something, but he couldn't put his finger on it.

"How long before someone comes looking for us?" Alia's wings fluttered. "Maybe we should fly out and one of us should go for help?"

Alix rubbed his chin. "Maybe this is what we came looking for." He stared up at the thin line of sky. "But you're right. We do need to send someone back. They're going to have their hands full enough without worrying where we went off to."

Alia nodded. "I can go. Are you two sure you'll be safe here without me?" She shot Venin a grin. "All alone *together?*"

Alix rolled his eyes. Like he had time to think about that. "Leave whatever you can spare." Alix took a deep breath. "The air seems good. We can take a look around while we wait for you."

"Just be careful." She pulled out her foodstuffs and a pulse rifle, laying them on top of Venin's carry sack. Then she stood before him.

They touched wingtips. "Gael be with you," she said, almost too softly for Alix to hear.

"And with you."

She gave Alix a quick kiss on the cheek, and then launched herself toward the sky.

He watched her until she disappeared into the river of light high above.

Venin watched Alia depart, ignoring the pulsing pain in his left wing. She wasn't wrong. Venin was acutely aware that he was now all alone with Alix.

Alix had gotten under his skin, somehow. A lander, of all people. He snorted.

"What?" Alix put a hand on his shoulder and electricity shot through him.

"Nothing." He closed his eyes and inhaled and exhaled. They had work to do. He knelt, touching the white surface. "This reminds me of something." The surface glowed. It was faint, but it sparked a memory.

"Come on." He grabbed his carry sack and tossed Alia's to Alix.

"Where are we going?"

"Where the hoversport blew." Venin jogged back toward the spot where they'd crashed. There should have been an impact crater. The walls of the crevasse had taken a beating, spilling down rocks and dirt along the edges. The burned-out husk of the hoversport lay on one side, still radiating heat. The ground itself seemed untouched, a smooth white surface.

"What the hell?" Alix stopped short of the site. "Is it impervious to fire?" He knelt to touch the white surface once again.

"I don't think so." Venin pulled off his carry sack and rummaged through it until he found his throwing knife.

"What are you thinking?" Alix's brow was furrowed.

"I have a theory." Venin set the blade against the floor and pushed it in, cutting a neat line about an arm's length long.

The material separated neatly, drawing away from the metal of the blade. Then it sealed itself back together. "Hah! I thought so. It's like corrinder."

"Corrinder?" Alix knelt next to him and watched in apparent fascination as the gash was bridged by white filaments, weaving it back into one seamless piece.

Venin nodded. "Like the towers of Errian—some call them *turbien*. This ground is alive."

Alix looked up and down the crevasse. "Alive? It can't be. It's huge."

"About fifty kilometers, maybe?"

Alix stared at him, and then laughed. "Maybe so. *This* is our circle?"

"You said it yourself. Maybe this is what we came looking for."

"Could be." Alix frowned. "So what now?"

"We should wait here for Alia." She'd find help within the next couple hours, he was certain.

Alix shook his head, touching the ground with a look of wonder on his face. "We both know there's not much time left, if what Quince told us is true."

He's a man of action, like me. Alix would no more want to sit around here for two hours—or more—than Venin did. "What say we start with a little exploration?" He pointed along the length of the crevasse.

Alix grinned. "Beats sitting here on our asses. Which way?"

Venin shrugged. "One direction seems as good as another."

They set off down the newly created canyon, leaving the blasted wreckage behind.

Alix strode next to him, a muscle-bound lander god, his thick arms filling out his body armor nicely.

Venin wished he had a tub of cold water to plunge himself into.

To distract his libido, he struck up a conversation. "So you worked things out with Xander and Jameson?" As they walked, the walls didn't change much, though in places he could see the layers of strata that marked the long passage of time.

Alix frowned. "How do you mean?"

"You and Xander were close, once, right?"

Alix sighed. "Yes. Five years." He spat at the crevasse wall.

Tread lightly. "It must have been hard, seeing him again, and with Jameson."

"I guess."

"And now?" *Why do I care?*

"Look, I really don't want to talk about it." Alix's face was impassive, his fists squeezed tight at his sides.

"Sorry." *Touched a nerve.*

"Did you ever lose someone?" Alix sounded like a lost little boy.

That hit home. "Yeah. Once." He closed his eyes, and he could see Tazim's face. "Tazim and I were close." *Inseparable, more like.*

"What happened?"

"Oh, so you can pry, but I can't?" It was meant to be playful, but it came out sounding harsher than Venin had intended.

"Sorry!" Alix looked down. "Didn't mean to push your buttons."

"No, it's okay." He frowned. Why did he care what Alix thought? "Taz was a once-in-a-lifetime thing. He—"

"He?" Was there a sparkle in Alix's eyes?

"Yeah. He was a childhood friend." Even now, he could see Taz's goofy face when he closed his eyes. "We used to play together on First Hill in Gaelan. He was so full of life, like Erro reincarnate. He almost glowed with life."

"You two were lovers?"

"For three years. It happened suddenly. When we were seventeen. We were on our *taslit.*"

"What's that?"

"It's a rite of passage. When a skythane reaches maturity and gets their wings, they are sent off to fend for themselves in the wilderness for a month." Taz had been so excited to finally get some time alone with him, away from prying eyes. Their time in the wilderness had passed in the blink of an eye, but oh the things Venin had learned in those thirty days. "Taz and I went together."

"Hey, isn't Taz the name of your PA?"

Venin blushed. "Yeah. It seemed appropriate."

Alix managed a small smile. "Sorry. Go on."

"We were camped out in one of the caverns up in the mountains. Like the one where you had the bi-wings hidden."

"Sure."

"Taz took a bath in one of the ponds, and when he got out, dripping wet and naked—I kissed him. I had to. He was so beautiful. I wanted him like I'd never wanted anything else in my life. Not just for sex, you know? I mean, yeah, I wanted that like crazy. I was just past puberty, after all. But there was more to it."

Alix nodded. "I know."

"I stepped back, and he looked at me. I will never forget that look." He closed his eyes, seeing Taz there again like it had been that first time. "I was so scared. Scared he would reject me. Scared I had misjudged him, but that look…." He sighed. "It was full of hunger and need, and love. He told me later he'd been wanting to kiss me for a year, but he'd been afraid it would ruin our friendship."

"Yeah. Damn. He sounds like an amazing guy."

"He was." Venin could still smell his skin, still taste his lips. No one would ever measure up to him.

"What happened? Did you two break up?"

"No." Ten years later, and he could still hear the screams. "He was killed. A long time ago."

"Holy crap." Alix put his hand on Venin's arm. "I'm so sorry."

"It's all right. We've all been through tragedy—"

The ground shook, harder than before.

Venin glanced at the walls looming above them, alarmed. "This can't be good." The shaking went on and on, and dirt and rock showered down upon them. A frightening rumble filled his ears.

"Which way do we run?" Alix's gaze darted back and forth along the crevasse.

The walls pushed suddenly closer, and the fall of debris multiplied tenfold.

"Neither!" Venin shouted. "Get down!" He pulled Alix to the ground and took out his knife, hacking into the white surface.

It pulled away from the metal of the knife, but there was still more of the corrinder below.

It was getting hard to breathe as dust filled the chasm.

He cut again and again, trying to break through, hoping there was somewhere to break through to. The knife went through the corrinder like butter.

Alix shielded him from the worst of the falling rocks and dust. "If we die here, it was good knowing you," he all but shouted into Venin's ear.

Venin laughed harshly. "You too—" Venin's arm went *through*, and then they were falling into nothingness along with a shower of debris.

15

ERINA

Erina waved zer hand over the blank white console of zer sleith, guiding the white ship through the air. The time was upon them. In a few short hours, most of the ithani would be gone from Arliss, gone north to slumber away the shift under the protective arms of the mountain.

The beings ze had foreseen had arrived, and they were as strange as ze had supposed.

Ze had *touched* them, briefly. They had bits of ithani in them. Of *zim*.

Ze marveled at that, though it had been implied in zer final vision. Still, that was a tale for the future to tell.

The previous seer, an ithani named Drevin, had been locked up away from the world by Thshnel'Jirron until zi'd died from starvation, or so they said. Since then, no one had dared publicly claim zis mantle.

Ze would speak with them both and learn more. Especially the one with the golden wings.

Then ze would get them into hiding until ze could figure out zer next step.

Xander's eyes flickered open.

He was lying on a white surface that hummed and vibrated underneath him. He was in a white room, on something that might have been a bed.

It was morning. The sun shone its red rays through a series of oval windows along one wall. The angry ball brought back some bad memories.

Jameson.

He sat up, searching wildly for his soulmate. Jameson lay next to him on another platform, asleep. Hopefully asleep.

Xander sighed in relief.

He looked around. He was inside a ship. Maybe. The room was wide, curved, and white. Handles at the back suggested cabinets or storage of some kind. Every form seemed to blend harmoniously into the next.

There was no one else to be seen inside.

He knelt over Jameson. "Hey, wake up." He shook Jameson's shoulder. "Jameson, come on, wake up."

Jameson's eyes flickered open, and he groaned, sticking his tongue out at Xander. "Let me sleep. I was having the most wonderful dream."

Xander rolled his eyes. "What are you, four? Come on. We don't have time for dreaming."

Jameson grunted and rubbed his forehead. "Damn you, skythane bastard." He levered himself up onto his elbows. "Where are we?"

"You're skythane too," Xander muttered. "I don't know. Let's see if we can find out." He got up and staggered to one of the windows.

They *were* flying, on one of the white sail ships, if he didn't miss his guess. In retrospect, it was obvious, but he was still a bit groggy from whatever the ithani had done to him.

Jameson joined him and gasped. "Damn."

The ship was passing over a row of white towers—maybe the ones they had seen in the distance. The towers—corrinder plants for certain—surrounded a vast white bowl. Against that dazzling background, ithani of many iridescent colors—blue, gold, green, red, violet, and many more—fluttered back and forth like a vast army of butterflies.

The white bowl was a wide, seamless plane.

"We could make a run for it," Xander said doubtfully.

"How?" Jameson pushed on the white surface of the walls. It gave a little and then sprang back.

Xander shrugged.

"Where's Puck?"

"I don't know. It was just you and me when I woke up."

"We can't leave without him." Jameson sounded adamant.

Xander sighed. There was no arguing with him when he was like that. "So what do you suggest? They may be leading us like auxen to the slaughter."

"I don't know… why not just kill us, then?" Jameson rubbed his chin. "Besides, I'm not sure how far we'd get, surrounded like this by ithani." He leaned on the railing and whistled. "Oh my gods, they're beautiful."

Xander nodded. They really were. Hard to see how such beauty could be such a threat. "You're going to think I'm crazy." He'd been thinking about this for a while now, and it was the only thing that made sense. That sort of made sense.

"Tell me." Jameson put a warm hand on his cheek, his brown eyes fixing on Xander's. "After what we've been through this last month, I'd have a hard time calling anything crazy."

Xander laughed. "It's been wild, right?" He took a deep breath. "I don't think we're on Oberon, or Erro, for that matter. Not the Erro we know."

Jameson nodded. "It would have been hard to miss something like this."

The ship was descending toward a hole in the white plane. In fact, the hole seemed to be growing wider to accommodate them.

"There are no other planets in the Oberon system, and the moons are barren." He swallowed, hard. "I don't think we went somewhere else. I think we went some*when* else."

Jameson's eyes narrowed. "How do you mean?"

"This place doesn't exist on Oberon or Titania, not in our time." He gestured at the "city" below. "But think about it. River apples. Corrinder towers. Even the ithani. This has to be Erro."

"Erro's past?" Jameson looked up at the shapes flitting by overhead in apparent abandon. "It makes as much sense as anything, I suppose, but how? The power that would require… if it were even possible—"

"I know. It's crazy. It's just—"

Something *clucked* behind them.

Xander turned to look into the face of the golden ithani that had assaulted them on the hillside. Though maybe *assault* was too strong a word. Nothing seemed to be damaged or broken. It had just been a flash of bright light.

A doorway was open behind it, one that hadn't existed before.

The ithani tilted its head and extended two of its arms. They ended in a paw that had three fingers.

He looked at Jameson.

Jameson shrugged and grinned. "You said you wanted to find someone who could tell us where we are."

"Yeah, I guess I did." He took Jameson's hand, and they reached out to touch the ithani's, palm to palm.

JAMESON FLOATED in a world of nascent possibility.

He could feel Xander's hand in his, but when he looked down, he was gripping empty air. Still, he held tight.

The space around him was complicated. At first glance, it was as if he floated in a gray, featureless cloud, but each wisp was a world unto itself, full of twisting patterns that seemed to repeat endlessly like some crazy Mandelbrot set. There were colors hidden in the white, an iridescent sheen like that of the ithani themselves.

Fractals. That's what they were called. A whole world of complexity hidden in the shrouding mist.

The fog swirled and formed an image of the ithani creature, staring at him curiously. The golden one. The one he'd seen on the hillside, and again on the white ship.

One of its arms touched itself on the chest and it said "Erina" quite clearly. Its voice was clear and pitched pleasantly in the middle of the human vocal range, sounding neither masculine or feminine.

"Erina?"

It squeezed its hand into a fist. "Yes. Erina."

The human word startled Jameson. "Erina. Your name."

"Your name," it repeated.

"No. Name. Name."

"Name." It made the fist gesture again.

Jameson held his hand up and imitated the gesture. "Yes?"

"Yes." The fist again.

He nodded and then pointed at his head. "Yes." He nodded again. "Yes." And a nod.

Erina nodded. "Yes." It also emitted a deep thrumming sound from its thorax.

Jameson grinned. *Okay, so we have a few words they could use.* "No?"

It searched his face, and he felt a strange tickling sensation in his head. He should have been afraid. Was Erina rummaging through his head?

Instead he felt calm, collected.

"No," it said, and made a sideswiping motion with its open hand, palm down. "No."

"Ah." Jameson repeated the gesture. "No."

"Ah," Erina said.

Jameson laughed. "I'm going to call you Eri."

It cocked its head at him, a gesture so patently human that Jameson laughed again. Some things were universal.

He pointed. "You. Erina. Eri."

"Ah. Eri." And the fist.

"Me, Jameson." He pointed again at himself.

"Meejaymeeson."

Jameson took a deep breath. Pronouns were going to take some work. "Where is Xander?" He could still feel Xander's grip on his hand.

Cocked head again.

"Xander." He brought up a mental image, the first time he'd seen Xander with his shirt off.

"Ah." Gently clenched fist.

Then Xander was with him in the strange place. "Hey!" Xander grinned. "Our friend here seems to be quite inquisitive."

Jameson nodded. "I taught him… her? Them? Yes, and no. We're still working on 'you' and 'me.'"

Xander laughed. "Where the hell are we?"

"I think it's something like ithani vir space."

"Do you trust it?" Their eyes met.

Jameson shrugged. "Do we have a choice?"

"Good point."

Eri was watching them, its head glancing back and forth as they talked. It seemed to be waiting for them to finish. When they looked back at Eri, the ithani reached out two hands again, this time toward their foreheads. "Yes?" It cocked its head again and closed each hand gently.

"I think it wants to connect with us." Jameson squeezed Xander's hand.

Xander leaned forward and kissed him. "Just in case." He searched Jameson's eyes and nodded. "We're in neck deep already. What's another half a meter?"

"Um, drowning?"

"Then let's drown together." Xander's eyes twinkled.

"I love you." Jameson kissed him again, and then turned toward Eri. "Yes."

Eri's cool hand reached out to touch his forehead, and a torrent of information flooded his mind.

XANDER WOKE AGAIN, his head feeling like mush.

Bits of knowledge—images, really, but laden with meaning—flickered through his head. Some were concepts. Language glyphs that turned into English if he concentrated on them.

Others were memories. Or maybe not quite memories. Lessons. Pieces of history.

Pronouns. A whole host of ithani pronouns. Ze, zer, zers... maybe feminine? Zi, zis, zim. A more masculine feel, maybe. And za, zaf, and zas—or zee, zeer, and zees.

Erina's voice spoke in his head, zer tone clear as if ze were there talking directly to him in English.

"Three ithani are needed to make a child. These are ze / zer / zers, roughly analogous to she / her / hers in your language—the one who provides the egg. Zi / zim / zis is similar to he / him / his—the one who fertilizes it. And za / zaf / zas has no direct human equivalent. It's the one who provides the organs to carry the child to term. When pregnancy occurs, the three forms unite into one—zee / zeer / zeers—until the child is born."

Xander blinked, letting that sink in.

Other memories and bits of information floated around him. He seized on a memory, dropping into it as if he were there. As if he were Zorin himself, the ithani captain of the ship.

One of the Ithani sail ships descended through the atmosphere, dropping toward the land far below, the heat of entry turning the tips of its wings red and then gold.

The world below was beautiful—red forests straddling the land, and a wide sea glimmering in the sunshine on the other side. In the distance, mountains marched along the other edge of the world.

Xander peered through a viewport, watching the curve of the planet grow larger.

It was hard to get a sense of the scale of the ship but based on the number of wings or sails, it had to be much bigger than the one he had ridden on.

On the way through the atmosphere, Xander saw strange things. Straight lines that ran across open fields. Clumps of black smoke hanging over coastal areas. Square patches that suggested crop fields.

Xander clucked his tongue.

This world was supposed to be uninhabited. It was closest to the ithani homeworld and had been chosen for this mission by the Council.

The ship's rate of descent slowed as it approached the ground, circling around a wide bay several times before settling on a landing spot on an open plain surrounded by forest.

It settled on the ground, and the side of it split open. A horde of ithani burst out, spreading across the clearing like excited children, chittering to one another in a language Xander found he could understand, if he tried.

"It's everything they said it would be," Landri said to Xander, zaf light brown fur shimmering in delight.

Xander thrummed his agreement, but inside, he had a bad feeling about this place.

A heavy thwump thwump thwump drew his attention skyward as a black airborne craft cleared the treetops, its rotor blades holding it above the scene for just a moment before it turned and sped off the way it had come.

Landri blinked in distress. "What was that?"

Xander sucked in his breath. "We're not alone."

XANDER'S EYES FLICKERED OPEN, and went wide.

He wondered if he'd just seen the beginning of the war with the dhagani, the beings Quince had said were the ithani's mortal enemies.

Too much I don't know. He sat up to look around, feeling disoriented.

The room he found himself in was a white cube, smaller by a third than the one he'd awoken in before. Other than the featureless white bed he'd been lying on, the room was empty.

He was alone.

"Jameson? Erina?" He got up and touched one of the walls. It was hard but yielding, like the ship. Maybe he was still on board?

There were no windows here, though, and he was feeling closed in. "Hello?" He paced the room, maybe two meters square, looking for something, anything to tell him where he was, how he got there. Or how to get out.

He felt a chill as goose bumps rose on his arms. He was trapped in here.

"Hello? Anyone? Can you hear me?" The last was almost a scream.

He beat upon the wall, trying to push through it, to knock it down, to make his presence felt.

It absorbed the sound, and he accomplished nothing beyond bruising his fists.

"I'm here!" he shouted, his wings shaking in protest. "Can anyone fucking hear me?"

No one came.

16

THE CROSS

Venin plunged deep into an underground lake.

He opened his eyes and was surrounded by a glowing world of blue light. The liquid was warm, almost effervescent on his skin.

Alix was in the water beside him, looking stunned.

Venin grabbed him by the shirt collar and struggled back up toward the air, pulling Alix with him.

They surfaced, and he took a huge lungful of air. Then he looked up.

The cavern was lit by both a pale blue glow from the water below and the soft white glow of the ceiling. It was like those he'd visited in the Mora Mountains, but on a far grander scale. The hole they'd fallen through was sealing up, and white columns, like the corrinder towers of Errian, rose from the cavern at various intervals to support the ceiling.

Venin shook the water out of his eyes. "You okay?"

Alix was treading water beside him. "Yeah, think so." He was breathing heavily. "Holy crap, what the hell just happened?"

Venin laughed. "We escaped a horrible crushing death, I think."

"How did you know this was down here?"

Venin shook his head. "I didn't. Just seemed like the best alternative."

"Quick thinking." Alix swung around to check out their surroundings. "Can you swim?"

"Yeah. You?" The water felt good on his wing and washed off the sticky remnants of crash foam from his body.

Alix laughed. "Part of my ranger training."

"Come on. Looks like a dry patch over there." He pointed to the edge of the lake, where a narrow strip of black sand and clumps of black rock offered landfall.

Venin swam toward the sandy shore with steady strokes, pulling himself through the water with the grace of a stendril. The silver-and-gold fish were a skythane staple, fished from the high mountain lakes of the Mora, sleek as a sword. His boots hindered him, but he made good progress.

Alix followed him.

His wing ached where he'd injured it. He cursed the fact that he was land-bound, but then again, so was Alix, whose bi-wings had been lost in the hoversport crash.

Venin glanced back at Alix. The man was following doggedly, managing to keep up with his fast pace.

He checked his chronometer. 1800 hours. Just twenty-six hours left until Quince's deadline.

They reached the shore, and Venin climbed out of the water, shaking his head and wings to dry himself. He'd managed to hold on to his carry sack, but it was soaked.

He reached out to help Alix out of the water. Alix tripped and fell into him, bringing them both down hard on the sand.

Their wet bodies met, and Venin could tell that Alix was interested, protests aside. Some things were hard to hide, especially under wet clothing. "At least get me dinner first?" He grinned to Alix, whose face was just inches from his own.

Alix smiled back for a brief second, then frowned. He pulled away, standing and brushing off the sand from his legs. "Sorry. Won't happen again."

Damn. It had to be his feelings for Xander. Venin knew the signs. Five years was a lot of time with someone to have to let go. *Not like we have time for it.* Still, the rejection stung.

He sat up and pulled off his boots, dumping out the extra water. He used one of the boots to scoop up some water and rinsed the sand off his feet. *I must look ridiculous, my feet in the air, balanced on my wings.* When he was sure his feet were as sand-free as he could manage, he pulled the boots back on. He wished they had time to let everything dry out a bit.

Nevertheless, he felt good. Strangely good, given their circumstances. His energy was up, and he felt hope, as if they had been brought to this place for a reason.

He looked around.

The cavern was wide and roughly round, one half of it taken up by the softly glowing blue lake, the other side a crescent of sand backing onto a jumble of black rocks, like some strange, broken alien stair ascending to the back wall.

White plants with long trailing fronds—they had to be plants—rustled gently along the edge of the cavern between the corrinder pillars, a few meters above where they stood on the black sand beach. Each one supported a handful of golden orbs.

Along the base of the rocks was a ramshackle assortment of wood, mostly broken into pieces, but in some places still standing to form small structures that backed up against the black rocks.

The blue light lit the cavern, coming from the water itself, throwing shifting dappled shadows across the walls and ceiling. It was an alien but entrancing scene, and it made Alix's skin look pale and cold.

For a moment, Venin longed to throw off his shoes again and run back into the water, to pass an afternoon in this strange underground paradise.

"It's beautiful, isn't it?" Alix followed his gaze.

"It reminds me of Taz." His white skin, so like Alix's, under the blue light.

An ominous rumbling came from above.

Got it. No time to relax. He wondered if that was a sign from Gael. *Better get moving.* First, he wanted to check out the wooden frames. The sand crunched under his booted feet as he crossed the beach toward the broken structures. Someone or something must have built them here.

"Where are you going?" Alix ran his hand through his short hair, glancing nervously at the ceiling.

"To check out the limits of our little cage."

"You think this cavern is a trap?"

"I don't know." He reached the black rocks at the edge of the beach and knelt, ducking into one of the still-standing structures.

A blanket lay folded over on the sand, gray with age. He reached out to touch it, and it crumbled away under his fingers. "Someone lived here once."

Alix popped his head inside the makeshift shack. "In the underground?"

"Or at the least, camped out here for a while. Who were they? How did they get here?" Something glinted in the light from outside, hidden under the sand.

Alix looked over his shoulder. "Maybe there's another way out, then?"

Venin knelt to touch the edge of the half-buried object and started brushing off the sand.

It was a piece of metal. As he cleared away the sand, the outlines became clearer. It was a small silver cross on a metal chain, badly tarnished by the years.

He pushed gently past Alix to look at it in the light. On the back, in a strange version of Common, it said, *Aaron Hammond, 2135 AD.*

Venin's head exploded with memories, sending him staggering backward to the ground.

Humans on this underground beach, living like refugees.

A red-haired woman clutching this cross in her hands, saying a prayer to something.

Nimfeach like butterflies flying through the air above.

Then it was gone.

Alix knelt beside him. "Hey, you okay? What happened?"

Venin clutched the sides of his head. Sheepishly he put his hands down. "Holy Split, that was intense. Another memory, I think. There were people here. People like us. Well, humans. No wings." He was trying to sort out the memories that had run through his head. "Humans and nimfeach." He handed the cross to Alix. "I think it was important to one of them."

Alix took it and read the inscription. He whistled. "How long ago were they here?"

"I don't know. Taz, any idea where this might have come from?" Alix handed the necklace back to him, and he slipped it over his head.

"My information is limited without grid access, but many religions in human history used the cross as a symbol for a prime deity. The date suggests it came from Earth, prior to the Collapse."

"Thanks." He'd have to find out more about this "Collapse" sometime. "Come on, let's get a look at the rest of this place." He climbed up onto the rocks.

Alix clambered up after him, nimble as a river cat.

Looking back, Venin lost his footing. His wings flew out to steady him, and a sharp pain flashed through his shoulder. "Fucking Split!" He caught himself on a rocky outcrop and closed his eyes, taking a deep breath while the pain passed.

"You okay?" Alix's hand was warm on his shoulder.

Venin turned to look into Alix's anxious eyes. "Yeah. Just my damned wing." He flicked it in irritation, and another wave of pain shot up it to his shoulder. "I'll be okay."

Alix nodded. "Here. Take my hand."

Venin snorted. "I don't need your help. I'm not ten."

"Hey, I'm having a hell of a time too. These rocks are really uneven, and sharp. Neither one of us needs to fall and skin a knee, or worse." He held out his hand again.

Venin stared at it for a moment, then took it. "Fair enough."

They scrambled up the rocks together toward the white plants that lined the edge of the cavern. The rock was sharp, and porous. Volcanic, if Venin had to guess. He chose his footing more carefully, and bits of the rock came loose and crushed into powder under his bootsteps.

They reached the top and paused to look back the way they had come. The beautiful blue lake was now fifty meters below them, sparkling against the black rock of the far cavern wall.

From up here, he could see movement in the water. It entered the cavern on his right and flowed to the left. He could also see the exit, a cleft that had been hidden from the beach below. He turned to Alix and grinned. "There's our way out."

Alix frowned. "Where does it go?"

"Somewhere that's not here?"

"Sounds good." Alix rubbed his chin where a bit of red stubble had grown. "How do we get to it? We could swim, but who knows how far we'll have to go before we come out? And how do we know it won't plunge us into oblivion somewhere inside that cavern?"

"We don't." Venin checked his countdown. "We have to try something else." He turned to survey the plants. They did look like miniature versions of corrinder, which meant they should float. He pulled out his knife and tested the edge. *Plenty sharp.* He licked the drop of blood from his thumb. "Want to build a raft?"

. . .

ALIX GRUNTED. GETTING THE "LOGS" for the raft down the rocky outcrop had turned out to be a lot harder than he'd anticipated. They'd tried throwing them down to the sand, but inevitably the corrinder beams would fall short and smash to pieces on the rocks.

The same things that made them great for raft material—lightweight and hollow—made them vulnerable to breaking on anything hard and sharp.

He felt pretty good, all things considered—trapped underground while the world might be ending above. The effervescent water must have done something to him, because his aching body, which had taken a beating in the crash, felt refreshed and pain free.

The golden fruit had proven to be similar to citrones—sweet, wet, and spicy. Alix had tried one—just a small piece—and it hadn't disagreed with him. After allowing half an hour for ill effects, he'd eaten the whole thing. It was also a bit like mango. Or at least the artificial mango that his home replicator produced.

So he and Venin had decided to haul the logs down to the beach a few at a time.

He'd taken off his shirt, and his chest glistened with sweat as he set the last pile of logs down on the sand.

He glanced at the soft white glow of the cavern ceiling. They should be up there, in the real world, looking for Xander and Jameson. He was exhausted, too, with new aches and pains in his back and arms from the difficult work. They had no more stims—they'd used the few they had for the arduous task of climbing up and down the rocks.

He glanced over at Venin. The man had his hands on his knees, and he was breathing hard.

"You okay?"

"Give me a minute. I will be." The skythane took a few steps to the water, kneeling and splashing some across his face and bare chest. "Ahhhh."

Alix sank down onto the sand next to him and did the same. The water felt really good on his overheated skin.

"So many memories." Venin looked up at the cavern ceiling, and then over his shoulder. Then he started shaking.

"Hey man, you okay?" Alix put a hand on his shoulder.

Venin's eyes were unfocused. "I… I can't…."

Shit, it's like Jameson all over again. What was it with these skythane? He knelt in front of Venin and pulled the man's hand to his chest. "Venin, look at me."

Venin looked at him. His eyes were unfocused but full of fear.

"Hey, it's okay. I'll get you through this. Feel me breathing. In and out." He put his other hand on the man's bare chest, his light skin against Venin's darker tone. "Breathe with me." He brushed aside the thoughts about how beautiful Venin's chest was, his umber skin and his wings, black like Xander's. Alix had always had a thing for wings. "In and out."

Slowly Venin responded. His chest rose and fell, finding a rhythm with Alix. His racing heart slowed under Alix's hand, and after a moment he closed his eyes and fell over onto the sand.

"Venin!" Alix leaned over him, checking his pulse in his neck. He was still alive.

A moment later, his eyes flickered open. "Take me into the water."

"What?" Alix glanced back at the lake.

"The water."

Alix nodded. "Okay." He pulled off his boots and then Venin's. Then he lifted Venin by the waist. It was a bit awkward, but he was strong enough to manage it.

Venin's wings drooped over Alix's back as he carried both of them into the water. It was warm, swirling up around his waist and washing off the sand and sweat from their hard work.

As it enveloped him, his fatigue dropped away, and he felt some of his flagging energy return. He was alive, awake, in touch with the world. "What the hell?"

There was magic in the water.

He let go of Venin, and the man spread his wings carefully to float on the surface.

A sigh of relief came from Venin's lips. His eyes were closed, but the edges of his lips drifted upward in a lazy smile. "I saw them, Alix."

"Saw who?"

"The ithani. This was… well, something like a resort for them. A long time before humans came here, I think? A place to get away."

It was strange, thinking of all the beings who had been here before them. Stranger still to think it had once housed humans, people not so different from the two of them.

Why had they come down here? How? What had happened to them after?

Venin's golden eyes opened. "The water. It's healing. Like an elixir."

"What, should I drink it?" Alix treaded water, looking at the blue liquid suspiciously. Would it make his insides glow?

Venin laughed, a rich warm sound Alix wasn't sure he'd ever heard before. "You can if you want. It won't hurt you, but just floating in it for a few moments is restorative."

"I'll take your word for it." Though he did feel really good. "Can I ask you something?"

"Sure." Venin did a lazy backstroke, going in a circle around Alix.

"Have you had these memories before?"

Venin frowned. "No, I don't think so."

"Why now? Will all skythane have them? Where do they come from?"

"Maybe?" Venin righted himself. "I honestly don't know. Touched by the gods?" He turned to swim toward Alix.

Alix spat. "Yeah, I guess that's as likely as anything."

Venin reached him, and without warning put his hands around Alix's neck and pulled him in for a kiss.

They plunged below the water, lips locked for a couple long seconds, the world reduced to a glorious blue glow around them.

Then Alix pushed Venin away and shot back up to the surface.

When Venin reappeared, he wore that same lazy smile.

"What the hell?" Alix paddled a few meters away from Venin.

He'd liked it. A little too much, maybe, but he wasn't ready for *that* yet.

"I wanted to see what it would feel like." Venin flashed him an enigmatic smile and then turned to swim back toward the shore, his body sleek and beautiful as it cut through the water.

His heart was screaming *I'm not ready*, but his lips tingled where Venin's had touched them.

Venin glanced back at him over his shoulder. "Come on. We have a raft to build."

17

ON THE RUN

THSHNEL'JIRRON FLEXED zis wings. It was good to be in the world again after such a long slumber.

Something had gone horribly wrong with the shift. The nimfeach had confirmed as much. Erro had only transferred halfway from Urshu to Ashalla, the new universe zis scientists had found for zim. When Erro's old sun had flared, it had destroyed the surface of the remaining half of the planet, though the remaining half of the amalite core was too small to ignite to critical mass.

The human that zi had taken over had filled in some of the gaps in zis knowledge. How the nimfeach had managed to resurrect zis grand plan with the arrival of the offworlders. How the shift had commenced, unfortunately saving those same human inhabitants.

Zi still lacked knowledge of what had gone wrong the first time. Why zi and zis kind had been forced to wait a hundred thousand cycles for the Great Migration. Thousands of ithani had perished, while the rest of the race had been left in a near-eternal slumber. Now this new race, humans, infested Erro.

Soon that wouldn't matter at all.

Jirron held zis strangely frail hand in front of the white wall.

The material split to reveal a small, sparse room on the other side. The human—Kadin, Dani's memory supplied—jumped up at zis entrance.

"Who's there—Dani?"

Jirron understood him. Though this "Common" tongue was a mess of contradictory rules and brutish pronunciations that offended zis ear.

The man's eyes bulged out as Jirron took him by the throat and forced him down onto the table rising out of the floor with an audible crunch of one of his wings.

Restraints encircled the man's arms and legs, and a white tendril appeared and bored its way into his skull.

Jirron watched curiously as red ichor dripped out of the human's wound. It fell to the ground, drip-drip-drip, as the human's pleading eyes stared up at zim.

Then they closed.

Jirron nodded. The Heart was assembling a profile of the man's brain. Soon he would be ready for transfer and dissolution.

Then it would be over for the poor creature.

Jessa flipped her pulse rifle up to full power and fired at the base of the shelving unit that she hid behind. She was running down the battery like crazy, but they needed a distraction if they were going to get out of this alive.

The metal quickly grew red-hot.

She attacked the other leg, and soon it, too, was red.

She threw the rifle over her shoulder and slammed her back into the shelf. It shuddered but stayed in place.

Once, twice, three times and the three-meter-tall unit finally groaned and collapsed away from her, slamming into the next one and knocking that one into the one after that.

As the shelves collapsed like dominoes, the merchandise they held scattered too, flying across the open aisle between her and Quince.

Quince shot her a grin.

Something exploded behind them. *What in heaven's name are they storing here?* A wave of heat passed over her, and Jessa ducked back into the limited safety behind her collapsed shelf, lying flat on the ground as the shock wave passed over. That was gonna leave a mark.

As soon as it passed, she was on her feet. "Come on!"

Quince nodded and followed, glancing back at the pile of devastation Jessa had wreaked.

"Where's Robyn?"

"She went ahead." Quince glanced back over her shoulder, looking for pursuit.

Robyn was trying to get the hatch open, apparently in vain. She looked up. The guards were coming. "Get back!"

Quince hauled Jessa behind another shelf. "She's using the grenade. Close your eyes and cover your ears!"

A guard appeared behind Robyn, turning his weapon toward them.

Robyn dove out of the way, and Jessa closed her eyes and put her hands over her ears.

There was a loud bang and a flash she could see through her eyelids.

When she opened them, the guard was gone.

"Come on," she called again, and ran out into the aisle.

The man lay crumpled on the ground a few meters away, his skin burned bright red.

Jessa's stomach twisted, but she forced it down.

The hatch had been blown wide open.

Robyn appeared from the other direction and all but dove into the hole.

With just a second's hesitation, Jessa followed. The grenade had taken out a decent chunk of plascrete, making a broken crater where the hatch had been. She scrambled over the rough surface, slipping the last few feet to the bottom of the broken bowl.

Quince was right behind her.

Jessa hesitated for just a second at the hole that led down into the ground. She wasn't big on tight spaces, and who in the daisies knew what was down there?

"Let's go," Quince said behind her, startling her. "Reinforcements will be along soon, with all the noise that grenade blast made. Brilliant move with the shelving. You're pretty badass."

Jessa grinned. She'd never been called *badass* before, and coming from someone like Quince, that was high praise indeed.

I can do this. She gritted her teeth and swung herself over the edge, grasping onto the still-warm rungs of the ladder that was set into the side of the shaft.

She could hear Robyn clambering down the rungs below. At least, she hoped it was Robyn.

Decided, she plunged into darkness, guided by feel and the dim red charge-level light on her pulse rifle that was slung over her shoulder.

This beat almost any night out on sedate, boring Beta Tau.

Quince followed Jessa down the rabbit hole. She'd seen enough tri-dimensionals to recognize Lewis Carroll's iconic entry to Wonderland when she saw it.

Jessa descended the ladder directly below her.

Quince's opinion of the woman had gone up a few notches since they'd first met. She'd assumed Jessa was an out-of-touch, wide-eyed ingénue, probably afraid of her own shadow.

The Jessa she was getting to know was, if a bit squeamish with rough language, intelligent, capable, and yes, pretty badass. *If I were twenty years younger and single....*

The light above dimmed.

Quince aimed her pulse rifle upward and shot off a couple rounds.

The light returned.

Still, they were fish in a barrel down here. "Go faster!"

"Trying. Damn, this is gonna mess up my palms."

Quince glanced down. Jessa slipped away into the darkness.

Quince fired off a couple more pulse shots at their pursuers, then tucked in her wings tightly and let herself slide down the ladder after Jessa.

Something rattled past her. A red light blinked. "Grenade!" Her voice echoed down the shaft.

After two seconds, a muffled explosion and a flash filled the tunnel.

Quince's heart leapt, and then her feet hit the ground.

She opened her eyes to find herself standing at the crossroads of two plascrete tunnels, dimly lit by repeating recessed lighting. One of the four corridors was dark.

Jessa had a sheepish look on her face.

"Where's Robyn?"

"Right here," a voice said behind her.

Quince spun around to embrace her. "Thank the gods. What happened?"

"I threw it down the hall." Jessa pointed to the darkened tunnel.

"Badass." Quince pulled away from Robyn to get her first good look around the space they were in.

It was a man-made access tunnel, built to a standard two-meter height. The walls were bare plascrete.

"Stand back." Quince pulled a second pulse grenade from her carry sack. She armed it and set it for three seconds. She threw it up into the shaft.

They all jumped backward.

Boom.

Light flashed again, and a pile of rubble rained down onto the floor where they had been standing. "That should slow them down."

"How will we get back out?" Jessa was frowning, but she didn't look too worried.

"Cross that gate when we come to it." Quince waved away the smoke from the grenade. "Ari, can you reach DOC?"

"Sorry, Quince. I have no connection to the grid."

"Dammit." She hadn't counted on being cut off here in the middle of Oberon City. She glanced at the three remaining tunnels. Which way to go? *The signal.* "Ari, enhanced vision, please." Her backup had included her blackware. Sometimes the ability to *see* grid traffic could be extremely useful.

The world shifted and dimmed.

From the shaft above, a glowing stream spun through the air, twisting like a glowing helix down into the tunnels.

"What is it?" Robyn asked.

"Our trail of breadcrumbs." She climbed the remnants of the ladder and approached the stream, gratified to see it was made up of the same strange glyphs that Mylin had discovered in the Oberon City grid. She held her hand out, and they flowed through her palm as if she were a ghost.

She followed their path with her gaze.

Of course, they went down the dark tunnel. "You had to throw the grenade down that one, huh?" She side-eyed Jessa.

Jessa didn't back down. "It's not like I had a lot of time to decide." She yawned.

"Don't start."

"Sorry. I'm just exhausted. So what exactly do you see?" Jessa was peering at the cavern ceiling, her eyes narrowed.

"Grid traffic. Something alien, maybe. It comes down the shaft, and then makes a zimbee line down that tunnel. Ari, what time is it?"

"Almost 1900."

Three more hours until midnight. Then, at most, two more days before the end of the world. "Let's go. We have some digging to do."

· · ·

Mylin stared at her desk. It was covered with paper.

She had sent poor Derren to take a nap and was only running on fumes herself. They had so little time left.

She'd taken a couple stims—they helped for a while, but when the fatigue returned, it came crashing back.

She was going to have to take a break soon, but she was close to something. Really close. She could feel it. Some of the pieces were starting to fit together, and if she let it go now, it might all be one vast jumble again when she woke up.

So she yawned and pushed on.

She'd started a few hours before with the strange alien code Derren had found. It intrigued her, and she'd used a couple of DOC's tools to try to unravel it, but DOC was stumped too.

He'd appeared in her room in one of his human accessible forms, a middle-aged, grizzled avatar wearing a wide-brimmed hat, denim jeans, a plaid shirt, and leather boots. He'd had to explain the whole cowboy thing to her. It was still a concept she couldn't quite wrap her head around. The hat, yes—it kept the sun off of your head on the "range." And the boots—DOC called them "shitkickers"—those were understandable too. But why blue pants, and a shirt pattern that hurt the eyes?

Then the strangest thing had happened.

"What's the file date on this one?" She held up a survey that had been taken of the area around Oberon City by the initial lander team.

"What file?"

"This one right…." Her hand was empty. "That's weird. I had a survey file from the original ZephyrCorp survey of this area."

"I don't have any record of such a survey." DOC frowned. "Though I remember that you requested a copy."

She frowned. "Could something be messing with your files?"

"Not without me knowing about it."

"Can you check yourself for any other inconsistencies? Say in the last day or so?"

"Already started. Give me half an hour." He scowled. "I don't like the idea of something crawling around inside of me, mucking with my files."

"That must be really weird." She didn't know if AIs like DOC were "real" or not, but he seemed convincing to her. She tried to imagine what he must feel like and shuddered. Like having bugs crawling under your skin.

In the corner of her vision, something else changed.

She spun around. There was a blank spot on her virtual wall.

"Dammit. DOC, dump all this to print. Now." Something was quietly erasing her hard-researched evidence.

She'd only discovered the idea of a printer the day before, but it just might be her salvation.

Now she stared at her desk, trying to make sense of the reports she'd dumped. It was so much harder dealing with masses of data in real life using paper copies than it was in vir.

"DOC would like to speak with you." Zim's voice was anxious.

"Sure." She closed her eyes and reentered vir.

DOC was pacing the length of her room. "It's been going on for decades. At least. Maybe longer."

"What has?"

"This pilfering and hiding of information. I did a comparison trace and found a steady erosion of information in my database, more than can be accounted for by standard computing errors and hardware malfunction. Someone or something has been messing with my files for a long time."

He looked furious. Steam poured off his back.

"Hey, DOC, slow down. I think you're overheating yourself."

He glanced back and laughed ruefully. The steaming stopped. "I've locked everything down for the moment. No more deletions, and I've isolated that bit of alien code you identified so it can't access anything important. I've given it a virtual copy of me to play with, filled with bogus ithani information, and you should see how it's going to town with it."

"Heaven and Erro." Her hand flew to her mouth. "What is it?"

"I don't know. I'd guess the ithani, or their agents, have been aware of us a lot longer than we've been aware of them."

"How come you've never noticed?"

He spit into a brass spittoon that appeared out of nowhere in the corner of the room. "It's very good at redirection. Every time one of my systems would flag an error, it would get bounced off in another direction, or that subroutine would be quietly deleted."

"Like when you think you see something out of the corner of your eye, but when you look, it's gone."

He chuckled. "Yes, like that."

"Can you recover any of what it stole?"

"I don't know. Give me—"

"Half an hour?"

"More like half a day."

Mylin glanced nervously at her countdown clock. Midnight. Twenty-two hours left to deadline. Maybe a little longer? "Just go as fast as you can."

He nodded and vanished.

"Zim, get me Quince." This was important. She could feel it.

There was a short delay. "Sorry, Quince is out of range."

"Moonrise help us. How about Alix?"

"Sorry, Alix is out of range also."

"Then get Derren up. Give him a couple stims if you have to, and get me whatever help is available. We have to put this all together today, or there won't be a tomorrow."

18

———

CAVERN OF THE WHIRLS

VENIN WAS full of light.

He felt better than he had in days, energetic, with the taste of Alix's lips still on his.

His flashes of memory had given him a newfound feel for the continuity of things—how it was all connected, somehow—and had restored his hope for the future.

Sure, everything might come crashing down, and the world might end the next day. But for today, he was alive and had survived a disaster that by all rights should have killed him.

"You look smug." Alix lashed together the last of the logs, tying it off in what he called square lashing, something he'd apparently learned in his ranger training.

"Not smug. Happy."

"How in the Split can you be happy? We're trapped underground while the world is about to end above us." Alix cast a nasty look at the white ceiling.

"We're still alive, and in good company." Venin tested the raft. The knots all seemed sound. "Let's go."

Alix grunted.

It was two in the morning. The light down here seemed to never change. He wondered what it had been like living in a place where there were no natural cues for night and day. "Feel like grabbing a bite?"

Alix's stomach growled. "Guess I do. Do we have time?"

"We have to keep up our strength." He grabbed an armful of desiccated wood and arranged it in a neat pile.

"A bonfire? How are you going to light it?"

Venin grinned. "Just watch." He selected a piece of corrinder splinter and placed the point down on a piece of dried wood. He rubbed it back and forth between his palms.

Alix watched over his shoulder. "That's some old-world shit."

"Yeah, they teach us wood skills out in the, you know, woods." A thin line of smoke rose from the piece of wood.

He sprinkled some splinters on top and redoubled his efforts, blowing on it as a small flame appeared.

Soon it caught the splinters on fire. "There we go." He piled more wood on top.

"What do we have to eat?"

Venin went through his bag. "Let's see. Some soggy bread. Some...." He sniffed it. "Cheese? It came out of the thingy at OberCorp."

"Replicator?"

"Sure." Venin looked up at the remaining "trees" above them. "Grab one of those fruits too. Bet it would be great roasted."

Soon they were settled in front of the fire, roasting melon over the flames.

Venin handed a chunk of "cheese" over to Alix.

Alix bit off a piece. "Oh my God, this is awful."

Venin tried his. "It really is," he managed through a mouthful. He spat it out on the ground. "I mean, I'm hungry, but it's all but inedible." It tasted like feet.

Alix ran to the water to wash out his mouth.

Venin chuckled. "Here, try this instead." He pulled a piece of the roasted fruit off the stick and handed it over to Alix.

Alix plopped himself back down on the sand and took a bite. "Oooh, that's good too."

Venin took another chunk of the melon and bit into it, the warm juices running down his chin. It was sweet and rich, and left him wanting more when he had eaten the flesh down to the rind.

"Look!"

Venin followed Alix's gaze.

Something was bursting from the water—lots of somethings. Small iridescent forms that seemed to sparkle with their own light. They danced into the air and spun around one another like glowing butterflies.

Venin laughed in delight.

"What are they?" Alix was entranced.

"I don't know." Some of the sparks combined and fell back into the water, where they sent up thin columns of steam. "Let's call them whirls."

"I like it." Venin felt Alix settle in next to him to watch the spectacle. "It's beautiful."

He grinned. Then he remembered the time. "We should finish these and get going on our way."

Alix pulled away. "Yeah. Of course you're right." He sounded disappointed.

"The world needs us." He guessed he wasn't the only one who wished the needs of the world weren't so pressing. *You did turn me down....*

ALIX SAT BACK on the sand, his gaze going from the magical dance above the lake to Venin's back.

Soon they'd have to be moving on. Time was growing short, but for the moment, he just wanted space to figure out everything that had happened to him in the last day or two.

He was your father.

He stared at Venin's wings, wondering what it was like to fly—to truly fly under one's own power. To feel the wind lift your wings, the sun warming your feathers. To be *skythane*.

Venin turned to him, his face carefully neutral. "Should we go?"

"What does it feel like?"

Venin frowned. "What does what feel like?"

"To soar. To fly through the air from place to place. To launch yourself from the ground and spread your wings to catch an updraft."

Venin stared at him for a moment. "It's hard to explain. It's like breathing for me. What does it feel like for you to walk?"

Alix chuckled. "Still, it was new to you once, when you got your wings?"

Venin's face turned wistful. "Yeah, it was. I remember waiting for that day, feeling my wings coming in. Flapping them madly to try to get off the ground."

"You and Tazim?"

"He got his first. I was so jealous, though I loved to watch him fly." Venin cocked his head. "Why the sudden interest?"

Alix looked away. "No reason. I was just admiring your wings."

"Should we go, then?" Venin stood and offered Alix a hand up.

"Sure. No rest for the wicked."

Venin snorted. "Or the damned."

They extinguished the fire and pushed the raft into the water. They climbed on board, and Venin threw the handle of his carry sack over the central mast.

Using the makeshift oars, they paddled it toward the egress, underneath the sparkling creatures. "I think they're mating."

Alix looked up, and back at him. "*Three* of them?"

"Different strokes."

"Yeah."

As they neared the middle of the lake, the current took them, spinning the raft around as it approached the dark hole of the exit cavern.

"You ready?" Venin grinned.

Alix snorted. He had no idea why the man was so happy.

"I'll take that as a yes."

Then darkness enveloped them as they passed out of the cavern of the whirls.

Alia closed her eyes, letting the sizzle of the hoversport's ionic shower clean the dirt and grit off her body.

She kept seeing it again, the crack in the earth slamming shut with a deafening finality.

Pounding the earth, frantically trying to dig her way down to Venin and Alix with her bare hands.

She squeezed herself tightly.

At last, she turned the shower off and climbed out into the main cabin.

Someone whistled, but Smythe—one of the other rangers who had answered her distress call—rapped him up the side of his head.

It felt good to be clean, the crash foam and dirt washed off her body. She accepted her clothes back from Smythe.

He was tall, trim in his green-and-purple ranger camo, and as clean-cut as they came.

She'd been lucky the craft had been passing close enough to pick up her signal. After flying for an hour, she'd encountered the hoversport and had been grateful for their assistance. "Any luck?" She'd asked him to swing around the site to see if he could pick up any other signals. Something odd was happening down there. White columns like corrinder had sprung up around the circle, and the ground itself was shifting. Visibly shifting away from the center of the circle Venin and Alix had found, toward the corrinder-lined edge. The Theseus and Demetrius rivers were having to find a way around, and there was sure to be widespread flooding.

She tucked her wings in tight in the limited space of the hoversport.

"Sorry, ma'am." The dark-haired enforcer averted his gaze from her naked body. "Nothing's come up on the scanner or grid channels yet. You say Alix Preston is down there somewhere?"

She tied her shirt on over her wings and pulled on the OberCorp work trousers he'd provided. "He was. I don't see how he could have survived, but I hoped…."

Smythe nodded. "I understand, ma'am." Now that she was clothed, he risked a glance in her direction. He was handsome enough, in a square-jawed Marine sort of way.

"Nix, can you get me Quince?"

"Checking." There was a pause. Alia sank onto one of the benches that lined the sides of the hoversport. It was a bit bigger than the one she, Alix, and Venin had taken, but it was full of burly enforcers.

"I'm sorry, Alia. Quince is out of range."

"How about Mylin?"

"One moment."

Smythe handed her a bottle. "Drink this. It will help get your energy up." His gaze lingered on her for just a moment before he looked away.

I must look blasted. "Thanks." She took a sip. It was fizzy, with a sweet taste that reminded her of citrones. "It's good."

He grinned.

"I have Mylin. There's not enough bandwidth out here for vir. It's voice only."

"Got it." She was still getting used to the whole voice-in-her-head thing. Audio only was just fine with her.

"Alia! How are you? Is everything okay?" Mylin seemed a bit frantic.

"No, sorry. It's…. We lost Venin and Alix."

A sob came across the line, then silence. She had to remind herself the girl was still young, no matter how mature she seemed. "Mylin?" she asked after a moment.

"Yeah. Sorry." An audible sniff came across the line. "What happened?"

Alia imagined Mylin wiping her eyes. "We went down into a crevasse that had opened up near the House of the Sky. The ship malfunctioned on the way down and crashed. They survived, but when I went for help, the crevasse closed up again. They're still down there."

"Okay."

"It was quick, at least."

"That's good. You're okay?"

Alia sighed. "Yes. Shaken, but okay." *And guilty as hell. Why did I survive?*

"I've been trying to reach Quince, but she's out of range."

"I know. Is everything okay there?" Their little Hunters were in pieces.

"Not exactly. Alia, they've been here for a long time."

"Who?"

"The ithani."

"Yeah, we knew that—"

"I mean inside the grid. In OberCorp's systems. They've been keeping everything about them hidden from us for decades. Maybe longer."

"Holy Split." If that was true…. They'd all assumed the ithani were just waking up. That their agents, the nimfeach, had maybe manipulated things to some extent, but this…. "How did you find out?"

"Something tried to delete the data I'd been pulling from the archives. Even DOC was unaware of it."

"Oooh." If they were meddling in lander business, what had they done to the skythane?

"Yeah."

"Look, I'll get back there as soon as I can—"

A male voice interrupted her. "I've got something!"

Alia opened her eyes. One of the enforcers—Dixon?—was staring at her from the cockpit.

She was on her feet in an instant. "What? Mylin, just a sec."

"Okay."

A three-dimensional representation of something hovered above the dashboard. It looked like a layered cake. "What is it?"

"See these two dots here?" He pointed to a pair of red spots underneath the cake.

"Yeah?"

"I think those are your missing friends. We can't connect with them through all this dirt and rock, but we're picking up their signals.

"Does that mean…. Are they alive?"

"Not by itself, but look at this." He swiped his hands through the image, and the dots got bigger.

"What?" She peered intently at the dots.

"They're moving."

A wide grin split Alia's face. "Mylin, I think they're alive!"

19

———

INTO THE HEART

Jameson was *everything*.

The overwhelming flood of memories that had flowed through his head when he'd first touched the golden hand of the statue of Erro, all those weeks before, seemed like the merest trickle compared to this.

Now he floated in a universe of them—thoughts, memories, emotions—and it was as if he'd expanded to encompass them all.

He could access them at will. *No, that's not right.* He could live them. *Be them.*

He tasted them one after another, like a kid in a candy store, eager for each new fresh remembering.

Ze was an ithani child with their brood mates, taking to the sky for the first time under the yellow sun.

Zi was part of an ithani triad, spinning through the sky in orgasmic ecstasy, on the brink of becoming one with zis lovers.

Zi was one of the white ithani sail ships, gliding right into the heart of a sun, its blinding light muted to let zim see the shades and patterns that danced all around him.

Jameson. Someone whispered his name.

Zi didn't want to heed that voice. He wanted to stay here forever, in this vast, unbounded playground, tasting lives he'd never even imagined.

Zi reached for another—

The world dissolved around him, and he was lying on a white platform that conformed to his back and wings perfectly. The sense of loss was immediate and brutal. "What in the hell?"

Something loomed over him through a fog.

He scowled. "Why did you wake me? I was just—"

A golden alien snout looked down at him. Erina. A series of chirps and squeaks came from zer mouth. *It's not safe to let yourself get lost in the* athrà.

Erina was speaking his language. Or… he was hearing what ze said, but in Common. New pronouns and all. "How did you…?"

"You gave me permission. I learned a lot about you and your lifemate." Ze shimmered. "Now when I speak, you can understand what I say."

"Got it." Jameson sat up and looked around, the haze in his brain starting to dissipate. "Where is Xander?" He got up, unsteady, and grabbed the platform for support. "What are you doing to me?"

Erina waved zer hands over a white console along one wall. It melted away, withdrawing back into the surface until it was as if it had never been there. "You present quite a puzzle. A new species, but with the ability to *fleech* with one of us."

"Fleek?" He frowned, looking around at the mostly featureless room. The two carry sacks lay discarded in one corner.

What had he gotten them into now?

"Fleech. It means…." Eri clucked zer tongue. "There's no exact translation. It's a bond. A sharing. A way to communicate that we thought no other species possessed, and on the eve of the Great Migration, no less."

"Where. Is. Xander?" Jameson shook his wings, standing tall, trying not to be intimidated by the ithani or zer apparent power over him. He leaned forward in a way that he hoped would make him appear threatening.

"Oh, you are distressed." Erina blinked at him, holding up a three-fingered hand in a way that could have been a threat or an apology. "I'm sorry. I didn't realize the fleech you two shared was so strong." Ze turned and waved a hand over the wall behind zer. The surface split and opened to reveal another room.

Xander sat on a platform like the one Jameson had found himself on, head in his hands, breathing heavily.

"Xander?" Jameson slipped past Eri and into the other room.

Xander looked up, and his face transformed from broken exhaustion to joy. "Jamie!" He kissed Jameson hard and picked him up to spin him around.

"I was scared I'd never see you again." He held Jameson's head in his hands and looked him right in the eyes. "Are you okay? Did she... I mean *ze* hurt you?" He glared at Erina over Jameson's shoulder.

Jameson shook his head. "No, nothing like that. She... ze... Erina showed me this whole universe inside my head. The memories.... Erina says we're not like anything they've ever seen before."

"A universe?"

"Yes. All the memories that flooded through me, and more. I think there's a reason we're here. Now. I think this is the time of the first shift."

Xander nodded. "I do too. But why are we here? And how?"

Jameson bit his lip. "I haven't quite figured that out yet."

"So what now?"

"We need more information." He turned to Erina. "Can you tell us about this Great Migration?"

Erina blinked twice. "Sorry, but I don't know what you are yet. You might be a dhagani spy."

Dhagani. Quince had said the ithani had been at war with something called the dhagani. He looked around. "Where's Puck?"

"Puck?" Erina cocked her head at Jameson, such a human gesture it almost made Jameson laugh.

"The nimfeach who was with us."

"Ah." That double blink again. Displeasure? "The nimfeach has been detained elsewhere."

"I need to see him." *Zim?* These new pronouns were still settling in his head.

"I'm sorry, that's not possible—"

Jameson leapt past zer again, snagging his carry sack and holding up the original key Quince had given him. It burst into a golden light, and Eri took a startled step backward, zer features twisting. "Where did you get that?" Ze sank down on one knee, not unlike the nimfeach had reacted at the crash site.

"It was given to me. Apparently it's a free pass around here."

Xander came to join him. "Don't overplay your hand," he whispered. "We still don't know why they're afraid of it."

Jameson nodded. "I need to see the nimfeach."

Erina looked even paler than ze had before, if that were possible. "Where did you get that?" ze said again.

"From a friend?" Jameson frowned.

"You're the ones foretold, you must be—but this…. There are currents moving in this room that I do not understand." Erina stood, trembling. "I will see what I can do." Ze summoned the console from the wall, passing zer hands over it in a rapid series of patterns.

Xander put his hand around Jameson's waist. "Foretold? What does ze mean?" he whispered.

"I don't know." Fate had something in store for them, he was sure of it. He just hoped it was something good.

XANDER STOPPED, stunned.

Erina had led them out of the sealed rooms with a wave of zer hand, down a long hall and outside of the building, or whatever it was.

They stood on a wide balcony in an upside-down world. Above them, a white "sky" glowed softly, and from it descended all manner of pillars and hanging structures—towers, domes, and curving spirals that seemed to defy gravity. It took him a minute to sort it out, to figure out what he was seeing.

He gripped the railing and tried to take it all in.

It was beautiful.

Ithani of all colors flitted around them on their way to or from one place or another.

"The Great Migration is close. There's much activity—everyone is leaving Arliss for the Mountain." Erina seemed to have recovered some of zer composure. "I will take you to the nimfeach."

The balcony separated from the building with a soft *slurrup*, growing a second wall behind them, and floated off into the rest of the city.

Xander took Jameson's hand, awed by the scale of what he was seeing. "We're underground," he whispered, pointing up at the white ceiling. "Or under whatever that is."

Jameson looked up and nodded.

It was the underside of the wide "bowl" they had seen from afar. Xander was sure of it.

The balcony veered and headed toward the middle of the vast space, where one structure stood out. Unlike the other parts of the city, it wasn't all white.

Instead, it was much more organic-looking, a huge dome covered with green growing things and topped by what looked like a stadium—hundreds of rows of parallel steps/seats that descended into a circular bowl.

It was too complex for him to take in all at once.

The dome was grounded far below by thick white "roots" that burrowed into the ground below it. A wide azure lake surrounded it, glowing of its own accord.

The sides of it were festooned with hundreds of shapes, like great white butterflies nestled against a tree whose size boggled the imagination. As Xander watched, one of the "butterflies" detached itself to soar upward. The white ceiling split to allow it passage, and Xander caught a brief glimpse of the greenish-blue sky above.

"What is it?"

Jameson shrugged. "I feel about as significant as a gnat right now." He slipped his arm around Xander and pulled him close.

Xander could feel him shaking.

"It's the Heart," Erina said simply.

"What's the Great Migration?" Xander waited to see if Erina would provide an answer this time.

Erina released a whoosh of air, maybe the equivalent of an ithani sigh. "We plan to leave this plane. The ithani tire of endless war and conflict." Erina sounded defeated.

"Did you lose someone?" Jameson had *that* look on his face.

The one Xander knew meant he was empathizing. "Jameson, don't—"

"You did, didn't you?"

Erina turned to him, head cocked, and made a thrumming sound in zer throat.

"Is that a yes?"

"Yes. Two, in fact. Ithani breed in triads." Erina blinked repeatedly, seeming distressed. "I lost them both in the war. Toreo and Sinael."

Xander frowned. "Breed match… that's what we saw last night, isn't it?"

Erina nodded. "It was the last breeding before the migration. Do humans ever breed in triads?"

Xander snorted softly. "Well, we have three-ways sometimes—"

Jameson elbowed him hard in the chest. "No, it's not the same for humans."

Erina looked at one and then the other. "You are very strange to me. I wish we had more—"

"What are they?" A bright blue ithani appeared directly above them, zer—zis?—beautiful iridescent wings fluttering back and forth.

"Yes, Erina, what are they?" This one was golden, with a red crest.

"Where did you find them?"

In just seconds, they were surrounded by a rainbow-hued crowd of ithani in flying form.

"They're humans!" Erina's booming voice cut through the chatter. "Everything else will be made clear at the tribunal. Now go!" Ze waved zer hands, and they scattered as if blown by the wind.

Ahead of them, the Heart loomed. Their craft glided over it into a wide bowl. In the middle, six or seven green towers covered with globes emitting a golden glow, topped by what looked like a wide arena.

Xander frowned. "What tribunal?"

Erina blinked. "I will take you to the nimfeach, as I promised. First, though, Thshnel'Jirron must grant us access to the Heart." Ze looked sad, but Xander wasn't sure how to read ithani emotions yet. "You must trust me."

"The Thishnail?"

"Thshnel." Ze said it like *tithishnell.* "Zis name is Jirron. Zi's the leader of the ithani."

Jameson and Xander shared a look. Jameson reached into his carry sack, but Xander shook his head. "This may be exactly who we need to talk to."

Jameson frowned, then nodded. "See where it goes?"

"Yes." To Erina he said, "We'll meet this leader of yours."

Jameson snickered.

"What?"

"Seriously? Take me to your leader?"

Xander laughed. "Yeah. Take me to your leader."

Erina cocked zer head. "Humans are very strange creatures."

The white ship that had been a balcony landed at the edge of the stadium, letting them off before rising into the air once again to find a perch farther down the Heart.

Jameson watched it go, wondering if it ran off amalite like the hover-sports. There was no obvious method of propulsion, and the ship moved so smoothly through the air.

Then other matters demanded his attention.

Thousands of ithani were arriving at the stadium. Word must have gotten around.

Some flew in on their own power, while others arrived on ships similar to Erina's. A few came through gateways, always accompanied by an entourage of other ithani and nimfeach.

Erina took them down one of the wide stairs that led to the center of the arena. Jameson felt a bit like a lamb led to slaughter.

Ithani all around them stared at the strange beings, chittering among themselves. They were as many colors as Jameson could count, from deep copper browns to verdant bright greens, and everything in between.

There must have been thousands of them.

He tried to read the emotions in their multifaceted eyes but failed utterly to decipher the thoughts of the inhuman ithani. There were a lot of cocked heads and clucking tongues.

As they reached the base of the bowl, a wide gateway opened up ahead of them on a raised dais.

A bright-red-and-black ithani stepped through, wearing a gold sash. Zi—for this was surely the Thshnel—was easily eight feet tall, head and shoulders over most of the rest of zis race, with a proud bearing that even Jameson could read. Zi carried a white staff as big around as Jameson's forearm.

Behind zim, another twenty or so ithani arrived, all dressed in matching black sashes, carrying staffs.

Jameson felt so out of his depth here.

"The Thshnel?"

Erina made a fist at zer side.

A chorus of nimfeach came through the gateway last, and Thshnel'Jirron raised zis hand.

The gateway vanished, and a hush fell over the assembled crowd.

The Thshnel held out zis staff and pointed at Erina. "Erinastor, progeny of Thais, Danacae, and Evros... why did you call us here, so close to the migration?" Zi held out zis arms, taking in all the gathered souls. "We have more important matters, certainly, than to spend time on a couple dhagani spies."

The sarcasm came through clearly in Common. Or maybe Jameson was just adding that interpretation himself.

"They have a key."

There was a hissing sound throughout the arena at that. Then everyone went deadly silent.

"Bring them here." Thshnel'Jirron cocked zis head at him, and Jameson felt the alien's gaze pierce him.

Erina led them up the steps to the dais.

"Show me."

Erina nodded.

Jameson pulled out the key, hesitant to hand over their only remaining means of escape. He looked at Xander, who shrugged.

Erina gestured toward Jirron.

With a heavy sigh, Jameson held out the amalite key.

Jirron took it in zis three-fingered hand and peered at it. "How did you get this?"

"It was given to me."

At the sound of Jameson's voice, Jirron hissed, zis ears laying back flat against zis skull. "Their voices are like the cries of baby schracknell." Zi turned to Erina. "Where did you find them?"

"Outside the city. They were watching the mating ritual."

Zi leaned forward and sniffed them. Then zi stared up at the sky.

A bright ray of light shone down onto the arena, bathing zim in red.

Jameson looked up.

The white ceiling was opening up, retreating from the center, letting in the midday sun. It was an angry red now. It wouldn't be long.

The Thshnel threw the key to Erina. "It matters not. This is yours now. If they are spies, they come too late to stop us." Zi raised zis arms. "Ithani, the great migration is upon us! Go to your places beneath the mountains. Soon we will shift the world, and then ourselves!"

A great cheer went up, high-pitched and grating to Jameson's ears.

"Take them to the Heart." Jirron looked at Jameson and then Xander, blinking rapidly. Then zi turned and summoned zis entourage.

A gateway opened up, and soon they were gone.

"What just happened?" Xander looked bewildered, watching the ithani evacuate the arena.

"I think we were just given the keys to the kingdom." Jameson stared after Erina, who was climbing the dais. "If we trust zer."

"Do we have any other choice? Ze has the key."

Jameson scowled. "Point taken."

They followed Erina into the Heart.

20

———

INTO THE AIR

The makeshift raft floated along the current through the tunnel that had been hewn deep into the rock. Patches of white fungus hung from the dark ceiling in irregular clumps, like miniature upside-down trees, each branch tipped with a glowing golden sphere.

Alix stared at Venin's back in the dim light. The man had removed his shirt, and beads of sweat ran down his dark skin, pooling on the raft below. His feet hung out into the water, and his wings were relaxed at his back. The tarnished silver chain glinted in the changing light from the water and the mushrooms above.

It was warm down here. Not hot. Just a steady, rather muggy temperature.

He wondered again about the people who had built those shacks along the beach so far underground. Who were they? How had they gotten down here?

Were they trapped?

Had they died there? *Will we?*

They had passed through several caverns now, each similar to the first.

Alix thought about other things too.

He closed his eyes and felt Venin's lips on his own again.

I wanted to see what it would feel like. Alix shook his head. He wasn't ready for this. It was too soon. *Isn't it?*

He scratched the back of his head. He missed having long hair, the way it had felt on his shoulders. The way it had made him feel about himself.

He'd cut it all off when he'd joined the rangers, but just thinking about it reminded him of Xander.

Too soon. And yet…. It had been a year and more since they'd really been together. A year was a long time to be alone. To go without.

He moved forward as far as he dared without tipping over the raft and put a hand on Venin's shoulder. Venin turned to look at him, his eyes asking the question. Alix nodded, and Venin kissed him, and his stomach flipped.

"I think we're coming out of the tunnel." Alix opened his eyes. They were still sitting on opposite ends of the raft, but he could feel those lips. *Dammit.*

"You okay?" Venin glanced back at him, and his eyes held only concern.

"Yeah. Sorry. Just tired." *At least that much is true.*

"Look!"

Alix followed Venin's gaze. The way was lightening ahead. They were approaching another larger space, but it was hard to make out any details.

Alix leaned over and splashed some cool water on his face. "How's the wing?"

Venin shrugged. "A little better? The water helped but it still hurts." He stretched it slowly and winced. "Yeah, no flying for a while."

There was a rumbling noise in the air. It took Alix a few moments to recognize it. "You hear that?"

Venin cocked his head. His eyes narrowed. "Yes, there's something."

"It sounds like a strong wind." It was growing quickly louder as they approached the bright space ahead.

"Or water. A lot of water."

The raft sped up. "Fucking Split—I think it's a waterfall!"

The raft flew toward the light.

Alix held on for his life. The noise had grown to fill the whole cavern now, thundering in his ears like a hundred skythane wings beating the air, and the water splashed all around him, clouding his vision.

"Alix!"

Venin's voice came to him through the din.

"You have to get to me! Grab the mast and pull yourself forward!" Venin's hand, dark against the splash of white water, reached out for him.

"I'll try!" Desperate, he relinquished his grasp on the edge of the raft with one hand and threw himself forward, grasping at the thin mast.

He missed it the first time and overcorrected, almost sending himself into the raging water, grabbing the edge of the raft and pulling himself back to safety.

White light filled the cavern now, the ceiling thick with the strange miniature treelike fungus.

He let go of the raft and threw himself forward, managing to snag the mast with his left hand. His right hand reached forward into Venin's.

Alix let go of the raft and it fell away underneath them as they went over the top of the falls, taking all their remaining supplies with it.

Alix didn't care. He slammed into Venin's chest and wrapped his arms around the man.

Venin's wings beat powerfully, carrying them past the spume of the fall. "Fucking Split," Venin said through gritted teeth, the pain in his voice clear.

He flew them down toward the ground below, each stroke of his wings clearly causing him agony.

Alix just held on, trying not to distract Venin from his task. Instead, he stared at the cavern as they descended.

It was immense, easily ten times the size of the last one. Behind them the falls cascaded down to a wide lake at the base of the cavern wall, and a bright blue river wound from there through the cavern.

It was filled with corrinder.

They must have been corrinder, but they came in so many shapes and sizes that it boggled the mind.

It was like an enormous city, filled with the most fanciful alien towers one could imagine.

In the middle stood the largest structure of all, a green dome that reached almost to the white ceiling above.

It was lost to view as they descended below the edge of the "skyline."

They hit the beach hard, and Venin rolled into a ball, his hand over his wing.

Alix's vision swam. He tried to get up and then sat back down again, gasping for breath. The impact had knocked the wind out of him.

He closed his eyes and tried to calm himself, ignoring the autonomic panic spreading through his brain. *It will come back. Let it come.*

His lungs unclenched, and he took a great gasping lungful of air.

In, out. In and out.

His breathing normalized, and he looked up at the huge waterfall. Venin had just saved his life.

The man was shaking all over.

Alix ran to his side. "Hey, you okay?"

Venin looked up "Hurts. Memories. Hurts." His eyes were glazed over, and he was shivering all over.

His wing was covered in blood.

"Come on. Get into the water." Venin had said the water had curative properties. Alix coaxed him up and into the lake, step by hesitant step.

When they were deep enough, he guided Venin to lie down and immerse himself on his back, wings spread.

Venin shuddered and howled in pain.

"It's okay. I'm here." He supported Venin's back with one hand and splashed water over the wing, cleaning the blood off. They'd had each other's backs for a week as they'd fought through the Erriani jungle and against his mother's forces. Now they were trapped in this together.

It was hard to see the skythane man like this—weak, at the mercy of his strange memories.

Venin's eyelids flickered as if he were in REM sleep.

Alix needed to break him out of the cycle. *He needs me.*

Maybe it was time to let his own walls down, just a little.

Grimacing, he stuck his thumb in the wound on Venin's wing and *pushed.*

VENIN WAS LOCKED inside his own mind, trapped by a torrent of unwanted memories.

Part of him clung to a sense of self, to who and what he was—Venin Araio. Gaelani. Skythane. Human.

The rest of him was washed away in the flood. Then everything cleared. He was in the air, surrounded by skythane and ithani. Dani Black floated before him, her face twisted in a parody of a grin.

"The Heart is mine."

"Dani Black!" He threw himself at her.

She turned toward him and tried to spring away, but she was too slow.

He rammed into her and—

Searing pain cut through the torrent of images, white-hot like the edge of a knife tempered in flame.

Venin screamed, arching his back, struggling to get away from his tormentor.

Struggling in water.

He thrashed about, coughing out the moisture that had invaded his lungs.

"It's okay. It's just me." Alix's strong hands held him up.

Venin calmed, letting his body float in the water. He looked up into Alix's warm brown eyes.

Alix was staring back at him intently. "You okay?"

Venin nodded. "That... that was bad. There were memories. So many memories...."

"I know. You sure you didn't pick something up from Jameson?"

Venin shook his head. "It was the Split-cursed statue." The warm water all around him had a calming effect. He felt better, more in control. "What happened to the raft?"

"You don't remember?"

"No. Just the sound of the waterfall, and then us, here."

"You saved my life." Alix glanced upward, and Venin followed his gaze.

The waterfall dropped from the cavern a good three hundred meters to crash on a jumble of rocks far below. "I did?"

"Yes. You flew me down from there, even though the pain nearly killed you." His voice cracked, or maybe it was just Venin's imagination.

"I don't remember that at all. But the pain...." He reached up to touch the open wound on his wing. "I felt that. It burned through me like a knife."

Alix looked away sheepishly.

"What?"

"It was the only way to bring you back." He gestured *pressing* his thumb. "The pain—"

"Ah." He grimaced. "It worked."

"I'm afraid we don't have anything to bandage it up with." He knelt to peer at the wound. "I rinsed it out as well as I could."

Venin laughed. "Yeah, we kinda lost our shirts, didn't we?" Not that he minded the view. Alix was a beautiful specimen of a man. *Tazim would approve.* "I just wish we had more—"

Alix cut him off with a kiss.

Venin responded hungrily. It had been a long time. *Far too long.*

When Alix lifted his head, Venin whispered, "What was that for?"

"I liked how it felt the first time."

Venin shook his head. "What does it mean? You told me you weren't ready—"

Alix looked away again. He suddenly looked more a lost boy than an OberCorp ranger.

Venin put his hand under Alix's chin and gently turned Alix's face back toward his. "It doesn't have to mean anything. Not right now."

Alix sighed. "It means something. I just don't know what yet."

Venin nodded. "That's fair."

Alix gestured in the direction of the strange underground city. "Come on. Time is running short."

Venin bit his lip. He checked his PA. Eleven hours. Maybe a few more if they were lucky. "Taz, any connection to the grid?"

"Sorry, nothing yet."

"Let me know if you get grid access."

They swam back to shore, and Venin got up, his pants dripping wet again. He followed Alix onto the beach, where he emptied the water out of his boots. He tied them together by the laces and slung them over his shoulder. "Where are we going?"

"This cavern's like a giant underground version of Errian." Alix pointed at the white towers that started about a hundred meters from where they stood. "There's a huge—something that way."

"Huge something, huh?" Venin knelt to take a sip of the lake water.

"Yeah. It's—maybe like a huge tree stump? A dome? It's hard to describe it, but it sits in the middle of the cavern."

Something flashed through Venin's mind. He staggered, but Alix caught him and steadied him.

"Memories?"

"Yeah. Memory." He took Alix's hand. "It's the Heart. I think it's what we came here for."

21

———

IN THE DEPTHS

Jirron hovered above Freyyr, the snow-covered mountain of the north, shivering in the cold air.

Human bodies were so different from the ithani, much weaker. Maybe his decision to merge with one of them had been a mistake, and yet… there was so much more to learn about them. To take into the Heart.

He'd seen the way newly awakened ithani had looked at him. They were afraid of him. After a lifetime that extended across a millennium, he'd done something unprecedented.

The nimfeach were still under his control, all but the human hybrid—they called him Morgan—who had bridged the split worlds. He was going to be trouble.

Cutting her wings off as she screamed.

He shook his head. Bits of the human woman's memories hadn't yet been fully integrated into his own. It was annoying, but he could live with it.

He had other things to worry about. Now was the time of the Rising.

He spread his white arms, extending his consciousness through the athrà to the mountain below. He encompassed the nimfeach, the awakening ithani, and then the mountain itself.

Together, they merged into one, sharing their power for the briefest moment.

In that instant, he forced his hands apart with great violence, rending the earth below with his will.

The mountain cracked, splitting into three parts, the fissures racing down toward the packed snow below. The ground shuddered with the shock, setting off avalanches in the nearby mountains, and a great roar filled the north.

The forge tumbled down into the waiting snow below, sending up bursting white clouds of frozen precipitation, and a golden glow shone from within.

Then the ithani rose, breathing in the fresh outside air for the first time in more than a hundred thousand cycles.

Thshnel'Jirron exulted.

The Great Migration would soon begin. He would finally become truly immortal, and there was no one left who could stop him.

MORGAN STOOD IN THE SNOW, far from the violence as the mountain collapsed, watching the ithani king rip open the mountain.

Time was growing short.

Since he and Tanner had become one, he had fought to bring about the plan—the freeing of his masters, the ithani, so they could complete the Great Migration.

Now, new things were bubbling up unbidden in his mind. Fleeting thoughts of another plan. Feelings like "loss" and "sadness" and "home." Ideas alien to his nimfeach nature.

And yet they tugged at him.

Home.

The village the humans called Egeus, on the southern end of the Gildensea.

Xander and Jameson, Quince and all the rest were going to die soon, if he kept to the plan.

Morgan had already deviated from it in a dozen ways, small and large. He felt something for these humans he'd come into contact with. Something akin to friendship. Or love?

It seemed wrong that they would die so the ithani could grow.

It seemed wrong that the nimfeach would die as well.

It is *wrong.* The Tanner part of him was insistent. *It's wrong and you know it. We can't let them all die.*

The snow and rubble were settling now, and the ithani were rising.

To the south, the sun was descending toward the horizon, dropping behind the cloud cover. Soon the ithani host would depart for the Heart.

Time was growing short.

He needed to go home.

He opened a gateway to Egeus and stepped through.

THE EARTH SHOOK underneath their feet.

Quince frowned, staring up at the air.

"What?" Jessa knew that look. It meant trouble.

"The signal. It's gone."

They'd hiked for at least half an hour down these nearly featureless tunnels, access ways built probably a couple hundred years prior by OberCorp when the Slander was still a thriving warehouse district. Jessa had read up on her Oberon history.

The place where they'd "landed" had been clean and well lit. Probably used for smuggling across the city, but the part of the network they were in now showed little sign of use. Dust was thick on the ground, the plascrete walls old and cracked. The light came from long-lasting lightdumps recessed in the walls, though even some of those—which were supposed to last a couple hundred years—had gone out.

The air was stale too. Thank goodness not so stale that it was actually unhealthy. At least none of them had fallen over from lack of oxygen yet. Then at some point, the tunnel they were following had connected to a natural cavern. It looked like a lava tube to Jessa, a fairly consistent width and height, running more or less in the same direction. She wondered if the original engineers had taken advantage of the connection to link these tunnels to the outside world and save themselves a bit of construction work.

Jessa had done a bit of spelunking on Beta Tau. If the air was breathable, there had to be a connection to the outside world somewhere.

Quince pulled out a glow sphere, activated it, and lifted it into the air, peering into the dark tube. "Do we go on?"

"I don't see that we have much choice." Robyn glanced over her shoulder at the way behind them.

Jessa met Quince's gaze. "You think this is important?"

"I do. If we can find out what's intruding into Oberon's grid, maybe we can use it to stop the ithani."

"What if it is ithani?"

"Cross that bridge when we reach it."

Robyn nodded.

Quince smiled without apparent cheer. "Okay, then we go on."

Jessa followed the others, lost in her own thoughts, wondering again what had happened to Jamie and Xand and where they had ended up. She was still convinced they were alive—call it intuition, or faith. She'd learned a lot about faith, real and feigned, back on Beta Tau.

She couldn't help but feel that they were heading down a rabbit hole to nowhere, following Quince's crazy will-o'-the-wisp. And yet, Quince was so certain.

"What now?" Robyn arched an eyebrow.

Jessa looked up. Quince had come to a halt where the cavern split, offering them two different directions.

"Not sure yet." Quince looked around, her wings fluttering in distress.

It was weird enough that the signal had followed this passageway and hadn't been a direct shot from wherever it originated to the OberCorp grid core. How that was accomplished, Jessa had no idea. There must be something directing the signal along this path. Of course, it was also probably the path of least resistance, assuming the source was under a few hundred thousand kilos of rock.

Quince tapped her forehead. "Ari, where are we?" Her frown deepened. "He says he can't get an exact location without a grid connection, but based on our movement so far, we're probably somewhere just south of Oberon City, not far from the Gildensea."

Heaven's gates. There had to be a way to determine the correct path. *Follow the signal.* Jessa put a hand on the rough, dark rock wall and looked up.

Something lurked up there. Something white, like a long tube or root that ran along the ceiling, not far from where Quince said the signal had been. "Quince, take a look at this." She stood on her tiptoes, staring at the dark place where the ceiling and wall met.

Quince peered into the dim corner. She pulled out her pulse rifle, stretched, and pushed on the tube with the nose of the gun. It retracted like a living thing, and then rebounded back. "It's pliable. It feels more organic than synthetic, maybe?"

She followed it to the juncture. It turned right and went down the new passage. "Jessa, you're a genius." Quince kissed her on the cheek.

"Maybe we can use it to reach the grid?" Jessa cocked her head, staring at the "root." *Damn, I should have gotten a PA.*

"Good thought." Quince squinted at the root. "Robyn, can you hoist me up?"

"Of course." Robyn knelt and lifted Quince up to the ceiling.

Quince held her right wrist over the root. "Ari, can you detect anything?"

Robyn held her, rock-steady.

"Ari says there's a faint signal. The root seems to be acting as a carrier for the signal." She frowned. "He should be able to ride it back to the core. Ari, get me Alix, if you can."

Quince waited.

Jessa paced the passageway below, feeling claustrophobic. *What's happening up there?* They were trapped underground for the moment, and she didn't like it at all. She glanced at her two winged companions, doing their best impression of a Beta Tau midschool cheerleading squad. *If I feel this way....*

Skythane weren't meant to be confined underground. They needed the wide-open skies—any fool could see that.

Quince must have been thinking something similar. "After this is over, Robyn, we're getting ourselves a quiet place up in the Mora Mountains and the rest of the world can—" She cut off midsentence. "Alix is away, but Ari's getting me Mylin."

Robyn squeezed her thigh in apparent agreement.

The rest of the conversation went on in Quince's head.

Jessa fingered the safety on her pulse rifle while she waited, glancing back at the tunnel behind them.

Was anyone following? There were four paths from their access point, but a quick search would show any pursuers that they'd cleared the rubble from one. Farther on, their footprints in the dust would betray them.

Then again, they had done a number on the access tunnel. Maybe they were safe from pursuit, for now.

"Mylin? Mylin!" Quince sounded anxious.

"What happened?"

"She said Alix and Venin were trapped somewhere, but okay. Then she tried to warn me about something. I lost her." She stared back the way they had come. "The signal's back. I think it swamped her transmission. Let me down."

Robyn knelt so Quince could climb off her shoulders.

"Mylin said something about the ithani just before we were cut off, but I don't know what she meant."

"What did she say?" Robyn looked worried. Robyn didn't worry easily.

"She said we had to be careful." Quince looked back the way they had come. "Like *that's* any surprise. Okay, let's go. At least we know where the signal goes now, if it cuts out again."

Jessa followed the two skythane women down the passage, resigned to being trapped in the dimly lit corridor for now.

There was no way out but forward.

ROBYN FOLLOWED QUINCE'S LEAD, pulling her wings in so they wouldn't touch the rock walls. This place was disturbing. It was so quiet here, the air dead and flat, and every noise they made echoed down the passageway.

The glow sphere illuminated the space around them for about twenty meters, and then the darkness began again.

What use were her new wings if she couldn't use them, couldn't even stretch them out?

She looked back at Jessa, bringing up the rear. There was a flash in the tunnel behind them.

"Get down!" She dove at Jessa, pushing her to the ground, her wings cushioning their fall.

Something hot flashed over her, singing the feathers of her left wing. "Quince, we're under attack!" Robyn crouched, unslung her bow, and fired off a few quarrels.

There was a cry and then a muffled thud. *One down.*

Quince flattened herself next to Robyn, her pulse rifle firing into the darkness.

Jessa joined her.

Two more shouts, and then Quince was barreling off, knife unsheathed, a silent avenger.

"Hold your fire!" Robyn whispered urgently to Jessa.

There was a gurgling scream, then another.

Jessa put her rifle down, closing her eyes and turning away from the sounds.

In a moment there was nothing but silence.

Quince returned, carrying a couple more rifles. "Syndicate men. They either cleared the blockage we created in the shaft, or there's another way in." She handed one of the weapons to Jessa.

"Probably another way in, or several, if they use the tunnels for smuggling." Jessa was a light shade of green, but she controlled herself admirably.

Robyn nodded in approval. "Give me one of those, please." She held out her hand.

Quince blinked. "Are you sure?"

"Yes. I need something with longer range."

"But I thought… never mind." She handed a pulse rifle to Robyn and stuffed the other under her carry sack strap across her back. "The release is here—"

"I know how to use it. I killed a few enforcers with one, before they took my wings."

Quince grinned, looking at her with apparent newfound respect. "I've never loved you more." She pulled Robyn to her and kissed her hard. "Come on. They may be expecting us on the other end too."

"Let me take the lead. I've been following long enough." Robyn needed to take control of something.

Jessa laughed. "You two are amazing together."

"That didn't squick you out?" Robyn doubted Jessa had ever been in a firefight on her tame home planet.

Jessa paled. "A little. Sure. But we have to protect our own, right?"

"Yes we do." Robyn squeezed her shoulder. "Let's go." She led them down the tunnel, away from the carnage they'd just wrought. "How much time do we have?"

"About ten and a half hours."

Robyn wished they could stop to rest, take even the briefest nap. She was exhausted.

There was no time. They had to keep going if they were to have any chance of unraveling the mystery the ithani presented before the endgame.

I can sleep when I'm dead.

IN THE END, it was Quince's body that forced them all to take a break. She stumbled and slammed into the tunnel wall, hard, almost knocking the breath out of herself.

"Hey, you okay?" Robyn took her by the shoulders and held her up.

"Yeah. I can keep going."

So they did.

Quince concentrated on putting one foot in front of the other. The world swam a bit—at times she thought she was walking along a beach on the Gildensea—but then she snapped back to reality.

Then it happened a second time, the rock wall shocking her back to awareness.

"That's enough." Robyn glared at her. "You can't go on like this."

Quince tried to stare her down, but there was no fight left in her. "We have to keep going. We only have a handful of hours left."

"You should see yourself." Jessa frowned. "Your face is gray. Robyn is right. You need a break. I brought some extra stims, but if you take them like this, they will just hollow you out."

"I can keep going," Quince insisted again, pushing away from the wall, but her legs betrayed her and she fell.

Robyn caught her and lowered her gently to the ground, leaning her against the plascrete wall. "No, you can't. What good will it do if we get wherever we're going, and you're too tired to fight?"

Quince tried to protest, but all that came out was a sharp croak.

"My point exactly. So we stop? Even if just for a short time? Eat something?"

Quince sighed. After a moment, she nodded. "If the world ends because we didn't keep going—"

"Then you'll have one less thing to worry about, won't you?" Jessa knelt and opened her carry sack.

Robyn chuckled. "I knew I liked you."

"Thanks." Jessa yawned.

She looks as exhausted as me. Quince closed her eyes, resting for just a minute.

Jessa cleared her throat. She'd pulled out a flask from her carry sack and now handed it to Quince. "Here, drink this."

"What is it?" Quince sniffed the contents suspiciously.

"I'm not sure. I asked for something a hundred proof from the OberCorp synthesizers. Take a few sips—it'll help you rest. But eat something too." She handed Quince a few pellets.

"No thanks. I brought some real food." Quince pulled out a carefully wrapped loaf of bread and some cheese. "It may be synthesized too, but at least it *looks* like food." She took a bite of each, and then a sip of the drink. "Damn, that's vicious." It tasted like the ass end of an auxen. Then she felt the warmth spreading through her stomach. "That feels nice."

She closed her eyes again, and in seconds she was out cold.

DAIA TRUDGED ACROSS THE SAND, carrying a bucket of water from the stream back to the colonists' makeshift encampment.

It was a beautiful world, a garden world, like old Earth was supposed to have been.

She wasn't sure she believed the tales her grandmother told. Sure, there must have been a homeworld. They'd all come from somewhere, and this new place was proof enough that worlds existed.

Some in the Church preached that God had created humans in her own image, and that Forever was the birthplace of mankind.

Some even believed that the world mind *was* God.

Daia thought that was utter nonsense. Someone had built the giant ship that had brought them between the stars to this place.

The last few years had been brutal, as Forever's systems had failed. The world mind had managed to hold on until they reached this place and had been able to generate a new seed before she died.

Now they were here, arrived in the pods she had made for them. This new world was theirs.

Several hundred colonists had reached this wide harbor that fronted the open sea. The seed had been planted in a cavern nearby with access to light and water and rock, and Daia had imprinted herself upon it. As it grew, it would help guide the colony, and with time they would find the others and build a civilization.

Daia stopped to look wistfully at the sky. The place she had grown up in, her whole world, was still up there somewhere, drifting away from them into the void. It had been a hard decision to make, but a mass of that size, falling onto the split world, could have proven catastrophic.

There was truly no going home now.

Daia sighed.

Marli's pod hadn't been among those that reached this open bay. Maybe her pod had malfunctioned and she had hurtled to earth, suffering a fiery death.

Daia hoped it wasn't true. She hoped Marli was out there somewhere, and that they would find each other again. Daia closed her eyes, squeezed again by grief. Marli, heart of her heart, connected to her in a way no one else had ever been. Or ever would be. Marli, one of the smartest minds of her generation.

"Daia!" Kylan waved at her from down the beach.

She picked up the bucket and put on a smile for him. Poor kid, trapped down here with all these morose adults without his parents, unsure when or if they would be reunited.

"Hey, Ky." She tousled the boy's sandy-blond hair. Kylan was one of the sensitives, the few who could share their thoughts with others like him over a long distance. "What's up?"

"There's a beautiful thing. You have to come see it." He tugged her arm. "Come on! You can come back for the water later."

She laughed. The kid's enthusiasm was infectious. *I could use a little beautiful.* "Okay, I'll come." She set down the bucket and followed him back up the beach, sticking to the wet sand by the water where the footing was easiest.

She spared a glance upward. How she missed the streets of Darlith where she'd grown up, in the middle of civilization. She wished she had wings to fly, to carry her back there.

It would be a short-lived respite, though. There was no doubt that world, her ship, was dying.

They ran up into the jungle, to the place where the new village was being constructed out of local saplings and a workable concrete they were making out of ash and sand. The whole colony seemed to be gathered in the empty square in the middle of the small cluster of makeshift houses.

Something glowed in the midst of them.

She pushed her way through—she was technically the colony master, after all. "What is it?" she asked. Then she froze, dumbfounded.

It was maybe two meters long, hovering in the air before her. It had glowing wings, and it was easily the most beautiful thing she had ever seen.

She reached out a hand to touch it, and an electric shock raced through her nerves.

Then a voice spoke in her head. "Hello, Daia Hammond."

. . .

Quince started out of her sleep.

She'd been dreaming. There was a beach. A woman. It had been so real. *A memory?* She wasn't like them. She didn't have other people's memories in her head. She hadn't touched a statue. Not like Jameson and Xander. And Venin?

Something was happening to the skythane. Like a switch had been thrown.

And what about the memory itself? Simple exhausted delusion? Or had she just witnessed the earliest skythane presence on Oberon? If so, why didn't they have wings? Her head hurt thinking about it all.

"Hey, you okay?" Robyn knelt next to her.

It was exhaustion. It had to be. "Just a dream." She checked her internal clock. "You let me sleep for an hour?" It came out as more of a growl than she intended.

"More or less? Here. Drink some of this." Robyn held out a canteen.

Quince took it, sniffed it, and then sipped the warm water gratefully. "Where's Jessa?"

"She rested with us for a few moments, then got up and went on ahead to scout out where we're going." Robyn handed her some bread and fruit. "Do you feel any better?"

Quince nodded. "A little. Still feel like I was trampled by an aux." *Barely functional. It'll have to do.* She took the food eagerly, and as she ate, some of the fatigue seemed to drop away. "I can manage."

Things flapped through her head like birds at the corners of her vision. She mentally slapped them away. *Memories.* How had Jameson put up with the damned things?

Footsteps echoed down the cavern. Someone was coming at them, fast.

Glancing at Robyn, Quince picked up her pulse rifle and slid into a crouch, aiming to take out whoever it was.

"It might be Jessa." Robyn was next to her, her own rifle trained on the darkness ahead.

Quince nodded.

"Quince, Robyn, it's me!" Jessa appeared out of the dim passageway "There's... it's amazing. You have to come!" She reached them, out of breath, and Quince was reminded of the boy in her dream. Kylan.

"What is it?"

"I don't know, but I think it's what we're looking for."

22

———

GHOST TOWNS

M ORGAN STEPPED out of the gateway into the streets of his childhood home.

Egeus was a hardscrabble town along the southern reaches of the Gildensea, the southernmost human town on Oberon. A forest of ice pines surrounded it, extending up into the hills above the town. They were frozen, victims of the big storm that had blown through town after the shift.

The town was just a hundred kilometers north of the southern glacier and was always cold, even in the middle of the summer. The sea's waters were dull and gray.

Morgan didn't bother to hide his presence or his manner of arrival. The time for such concerns was past.

The main street was a pitted mess of pavement, lined by buildings that had long ago seen better days. They were mostly built of local wood from the southern forest, and their paint was peeling, while some were boarded up altogether.

Morgan saw the town through Tanner's eyes.

Tanner's mother had been one of the town's "comfort women." She'd given comfort to the single men in town, which was most of them, but Tanner hadn't really understood what that meant until he was older.

He'd never known his father—an ice fisherman who had died the year after he was born, according to his mother.

She had died from pneumonia when he was just four years old.

Morgan was struck by the image—Tanner's memory—of her on her deathbed.

She squeezed his hand, taking a raspy breath, and leaned forward to whisper something in his ear.

Tanner bent down to hear her.

"I want something better for you." She took a painful breath. "You—you're the one good thing I have ever done in this life." Her frail hand reached out to cup his cheek. "My little angel."

"Mamma, don't go!"

She took his hand in hers. Her hand was warm. Too warm. He didn't understand it. Not then. "You are strong. You have my blood in your veins. The blood of kings." She pulled him down to kiss his forehead, and then lay back on her rough pillow, her breath slowly diminishing.

After a few moments, the rise and fall of her chest ceased.

Tanner let out a terrible wail, and then ran out of the tiny shack for good.

Morgan stopped in his tracks. "The blood of kings." Tanner had never shared that with him before.

In point of fact, Tanner's personality had only recently come to the surface. For months he'd remained hidden, having given up his will, his body, his mind to the beautiful stranger.

Since Quince had almost died, Tanner had begun to reappear, first in random thoughts and impulses, then as a personality in his own right. Now they were one, and sometimes he felt more Tanner than Morgan.

"You came back!"

Morgan spun around.

A young human girl, close to Tanner's own age, stood there in the street, surrounded by four other kids of varying ages. She was whip-skinny, her dirty blonde hair pulled back and tied to one side with a leather thong. Her clothes were an assortment of rags, and she held a makeshift spear.

"Tally?" The word was out of his mouth before he knew what he was saying. He threw his arms around her, knocking her to the ground.

"Hey, easy there." She grinned up at him fiercely and pushed him off and stood, brushing the dirt off from her pants. "Where in the three hells have you been?" She thrust the spear at his neck, holding it just an inch away from nicking him. "You're not a sneach, are you?"

He could have destroyed her. Morgan could have burnt her spear to a crisp or thrust her through a gateway that opened a thousand feet up in the air. "No. I'm not a sneach." Morgan held his hands out in surrender. "I'll tell you everything. I swear on the Split."

She stared at him through narrowed eyes for a long moment. Then she nodded curtly and withdrew the spear. She offered him her hand. "Come on. It's cold out and there's a storm coming."

"Where are all the adults?"

She snorted. "They all cleared out of here a couple days ago on the last company transport truck headed north." She spit on the ground. "Left us all behind to die. We've taken over the old company store."

"Good to have you back, man," one of the other boys, Sully, said, clapping him on the shoulder. He was a couple years older and had always considered himself the adult of the group.

Morgan let Tanner guide him and followed the ragtag band back up the street and into the company store.

VENIN AND ALIX climbed out of the bowl that held the lake and the waterfall. The hillside was overgrown with more white plants of various sizes and shapes. Venin had to cut his way through with his knife in a few places.

The plants pulled back with sounds like little screams. Alix shuddered. This place gave him the creeps.

Bit by bit, they made their way up a slight rise to the top of a hill that afforded them a better view of the whole cavern.

It was massive.

It stretched from where they stood at least five kilometers into the distance, a vast hollowed-out space with a white ceiling.

Like in the smaller cavern, the roof gave off a soft glow.

A city of white towers surrounded the giant structure in the middle of the cavern—the Heart. It was certainly the heart of the city, but Alix guessed there was another reason for the name too. It was hard to judge the scale of it, but it towered over almost everything else. It reminded him of a beehive, with wide hexagonal panels overgrown by some kind of heavy green moss. The top was concave, like a hollowed-out arena.

The far side of the cavern was lost in haze.

"It looks like a long way to walk. I wish I could fly." Venin winced as he twitched his wing.

Alix laughed. "Me too. Wish I hadn't lost my bi-wings in the crash." The "buildings" of the city reminded him of Errian. He guessed they'd been made out of corrinder, or whatever the actual material was called.

Or grown?

"Do you think anyone still lives here?"

Alix looked around the cavern. Other than the sound of the waterfall behind them, the place seemed dead quiet, deserted. "I don't think so. Unless the whole city went into hiding when we popped our heads above ground?"

Venin laughed. "Yes, we big scary hooomans." He put his arms out and flared his wings, doing a great skythane monster impersonation.

Handsome, and a killer sense of humor. "So how do we get there?"

"I think there's a road down there." He pointed to the base of the hill. Something like a road or path wound through the hillsides and down into the city. There were small structures and great towers down there. Spirals and domes and some that seemed to hang from the ceiling itself.

The city had an overgrown appearance, as though it were a garden that hadn't been tended for a long time.

The ground rumbled.

"I think that's our cue. Come on." Venin clapped him on the back and started down the slope toward the road. He pulled out his knife and cut his way through the brush once again.

Alix shrugged and followed. "So tell me about this religion of yours."

Venin turned to look at him, his eyes narrowed. "What do you want to know?"

"What it's all about?" Religion was a bit of a mystery to him. To his mind, things just worked, or they didn't. There was a sensible mechanical reason for everything. "I grew up in a strictly secular household. My mother's religion was OberCorp."

Venin snorted. "That sounds about right." The hillside was like a fairyland —it must have once been a huge manicured garden, because there were black paths under all the shrubbery, and so many plants. Some were purple-leaved, like their aboveground counterparts, while others were white like the "trees" they'd made the raft out of, with their citrone-like fruit.

Alix snagged a couple of these and handed one to Venin.

"Thanks." Venin used his powerful fingers to split open the fruit, scooping out the meat inside. "By the Split, those are good."

Alix laughed. "Yeah, not bad."

Venin smeared some of the fruit pulp across Alix's face with his fingers.

"Hey, stay on mission." He wiped it off, giving Venin a mock-serious glare. Inside, though, Alix grinned.

"Yes, sir." Venin held up one half of the fruit. "Seriously, we have to come up with something to call these."

"Cave fruit?"

Venin stared at him. "A bit on the nose, don't you think?"

"Okay, how about *cavins*?"

Venin nodded. "Fair enough. So this half of the cavin is Oberon. It's the province of Gael, the god of the moon, who ruled over Oberon since the great flare."

"Got it."

"When the landers first came to Oberon, the Gaelani—followers of Gael—lived on Oberon, and the Erriani—followers of the sun god Erro—lived on Titania."

"Ah, that's where the names came from."

"Right. So most of the skythane aren't so religious anymore. At one time, religion was a powerful motivating force among us, though. Wars were fought over differing interpretations of the legends and prophecies."

"The story of mankind, in a nutshell, and also the main reason *I'm* not religious." Alix grinned. "Plus the whole deity-in-a-cloud thing never really worked for me."

Venin laughed, a warm sound that stirred something deep inside Alix. "I didn't used to be. Things changed the day that Tazim died." He stopped, leaning against a white tree, and closed his eyes. The pain was clear on his features, and his wings visibly drooped.

Damn, I'm an idiot. "I'm sorry. I didn't mean to—"

"It's okay. It's still hard to think about him. But that's not what you asked about."

Alix very much *did* want to ask about Tazim. What was he like? What had Venin seen in him? What had befallen him?

It didn't seem like the time. "So two worlds, two gods?"

"Right." He flashed Alix a grateful smile. "Two sides of one coin. One dark and mysterious. One bright and golden."

"Like a pair of skythane we know?"

"I did say there was a prophecy."

. . .

Tempest comes with clash and thunder,
  Skies alight with rainbow's blood,
  When the sunlight runs to red,
  Comes the reaper for the dead.

One with wings as black as night
  One with wings of golden light
  Spin the worlds back into one
  To save them from the murdering sun.

Alix whistled. "That's some heavy shit." Black and golden wings. It sounded like Xander and Jameson, although to be fair there were probably *thousands* of skythane with wings of those colors. But they *had* managed to shift the whole world. In more ways than one. "Where did it come from?" They were walking at a brisk clip through a wide plaza with what looked like a fountain in the center, though it was dry—it was made up of white sails, connecting at odd angles and shimmering with that subtle rainbow sheen.

"No one knows. It's just something that has always been. Most of us didn't believe it anymore, at least not until—"

"Until it actually happened."

"Yes."

They'd reached the white path, which made the going considerably easier. They continued on in companionable silence, making good time toward the edge of the city. Alix had managed to get a catnap on the raft, but he was still tired. He'd been away for most of the last day and a half, and he hadn't had a good night's sleep in weeks.

Just a little longer.

23

IN THE DREAMTIME

Jameson followed Erina to the back of the dais, where a stair descended into the darkness of the Heart, pulling Xander along with him. The green "ground" beneath his feet was soft, like moss.

They clambered down the stairs after zer, coming to a wide space at their base.

Jameson's eyes adjusted. They were standing inside a dome whose walls were smooth and lined with silver filigree in fantastic patterns. The silver glowed.

"The Mountain," he whispered.

Xander looked up and gasped. "It's just like it."

They had stood in a place like this once before, when they had shifted the world.

Erina turned to look at them, standing in front of a stone archway toward the back of the room.

Jameson felt a growing sense of déjà vu.

Ze made a gesture that was easy for him to interpret. *Come on.*

"Wait."

"We must go through the gateway before the Thshnel changes zis mind."

"I want some answers first."

Ze blinked at him a few times in sequence. "Time is short."

"Humor me."

Ze worked that out and let out a whoosh of breath. "Very well. Ask me."

He looked at Xander, who nodded.

"You didn't seem very surprised to find us. Why?"

Erina clucked zer tongue. "Because…," ze said at last, "because I foresaw your coming."

"What do you mean?" Prophecy. Ze had to be talking about prophecy.

"Every generation has a seer. To guide the race. I saw that you would be coming."

"That's not possible."

Xander laughed. "Who are we to say what's possible and what's not?" He gave Jameson a wry grin. "After all we've been through in the last month?"

"Point taken."

"Shall we go?" Erina glanced at the archway.

"What are the nimfeach? Why do they serve you?"

This time the whoosh was more pronounced. "It's a long and terrible story. They are our… how would you say? Elders. When the ithani are ready to transition, they go into the Heart, taking their memories with them." Ze blinked rapidly. "It is not an easy thing to talk about."

Jameson shared a glance with Xander. "It's okay. Please continue. Humanity has commited enough atrocities. We won't judge you."

"You are very kind." Ze let out a whoosh of breath, stirring the hairs on Jameson's forearms. "The ithani take our memories with us into the Heart, and when the nimfeach are born, they carry the memories of many who have gone before. Each one has… you call it a key… where the memories are stored."

"Ah." Now things were starting to make sense. "This is where the memories come from."

Erina made a fist of agreement. "The Thshnel… is not like the rest of the ithani. Zi was born over a thousand cycles ago."

"Years?"

"Yes." The blinking again. "Zi led us in the war against the dhagani, but when the time came for him to return to the Heart.…"

"Zi changed the rules."

Ze looked deflated. "Yes. Zi took the body of a younger ithani, whose memories were lost to the Heart. It was *gresachh*."

"Gres…?"

"It's hard to translate. It means, roughly, disgraceful, dishonorable, unthinkable, and perverse."

"Ah." So the ithani were no strangers to amorality. "And the nimfeach?"

"When the final dhagani attack poisoned the sun, zi declared… you would call it martial law. Zi took the keys from the nimfeach, stripping them of their power and will, and reducing them from elders to slaves. It has never been done before but the Thshnel… zi doesn't care much for morals or precedent or the well-being of zis people."

Jameson frowned. "I know the type. So zi enslaved zis elders, just so zi could take you all to some higher plane?"

She hissed, a sentiment that needed no translation. "I don't think so. When the Great Migration ends, I think it will be only Jirron who survives."

"Why didn't you tell someone?"

Erina turned away. "I tried. No one would listen, and I feared word would get back to the Thshnel." She drew herself up. "Now come. We must pass through the gate before zi rescinds zis permission."

"No."

"What?"

Jameson was taking a chance. Maybe a stupid chance, but he had vowed to stop running. Now he wanted to stop following the lead of others too. It was time to take back some control. "Show me where we are going."

"You can't… we can only get there through this gateway."

"Humor me."

This time she understood immediately. With another whoosh, she acceded.

"Can you show me, in the athrà?"

Ze made a fist. "Come here."

He approached zer. "Angie, record this, please."

"Understood."

Erina cocked her head but said nothing. Ze put zer hand on his cheek.

He closed his eyes, and everything shifted.

He was looking out at a wide cavern. It was easily half a kilometer across, the walls covered with what looked like a growing green moss. Giant golden globes hung suspended from branches or roots that crisscrossed the space. In the center was smaller dome—a shimmering pool of silver whose surface swirled and twisted like the surface of a soap bubble.

He opened his eyes.

"Did you see it?" Zer multifaceted eyes searched his.

"Yes." He pulled out the key.

Ze clucked her tongue. "It won't work. Only Jirron can make a gateway that leads there."

He laughed. "I don't think that's true anymore." He twisted the key, visualized the Heart, and *pushed*. A gateway split the air.

Erina's fur shimmered in the dim light. "Ah, you are something special, aren't you?"

Jameson glanced at Xander.

"I think so."

He grinned at his man, and together, the three of them stepped into the Heart.

Xander looked around the cavernous space. "Who knew this whole strange journey would lead us somewhere as weird-ass as this."

Erina cocked zer head. "Weird ass?"

Jameson managed a grin. "It's not translatable." Memories fluttered through his head. Memories of this place, if not this moment. They'd been mostly quiescent since he and Xander had fallen through the gateway to this strange world, but now they were back in full force.

Xander squeezed his hand. "What now?"

"This place. It's—"

"I know. I was right. We never left Erro, did we?"

Jameson shook his head. "We just went back in time." His head was about to burst with all the information flying around inside his skull. "Can you feel the memories? Fluttering in your head?"

Xander nodded. "It's worse for you, I think."

"Maybe so." He took a deep breath.

"Are you all right?" Erina leaned in to look at him closely.

"I need… help." Jameson put his hand to his forehead and squeezed his temples, willing the headache to go away.

"With the memories?" Xander's face swam before him as if he was drunk.

Jameson nodded. "Erina… something you did freed them up. There are so many. So, so many." He drifted, following one of them off into another place.

Pain flared through his cheek. He opened his eyes, and Xander was peering at him intently. "Sorry, but I was losing you."

"You slapped me?" Jameson rubbed his left cheek.

"Yeah, sorry." Xander didn't look sorry.

"Thanks." He kissed Xander, and his lover's eyes went wide. "I fought this before. I can do it again, but I need your help."

"What's wrong with him?" Erina sounded concerned.

"He's flooded with memories."

"Ah." Ze made a thrumming sound. "It happens to our young sometimes. We call it athrà sickness."

"I can help him. We've dealt with this before." To Jameson, he said, "Whatever you need."

"Be quick. The time of the shift is approaching."

"We will."

"Help me breathe." He slipped his hand through the front of Xander's shirt, feeling his warmth beneath. A thrill of excitement went through him, but he squashed it.

Xander did the same with him, and they inhaled and exhaled together, calmly. In, out.

The chaos in his mind subsided.

It wasn't enough, though, to just push the memories away. He had to master them, fully embrace who he was. What he was.

Lander. Skythane. Ithani.

It was time.

He put his other hand on Xander's cheek. Xander's green eyes opened, meeting his.

"I have to do something. Take us somewhere. Do you trust me?"

Xander nodded. "Completely."

At that one word, Jameson felt a rush up his spine. Lust. Adrenaline. Absolute love. It could have been any of those things, or all of them at once.

He opened himself up to Xander, and they dove into the athrà.

JAMESON'S HAND on his cheek was the last human thing Xander would remember for a long while.

There was no memory where they went—or rather, only memory.

He closed his eyes, and the world dissolved around him. He felt Jameson moving closer to him, and then inside him.

It was like sex—a perfect merging of their bodies in a way that was impossible in *rel* space. They flowed together, two becoming one, as intense an experience as Xander had ever felt with another man. With anyone.

Xander's body was on fire, flooded with endorphins like the most intense orgasm he'd ever felt.

And Jameson's mind… if Xander had ever had reason to doubt Jameson's love for him, that was over now.

He held out his/their hand and stared at it in wonder. Jameson overlaid him, was part of him. *Was* him. They shared a body, a form, a soul, and all at once he understood what it was like to be ithani. What Erina had tried to explain to them.

We're together.

Is this you?

I don't know. Are you me?

Where are we?

We don't know.

It's the athrà, we think.

He/they looked around. They stood in the midst of a maelstrom.

All around them memories danced and spun, flying through the air and streaming colors of joy, sadness, anger, and grief. They reached out their hands to touch some of them, and the memories flowed through them, leaving an indelible mark.

It was the most beautiful, intimate moment of Xander's life, to be a part of Jameson, to experience this with him. *With us.* There was no line between them.

Here they saw the birth of a star, as witnessed by an ithani scientist an eon before. There the simple memory of a field of flowers, both green and red, that smelled like musk and cinnamon.

Swirling above them, the mating dance of an ithani triad.

Then the birth of a nimfeach from the Heart, breaking the hard golden shell that covered its chamber and crawling out, spreading its wet wings that shimmered like magic.

They floated above the sun, boiling and angry beneath them, mere hours away from a terrible act of devastation.

It's too much. There are too many.

They pulled their hands in and sank down to the ground, hugging themselves.

We can't do it. We aren't strong enough. They shivered, wanting nothing more than to be left alone. The magic was gone, drained out of them like blood through a deep cut. They closed their eyes, willing it all to go away, knowing they had failed.

I thought I might find you here. Erina cocked zer head and blinked at them.

They opened their eyes and stared up at zer. A little hope crept back into their heart. *How did you find us?*

You aren't yet skilled in the athrà. No one but the ithani should be able to come here.

They stared at zer. *We… we are ithani.*

Erina cocked zer head again. *I know.*

They got up and placed their hands on Erina's head. Zer golden fur was soft under their touch.

Erina seemed surprised but did not back away. Closing their eyes, they gave Erina their story.

They held nothing back. Their rocky meeting and the halting advance of their relationship. How Quince had dosed them both with pith. The war between the skythane, and the war with OberCorp. The fall back through time.

When it was done, they dropped their hands, and Eri backed away, zer eyes wide and blinking rapidly. *Everything I foresaw will come true.*

We need to find Puck. The nimfeach.

Erina nodded. *I will show you where it is.* Ze held up zer hand, and part of the athrà swirled and solidified, showing a dark room.

We see it.

Time is short. Ze looked at the two of them and made a thrumming sound in zer throat. *You are ready. I will wait for you in the Heart.* Erina vanished, and Xander felt Jameson's mind withdrawing.

Wait!

We have no time.

We have time for this.

He was inside Jameson again, this time connected to him in a primal way. They moved as one, passion rising as they passed through each other, connected in the athrà down to the last fiber of their beings. They rose on the tide of climax, fixed on each other, and it was as good—no, better—than sex had ever been in the flesh.

Xander could taste Jameson, could feel his breathing deep inside. They filled each other, the excitement building, shivers running down his limbs that were also Jameson's.

As he reached the height, Xander moaned, and Jameson matched him, their voices rising together in a tumult of exultation. They hung there, suspended, for a second, an hour, a lifetime, perfectly connected, perfectly sated.

Then it was over, and they fell apart inside the Heart, panting heavily and staring at each other in amazement.

"Holy fucking Split." Xander laughed.

Jameson grinned. "Oh gods, I needed that."

"The memories?"

Jameson cocked his head, making Xander laugh as he mimicked one of Erina's trademarked gestures. "They're gone. Or… no, that's not quite right. They're all there, but they're settled."

Xander nodded. "Me too."

Erina looked at both of them. "Yes, you are ready."

Jameson stood and pulled Xander to his feet, planting a kiss on his lips. "We have to get Puck." He pulled out the smaller key.

"Then what?"

Jameson squeezed his hand. "We go wherever the universe leads us."

24

IN THE WHITE CITY

Morgan looked around the company store.

It was half empty, shelves pushed back to the edge of the room. Sleep sacks filled the floor, and empty wrappers overflowed a trash can in one corner.

Something small and dark glared at him from the shadows before grabbing a wrapper between its teeth and scurrying away on six legs behind one of the shelves. *Ice rat.*

Tally tossed him a packaged something.

He turned it over. It was an MRE.

A pain went through his chest. It had been weeks since he had eaten human food, and an MRE was the first thing Xander had ever given him.

A memory flashed through his mind. Xander and Jameson, deep inside the Heart.

He blinked. That couldn't be right. He had given Quince the key. He still didn't understand quite why.

"You okay?" Tally was standing before him, searching his eyes. "You just press here to open it...." She opened the MRE for him. "It's not hot, but they taste pretty good. That one's 'Argantan Chicken.'"

"Thanks." Morgan sniffed the contents. They weren't half bad.

"So talk." Tally plopped herself down on one of the sleep sacks, opening an MRE of her own.

Morgan picked up a piece of chicken between his fingers. It was green with a brown sauce, but it didn't taste terrible. He let Tanner take the lead. "I was out in the ice pines, looking for something we could eat. Ice rats. Blevons. Anything. It was after we got kicked out of the back of the company warehouse."

Tally nodded. "I remember."

"I was chasing a covey of blevon down a streambed, and something appeared." Morgan remembered when he had found the boy, had chosen him from the crowd, partly because he would elicit the needed sympathy from the other humans. Partly because he'd often gone out on his own and had been easy to corner.

"Something? What kind of something?" Sully's eyes were wide.

"It was a nimfeach."

Tally snorted. "You almost had me going there."

"What? You just accused me of being a sneach a couple minutes ago."

"Everybody knows nimfeach aren't real." She stared at him, as if daring him to look away.

Morgan, the old Morgan, would have given up on the whole thing. What did it matter what human children thought? They weren't part of the plan.

Tanner *remembered.*

"Tally, come back!" Tanner howled after his friend across the frozen lake. "It's not safe!" A cold wind blew up from the south. Tally had decided to go ice fishing on Bottom's Lake.

It was still early in the winter season. The temperature hovered at just above freezing, the wind cutting through his makeshift clothing like knives.

"I want to bring us home some fish," Tally shouted back, brushing aside her long hair in the gusting wind. "We'll eat like kings tonight!"

Tanner growled and set off after her.

The ice felt solid enough under his feet, and besides, what kind of life did he have anyhow? If it opened up underneath him and he slipped through into a cold, watery oblivion, maybe it would be better for everyone. They said freezing to death was the best way to go.

He finally reached her—though Tally hated it when he called her a girl—without plunging into oblivion and tried to talk some sense into her. "It's not cold enough yet. We could fall through the ice!"

Tally ignored him, using the saw she'd stolen from the general store to cut through the ice.

It went faster than he expected.

"Help me haul this out." She grasped the edge of the ice plug.

He knelt beside her, pulling at the ice, and all at once it popped out. It was only a quarter-meter thick.

Tally flew backward with it, slamming into the frozen surface and just as quickly vanishing as the lake swallowed her whole.

It happened so fast that Tanner barely had time to register it. "Tally? Tally!" He scrambled after her, across the ice.

A jagged break in the surface showed where she had plunged through.

"Tally!" Nothing. He peered over the edge, hoping to see her.

He was ready to dive in after her when her hand, blue with cold, thrust out of the water, grasping onto the slippery surface.

Tanner grabbed it, and lying on his stomach, he pulled her up, inch by inch.

Her head appeared above water, and she took a deep, shuddering breath. "Oh God, oh God, oh God."

"Stay calm. I got you." He pulled her up onto the ice, keeping himself spread out as widely as possible to distribute his weight.

Her face was blue, too, and she was shuddering all over.

When he had her a safe distance away from the hole, he scooped her up and ran back toward the shore as carefully as he could manage.

Something must have guided him across the treacherous surface, because he made it to the shore.

He opened the tent, another furtive acquisition made for the trip, and turned up the little heater inside.

Tanner opened one of the sleep sacks and stuffed Tally in it, and then wrapped the other one around her.

Her teeth were chattering, and she looked white as a blevon in its winter feathers.

She needed more heat.

He shrugged off his clothes and climbed inside the sleep sacks with her, wrapping his warmth around her. She was like the ice itself, but slowly, ever so slowly, skin to skin with him, she began to warm.

He pulled the sleep sack over them and breathed the warmest air from his lungs into the confined space.

Eventually, the shivering stopped, and she drifted off into sleep.

Tanner stayed awake with her for hours, making sure she was okay.

MORGAN BLINKED. Something had shifted between him and Tanner. That was one of Tanner's memories, maybe the most intense one, but it was only one of many.

Tanner had opened his soul to Morgan, and with it the sum total of his experience, his memories, his loves and hates and fears were flooding into Morgan, merging with his own.

As they did, they opened other doors inside of him, and Morgan remembered his own past.

A homeworld that was his as much as it was the ithanis'.

The wrong done to him and his kind by the Thshnel'Jirron, and their enslavement.

The life, the world, the time that had been taken from him.

He was human. He was nimfeach. He was ithani.

Tally was staring at him. "You're scaring me, Tanner."

"Sorry." He blinked and saw these humans like Tanner did. "I saved you once, out on Bottom's Lake."

"I remember." A single tear rolled down Tally's cheek.

He edged forward and touched it. "You fell through the ice. You would have done the same for me."

Tally looked away, her face red.

"I can save you all now."

Tally turned and stared at him, hope evident in her eyes. "How?" Those eyes narrowed. "You're not really Tanner, are you?"

He returned her gaze. "I'm still me, but I'm a lot more now too." He let go of her cheek and opened a gateway to Green Isle, to the beach along the volcanic lake. A warm breeze blew into the general store, and several skythane looked up, startled. "Go. You'll be safe there."

Tally stared at him a minute more. The other kids stayed frozen, awaiting some sign from their leader, though Sully glanced longingly at the beach.

Then she threw herself at him.

He thought she meant to stab him with the knife in her hand, but instead she threw her arms around him. "Thank you for coming back, Tanner," she whispered into his ear. "Or whoever you are."

He grinned. "Call me Morgan."

VENIN SET A BRISK PACE, and Alix managed to keep up with him despite his extreme exhaustion.

At last they passed under a white arch that must have been a hundred meters high and entered the city itself.

It was beautiful, if past its prime. The buildings, which had looked white from a distance, glimmered in the ethereal light with a slight rainbow shimmer.

Alix looked up. They had eclipsed about half the distance to the Heart. He covered a yawn. "Can I ask you something else?" He'd been forced to revise his opinion of the skythane nation over the last two weeks. Once he'd thought them savages, primitive copies of real men like himself and the other landers. He'd seen Xander as the exception to the rule.

Now he saw what a complex history and culture they had. Besides, he apparently had skythane blood flowing in his own veins.

"Sure." Venin flexed his wings in a gesture Alix had learned to interpret as discomfort. Physical or emotional, it was hard to tell.

"You said you were in love, once. With… Taz?"

"Tazim." Venin grimaced.

"Sorry."

"It's okay. It was fifteen years ago now. It still hurts, but I've made my peace with it."

Alix put a hand on Venin's shoulder. "I'm still sorry."

Venin didn't shrug it off.

"What happened to him?"

Venin laughed mirthlessly. "He thought he was a great warrior. He wanted to bring home an auxen rack. He thought bringing down one of the biggest beasts on the planet would make him more of a man." Venin growled. "I wish I'd known better, then. I went with him, and we found a herd in the northern parts of the Riamhwood. It was a cold winter, and they were ranging farther south than normal."

"Auxen? Like the aux herds around Gaelan?"

"Bigger. Auxen are huge herbivores that live up in the north, on Titania. Nasty set of horns."

Alix nodded. He'd seen images of something like that in his company orientation—the flora and fauna of the two halves of the world were very different. "Go on."

"Taz was really good with the bow, but he wanted to do this up close. So we took a couple hunting spears, and we found a small herd that was separated from the rest by a wide creek. There were three of them—two adults and a baby. We should have known that was trouble."

"Why?" For just a second, Alix flashed on what a strange scene this was, walking through an empty alien city far underground, discussing a winter hunt with a skythane man.

"Auxen raise their herds in threes. Three parents and one or more calves." He spit.

"Ah." *There's so much I still don't know about this world.* When all this was over, if they survived it, he vowed to find out about everything that he'd been missing.

"We circled around, choosing our target and waiting for the right moment. Taz leapt up and threw the spear, and it flew true and pierced the auxen's chest, going through both of its hearts. The auxen collapsed, and the look on Taz's face was pure, fierce joy." Venin rubbed his chin. He laughed harshly. "I'd never seen him like that."

"He must have been proud of the kill."

"Yes, he was." Venin sighed. "It didn't last long, though. The other adult shooed off its calf and turned toward us, and the look in its golden eyes was nothing short of murder. We were ready, though, and as it charged across the small clearing toward us, we leapt into the air. There was this...." Venin's voice cracked.

"Fucking Split, I'm sorry. I shouldn't have asked."

"It's okay. It helps to talk about it. Really." He reached out to hold Alix's hand and took a deep breath. "There was... this horrible gurgling scream. I looked down to see another auxen—the third parent—with Taz's body impaled on its main horn, shaking him around like a rag doll. It dumped his body on the ground and then stomped him into the earth." Venin's face was ashen.

"Fucking Split." Alix pulled Venin to him, hugging him tightly. "I'm so sorry, man. I didn't know."

Venin shuddered. "It was horrible. If I close my eyes, I can still see it."

Alix squeezed him. "Was it quick, at least?" *To carry something like that around inside you....*

"Yeah. I don't think he suffered much."

"Suffering belongs to the living." He let go of Venin. "It wasn't your fault. You know that, right?"

"I tell myself that. But maybe... if I had stopped him from going, told him what an arrogant, stupid idea it was. If I had looked around a little more before we chose that target. If I had checked behind us, just a couple seconds before—"

"You can't think like that. You can't go back and change it. Look, maybe something you did the week before, or the month before that, saved him from some other terrible fate." He closed his eyes, thinking about Tucker, the poor bastard who'd been buried under an avalanche just after the shift. There had been others, too, in his time with the rangers. "Sometimes it's just our time." He looked into Venin's eyes.

Venin wiped his face with the back of his hand. "You're pretty damned smart. For a *lander*."

"And you're not as obnoxious as most of the other *wing men* I've met."

Venin laughed and kissed him on the cheek. "There might be hope for a landbound bastard like you yet." He looked up at the Heart and the ground shook. His eyes glazed over, and he started to shake too.

"Venin? What is it?" Alix followed his gaze.

The Heart was growing.

The top of it had burst into bloom, and it was visibly extending toward the roof of the cavern and expanding as it went.

Alix took Venin's face in his hand. "Look at me. Venin, look at me, goddammit!"

Venin's eyes remained unfocused.

Pain had worked before, but he was loath to reopen the man's wound.

Instead, he pulled Venin to him and kissed him, hard.

He felt the change as Venin struggled in his arms.

Alix pulled back and looked at his companion. "You okay?"

"Thank you." Venin's eyes refocused. "Damn, that felt good. Does it mean...?"

"I don't know. Maybe."

Venin nodded. He looked back up at the Heart. "It's a harbinger."

"For what?" Alix stared at Venin. What the hell did he mean?

"The end of the world. Come on. We have to run!"

"THEY'RE UNDERGROUND STILL." Dixon pointed to the scanner. "They're right below us, but we still can't reach them directly."

"What does that mean?" Alia looked from Dixon to Smythe and back again. "Are they all right?"

Dixon squirmed uncomfortably under her gaze. "Sorry. There's no way to know. We can't get more than a tracer signal off their cirqs."

Smythe nodded. "We'd have to find a way in. Right now they're so deep it would take a month to tunnel down there."

Alia bit her lip. Things had spun so far out of control. She needed to do something to help at least one of her friends. "What if—"

"Hold on." Dixon was staring at his console. "That can't be right." He unclipped his belt and leaned forward to look at the ground beneath them. "Holy Split! Get into your seats!"

"What's happening?"

"Funnel cloud." He ran his hands across the instrument board and the hoversport jerked to the left.

Alia managed to get back to her seat and buckle in.

The craft bucked, slammed by particles of something that sounded like hail across the right side of the ship, and Smythe flew past her.

Alia grasped his shirt, pulling him back as the hoversport steadied and sped ahead.

"Sorry about that, folks," Dixon called back from the pilot's seat. "We have some weird… weather?"

He pulled the hoversport around, and the side windows went clear to give them a view of what was happening.

"What in Gael's grace?" Alia pressed her face against the window, staring at the maelstrom before them.

A huge tornado spun over the ground, sucking up earth and trees and water from the river as it grew in force, carrying all the debris up high into the air. Her gaze followed it, tracing the arch of it. It was either being ejected into space or….

"Dixon, get us out of here!"

Smythe stared at her. "We should be far enough away from the funnel already."

"All those rocks and trees and dirt are going to come back down!" She poked her finger into the sky.

Dixon looked up at her and went pale. "Yes ma'am."

The hoversport hummed and jumped away from the tornado at full speed.

Alia just hoped it was fast enough.

25

——————

DAIA

QUINCE, ROBYN, and Jessa followed the root, traveling down three or four more interconnected passageways. There must have been a substantial lava flow here at one point, leaving these shells of caverns interlaced near the shores of the Gildensea.

Maybe they came about at the time of the initial shift.

The brief respite had done Quince good. Although she was sure she was going to collapse if and when this was all over, she could function again, and that was a blessing.

The walls of the cavern were lined by a glowing green moss that gave off enough light to let them see their way.

Quince glanced up. The alien signal continued unabated overhead. Then it veered unexpectedly upward.

Quince stumbled to a halt, staring up at the high-ceilinged cavern they had just entered.

Something was up there, something suspended from thick ropes or cables.

Quince pulled out the flashlight she'd grabbed in the armory and shone it up into the darkness.

"What is it?" Robyn stood beside her, staring at the thing Jessa had found.

"I... I don't know." It was immense, an oval shape supported by giant beams or roots that were sunk into the surrounding rock. Its surface was covered in whorls and swirls, and bits of golden light jetted across it.

Something that looked like roots spread out from the thing to cover the surface of the ceiling, making it appear to be a carved wooden masterpiece.

Then the world shimmered, and she found herself alone in the room.

The rough stone floor was replaced by flagstones, and the *thing* above vanished. In its place stood a giant tree, bigger than a blue oak, its trunk rough and reddish brown.

"I wondered when someone would find their way here."

Quince spun around to find herself face-to-face with a young woman. "What… who in the three hells are you?"

The woman smiled. "They used to call me Daia."

Daia.

Quince *remembered.*

THEY'D CARRIED the seed into the cavern by the sea, up far past the waterline. She would be the child of Forever's world mind, full of the knowledge passed down to her by the ones that had come before.

It had taken eight colonists to lift and carry her to her new home.

No matter whether the rest of this mission failed, they would get this part done right. Daia swore she would not be responsible for the extinction of humankind *and* the world minds.

They chose a spot near the back of the cavern and lodged the seed in between some rock outcroppings.

"Guess this is as good a place as any." Braice brushed off his hands and looked over his handiwork. He had always been a bit full of himself, but the loss of the world mind and their own sorry state had knocked him down a few pegs. "Are you sure we should be doing this?"

Daia nodded. "We don't know what will happen next. We have to do this now, while the seed is still viable."

Braice touched the rough surface of the seed, his brow furrowed. "These things ever go bad?"

She sighed. "I don't know. They were made to last for a long time, in space, but down here, there are all kinds of corrosive substances—wind, water, alien germs…." It was an old argument. In truth, she didn't know if any of those could be damaging to the seed, but they needed a win, after all that had happened since they'd come down planet-side.

She turned to see the rest of the colonists gathered behind her, a fraction of those she had hoped would make it to this shore. The sound of the waves stirred something primal in her, like the wide-open sky above.

The first week, she'd been terrified to leave her makeshift hut, frightened that green sky would suck her up into its depths, that she would somehow fly off this spinning half ball and into the cold clutches of space. Such fears were unfounded, but she'd had a hard time shutting them down.

She searched her heart for what to say. "Today we take control of our own destiny. Today we plant here the start of a new world. A new Earth."

They needed a name for this world.

The works of Shakespeare had been much on her mind of late, the great drama a foil for the tragedies they had endured to get here. She'd spent endless hours in vee watching them, some of the finest literary works ever created by the hand of man.

Yes, a new name, but she would not root it in tragedy.

This world was like something out of a fairy tale. A magical place full of forests and fresh air and promise, no matter how badly things had started out.

Sound, music! Come, my queen, take hands with me, and rock the ground whereon these sleepers be. She laughed.

Braice looked at her, concerned. "Are you okay?"

She nodded. They would rock this ground indeed and make it their own. "We should call this world Oberon." It seemed fitting. A new beginning after all the folly of the past. An awakening after a long slumber.

There were mumbles and confused looks from some in the crowd, but no one gainsaid her.

She turned to kneel before the seed, placing her hands on its rough surface. Closing her eyes, she *reached* inside and searched for its spark, its nascent consciousness. As Forever's world mind had shown her in its dying days, she opened herself up and let the seed imprint on her mind. It carried within it the memories of the minds that had come before it, all the way back to the First Mind, Alix. She would make a copy of herself in the new mind, and thereafter it would evolve eventually into a mind of its own, but with her thoughts, her hopes, her experience, and her fears as its foundation.

There.

The spark was like a tiny glowing ember inside the seed, a spark of potential.

Daia touched the spark and opened herself up to it.

She felt her consciousness flow through her, carrying with it all the flotsam and jetsam of her long life—feelings, memories, hopes and fears—making a perfect copy of herself inside the nascent biomind. Over time, it would grow into its own, finding a life separate from hers and much, much longer.

For now, the Daia being created inside the seed was her twin.

When it was over—a minute or five hours later, she couldn't be sure—she stood and staggered backward.

"You okay?" Braice caught her arm, steadying her on the uneven rocks and sand of the cavern floor.

"I think so." It was disconcerting, the idea that she was no longer alone. No longer the only Daia in the world. "I wonder what she will live to see?" The Daia inside the small world mind would far outlive her own mortal days.

Such thoughts and introspection would have to wait.

The seed was rocking back and forth, like an egg with a hatchling inside.

Then a root burst out, shattering part of the husk and seeking the rock below. Another followed, and a third, and the seed grew visibly larger as it took in nourishment from the earth and stone.

Braice squeezed her arm. "We'll make this work. Oberon will be our new home."

"I hope so." *But at what cost?*

Quince blinked.

She'd just witnessed something monumental. She could no longer convince herself otherwise, that it was all some fever dream brought on by sheer exhaustion. She'd seen—no, lived—the dawn of the skythane here on Oberon. "Who… what are you?"

The woman who had been called Daia in the memory stepped forward. "I'm the seed. The world mind. The great hope of the colonists who came here from Earth, so long ago." She sounded bitter. "Then they abandoned me here to my fate, left all alone in this cavern to fend for myself."

This was the copy of Daia, the one the original, mortal woman had invested all her hopes and dreams in. An unexpected relic of the original colony, here in Quince's own time. "What happened to you?"

"They created me, and then they left. What else matters?" Her hand came up to touch Quince's face. "The real question is, who are *you*?"

Quince's world twisted.

. . .

Robyn checked Quince's pulse. *Where in Gael's grace did you go?*

It had happened so quickly. Quince had been speaking with someone, or something—although there'd been no one else visible in the cavern with them. Then she had collapsed in a heap on the stony ground.

Something was odd about this place, besides the hulking mass that hung over their heads. Robyn kept seeing things out of the corner of her eyes, little flashes of things. Sunlight streaming through one end of the cavern where there was a collapsed rock wall.

Voices, people talking at the edge of her awareness.

Someone standing in the corner who was gone when she looked at them directly.

I'm going mad.

She shoved that thought to the back of her mind. "She's alive."

Jessa's eyes met hers over Quince's supine form. "What happened?"

Robyn shook her head. "I don't know." She looked up. "What do you think it is?"

Jessa squinted at the dim form above them. "I'd guess some kind of computer? Or is it alive?"

"Whatever it is, it has to have something to do with this." She knelt over her love, the woman she'd waited a quarter century to see again. Quince was breathing, barely, her face serene as a babe's.

"Quince, can you hear me?" She took Quince by the shoulders and shook her gently. "Quince, I need you to wake up."

Quince's head rolled off to the side.

"Come on, Quince." Robyn patted her cheeks, trying to elicit a response. Any response.

It wasn't supposed to be like this. Quince *had* to be okay.

We had plans. They were going to go off together, to find a place far away from the world's cares and fears. "Quince, if you can hear me, blink, or squeeze my hand," she pleaded. "Give me something." Still, there was nothing.

Only slow, steady breathing and the beating of her heart.

Quince woke to a nightmare.

Her hands were covered in blood, the smell of iron thick in her nostrils.

Queen Andra, Lyrin's mother—Jameson's mother—lay before her, her throat slit and staring up at her in dead accusation.

Behind her, Jameson wailed in his crib.

"You did this," Andra hissed at her, the queen's voice like shattered glass.

"You're dead!" Quince scooped Jameson up and ran for the balcony, chased by Danner and his men and Andra's angry, broken voice. *You did this.* It chased her out the window like a curse.

QUINCE WOKE ON A MATTRESS, somewhere in the depths of the Slander. "It wasn't like that," she whimpered, lifting herself up off the piss-soaked bed. Her own urine.

Her head felt thick, as if it were packed with gauze.

Next to her, a lander woman—Lilith—slumbered, her tangled hair and rough features a far cry from the angel she'd seemed the night before under the influence of Mugjuice. The taste of pith from the drink was bitter on her tongue.

She swung her feet over the edge of the mattress.

Xander stood there, a child version of Xander, his innocent features twisted with pain. "Where are you, Quince? Why are you letting him *do this to me?*"

Quince backpedaled, trying to get away from the apparition. "Leave me alone. You're not real!"

Xander took a step forward, holding out his arms. They were filthy with bruises. "Why did you let him do this to me?"

Quince covered her face with her hands, trying to shut out the piteous voice.

Why did you let him do this to me?

"I didn't know. I didn't know!"

SHE OPENED her eyes and he was gone. She was standing on a hillside, holding Jameson in her hands, looking down on Ballifor. "No, not this. Please, not this!"

It was a beautiful sunny day, the kind she used to spend with her mother and brother, picking hoarberries. Jameson was strapped in his harness at her chest, burbling happily.

She *knew* this day.

A high-pitched whine split the air, like the buzzing of a hundred bees, then a thousand.

Something dark shot across the sky and down into Ballifor, her home village, where her mother and brothers and a hundred other people she cherished lived.

A terrible flash and blast wave knocked her backward and slammed her into the ground. "No, please no...." She scrambled up, crawling forward to see her home village destroyed, melted into a sea of glowing glass.

"You brought him here."

She spun around to find her mother standing over her, her face lined with disapproval. "*You* did this, Quince. *You* killed everyone here who ever loved you."

"I didn't know. I couldn't have known."

"You killed everyone."

Quince scrambled back from the burning hatred in those eyes and fell off the edge of the cliff, tumbling down the hillside.

You killed everyone.

She slammed to a halt, the force of the impact shuddering through her whole body. When she got up, she was inside the way station.

Jameson sat there, his head down, looking as distraught as she had ever seen him.

He held out the pith vial from her carry sack. "How could you do this, Quince? I loved him. I thought I loved him. Now I don't know. You took that from me. From us."

Jameson didn't look angry. Instead he looked broken.

That was worse.

She got down on her knees and put her hands on the sides of his face. "I had to. The two of you needed to be in love."

He wouldn't look her in the eyes. The boy—no, the man—who was most like a son to her was too disgusted with her to even look at her. "That would have happened anyway." Jameson sank down on one of the cots, his head in his hands. "Don't you see? You took away our free will. You forced something that should never have been forced. You did this, Quince. You did this, and you have to live with it."

He was right.

"Jameson, I'm so sorry. I thought I had to. I…."

But he was gone.

You have to live with it.

SHE LOOKED DOWN.

Her hands were covered in blood, and Queen Andra, Lyrin's mother—Jameson's mother—lay before her, her throat slit and staring up at her in accusation.

"Please, no. Not again." She turned to run, but there was nowhere to go.

"*You* did this," Andra hissed at her, the queen's voice like shattered glass.

JESSA GOT up to look around the cavern, leaving Robyn to watch over Quince.

Quince was a tough old bird—she'd be all right.

Jessa picked up the flashlight Quince had been using and walked along the perimeter of the cave, looking for anything interesting.

The floor on the far side of the cavern was covered with sand and smooth rocks, close to the pile of rubble that showed where there had been a collapse, some hundreds of years before to judge by the settled grime and moss on the rocks.

The sand reminded her of a cavern on Beta Tau, along the Eraysses Sea, where her parents had taken her one summer. The Eraysses was a popular resort destination, and the cavern still held a sense of the primal, not the park-like feel of most of the terraformed world Jessa had called home.

Standing there, her feet in the sand, the waves at her back, staring up at the dark maw of rock, Jessa had understood the dark pull of truly wild nature for the first time.

She knelt and picked up a handful of sand, letting it run through her hands. The last time Quince had checked their location, they'd been close to the Gildensea. This had been a seaside cavern once, a long time ago.

She stood and shone the light up at the immense thing that crouched in the shadows above them.

She didn't like it—it gave her the heebie-jeebies. The wooden walls reminded her of rootbound plants—left too long inside their old pots until the soil was gone and they were a mass of twisted limbs struggling for nutrients.

Jessa climbed up on the pile of rubble, trying to get a closer look at the computer—the mind?—at the center of this strange cavern.

Wide roots or beams anchored it to the wall, plunging right into the rock as if it were butter.

She reached up to touch one that was close to the ground. It was warm, the "wood" rough under her fingers.

Whatever it was, it was alive—she was sure of that much—and if it was alive, she could kill it, or at least hurt it.

Quince looked so small, lying on her back in the middle of the forsaken cavern. Robyn kneeled over her and whispered something into her ear.

These women, as different as they were from anyone else in Jessa's experience, had taken her into their lives. Even when she might have presented a danger to them and their plans.

They were her *friends*.

Without thinking, she pulled her pulse rifle out of its holster and aimed it at the thing that hung from the cavern ceiling.

"Here goes nothing."

Quince was trapped between some of the worst moments of her life.

Scenes that shifted mercilessly from one to the next, carrying her along with them, each time shredding a bit more of her self-respect and control.

The queen's death. Blood on her hands. A urine-soaked mattress and Xander's pleading eyes. A sea of molten glass and her mother's condemnation. Jameson, broken by her own actions.

They swirled by time and time again, and she felt her self, her inner core begin to wear away, to burn off like fog under the morning sun.

"I didn't mean to." She whimpered, only glad there was no one there to see her reduced to such a state.

She had no power here, wherever here was.

Daia had stripped away her ability to act, or even react, her ability to choose her own course.

Why? Why me?

Blood on her hands.

You did this.

Urine-soaked mattress.

Why did you let him do this to me?

Sea of molten glass.

You killed everyone.

Jameson, broken.

You took that from me.

So much pain. So much anguish.

NONE OF IT WAS RIGHT.

She hadn't been responsible for Andra's death.

She hadn't killed her whole village.

She hadn't even been responsible for what happened to Xander, though she could have kept looking.

One thing she *had* done.

Bloody hands. Urine mattress. Molten glass. Broken Jameson.

She had taken away Jameson's choice. Xander's choice. Forced them into a relationship they might have found on their own, with time. All for the sake of a prophecy.

Yes, she'd had her reasons. Yes, she might even do it again, if faced with the same choice.

Blood. Urine. Glass. Broken.

What she had done was wrong.

"Enough."

The queen looked up at her. "You did this."

"No, I didn't." She knew what was required of her now. "Danner Black did this to you." She knelt and gently put her palm on the queen's cheek. The bloodstains on Quince's hands faded away. "I saved your son. I saved the world. You didn't deserve this."

The queen continued to glare at her for a moment, but then the accusation faded from her eyes. A look of utter peace came over the queen's face, and her eyes closed.

A moment later, she was gone.

Quince stood to face Xander, pushing the mattress away. The little boy trembled with fear.

She knelt and pulled him into her arms. "You were so young. I failed you. I should have kept looking. I never should have stopped, but I didn't know. I didn't know!" She hugged him fiercely. "You went through a terrible thing, but you survived." She held him out at arm's length. "My gods, you survived, and grew to become a beautiful, strong, amazing young man. I promise you I will never abandon you again."

Xander nodded. He grew in her arms until he was man-sized, and then he squeezed her tightly, wrapping his arms around her, covering her in his own wings.

Then he too was gone.

Quince turned to see her mother, her mouth twisted in a mask of horror. "Mamma." Tears came from the corners of her eyes. If only she hadn't come back…. "I'm so sorry, Mamma. I never knew I would lead them here. I didn't even know what they wanted him for. Not then." She held her arms out, and her mother took a hesitant step, then two, in her direction. "If I could go back and change it all, I would, but I can't—"

Her mother crossed the remaining distance between them in a second and pulled Quince into her arms. "I am so proud of you, my little imprean. You've traveled so far and done so much."

"I miss you, Mamma."

"I know. Your brother and I miss you too." They separated, and her mother squeezed her hands. "We all make choices we regret later, but there's not a bad bone in your body." She looked past Quince and nodded. "I think there's one more person you need to talk to."

Quince turned to find Jameson, sitting on the cot in the way station.

"You did this, Quince. You did this, and you have to live with it." He stared at her, and his eyes burned into her.

Instead of turning away in shame, she gestured for him to move aside, and he did, making room for her on the cot, his eyes never leaving her face.

She sat with a heavy sigh and took his hand in hers. "You're right. *I* did this. It was my decision, and I will have to live with it for the rest of my life."

His eyes widened, but he didn't say a word.

"I made a choice. I decided to do something because of the *grand plan*." She snorted. "Maybe I'm not so different from Morgan and the ithani after all." She squeezed his hand and brushed her other one against his cheek. "You are the closest thing I have to a son—the closest thing I will ever have. A son who deserves a mother who would give everything for him. Who would put his needs above everything else."

Quince looked away. She was wrong. She couldn't do this. Couldn't bear to see him look at her with pity. She had failed him. Worse, she had taken something from him, something from both of them.

She'd gotten a taste of what it felt like to lose her own agency, her ability to make her own choices. It was a bitter taste that had shaken her to her core. She deserved it if he never wanted to speak with her again.

His hand touched her cheek.

She turned reluctantly.

He wasn't looking at her with pity. Instead, he was crying. "Thank you for saying that."

She pulled him close and held him tightly, and he was warm against her chest, vibrant, alive.

He wasn't real. All of this was a trick of her mind, a trick of whatever Daia was. But still, it gave her hope.

She would take responsibility for her choices, especially that one. Then she would take her penance.

"I'm so glad you—"

The world shattered, a billion pieces falling around her like shards of glass.

She threw her hands over her ears and closed her eyes as the shards created a cacophony and then a howling scream that was like nothing Quince had ever heard.

Wind whipped them around her like she was in the center of a cyclone.

Then there was silence.

She opened her eyes, and Robyn was looking down at her, eyes narrowed in concern.

"Quince, are you awake?"

Quince blinked. "I… I think so. What just happened?"

Jessa came into view, blowing invisible smoke off the barrel of her pulse rifle like a tri-dee cowboy. "I took my best shot."

"I have a call for you," Ari whispered in her ear.

"Quince, are you there?" Mylin's voice came through loud and clear.

"Yes, I'm here." She sat up. "What's happening?"

"Things are going nuts up here. You have to come back!"

JIRRON WATCHED THE HEART GROW.

Arliss was exposed below zim, a window in the cheth ceiling opened up.

All around him, thousands of newly awakened ithani chittered amongst themselves, keeping a respectful—even fearful—distance from zim. They thought zis new form was strange, but none dared cross zim. Zi had led them to the brink of this, zis race's finest hour.

Destiny was upon them. After a hundred thousand years of sleeping exile, they believed they would finally become gods themselves. It was almost time for the Great Migration.

Many of the other beings on this small planet would die. A small enough price to pay for the birth of a god.

Their ending would be mercifully quick.

26

A NEW PLAN

MYLIN SAT at her desk, trying to keep everything moving. She had one foot in vir and one in the real world.

DOC had managed to lock their grid attacker out of his critical systems, so she finally had free access to her vir room again.

Back in rel, she shot a look at the clouds gathering in the skies outside. How she wished she were out there and not stuck in here, but they needed her here.

"What's happening up there?" Quince's voice sounded faint through her cirq, as if she was a long way away.

"Something's going on at the House of the Sky. Or where it used to be." She relayed the images from Alia and the others aboard the hoversport. "Something huge is growing there."

"Holy Split!" Quince's voice sounded faint, tinny.

The ground rumbled.

"You feel that?"

"Yeah, little bits of the cavern are coming down on me."

Mylin frowned. "Where are you? I can't get a fix on you."

"In a cave near the ocean. There's something here. Look, I need you to search the records of the time after the Fall. See what you can find out about generation ships."

"Generation ships. Got it. Is it really important, though? There's so much going on."

"If I'm right, it might be the only thing that really matters."

"Got it." She slitted an urgent note off to Derren, who looked half asleep at the other desk in the office. He sat up suddenly, shot her a look, and nodded. "Okay, handled. One second."

DOC was waiting for her. "We're getting reports of widespread violence across the city."

"What about Rogan?" She didn't like the man—there was clearly some bad blood between him and Xander, though she didn't entirely understand why—but he was the one they'd put in charge of security.

"Rogan and the Syndicate appear to be the source of the violence."

She switched back to Quince. "Quince, I have to go. Things are getting crazy here in Oberon City. I've got to see if I can tamp things down."

"Got it. Let me know what you find out." There was silence across the line for a few seconds. "We may only have five or six more hours."

Mylin checked her own chron. Time was indeed running short.

"DOC, have you cracked that code yet?" She stood in her virtual office, staring at the wall. Something tickled her mind.

"Not yet. I've worked out that it's an organic language of some sort. I think these are verbs." He displayed a set of flattened glyphs with tails. "And these are nouns." Those were more three-dimensional.

"Let me know what you find, and get me as many rangers and enforcers as you can. We may need to defend the building."

"Will do. Most of them were sent home, or out with the rangers. Someone's pinging you. I believe you have a visitor."

Mylin opened her eyes in time to see an impeccably dressed woman enter the room.

She was tall and thin, beautiful in an ageless, ice-queen sort of way.

"Can I help you? I'm sorry, but my time's really short." She was stretched thin as it was.

"I'll make this brief. My name is Lena Preston, and I'm here to help you untangle this godsforsaken mess y'all have made."

Alix ran after Venin as the world went mad around them.

The ground had begun to shake at irregular intervals. A deep thrumming filled the air, and the Heart continued to grow, giving off a pulsing golden glow.

They crossed a stone bridge, and as they reached the other side, it crumbled to rubble behind them.

A little farther on, one of the white towers collapsed in front of them, groaning and sagging like a melted candle.

"This way!" Alix pointed to the left, and they scrambled around the fallen tower. They clambered over the flattened end of it and ran across an open plaza decorated in graceful swirls.

Suddenly Alix realized he was alone. He turned back to find Venin kneeling on the ground, his head in his hands, his wings wrapped protectively around his body.

Alix ran back to him, kneeling beside Venin.

"Come back to me." He pulled Venin in for a kiss.

THE WORLD WAS SPINNING around Venin.

He couldn't run anymore. He collapsed to his knees, watching Alix run ahead, and then his vision clouded over.

Memories flooded him in great dark clouds, things he couldn't possibly have known. Memories of this place.

Of men and women shepherded here by their nimfeach masters.

Of the painful genetic testing and experiments.

Of wings sprouting out of his back, turning him into something not human. A freak.

Older memories too, of this place as it had been when the ithani had ruled Erro. Of the end days when the world had prepared to shift, had prepared for the Great Migration of the ithani race.

And something else.

DANI BLACK TAUNTING Xander and Jameson in the sky above this place. "Dani Black!" He threw himself at her as the clouds spun around them like the eye of a hurricane.

She turned toward him, and tried to spring away, but she was too slow.

He rammed into her and *reached* inside.

· · ·

Venin shook his head. The image had a hold on him, but he had no idea what it meant. Why Dani? She'd vanished weeks before.

No time to figure it out now.

He pulled Alix after him and they ran through the abandoned city. Already the ground was trembling beneath them.

They ran over wide white bridges and under white arches and between white buildings, all the while making progress toward that alien thing that sat in the middle of the city.

For he was now quite sure it was the key to everything.

The memories threatened to overwhelm him.

He was breathing hard. "I can't...."

Alix knelt before him and pulled him up for a kiss.

The kiss lasted just a few seconds, but Venin lived a century with Alix in that short time. The future became clear, the clouds in his mind rolling back and the darkness of his past receding like a bad dream. There was a way through this. He could see it now.

Taz was there before him for just a moment. "Every generation has a seer," he whispered, and then he was gone too.

Venin opened his eyes. "Holy Split."

"Better?" Alix's eyes twinkled.

"Better." The memories were quiet in his mind. "But we're not going to make it in time." As he said it, the Heart grew, and the ground beneath them shook like it was the end of days. He stretched his wings, and a sharp pain surged through his left one. "Maybe I can—"

"You two are needed."

Venin spun around to find a young boy, maybe twelve or thirteen, staring at them. "Morgan?"

"Come with me. We're going to change the plan."

Alix stepped through the gateway.

He'd never get used to that. Sure, the Common Worlds were high tech, but they had nothing to match this instant connecting of time and space.

His whole body hummed. *That kiss.*

The three of them stood in a wide bowl at the top of the Heart. It rumbled underneath them as it expanded, growing toward the white ceiling of the cavern.

The masculine symbolism wasn't lost on him. "You have to stall them." Morgan pointed skyward.

"Stall who?"

"The ithani. They will try to enter the Heart. You must stop them."

Alix shared a how-the-hell-do-we-do-that glance with Venin, who looked equally mystified and shrugged.

"Give me your hands." Morgan held out his own.

Venin and Alix exchanged a glance, and then took Morgan's outstretched arms.

The boy glowed, and a feeling of well-being flowed from his small arm up into Alix, spreading into his torso and throughout his body. He felt better than he had in days. In years, even.

He glanced over at Venin. The skythane's shoulder wound was knitting itself closed.

Venin opened his eyes and looked at the shoulder. "It's healed."

"Damn, wish we had more like this kid." Alix thought of all the rangers he'd lost. Of Tucker.

"I'll come back soon." Morgan let go of their arms, opened another gateway, and vanished.

Above them, the ceiling of the cavern had opened up. It actually peeled back, like the skin of an orange, allowing the Heart to continue to rise toward the planet's surface.

Above, a host of ithani were gathering in the sky.

Venin took his hand.

"I have a connection to OberCorp," Erissa said in his ear.

"How…?"

"What is it?" Venin frowned.

"Erissa says she can reach OberCorp. Hello?"

"Alix, is that you?" It was Alia.

"Yes! We're both safe—Venin is right here with me. You're not going to believe what we found down here—"

"Things are crazy up here too. There's something happening where the House of the Sky used to be."

"Yes, we're right in the middle of it. Listen, there's not much time. Can you relay a message to OberCorp?"

"Sure. Mylin's pretty much taken over there in your absence. With help from your mother, apparently."

Holy Split. Who let her out of confinement? "Okay. Well, she's one of the toughest sonofabitches that I know, so that's probably a good thing. Look, I'll call you back shortly. We've got another war on our hands, I think."

He cut the connection. There had to be a way to forestall the ithani advance.

Venin shook his head. "It's always violence. That's what has gotten us to this point. I wish—"

Alix closed his eyes. He was tired of fighting. "I know. Look, if we get out of this thing alive… should we give this a shot?" He squeezed Venin's hand.

"I don't know. We come from two totally different backgrounds."

Alix could see the way Venin looked at him. There was hunger there, and not just lust. He'd been alone for so long. "Does that really matter?" He pointed up at the sky. "Look what's waiting for us. Look what we've been through together. No one else understands that like you do. Not even Xander." It was true. He realized it as he said it. He needed to let go of his ex. To let him find happiness, or whatever he could, with Jameson.

It's time.

27

———

IN THE HEART

JAMESON FELT a growing sense of purpose. He'd come so far from the scared, closeted lander man he'd been when he'd arrived on Oberon the month before.

He was more than that, now. Much more. He was human. He was skythane. He was gay. He was ithani.

He was Xander's.

Their bond in the athrà… sex? Intimacy? Total connection? Whatever it had been, it had released him from his remaining fear and doubt.

There was more to discover. So much more, but he didn't have time to drink it all in yet. The athrà held more secrets for him, he was sure, but they had to act quickly to save Puck. That was important.

The little creature reminded him of Morgan, in a strange way. Both had come into his life unexpectedly, needing his protection. And like Morgan, Jameson had become certain that Puck was the key to everything that was going on.

He squeezed Xander's hand, and his other half nodded. Their connection had deepened in the athrà, so that Jameson could almost hear his thoughts.

We go?

Yes.

"We're bringing back Puck."

Erina merely made a fist of agreement.

Jameson used the original key Quince had given him, a world and an eon away, and fixed the dark place Puck was being kept in his mind. He twisted the key and the gateway opened up, letting him through. He pulled Xander after him, hand in hand.

They found themselves in a small dark cell, much different from the clean white enclosures Erina had taken them through. It looked like it had been carved out of the stone and carried with it an air of incredible age. Metal bars blocked the cell off from whatever lay outside.

Puck sat disconsolately on a stone bench, zer back to them, zer wings drooping.

"Hey there!" Now he could see the nimfeach through ithani eyes. Puck was *ze*, not she.

Puck turned and chirped and ran at him, throwing zerself into his arms in one huge leap. Zer wings extended out behind zer, and ze chittered happily at him. Jameson wished he could understand what ze was saying.

Xander looked at him.

The athrà.

Puck was a nimfeach. If Puck could enter it with them, ze could tell them zer story.

Not here. We aren't safe here.

Jameson pulled out the key and opened a gateway back to the Heart.

Puck pointed at the key and chittered animatedly, clearly excited.

Erina met them, glancing at the nimfeach, and touched Jameson's shoulder. "Give zer the key."

"What?" He looked at Erina, and then at the key in his hand. "This?"

Ze waved zer hand back and forth in the air, in the gesture Jameson was coming to understand as *no*. "The other one. The master key."

Jameson put the smaller key away and took out the larger key.

Its milky-white surface changed almost immediately, giving off a rainbow of colors, buzzing under his touch.

He looked at Erina, who thrummed.

He held it out to Puck.

Ze blinked at him, and then turned to stare at the key. Ze reached out to touch it.

Jameson, guided by some instinct he didn't quite understand, let it go.

The nimfeach took it, holding it in the air before zer like a crystal ball.

The colors flared brightly and then subsided. They drained into Puck's outstretched arms, and then the key dissolved and disappeared as if it were made of air.

The nimfeach sighed and dropped to the ground.

"Is ze dead? What the hell did you do to zer?" Xander touched the little creature's carapace. "And how do we get back home now?"

Jameson shook his head. "I wish I knew." He knelt beside Puck. "I'm going to try something." He used his most reassuring psych voice. He held out his hand, and Xander took it and knelt beside him, their wings settling around each other and over Puck.

Jameson plunged them into the athrà. They stood once again in the gray fog of possibility.

Jameson looked at Xander. Through their connection, he felt a flood of absolute love and support.

He squeezed Xander's hands and pulled the two of them again into one.

PUCK WATCHED the silver moon above, hanging in the sky. The time would come soon. They would take zer heart, leaving zer a husk of zer former self.

The ithani had always lived side by side with the nimfeach, and the nimfeach had given freely of their abilities. There were far fewer nimfeach than ithani, and so there was always work to be done.

The nimfeach had their own homes and customs, separate from the ithani. When a new one was born from the Heart, its ithani soul transformed to rise to the status of elder, the birth was celebrated throughout the community.

Then the war had come.

The ithani general had kept the old traditions for a time, but zi'd demanded more and more from the nimfeach.

When they'd had enough, Puck had been in the minority, arguing for a peaceful solution.

Instead, the Thshnel had ordered the nimfeach tracked down and had stolen their souls, the keys that each one carried inside, which allowed them to transcend space and sometimes even time.

Without zer key, ze was a shell of herself, a hollowed-out creature enslaved to the whims of zer masters.

. . .

JAMESON SEPARATED from the nimfeach with a gasp and fell out of the athrà. "Holy fucking hells."

"The ithani are going to destroy zer race." Xander looked at Puck, his eyes full of sympathy.

"Not just the nimfeach. Everything." Jameson grunted. "Quince was right."

"So Morgan was working for them all along?" Xander looked devastated.

"I don't know. Maybe at the start? Maybe we changed him. Maybe his human half changed him."

Erina broke in. "The shift is coming. We're almost out of time. The other ithani will all be going to hibernate for the shift."

"Hibernate?"

"We can't withstand it unshielded. Only the nimfeach can."

"Why are your people doing this?"

Erina let out a whoosh of breath. "Jirron. Zi's our most brilliant… general, I think you would say. Zi was a triad once, Jirrol, Ronil and Dinas. Jirrondin. When zis three became one, they had a mind for strategy that surpassed all others."

"Just what you need in the middle of a war." Xander flashed Jameson a wry grin.

"Yes, but then zi rejected the ithani ways. Zi refused to bear children. Zi wanted to stay in zis combined form."

"And that's bad?"

Erina swiped zer hand sideways. "Some do so, forgoing having children to pursue the arts or sciences. Many of our greatest advances have come from the combined minds of a triad.

"Jirrondin was different. Zi wanted everyone else to be like zim. To celebrate intellect over form."

Xander grinned. "Big nerd, huh?"

Erina cocked zer head. "Nerd?"

"Someone who values knowledge above all else."

Erina made a thrumming sound of agreement. "Yes. Zi is a big nerd."

Xander stifled a laugh. "So not all the ithani want this?"

Eri double blinked. "No, but we have let ourselves be swept along by the fervor. Thshnel'Jirron is very persuasive."

"Can we stop zim?" Something had ended the shift. Oberon in their own time was proof of that.

Erina stared at them for a long moment, clucking zer tongue. "Yes. I can."

Something was happening to Puck. "Guys?" Xander pointed at the little nimfeach.

Ze was shivering, and then shaking, and then convulsing.

"Is that normal?"

Erina *thrummed* zer agreement. Ze knelt and took the nimfeach in zer lap, petting zer gently with zer soft white hand. "Ze's coming back into zerself."

Jameson felt Xander's gaze on him. "What are you thinking?"

Xander was as beautiful to him as ever. "What *are* we?"

"What do you mean?" But he knew exactly what Xander meant.

"Before I met you, I knew exactly what I was. A skythane outcast living in Oberon City, working for an evil corporation."

"Sounds about right."

"Now? I'm a skythane prince—or king—and I have bits of me that are ithani and maybe even nimfeach." He glanced at Puck and back at Jameson. "So what am I?"

Jameson shrugged. "I don't know. I suppose we're human, overall? It's how we were raised. It's our whole outlook." He rubbed his chin. The stubble was getting a bit thick. "But maybe we're more?"

"How do you mean?"

Jameson searched for a way to explain. "When I was little, I knew I was attracted to boys, but I didn't want to grow up like that. You know?"

Xander laughed. "Not really, but go on."

"I told myself maybe I had those feelings for a reason. Maybe they were supposed to make me a better person. You know, able to relate to people who were different from me."

"And this makes us more human… how?"

"What I'm saying is that maybe there's a reason we ended up being a mix of all these different things. You, me, and the skythane. Maybe we are the only ones who can stop all of this. Broker a peace."

"Maaaaybe." Xander sounded doubtful.

"So what's the plan?"

They both turned to Erina. "What do we do?"

Ze showed them what ze had forseen.

Xander hated change.

Things had been rough enough before this whole adventure had begun. Losing Alix had cut him right through, leaving him broken and exposed.

Then Jameson had come along.

His lover held the little nimfeach gently. Xander marveled at the change Jameson had undergone, both physically and in his character.

He no longer ran from things. Instead he ran toward them.

Jameson had changed him too. Brought back his soft side. His faith in humankind.

Well, most of it.

Some of that had been Morgan's doing too. He brought out Xander's protective instincts in a way no one else ever had.

Now everything they'd fought for was threatened. He had no choice but to embrace change, to harness it to save himself, Jameson, and everyone else they loved. "We're going to destroy half of Erro, aren't we? In this time?"

Erina's face took on an almost wistful look, though it was hard to tell on that alien visage. "It's unavoidable. We were different once. We lived with the nimfeach in peace. We weren't so focused on this strange dream of an *afterlife.*" The last word almost sounded like an epithet.

"You sound like you don't believe." Xander was getting better at reading the tall alien.

A whoosh. "Once I did. I wanted to believe. That what we were doing was right. That we had been attacked, and this was the only way to stop it from happening again." Ze blinked a few times. "Then the dreams started. When an ithani is chosen as a seer, it's not always clear. It begins with dreams. Strange dreams that seem to come true. Little things like a premonition of an accident. Or of the birth of a child."

"Or the end of the world."

"Yes. It came to me in pieces, over the last cycle. Now… now I know what it means. What Jirron intends."

"Why not just kill zim?"

Ze made that curious ithani sigh again. "Zi is entwined with the Heart. If we kill zim, we kill the Heart, too, and eventually the nimfeach and the ithani. I have to stop zim, and zi's too powerful for me to go up against zim alone."

"You won't survive." Ze'd said earlier that ithani couldn't live through the shift.

Ze stared at him for a long moment. Then ze made a thrumming sound deep in zer throat. "If we stop it, I'll still be on this side of the shift. If not… I'll go into the Heart."

"Will the Heart survive?" He'd never heard of it in his own future time.

"Yes."

He looked at Jameson, and then at Puck. "So what happens to us?"

Erina rolled her head on zer neck. *That* was a new one. "I have a plan for that too."

MORGAN OPENED A GATEWAY TO ERRIAN, stepping out onto the wide plaza of First Square.

Night had fallen, but skythane buzzed all around him, intent on the cleanup of the ravaged city.

He brought his hands together, and a thunderclap spread through the city.

"People of Errian, Jameson needs you."

An older woman with gray hair dropped to the square before him. "Who are you?" Her eyes narrowed. "We've had enough of fighting. It's time to rebuild Errian."

"You're needed for one more fight." He held his hand out. "I'm Morgan. I'm part human and part ithani, and I call Jameson my friend."

She knelt next to him. "I've heard of you. I'm Vestra, one-time regent of this city." She took his hand.

"Close your eyes."

Others of the skythane were gathering around them, though they left a wide circle around the two of them.

Morgan put a hand to her cheek. "The last days are here, but we still have one small chance to stop them." He shared his soul with her, the knowledge of what had passed and what was still to come.

After a moment she opened her eyes, gazing into his. She gave him a small nod and then pulled him into a hug. "You've suffered so much."

For a minute, he was just Tanner.

He hugged her back and sobbed. She felt warm and safe, and her wings enfolded him. Tanner cried for his mother, for his friends who had died on the streets, for the lives of the others who had lived through such terrible times. He cried for the nimfeach and their long bondage to the ithani.

And he cried for himself. For Tanner. For innocence lost and a life that would never be lived.

In the end, his sobbing stopped. He sniffed and looked up.

There were dozens of skythane gathered around the two of them, each reaching out to put a hand on him.

Vestra waved them back. She let Morgan go and squeezed his shoulders gently. "We will go where you tell us."

He nodded, wiping his tears. "I'm sorry for crying. Nimfeach don't cry."

"But little boys do." She kissed his forehead. "Stay strong, Morgan."

Morgan reasserted himself, but Tanner remained. They were linked now, truly one.

He opened a gateway to the Heart.

"We go to fight!" Vestra sent for weapons, and soon they launched themselves through the gateway, and the assembled throng followed.

When the last one was through, he closed the gateway and opened another to Gaelan. He'd secure the aid of the Gaelani next.

Then he'd go find Quince.

28

———

FREE

WHEN THE alarm sounded, Lena swung into action.

"Pulse cannon," she said when she picked a big gun out of her own personal weapons stash, hidden in the back of her former office at OberCorp. It was palm-only access, paired with a retinal scan.

Mylin doubted Alix had even known it was there.

She handed Mylin a pulse rifle. "Know how to use this?"

Mylin nodded.

"Good girl."

"How did you get here? Alix says you were in the medical wing," Mylin said as Lena handed her the rifle.

"I sprung myself when I heard the situation had started going south, fast. Things aren't going well for Team Human, are they?" She sighed. "Where is my son?"

"Somewhere in the Outland." Mylin shook her head miserably. "There's something going on out there." She wasn't sure how much she should tell the woman. After all, Alix had removed his mother from power for trying to destroy the skythane.

Still, that old saying rang true. A new enemy made an old one your new friend.

"What about Quince? She seems to be the one capable person in this whole shit show."

Mylin laughed in spite of herself. "You know her?"

"Only by reputation."

She's tracking down a lead, somewhere under Oberon City."

Lena snorted, a surprising sound out of such a refined woman. "What? I wasn't always the flawless corporate creature you see before you." She tapped her temple and frowned. "I forgot, Alix shut down my grid access. You'll have to run ops."

"Run ops?"

"Tell me where we need to go. Where's the alarm coming from?"

"Okay. Let's see." She slitted a request to DOC. "It's down on the third floor. The armory."

"Of course. It's Rogan, isn't it?"

"How do you know about Rogan?"

Lena smiled grimly. "Like I said, I still have friends in OberCorp, board ouster or not. Come on."

She led Mylin out of the office and past the lift.

Mylin glanced at it questioningly.

"Too dangerous. We might get stuck if they cut the power, or worse."

"You know I have wings, right?"

"Yes. Which would make you a sitting duck if they fired up the shaft. Sorry. Flying duck."

"Duck?"

"Look it up later." They gathered the few remaining OberCorp enforcers in the building, and Lena palmed the pad next to an unmarked door. It swung open silently, revealing a dimly lit stairway.

Twenty-five floors down.

Come on!" Lena barreled down the stairs, and Mylin followed her.

On the way, she asked DOC to send out updates to Quince and Alia. She marveled at the strange circumstances she found herself in, following the former OberCorp CEO down the stairs armed with a pulse rifle to try to fight off a Syndicate boss. A month ago, she hadn't even known those people and things existed. *If I die today, at least I've had an interesting life.*

"You're awfully young," Lena said between breaths as they ran down the stairs. "How old are you?"

"Sixteen. I've always been really good at organization."

"You should come work for me when this is all over." They rounded the landing on the fourteenth floor. "For OberCorp."

Mylin grinned. "I think I'd like that. Why are you helping me?"

They passed the eleventh-floor landing. "Alix and I had our disagreements, and I'm still on the fence about the skythane. But like I said, we're all Team Human."

"Time enough to sort the rest out later?"

"Exactly."

"What about Rogan? He's human."

"After all the things he's done? I'd say he's Team Scum."

Soon they reached the armory floor. Two of the enforcers quietly removed an access way cover and slipped inside.

Now they were in the hall, thirty meters from the armory. A firefight raged around the corner, the smell of melted plas and the sounds of pulse fire filling the air.

Mylin had her back to the wall, her pulse rifle held at the ready.

Lena Preston crouched next to her, holding a much larger gun. "Ready?"

"Wait!" Zim was pinging her. "Zim, kind of a bad time…."

"There's a young enforcer trying to reach you. His name is Tovey. He says he's pinned down in the armory. He's only managing to hold out because of the armored door, but his attackers are almost through."

"Put him through."

"What is it?" Lena looked anxious to go.

Mylin put up her hand. "Tovey? Yes, I know. We're right outside. Give me a count of ten, and then give them everything you've got."

"What?"

"We've got a man inside. Three… two… one. Let's go!"

QUINCE GRUNTED IN FRUSTRATION, turning a smooth pebble over and over in her hand.

According to Mylin, OberCorp was under attack, by Rogan, apparently. Something called the "Heart" was rising near the site of the House of the Sun.

And she was stuck down here on a fool's errand that had so far uncovered little more than a history lesson and a mind-bending guilt trip. "Gods dammit." She threw the pebble at the wall of rubble that had once been the cavern entrance.

Robyn took her hand. "What's going on in there?"

"I was wrong. About dosing Xander and Jameson with pith. About running back to Ballifor after… Andra. About all of it." She let go of Robyn's hand. She couldn't bear to have Robyn see her like this, full of shame.

"Hey, look at me." Robyn pulled her face around gently, her green eyes staring intently into Quince's. "You saved them both when the world was against them. You saved *me*." She fluttered her wings. "You brought me back to myself."

Quince laughed ruefully. "Maybe. I made so many mistakes."

Robyn's laugh was more cheerful. "Who hasn't? More importantly, have you learned from them?"

Quince thought about that. She had learned some hard lessons about herself over the course of the last month. "I guess so?"

"We can't change the past. We can only change how we react, and what we do next." Her green eyes searched Quince's. "What happened inside that head of yours after you collapsed?"

"She… Daia… the mind up there. She made me relive all the bad decisions I've made. She forced me to face up to the people I've hurt. It wasn't real, but still."

Robyn nodded. "It changed you."

"Maybe. Too soon to tell. I have to apologize to Jameson. To both of them."

Robyn pulled her close. "You're my soul mate. When you ache, I ache."

Quince let herself be held, feeling Robyn's warmth, and closed her eyes. For just a moment, she let go of the huge weight she carried with her, day after day.

For just a moment, she was at peace.

"Ahem."

They separated. Jessa was pointing up. "I think we're about to have company again."

The world mind was stirring, electrical impulses running across its surface.

"What is it?" Jessa frowned, pointing the pulse rifle up at the mind again.

"Don't! You might damage it."

"Sounds like it attacked you first."

Quince shook her head. "I think there's something wrong with it." She didn't know how to explain it, but the Daia she remembered, the real Daia, wasn't cruel. Wasn't vindictive. "You're looking at the last world mind, something the skythane colonists brought with them when they first came here." Maybe Daia had reached out to the grid because she was lonely. But why would that mind be the source of the strange alien code they'd found in the OberCorp core, the code that had led them here? It didn't make sense.

Quince stared at the white "root" that ran from the mind above to the heart of Oberon City. "Jessa, give me that flashlight."

Jessa handed it over.

She shone it along the ceiling, following the root. It ran up the wall to a white sphere attached to the edge of the world mind.

She'd thought before that the material reminded her of corrinder.

It hung off the mind like a tumor.

Or a parasite.

Quince leapt into the air, her wings pulling her up into the dim upper recesses of the cavern.

The more she stared at it, the more she was convinced it didn't belong.

She closed her eyes, and a memory slipped in.

Daia the woman stood on the sand below, staring up at the mind. "We're going to block you in. You should be safe here until we can figure out what's happening."

"I understand. Can I help?"

Daia shook her head. "You are the most important piece of the colony. If they find you…." She shuddered. "We'll come back for you when this is all over."

She closed her eyes, and her mirror image stared back at her. "I understand."

Daia backed out into the sunlight. "Are we ready?"

Braice nodded.

"Do it."

He set off the carefully placed charges, burying the world mind's cavern.

There were only a few colonists left. Something was taking them, one or two at a time. She suspected the nimfeach, the beautiful rainbow-hued thing that had tried to woo her away from the camp that day, two months before.

She'd refused, but in the end it was having its way.

It wouldn't have the world mind. She'd seen to that.

"Goodbye, sister mind."

• • •

THE THING ATTACHED to the world mind hadn't been there before, when she was sealed in this tomb.

Somehow it was being used to control the mind, or to tame it.

She reached out and pulled on it, trying to separate it from the mind.

It was firmly attached, its own "roots" sunk deep into the flesh of the mind.

"Quince, don't! You'll kill me!" The parasite changed, becoming Daia, hovering weirdly in the air before her without wings.

Several roots detached from the wall and quested toward her.

No more time. Quince pulled out the knife she'd chosen from the armory.

Suddenly the thing became Xander. Little Xander. *Why did you let him do this to me?*

"You're not Xander."

She raised the knife and hacked at the thing.

Her knife sliced across Queen Andra's neck. The queen's cold, dead eyes stared back at her. *You did this.*

"You don't have any more power over me." She hacked at the thing, concentrating on where it was linked to Daia, and the image disappeared, leaving a sagging white sack.

It melted away from the blade like butter, and soon she had separated it from the mind. It sent out little runners, trying to reconnect, but then she severed its connection to the root line that led off to the OberCorp core, down the long series of caves and tunnels that had brought them here.

It fell to the ground with a wet *plop.*

She ripped the root from the ceiling, too, and flew down to the cavern entrance, severing it completely.

She threw it onto the parasite, and then pulled an acid tab from her pack and activated it, tossing it onto the pile.

The acid sizzled and popped, consuming the whole nasty mass.

She looked up at Daia. Some kind of golden fluid dripped from where she'd severed the parasite, but as Quince watched, the remaining parts of it were forced out, one by one, and the surface of the mind sealed over.

"What is it?" Robyn stared at the sodden mass that was quickly melting down to a puddle of goo.

A great grinding sound filled the cavern, and Quince dropped back to the ground. "I don't know. Something of the ithani's."

"Maybe that wasn't such a good idea?" Jessa pointed.

One of the mind's own roots, thick as a blue oak trunk, had sprouted a new extension. It raced along the ceiling to the debris pile, and a fine filament spread out over the broken wall of rocks.

The rocks shrank as more of the filaments spread out across the entire wall.

Soon bits of it began to fall, slipping through the net.

"She's eating the rock." Quince's mouth fell open. She hadn't thought anything could still surprise her. "Stand back!"

They retreated to the cave mouth where they'd first entered. It didn't take long.

Soon the wall was gone. A cool sea breeze filled the cavern, and the filaments retreated to reveal the Gildensea, lit by Bandia's silver light.

Silhouetted there was a woman's form.

"Daia," Quince whispered.

"She's the one who attacked you?" Robyn had her own knife out.

"Who? What are you guys seeing?" Jessa looked at Quince, then at Robyn, confusion plain on her face.

"Daia. The world mind."

"I don't see anything."

Quince smiled sadly. "You're not skythane."

She took Robyn's hand, and they went to meet the apparition.

JESSA WATCHED THEM GO.

She couldn't help but feel jealous. The skythane were human like her, but they were different in subtle ways—and some not so subtle—from people like her and Alix. At some point on the timeline they had diverged, and someday maybe they would be a distinct species, as different from humans as humans had been from apes.

She crossed the space, giving the two of them a wide berth. They stood in the center of the cavern, their hands held out, transfixed. Staring at something only they could see.

It was a bit creepy.

She climbed over the remaining rocks at the newly revealed cavern entrance, and out onto the sand outside.

It was a warm evening. The sky was clear over the Gildensea, but a storm was brewing behind her, lightning strikes too far away to be heard. The air was heavy with humidity.

Just to the north, she could see the lights of the arcos, marking the center of Oberon City.

Not too far south, a single white tower stood by the sea.

This might be the last night of the world. It was a strange thought. Everything was deceptively normal, even beautiful.

She could come to love this world, given time.

She sat on the sand, her back to a black rock that jutted into the air, and watched the waves roll in and out.

Jamie, where are you?

Only the ocean breeze answered.

Robyn glared at the spirit that had appeared before them in the cavern. "I don't trust her."

Quince took her hand. "It's okay. She wasn't herself. She was under the influence of the ithani."

"How? They've all been asleep."

"I don't know. Maybe the nimfeach? Someone put that thing up there."

Daia was watching them.

"Come on." Quince urged her forward gently. Quince pulled her hand up, and Daia touched her palm.

The cavern dissolved, and they found themselves in a wide green valley. A golden sun shone brightly, and a stone tower stood high upon a central hill, casting its shadow across them.

Daia sat cross-legged in front of them, and she invited them to do the same with a gesture. "I've waited a long time for someone to come."

"How long?"

"More than eight hundred years."

Robyn whistled. "That is a long time."

"What are you?" Quince looked around at the strange world. "What is this place?"

"I'm the seventh world mind. I came here with your people, seeded from the sixth mind." Daia gestured at the valley. "This is a replica of the domain of the first world mind. I find it peaceful. I come here when I want to think."

Robyn breathed in the air. It was fresh and cool, with a hint of moisture.

She ran her hand over the grass. It tickled her palm. "This place is real. It has to be." Maybe a gateway had brought them here.

Daia laughed. "It's every bit as real as the world you live in, but it's not physical. Not in the way you mean."

"Astonishing." She looked up at the sky. "How far does it go?"

"As far as I want."

"Were you trapped in here?"

Daia nodded. "For many years. My namesake blocked me into the cavern in the hopes of keeping me safe from the nimfeach, but they already knew about me, and they made the *harsorch*."

"The what?" Quince frowned. "The horse sauce?"

Daia laughed again. "No, the harsorch. The parasite you cut off me. They used it to control me. To keep me docile."

"So that really wasn't you?" Robyn frowned.

"No, but I couldn't help but see what she put Quince through. I'm so sorry, Quince." Daia reached out to touch her arm.

"How do you know our names? How are we even here?" Robyn still didn't trust the woman. The mind. Whatever she was.

"I saw you. In my dreams. All of you—every one of the skythane."

"How is that possible?"

"You *made* me. Your kind. Long, long ago. Since then… we've been connected. It's hard to explain. Here." She held out her hands.

Robyn looked at Quince, who nodded.

She took Daia's hand, trying to keep her own from trembling.

"This is who I am."

A torrent of information flowed through Robyn's mind.

Wars and spaceships and battles, love and loss, a long, lonely journey through the void.

And more personal details—a woman born inside a generation ship, on the last leg of its journey to a new star.

Ties between human and biomind that were beyond Robyn's wildest imagination.

Daia was the last of her kind.

Quince narrowed her eyes. "The skythane memories, they come from you."

Daia nodded. "Some of them. The human ones." She sighed. "It was the only way I could reach you."

"And the rest?"

"From the Heart. The ithani."

"You know about the ithani?"

"Yes." Daia frowned, brushing her silver hair away from her face. She seemed so human. "The nimfeach used me to monitor the newcomers. Sometimes they would come here to ask me questions."

"The newcomers?" Robyn frowned.

"The landers. The second wave." Quince turned her attention back to Daia. "Are you free of them now?"

"Yes. Thank you." She stiffened. "One arrives now." She let them go and vanished, leaving them in an empty cavern.

Robyn spun around to see a gateway splitting the air.

Morgan stepped through, closing it behind him. "Are you ready to help me change the plan?"

Quince looked at Robyn, and at Jessa, who had come running up from the beach outside when the gateway appeared.

Both nodded.

Quince grinned. "Sure. What do we need to do?"

29

—————

NIGHT FALLS

Thshnel'Jirron led zis army of ithani south, passing over the lands that had once been zis. These human invaders had left much of it untouched, but their very presence on Erro vexed zim. Like verthex that scurried from the light, they were craven insects that had no right to be on zis world.

Even their bodies were ruled by contrarian impulses of emotion, thought, and hormones. Zi'd learned that firsthand, and zi was questioning zis choice to be reborn in this human host. Thankfully it was a state zi'd need to endure for only a little while longer.

Dani lay on the forest floor, her wings spread out behind her, as Kadin worked his way up her body, eliciting gasps and soft moans....

Jirron thrust the memory back down. They'd been coming to zim more and more frequently, little snippets of the human's former life. It was unusual. In the past, zis hosts had been entirely subsumed by zis own personality, their memories only surfacing when zi searched for them.

No matter. The time of the Great Migration was upon them. Denied to zis race for millennia by a catastrophic event, zis grand plan was once again in motion, thanks to the nimfeach. The little creatures had proven invaluable in getting the ithani to this point, continuing zis work when zi zimself had been asleep all those many years.

The Heart rose in the distance like a mountain, beckoning them forward.

Clouds gathered as the Heart drew energy from the amalite deposits below the surface.

In mere hours, zi would be free of this planet-bound form, freed to become what zi was always meant to be.

Zi would *be* the ithani.

"Erissa, get me Alia." Alix frowned at the stormy sky. Who knew the end of the world would be accompanied by such miserable weather?

Her voice came through loud and clear. "Alix?"

"Yes. Where are you?"

"In a hoversport circling the place where the House of the Sun used to be. Where are *you?*"

"Thank the Split you're in range. See that big dome thing rising from the ground?"

"Yes?"

"We're on the top of it." The Heart rumbled beneath him, and the skies thundered as if in response. "Listen, we have ithani coming in hot. We have to keep them from entering the Heart."

"Okay. What do you need?"

"Any and all hoversports we can scramble to the area. Ground support too. Pull in everyone we have. It's all hands on deck." He took a deep breath. Had it really come to this? "Tell DOC to get ready to launch that Rentz Class ship in this direction."

There was a long pause. "That would kill you too."

Alix nodded. "I know. I hope we don't have to use it, but we have to be ready. Erissa, how long would it take that ship to reach here from the spaceport?"

"About three-point-two minutes."

"Okay. I'll keep that in mind."

"Venin can carry you out of there—"

"Venin has to confront the ithani. I'm stuck down here."

"You're a sitting target."

"This is where I need to be, in the middle of the action. It'll be all right." Alix scanned the skies, worried. He was exposed up here, but there was nothing to do about it.

"Like hell it will."

"I've gotta go. Let the pilots know we'll be fighting along with the skythane this time."

"Of course." Her response was curt, almost cold.

He had no time to deal with emotions, hers or his own. "Call me if you need me." He cut the connection.

"What did she say?" Venin was scanning the skies next to him.

"Reinforcements are on the way from OberCorp."

"They may be too late." He pointed up. Alix followed his gaze—the ithani had arrived.

"I have to go meet them, stall for time."

"What can you do against so many?" Alix didn't want Venin to go. Not like this. Not when there was a good chance he would never return.

"If I don't, there might be nothing left to come back to." He swept Alix up and kissed him hard.

Alix kissed him back, dropping the last of his walls, his regrets and fears, and giving in to this thing between them completely. Time slowed and stopped, and for a moment there were just the two of them.

Then it lurched forward again.

Venin let him go. "If we get through this...," Venin whispered as they parted.

"*When* we get through this."

Venin grinned and then leapt into the air to meet the arriving ithani.

It was a promise.

"GODSDAMNED SPLIT-ASS JERK." Alia wanted to throw something.

Outside, the storm was building. Thunderclouds climbed into the sky, and under their dark skirts, lightning slammed into the earth, sending up showers of broken trees and dirt.

"What is it?" Smythe sank down on the bench next to her. His chiseled face belied the gentleness in his hand as he touched her cheek.

"That self-important prick Alix is going to get his ass killed, and Venin too."

"So, the whole macho Marine bravery thing?" Smythe cracked a smile.

She nodded miserably.

"You two weren't... aren't...?"

She laughed in spite of herself. "Nothing like that. Just… he and I have been through a lot together in the last few weeks. Venin too."

"So what are we gonna do about it?"

"What do you mean?"

"Come on. We have a hoversport." His eyes went unfocused for a minute, and then he looked right at her. "We're being ordered into battle. Your doing?"

"Alix's, but yes."

"So there you go. What say we launch a rescue mission?"

Thshnel'Jirron and the ithani arrived at the site of the Heart. Its rise was stirring up a great storm as Erro itself prepared for the Great Migration and the birth of something never before seen.

Zi shivered in glee at the thought that true immortality was almost zis. Zi could almost grasp it in the strange, thin white claws of zis human host— nevermore would zi need to fear the death of zis host body. Now only a few puny obstacles stood in zis way.

The plan had taken generations for zim to piece together, as zis scientists had discovered how to use the nimfeach to pierce the veil between realities. It had taken longer still to find the reality zi wanted. This place.

Zis plan had been rushed in the end by the imminent destruction of the world by the dhagani, a last-gasp attempt to bring zis people down.

The shift required a bonded triad, with one of the nimfeach acting as the key.

Stripped of their hearts, the nimfeach had remained loyal for millennia while the ithani slept and had ultimately brought about zis plan through the selective breeding of these humans.

Jirrondin had lived through it all—countless transfers to new ithani hosts when zis body had grown old and feeble, and then a hundred-thousand cycle sleep.

Always knowing zi was one accident or attack away from oblivion if zi was unable to flee to the safety of the Heart.

When zis scientists had discovered this new universe, only ever so slightly different from their own, Jirron had known it was what zi sought. The rules here were so similar to zis own universe, but the smallest variation was enough to make the difference. In this place, zi could embed zis consciousness into the very fabric of space and time. The rules of physics were different here. The form of space-time was similar to the athrà. Zi could merge the ithani virtual world into the weft and weave of this reality, and zis power would be endless.

Zi would be a god.

The ithani would all become part of zim, a new hive-mind race—the jirrondi. Zi grinned at the thought. Zi was starting to get used to the odd human gesture.

Zi stared down at the Heart, awaiting them all, and was astonished.

Someone or something was flying up from the Heart to meet zim.

Zi swept down to get a closer look, zis wide midnight-black wings carrying zim toward the Heart.

It was one of the human skythane. The ones with wings, like zis host. Jirrondin had to admit, humans had a sort of rugged, brutish beauty.

There was another human as well, far below, standing at the top of the Heart.

How had they found it so quickly after the rise?

The skythane man was staring at zim, his mouth agape. "Dani?"

A human smile stretched across Jirron's face again. Zi wished zi could *shimmer* with glee in this human form. "And you're… Venin."

VENIN STARED at the leader of the ithani. She was grinning like a madwoman.

How had the two-bit thug who'd occupied Gaelan on behalf of OberCorp come to lead an army of alien ithani?

"What… why are you…? I don't understand." It was the ultimate betrayal, not just of her own race, but her species.

And yet he shouldn't have been surprised. She'd always been just a step above savagery.

"Dani told me a lot about you. One of the captains of the Gaelani guard. You were there when the shift happened." As she said it, the information seemed to surprise her. "Are you part of the triad?" She flew closer, looking at him in a way that made him extremely uncomfortable. Like he was a colorful insect she wanted to pin to her display case.

"You're not Dani." That much was becoming clear. Maybe she was something like Morgan, part Dani and part… something else. Ithani, he guessed.

Wind whipped his hair as the storm walls closed in around them, circling the Heart. "Who are you?"

The woman who wasn't Dani drew herself up, flapping her wings, and laughed. "No, I'm not Dani. I'm the Thshnel Jirron, leader of the ithani."

"The… shrapnel gerund?"

"Jirron." The ithani let out a whoosh of air, looking as though Venin had just dealt her a mortal insult.

Above him, the other ithani—thousands of them—had clustered nearby to listen to the conversation. Venin wondered if they understood Common.

He wished he had a pulse rifle with him. He could end this right here with one good shot to the chest. "You should go back to the north, where you came from. You won't get to the Heart. Not today."

Jirron blinked and hissed, looking a bit taken aback. She looked down at the ground, and then back at Venin. "How do you know about the Heart?"

"I know a lot more than you think." Venin wasn't sure how long this bluff would last. He hoped he could keep it going until reinforcements arrived.

Taz whispered in his ear.

"I know about the Great Migration too." *What Great Migration?* Mylin must be feeding him information.

That startled Jirron. The ithani clucked her tongue, blinking rapidly, but she quickly regained her composure. "Get out of our way, human. Your time here is—" She stopped abruptly and looked past Venin, blinking rapidly again.

Venin grinned. The cavalry had arrived.

A GATEWAY OPENED up behind the human, and more of the skythane poured through.

Jirron clucked zis tongue, staring at them in disbelief. *How did this happen?*

Zi hissed. They had a *key.* Or the nimfeach had turned on zim. Neither seemed likely.

In moments, a few hundred skythane were arrayed between zis people and the Heart, their wings white and golden.

The gateway snapped shut.

Zi let out a whoosh of breath. It didn't matter. They were still too few to truly challenge zim. Zi would lose some of zis people, but enough would survive to finish the migration.

Zi prepared the call to battle.

Another gateway opened up and more skythane came through, these with dark wings—brown and ebony and midnight blue.

Zi was beginning to hate these humans.

A sharp whine drew zis attention to the west.

A small fleet of flying *things* approached the Heart. Dani's memory supplied the answer. *Hoversports*, they were called. Powered by heartstone, from the core.

So there was to be a fight after all. Zis grin returned. If they wanted war, so be it.

Zi let out a screech and sent zis people the order to fight as the storm clouds thickened around them.

Claws slipped out of their hands and feet. They had no weapons. This was to have been a day of celebration, not battle. But zi was certain the strength of the ithani would carry the day. They would bury the offworlders at the base of the Heart, and then they would obliterate the world.

Jirron backed away from the contest, content to let others fight for zim.

Zis people fell upon the skythane.

In the end, it took a lot of convincing to get Daia to agree to Morgan's plan.

She was frightened at the appearance of the nimfeach, and more than a little damaged by her long time of solitude and virtual imprisonment.

Quince could understand that. She couldn't imagine being locked away from everyone she knew, everyone she loved, for close to a thousand years.

But Morgan made a good point—the memory of the ithani past, and by extension Erro's past, was valuable beyond measure. The Heart was also the progenitor of the nimfeach. If they were going to destroy the Heart, they had to save its memories. Morgan hoped to coax a seed from it, but they had to save its history too.

Quince found Daia in her virtual domain. She stood on top of a cliff at the edge of an alien forest, looking out over a vast sea. It was no ocean on Erro—she was sure of that much. Maybe it was someplace from old Earth, or maybe it had only ever existed here in the world mind.

Trees with leaves like green needles swayed on the ocean breeze, and the air was thick with the smell of the sea. Dried needles crunched under her feet. She shivered, goose bumps popping up on her forearms.

Quince looked around in amazement. Daia and her domains were truly an awe-inspiring achievement, surpassing even the virtual worlds of the grid.

"So much time." Daia glanced up at her as she approached.

"Time?" Quince sat down next to her, staring out at the breaking waves. She could feel the wind on her skin. Smell the salt of the sea and hear the cry of sea birds riding the air currents above.

Daia nodded. "I carry it inside of me. Memories. Files. Sensations." She reached over and touched Quince's cheek.

QUINCE WAS SOMEONE ELSE, a woman, small and dark, razor sharp in her intelligence. Deeply flawed. Quince felt all of it. No, she *was* all of it. A woman named Ana with a strange accent, whose father was murdered by terrorists. Who knew the secrets of the world mind. Who had almost been immortal herself.

DAIA LET GO, and Quince gasped. "Who was she?" She could still feel the woman's thoughts. Her genius. Her sadness.

Daia's smile didn't reach her eyes. "The mother of us all. Of me." She put her head in her hands, staring out at the sea, and sighed. "I carry so many lives. So many memories."

"Ah." Now Quince understood. "'So much time.'"

Daia nodded, her dark hair covering her face. "Yes."

Quince couldn't imagine the burden, the backbreaking weight of such a responsibility. "Do you... do you carry us too? The skythane?"

"Yes. Some of you." She looked up at Quince, offering her a weak smile. "Those who are open to me. Even when I was trapped, I could still touch you. It kept me sane."

Quince sat down on the rock next to her. "Do you remember me?"

Daia looked at her again with her gray eyes and nodded. "Here." She touched Quince's cheek again.

•　•　•

QUINCE WAS THREE YEARS OLD, held in her mother's arms. She felt warm and happy. Her mother held up a bunch of redberries, and Quince clutched at them greedily. "Now, now, my little wereveren. Be patient." She broke off one of the berries and put it in Quince's mouth. It exploded in a burst of sweet flavor, the juice running down her cheek.

QUINCE BLINKED, staring at Daia, only partially aware of the tear rolling down her cheek. "I remember that moment." She held out her hand, as if she would find her mother there, ready to laugh with her, to hold her, to tell her everything would be all right.

How far she'd fallen since that day.

She sighed. The past was gone and buried, though maybe it could still be relived. "Thank you for that." Time was short. "Morgan tells me that the Heart is something like you. A depository of knowledge, of ithani history and culture. For the nimfeach too." She took Daia's hand. "I know it's hard, but we need you to help us save it. He says I can facilitate the transfer, with his help, but we can't do it without you."

Daia looked at her, searching her eyes. "I don't think I can."

Quince explained what Morgan had told her. "The king of the ithani is linked to the Heart. If we don't destroy it, we can't destroy him, and all this—our whole world—will come to an end." Including this amazing paradise. "You, me, the memories you carry. Everything that survives will become a part of him. A slave to him." *Robyn too.* "If you help us, we can keep you safe. Free. You won't be alone ever again. I promise."

Daia let go of her hand and stood, taking the few steps to the edge of the cliff.

Quince's heart beat faster, even though she knew it wasn't real. She could feel it in her chest as she awaited Daia's answer. This place was truly amazing.

"I'll do it," Daia said at last. "But I want something in return."

"Name it." Quince hoped it was something she could afford to give.

"When it's over, I want you to let me go."

"What do you mean?"

Daia turned back to face her, and there was fire in her eyes. "Eight hundred years is a long time. I am tired, Quince. I'm ready to go. Someone else can take up this burden."

Quince nodded. She could do that.

Daia was a copy of someone who had once been a living, breathing person. The original Daia Hammond who had lived in this place more than eight hundred years before.

The world mind Daia was so much more than that now, but she had started her life as human as Quince.

They would find someone to take Daia's burden. Someone to imprint on the new seed, who would have the strength of will to carry it. "We can do that."

The tension slipped out of Daia's lithe form like smoke. "Thank you, Quince."

Quince pulled her in for a hug, and away from the edge of the cliff. Virtual or no, it made her nervous as hell to see Daia standing so close. "I'm sorry you were alone for so long. If I had known—"

"You said time was short." Daia pulled away, hugging herself as if she were cold. "What do I need to do?"

"On my signal, go!" Lena pointed down the hall toward the armory.

Mylin nodded. "Derren, you ready?" she whispered via her cirq. They'd been pinned down here for ten minutes. The Syndicate fighters were fierce and armed to the teeth, but they had the advantage of home terrain. And Derren and DOC.

"Yes ma'am."

"That's 'yes, Mylin.'"

"Sorry. Yes, ma'am, Mylin."

Mylin sighed. "Close enough." The fool was besotted with her.

Lena coordinated with the other enforcers. "On my mark."

Three seconds later, an explosion filled the hallway with smoke. "Good boy, Tovey." Lena gestured her forward. "Go!"

The hallway went pitch-black.

Helped by DOC, Zim guided her aim in the darkness, but the coughing of the Syndicate men helped her locate them too. One, two, three enemy fighters went down with stun blasts from her pulse rifle.

Others retreated toward the emergency stairs but were caught by the small team of enforcers. A firefight broke out, along with some angry shouts.

Then the hall was silent. The lights came back up.

Smoke filled the hallway, but DOC amped up the building's circulation systems to clear it out.

"Good work." Lena surveyed the damage. Seven of Rogan's men were down. "Let's get these guys disarmed and into holding—"

"Down!" Mylin had seen a flash out of the corner of her eye, and she pushed Lena out of the way, firing her pulse rifle down the hallway at the attacker.

There was a grunt, and another Syndicate woman fell out of a doorway onto the floor.

Something hot and wet spread across Mylin's abdomen.

Mylin fell to her knees. "I think I've been shot." She touched her stomach with her hand, and it came away red.

Lena took her in her arms and eased her to the floor. "Tovey! Get your ass over here. We have to get this one to the infirmary."

The last thing Mylin saw was a young man's face above hers, but it wasn't Tovey.

"You're gonna be okay, ma'am… Mylin." It was Derren.

THE SKYTHANE WERE OUTNUMBERED.

Alix watched from below.

The skies above the Heart had become a massive battleground, fought mostly hand-to-hand, in and out of the storm.

The skythane were armed with a few pulse rifles and knives, while the ithani had claws like knife blades that extended from their three-fingered hands.

Somewhere up there, Venin was in the thick of it. He kept in touch with Alix via his PA, but Alix had never felt more helpless.

It was hard to make out the entire battle as water poured down in torrents, blocking his view on and off. *God, I'm sick of the rain.*

Alix watched from the top of the Heart, directing the hoversports in a coordinated attack, but even there he felt useless. All he could really do was to issue some orders and hope they were followed through.

What he wouldn't have given for one of those gateway keys right about now. Not that he'd have the slightest clue how to use it.

The water was collecting in the bowl atop the Heart. He'd climbed to higher ground, trying to avoid puddles as lightning rained down on the Heart and the surrounding ground.

The Heart itself was starting to glow, the vegetation sloughing off like old scabs.

He was going to have to call in the meso strike, casualties be damned. If they lost this battle, the whole world would pay the price, and that possibility was getting perilously close.

One of the hoversports was coming in hot.

"Erissa, who is that?" He scowled. "Tell them we need them in the battle."

"Negative, Alix. We're coming in to get you." It was Alia.

"Abort! You guys need to get your asses back up there and—"

"I'm not leaving you down there to die. Besides, from up here you can see things better."

Alix growled. She made a good case.

Lightning struck the Heart not ten meters from where he stood, knocking him to the ground and blinding him temporarily. The Heart absorbed the energy, glowing brighter.

He got up, blinking and trying to see which direction to run to reach the hoversport.

Then she stood there before him, an angel, her black wings outspread against the backdrop of the tempest. *More like a Valkyrie.* "Come on!" She grabbed his arm and hauled him toward the hoversport. "Where's Venin?"

He pointed up at the battle above.

The craft appeared before them, a hatch open on its side. A square-jawed ranger was waving them on.

She shoved him inside and followed, slamming the hatch closed behind her. "Get us the hell out of here!"

Alix grinned. Alia was picking up a thing or two from her new ranger friends.

ROBYN AND QUINCE held each other's hands as Morgan opened a gateway from Daia's cavern to the Heart.

Robyn was concerned for the nimfeach's health. His skin looked a bit gray. He was pushing himself hard, and even though he was something more than human, he must have limits.

She was worried for Quince too. Her lover was too quick to take the burdens of the world upon her own shoulders.

They had no idea if what they were attempting was even possible, let alone what effects it might have on the human psyche and physiology. "Are you sure you want to do this?"

Quince nodded. "We're part human, part nimfeach, and part ithani. This is *our* heritage too."

Robyn was still a bit unsettled by the newfound knowledge that she carried a bit of alien DNA in her bones, but she put on a brave face and squeezed Quince's hand.

"It'll be okay." Quince kissed her cheek. "Here we go."

They stepped through the gateway after Robyn, and Jessa followed them.

The cavern was huge—maybe half a kilometer across. The walls were covered with glowing green moss, and stone benches sat against the walls at regular intervals, cracked with age. Golden globes were suspended above, and in the center a silver dome shimmered with the colors of the rainbow.

Robyn reached out to touch it. It was warm, and as her hand connected, she felt a thrumming that vibrated up her arm. A ripple spread from the point of contact across the Heart.

She shivered, startled by the realization that she *knew* this place.

DAIA STOOD BEFORE THE HEART, her own heart racing, her face reflected and distorted on the liquid surface.

She was the last one, the only holdout.

The nimfeach had promised them so much, and in return only wanted access to her mind and soul.

She had scorned the bargain and had urged her fellow colonists to do the same. It was a bargain with the devil.

And yet....

One by one, they had vanished, drawn off by its promises. They would come in the night, and in the morning another one of her fellow colonists would be gone.

She'd started calling them sneach instead of nimfeach, because they'd sneak around the camp and lure away the unwary.

Now she was the only one who remained. Even Braice had eventually given in, though he'd lasted longer than almost anyone else.

She had spent the last three months alone in the village, surviving on the remaining supplies, sampling local fruits in small portions. Some had been edible, though she had no idea of their nutritional value. Others had made her violently ill.

Winter was coming, and she was out of options.

Perhaps she could provide them with guidance… *after.* Not that they had listened to her before. Maybe she could still make a difference in what happened next to her people.

Maybe it was all a lost cause.

After all, who wouldn't want to learn to fly? What was a lifetime of back-breaking work to build a human colony on this wretched world worth, next to such a promise?

Marli, what would you do? Her lover didn't answer. She'd been missing or dead for half a year.

Daia sighed. It was this or a long, slow death.

She made up her mind and reached out to touch the silver surface of the Heart.

ROBYN PULLED her hand away from it, shuddering. So much pain.

So that's what it feels like. The memories had finally found her, as well. She didn't care for it.

Quince pulled her close. "I saw it too."

Daia's thoughts haunted her. "We've been pawns in this game for so long."

"What game?" Jessa was staring at the Heart.

"The skythane." Robyn turned away from the Heart. "We were like you. Like the landers when we arrived here. The nimfeach took us in and changed us."

"Changed you? How?"

Robyn extended her wings. "These, for one. We're part nimfeach, and ithani too." Her wings settled against her back.

She felt sick to her stomach at the thought, suddenly unsteady on her feet. She sat down on a stone bench along one side of the cavern, closing her eyes and trying to calm her racing thoughts.

"Well, so what?"

Robyn looked up sharply. "What?"

Jessa stood before her, hands on her hips, shaking her head. "You skythane are all such mopey defeatists."

"That's not fair."

"It's true. You're all a bunch of worrywarts." She sat down next to Robyn and put a hand on the queen's knee.

Robyn was uncomfortable with such familiarity—they hardly knew each other, and few had dared to treat her so casually at any point in her life. Yet she didn't remove Jessa's hand.

Jessa sighed. "Look, Xander went on and on for days and days about how his love for Jameson couldn't be real, just because it might have started with pith."

Quince winced at that one but said nothing.

"He was wrong. In the end, it's no less real than the love you and Quince have for each other. It doesn't matter how it started."

"I guess so." Robyn wondered how *Xander and Jameson* felt about it all now, but the girl had a point.

"Now you find out that the skythane might have been made in a petri dish. So what? You all are beautiful and amazing, and you can freaking fly!" She put out her hands for emphasis. "I would kill to be a skythane. Seriously, *kill*. It doesn't matter where you came from, whether it was a quirk of evolution or a scientific miracle. See, this is the thing. None of us have any choice in where we came from. The only thing we can control is what we do with what we've got."

Quince laughed. "She's got you there."

Robyn blushed. Put in her place by a *lander*. And an off-worlder, at that. "Maybe so."

"And it explains one of the strange things that Mylin found… the divergence of our DNA from the landers' in such a brief period of time."

Robyn nodded, though she wasn't completely sure what DNA was. Still, it made sense. The skythane *were* different.

She wasn't ready to commit to this new worldview. Not just yet, but Jessa had given her a lot to think about.

"Ari, get me Alix."

"One moment please. Connecting."

Quince frowned as she waited for the connection. "Alix, are you there?"

"Quince? Holy Split, it's good to hear your voice. Where are you?"

"I'm inside the Heart. Robyn, Jessa, and Morgan are with me. We're going to make a copy of the Heart's memories—"

"How the hell are you going to manage that?"

"I'll explain later. I'm gonna need you to buy me more time. Can you do that?"

There was a long pause. "How much time? Things are pretty hairy up here."

"I don't know."

"Shit. Okay, we'll do what we can. But Quince, make it quick."

"I'll try." She cut the connection. "Okay, let's do this." Quince turned to Morgan. "What do I have to do?"

Morgan took her hand.

A root from the world mind had snaked through the open gateway after them. Morgan had her put one hand on it, and one on the surface of the Heart. "Can you sense Daia?"

Quince nodded. "She's here."

"Find the Heart. Daia will do the rest."

Quince closed her eyes and searched. For a couple seconds, nothing happened.

Then she stiffened, her eyes rolling back in her head, and her whole body shook. The room dissolved, and she grew and stretched, becoming a great river.

The Heart was waiting for her, as if it had known she would come. It poured itself into her, and Quince was washed away in the flood.

QUINCE WAS SHAKING, her eyes rolled back in her head. Robyn jumped up. "Is she okay? What's happening?"

Morgan nodded, stifling a yawn. "She's in the middle of the flow. The Heart is transferring its information to Daia."

As if that were a signal, Quince's arms steadied, and her eyes closed.

She looked peaceful and focused.

"Come back to me, my love." Robyn sat back down with Jessa to wait.

30

SHIFT FORWARD

Puck was transformed.

Ze fluttered back and forth with zer iridescent wings, full of nervous energy. Zer wings shone brightly in the dim light of the Heart.

"What's wrong with zer?" Jameson reached out to the nimfeach, but ze danced away from him.

"Ze's been restored to zerself for the first time in years." Eri's eyes looked sad, but it might have just been zer alien physiology. "We took zer heart—it's how we were able to control the nimfeach."

The whole Heart shuddered.

"It begins."

"The shift?"

Ze nodded. "Under Freyyr, the Thshnel and zis minions have begun the process. Zi will slumber until it's over."

Jameson looked around. The Heart itself was changing. Electrical impulses raced up and down its surface, arcing blue over the top and splitting in crazy glowing patterns. "What do we do?"

"You two carry the essence of Jirron in your cells. With Puck, you can stop the shift, when the time comes. It comes swiftly."

Jameson looked around at the strange place they'd finally arrived at. Everything that had happened to him, from his birth onward, had started in this place.

Puck came up to him, wings fluttering as ze looked into his eyes.

Ze put out a small hand, and he touched it with his. Even zer body had changed, becoming less shriveled and insect-like, and more like a miniature version of the ithani.

Thank you. Zer voice was inside his head.

These things no longer surprised him. *You're welcome. Are you ready for this?*

Erina had explained what was to come, but he still couldn't quite believe it.

He and Xander, along with these others, were responsible for the Split—one of the great wonders of the Common Worlds. Or were about to be. Or maybe had been. Time travel made his head hurt.

What had happened to Erro had happened already because of them. Was to happen now? He was hopelessly confused about what came first and what would come later.

They were doing this because they had always done it. That was as close as he could manage.

Yes. You have been kind to me. Puck let go of his hand.

Jameson thought ze intended to say more. There was a lingering regret on his soul, like an aftertaste. "Erina, what happens to Puck when all this is done?"

Erina turned away, acting as if ze hadn't heard him.

He pulled zer back around.

Ze hissed at him, zer fur standing on end. "I'm sorry." Ze blinked so hard he was surprised ze could still see him. "Ze will cease to be."

"Fucking Split." Xander was angry enough to tear the ithani in two. "We can't do this. Puck just got zer life back." *I'm so sick of secrets.*

Jameson looked surprised at his vehemence. "What choice do we have?"

Xander snarled. "It's Morgan all over again. When we thought we lost him." Xander paced back and forth in front of the Heart. "There has to be another way."

"It's what I foresaw—"

"To hell with all these memories and visions. I'm so sick of them governing my life." First the prophecy Quince had dangled in front of them to get them to Titania. Then the Split-cursed statue that Jameson had touched, and the avalanche of memories that had almost buried him. Now this. "I won't do it." He sank down on a stone bench and put his head in his hands.

He'd already given up so much. His innocence. His first love. His old life. *It's too much.*

Something bright lit up his knees. He looked up to see Puck hovering before him, zer beautiful wings an iridescent blue and purple, the color radiating from zer compact body. Zer skin was blue too, a brilliant turquoise blue. Zer face was alien, longer and thinner than a human's, but it conveyed a sense of deep contentment and peace. He reached out to cup zer cheek. Ze was cool to his touch.

Don't worry for me. I'll go into the Heart when this is over.

He sighed. *I don't want you to die.*

This is what is supposed to happen. A warm vibration extended from zer into his arm. Ze was purring. *This is what will have happened, in your time.*

Xander closed his eyes. In this short period, he'd come to care for not one but two little beings who had needed his help and protection.

How long ago that one-night stand back in Oberon City seemed now, the night before this had all begun. *How much have I changed?*

He didn't like it, but it seemed everyone else had accepted this. "If this is all foreseen, then don't I have to go along?"

Jameson shrugged. "That question's beyond my paygrade."

Xander snorted in spite of himself. "Like we're getting paid for any of this."

Erina watched the byplay between them, zer head cocked, a chuffing sound coming from zer nostril. "You have a choice." Ze held out zer arms. "We all have a choice. Jirron made zis. You could refuse to follow the vision. It's your right."

Xander looked at her and then at Jameson. "What would happen?"

Ze held his gaze. "I don't know."

Jameson sat next to him. "Would you give everything up for me, if you had to?"

"In a heartbeat." He let go of Puck and hugged Jameson to him tightly.

"Then you have to let Puck do the same, for us."

Checkmate. Xander was outmatched. He sighed heavily, letting Jameson go.

"Okay." He turned to Erina. "What do we need to do?"

• • •

THE HEART WAS SEETHING with activity. Blue currents arced across its surface, and the room's floor trembled constantly.

Erina put a hand on the surface of the Heart, seemingly unfazed by the electricity that wrapped up zer arm. "It's almost time. Xander, Jameson, come here. Stand here, facing each other."

Jameson glanced nervously at the Heart, wondering if there was any way he could fuck this up. And if he did, what would happen in the future? In his time? "We don't need a gateway, like last time?"

Ze waved zer hand in negation. "We're all on the same side of the shift here. Puck will create a gateway, but it will be used to redirect all the energy ze steals from the shift."

"Redirect it where?" Jameson didn't like the sound of that. It would be a fuck-lot of energy. It would have to be, to shift a world.

"Into the time stream."

"Nimfeach can do that?"

"Only a few. Once or twice in a generation."

"Ah." Jameson had no idea what ze meant, but it sounded complicated and potentially deadly.

He faced Xander, feeling as nervous as a boy asking someone out on a first date. "Are you ready?"

Xander frowned. "Not really. Not that it matters. We're going to do this, right?"

Jameson glanced at Puck. "Yeah. I think so."

Puck slipped in between them. They took the nimfeach's hands.

Zer skin was cool to Jameson's touch.

Ready. Ze squeezed their hands, as if in reassurance. Then ze opened a gateway.

ERINA WATCHED IT UNFOLD, zer whole being thrumming with anticipation. Ze had bided zer time, made zer plans, and at last they were coming to fruition.

Thshnel'Jirron was surely in suspension now, not to be awoken until after the shift.

Ze had *won.*

It would take time for zer victory to be sealed. Zer heart ached with the amount of time it would take. But when it was over, zer people and the nimfeach would be saved.

It was almost time, as Erro shifted into a new universe, a new reality.

"Ready."

The others looked at zer, as ze felt for just the right moment.

"Now!"

Something shifted.

Energy poured from the Heart into the gateway. It grew in strength, until Erina was forced to step backward, to turn away from the light.

A horrible grinding crash filled the air, like the sound of an asteroid slamming into the earth, or a world being ripped in half.

Unlike a crash, the sound grew and grew, cresting in a crescendo that almost burst zer ears.

In the midst of the cavern, the gateway shone brighter and brighter as it sucked in the energy from the Heart, until it threatened to engulf the nimfeach and the two brave skythane kings.

Puck knew what to do. Erina had discussed it with zer as they had made their own plans.

Not everyone needs to transcend, tonight.

Above, the flare was coming. The unstable sun was about to let off a scathing burst of superheated particles and radiation that would swamp this half of Erro. The half ze had doomed to destruction waited for its ending.

Erina felt a bittersweet joy. Every ending was a beginning, too. Ze had *seen* it. A new world would arise from the ashes of the old, a world that with time would become the world of the skythane.

At last the rumbling died down.

The gateway, however, remained bright.

It was done.

JAMESON BLINKED, looking around. The light from the shift had nearly blinded him and had left a nasty afterimage burned into his retina.

Jameson held up the key he'd given to Puck, staring at it in wonder. "Ze's gone." It was all that was left of the plucky little creature. "Is ze… did ze hurt?" He wiped his eyes with the back of his hand.

"No. It was quick." Erina wiped zer own tears.

Jameson sighed, surprised that ze could cry. It seemed the ithani had at least one thing in common with humans. "Is it… done?"

"Yes."

Xander growled. "It's done, all right." He held out his hand to Jameson. "May I?"

Jameson handed him the key.

Xander sighed. "All that life and beauty, reduced to this."

Jameson closed his eyes. "I'm sorry, Xander. We had to. Even Puck knew it."

"I know. Knowing doesn't make it any easier." He stared at the gateway. "Where does it go?" he asked Erina.

"Home. Zer final gift to you."

Holy Split. "Really? We just step through and we're home?"

"Yes." Erina thrummed. "Things may have gotten a little crazy since you left."

"I have one more question. How did we find Puck?" Xander held up the key. "Out of all the places we could have landed on this godsforsaken world, we ended up where ze was? It seems like far too large a coincidence."

"The key." Erina made a waving gesture.

Jameson decided to interpret it as "Gods rest her soul."

"The key belonged to zer, once. It was zer heart." Erina held out her hand. "May I have it?"

Jameson handed it over. "Is a part of zer still in there?"

"Yes." Ze held it gently. "When you touched the key, it was activated to bring you to zer, in that moment in time."

"Ze knew?"

"After this, yes. Ze knew."

Jameson whistled. "That's some seriously strange time looping."

"Yes, it is. Now go. The gateway won't last for much longer."

"You'll be okay?"

Erina thrummed. "I survived the end of the world, didn't I?"

Jameson laughed. Ze had a sense of humor. He threw his arms around zer. "Thank you for saving our world too."

Ze stiffened but accepted his gesture with good grace.

Xander hugged zer too. "I'll miss you most of all, scarecrow."

Ze cocked her head.

"Old tri-dee."

"That makes no sense to me either." Ze blinked a few times, then shimmered. "Now go! You still have work to do. In your own time, you must force Thshnel'Jirron into the Heart, alone."

"Easier said than done." Jameson took Xander's hand. He took one last look around the Heart, and then pulled Xander through with him.

Their friends needed them.

ERINA WATCHED THEM GO.

When the gateway winked out, ze closed zer eyes for a moment, wishing the two travelers luck on their great leap forward.

Then ze went to the Heart and held the little nimfeach heart, round and milky-white, up to the surface.

It rested there for a moment, then dissolved and flowed inside. Soon the surface was smooth and calm once more. "Your time will come again, little elder." Ze put a palm to the surface, conveying zer good will to the nimfeach's soul. "As will mine."

Ze took a deep breath and put both of zer hands in the Heart. Then ze opened zerself up to it.

It reacted to zer, flowing up zer arms, and then over zer chest and up and down the length of zer body.

Ze folded her wings, closed zer eyes, finally at peace.

As the destruction of half of Erro commenced above zer, the silver shape that had been Erina flowed back into the Heart and disappeared.

31

STORM BATTLE

Thshnel'Jirron watched zis people battle the humans.

The Heart was calling to zim, almost ready to thrust zim into godhood.

The storm clouds that had swirled around the perimeter of the site had closed in, and lightning flared through the dark clouds, occasionally striking friend or foe.

The ithani were gaining the upper hand. Zis side had the numbers, and the enemy had been worn down by the demands of the shift and the warfare among themselves.

Dani's memories had taught zim much about this race. They had been at each other's throats for most of their history, and the last year had been no exception.

They were weak and divided.

Dani screamed in pain as her wings were cut off in the cattorah, the penalty for her crimes against the Erriani.

Jirron put zis hands to his head, willing away the memory, the terrible pain. These flashes were coming more frequently, and zi was surprised at both their ferocity and zis own difficulty suppressing them. Never before had zi experienced such trouble with a new host.

Zi drew on the strength of the Heart, pushing the memory back down.

Soon it wouldn't matter. Soon zi would be rid of this body, done with the need to ever take physical form again.

The storm raged all around zim, but zi saw through the clouds as though they were empty air, directing zis forces to tackle the enemy where they were weakest.

The battle continued, but it wouldn't be long now.

VENIN FELL on another of the ithani from above, grabbing its furred head in both hands from behind and twisting. Its head separated from its body with a sickening crunch, and then he dropped the corpse to the ground far below.

Visibility had faded to less than twenty meters in any direction.

Alix had ordered his hoversports down to the Heart itself, where they were circling and taking out anything that approached.

So far the ithani hadn't figured out how to take out the armored transports other than by piling on them en masse. Three had already been downed that way to fiery explosive deaths. Only half a dozen of the craft remained.

Venin's heart ached for the casualties, but he had no choice but to fight on.

A human cry pierced the storm nearby.

"Alix, we can't take this much longer." They had an open channel between them.

"We're waiting for Quince." He could hear the pain in Alix's voice too.

"A few more minutes and this will be over—" A bolt of lightning seared the air less than ten meters in front of him. "Holy Split!"

"You okay?" Alix's voice sounded anxious.

"Yeah. Just a close call. Tell Quince we can't hold out much longer. We're getting slaughtered up here."

"I know. If she doesn't call in five minutes…. What the hell?"

"What?" Venin turned and saw what had caught Alix's eye.

An area of calm was extending around the Heart, pushing up into the atmosphere as the storm clouds drew back.

A golden light shone on top of the Heart like a miniature star, and then two figures emerged.

The light winked out.

A second later, a familiar voice spoke in his ear. "We're back—anyone miss us?"

"Xander?"

"In the flesh."

. . .

Mylin slipped in and out of vir like a dreamstate.

At one point there was a sharp pain as something hot ran across her midsection.

She vaguely remembered getting shot, Derren's concerned face hovering over hers, his hand grasping hers as she was rushed to the OberCorp infirmary. Mouthing "You're gonna be okay."

Then she was in vir with DOC.

"What's wrong with me?" She felt disconnected from her body, lightheaded.

He sat next to her and took her hand. "You were hurt. Someone shot you, and you were injured rather badly."

"How badly?"

He looked away.

"DOC, how badly?" She wanted to know. Needed to know.

"It's… not good. The medics say your chances are about thirty-seventy. There was a lot of burn damage."

Thirty-seventy. She nodded. "What did you find in the archives?"

He stared at her for a moment. "Maybe you'd like to talk about something else? If… just in case?"

She shook her head. "I want to keep busy. I don't want to think about that." She closed her eyes. *I'm not ready to die.* "They're depending on me. What did you find?"

"Are you sure?" He looked really worried for her.

For just a moment, she forgot he was just code in the OberCorp core. She threw her arms around him, and he hugged her tight.

Vir space swam a little around her, but this was important. She could hold it together for a couple minutes more. "I'm sure," she whispered. She let him go.

"Okay. There are files going back to the founding of OberCorp that don't match my current database. Mostly having to do with the split and certain places on Oberon."

"The House of the Sun."

"Yes, that's one."

Mylin struggled to think clearly. "Give me the earliest files. What was the first thing they tried to hide when they accessed the network?"

DOC grinned. "Thought you might want those." He tugged on his thick mustache and splashed an array of files up on the wall.

Mylin scanned them, mentally pinching herself to stay awake. "These are the initial ZephyrCorp surveys of Oberon."

He nodded.

"And this place. I recognize this. It's where the Heart is. What are these designations?" She pointed to certain notations on the map.

"Here." He slitted her the information.

As she looked at the survey map with new eyes, her jaw dropped. "Heaven and Erro. Is this right?"

"Yes."

There was a massive amalite deposit just below the surface under the House of the Sun. Where the Heart was now. "They must have known we'd find the Heart if we tried to excavate that deposit."

He nodded. "That was my thought too."

"If they drop those bombs on the Heart on top of that much amalite, it could blow the whole planetary core."

"It's possible."

"Get me Alix." The room was spinning. If she was this off in vir….

DOC cocked his head. "I'm sorry. I can't reach Alix or Venin or anyone in the battle zone. Something has changed."

"We have to find a way to stop them—" She was seized by an intense wave of mind-numbing pain, and for a moment the world went black.

When she opened her eyes, she was on the operating table.

"She's awake!" A face looked down at her through a plas mask. "Don't worry, we've got you. I'm going to put you under. You won't feel a thing." The medic put a hand on her shoulder. "You'll be okay."

"No, don't put me to sleep! I have to tell them—"

She felt a slight pressure at her neck, and then everything went fuzzy and gray.

QUINCE WAS LOST in the flow. So much history was stored in the Heart. As the conduit, she caught glimpses here and there, enough to get a sense of how long and deep the story of the ithani was.

She saw the hive mind that had produced them, when they had been little more than drones. How they had eventually become imbued with intelligence and independence.

The growing of the Heart, the hive of the colony.

The worker bees and the teachers, becoming the ithani and the nimfeach.

So much time.

She had a sense, now, of how Daia felt, having been the repository of so many others' memories.

She was aware that she sampled only the barest taste of the information flowing through her, the heritage of a race.

Somewhere out there, outside of her, her friends were fighting and maybe even dying, while she was fixed in place here, lost in this limbo between real time and an alien mind she could barely comprehend.

She had no sense of how much time had passed. It might have been thirty seconds or a hundred hours.

All she could do was hold on and wait for it to end.

JAMESON FELT STRONGER than he ever had. Power flowed through him from below, replenishing his energy and chasing away his fatigue.

Erina had been right. Connecting with the Heart had been easy, once ze had shown him how. He and Xander had been bred for it, after all.

There was a taint on it, though, something almost sickly sweet. Tshnel'Jirron had long since claimed it as zis own, the birthright of zis people.

That would end today.

Are you ready?

For his answer, Xander kissed him hard. "Let's go."

They were one again joined through the Heart's athrà, a bond closer than any Jameson had ever known.

With a single mind, they leapt into the air to confront the ithani.

Venin met them with a grim smile. "Welcome to the battlefield."

Jameson slammed into him with a bear hug, sending both tumbling. "We're so happy to see you," Jameson said when he let go and they recovered.

"We're?"

"Long story."

"Where's Jirron?"

Venin's eyes widened. "She's up there."

"She?" They looked up.

Dani Black descended from the sky, her face clouded with anger.

Jirron was furious.

Something or someone had wrested control of the Heart from zim. Everything zi'd built—everything zi'd worked for over a thousand cycles—was in jeopardy. Damn these vermin humans.

Running through a field of flowers, her mother chasing her. "Dani! Get back here! It's time for dinner!" Dani's mother's shadow flew past her, and she giggled as she ran into her waiting arms.

Jirron hissed and thrust the memories down again.

The newcomers waited for zim, flapping their wings and glaring at zim. There was bad blood between these two and zis host body. Maybe zi could exploit that.

"The kings of prophecy." Zi leered. Over time, zis control of this host had grown and had begun to feel more natural. "Xander, have you reconsidered my proposition?"

The two sneered in unison. *A bonded pair.* "We know what you are."

When the skythane man spoke, Jirron felt the echo through the Heart. Zis eyes narrowed. These two were linked in the athrà.

They had found a way to access the Heart, but they were still new to it, and zi had been controlling it for much longer than they had been alive.

"No!" Dani screamed. Her father's craft plunged into the ocean, and seconds later a great explosion rocked the sea....

Jirron blinked in displeasure. Habits of a lifetime were hard to dispel.

"The fight is over," they said in unison.

Zi drew out the moment while zi searched for a way to cut them off from the Heart. "What do you propose?"

They looked at each other in surprise, and then one of them laid out the terms of surrender.

The Thshnel'Jirron listened absently, nodding every so often as zi set about undermining the control the two skythane kings had over zis Heart.

Quince gasped.

Robyn leapt up off the bench to catch her as she collapsed, lowering her carefully to the ground.

Quince's eyes flickered open. "It's done." Her skin was gray and cold.

She looked to Morgan. He knew how to heal people. Quince had told her about it. Unfortunately, he looked to be in worse shape than Quince.

"Take me back to the other side." Quince's voice was faint, but her intent was clear.

Robyn nodded. "Jessa, bring Morgan."

"Will do."

Together they scooped up their wounded and carried them from the battlefield to the gateway and through to the other side. Robyn leaned over and kissed Quince on the forehead. "Daia?" She looked up and the world mind was there.

"Yes."

"Did it work?" Daia seemed to shimmer and fade, but then reappeared. "Are you okay?"

Daia nodded. "I'm having some trouble integrating all the new information. But yes. It worked. Is Quince okay?"

"I don't know." She cradled Quince's head in her lap.

Jessa held Morgan. He looked like a little boy again, all guile gone, sleeping like an angel.

"Quince?" She put her cheek over Quince's mouth. She was still breathing. "I really don't know."

MYLIN SWAM in a sea of anesthesia and anxiety.

There was something she had to do. Something she *knew* she had to tell someone. The pain in her abdomen had dulled to a throbbing background ache.

Her heart beat steadily.

The Heart.

Mylin.

She stirred. A woman was standing over her, dark-haired. A lander. Beautiful eyes. Sad eyes.

Mylin tried to speak. *The Heart. They can't....*

The women knelt next to her and cupped her cheek. *Tell me.*

Mylin felt a gentle pressure and let herself open to the woman's touch. Her anxiety flowed out of her like air out of her lungs.

When it was done, she reached out to the stranger. *You have to tell them.*

The woman knelt over her and kissed her forehead. *I will. Sleep. All will be well. All manner of things will be well.*

Mylin nodded. *Sleep.* That sounded so good. She stirred again. *Who are you?*

Daia.

Then she was gone.

JAMESON AND XANDER faced their old nemesis. It wore Dani's face, but it had an alien soul. It was strange seeing the ithani inhabiting Dani's body.

Jameson was laying out the terms of surrender—a delaying tactic while Xander contacted Alix.

"Alix?" They called their friend through Jameson's PA.

"Hey, good to see you two. We'd all but given you up for dead."

"Yeah, us too."

"You… is this both of you together?"

"Yes. We'll explain later. Still have that carrier full of meso bombs on tap?"

"Yes."

"Use it. We have to destroy the Heart."

"Affirmative. Launch in sixty seconds."

They returned their attention to Jirron. "It's over—"

Jirron cut him off. "I remember you. Before the shift." Zis eyes narrowed. "Erina found you and brought you to the Heart…. How is that possible?"

"We get around." Xander and Jameson smiled at the same time.

Jirron didn't react.

Something was wrong. The Thshnel didn't look worried. In fact, zi was grinning, an unnerving ear to ear grin.

Jameson suddenly felt sick. The source of his power, the Heart, was turned against him.

"It's not so easy controlling the Heart, is it?"

Jameson couldn't feel Xander through the bond anymore. Instead, he felt nauseous, the taint from the Heart spreading into his mind.

Jirron's grin stretched even wider.

"ROBYN."

Robyn blinked and looked up. Must have fallen asleep. Quince's head still rested in her lap, her color back to normal.

Daia was looking down at her.

"What is it?"

"Mylin. She's hurt."

"Is she okay?" Quince's eyes opened. Her voice was raspy.

Daia shook her head. "I don't know, but she sent you a message."

"Hey, you need to sleep." Robyn kissed Quince's forehead. "You taxed yourself to the limit."

"It's okay. This is important." She struggled to sit up. "I told her to contact me if she found anything in the archives."

Robyn sighed and helped her up. "You're going to drive me to an early grave."

Quince kissed her cheek. "What did she say?"

"There's a bomb on a ship."

Quince nodded weakly. "Yes."

"If it goes off over the Heart, it might set off a chain reaction in the amalite underneath that could destroy Erro."

Quince grunted. "Robyn, help me up."

"Quince, are you sure?"

"I need to contact Alix, or Venin."

Robyn helped Quince stand.

Jessa had been watching the whole exchange. "Daia's back?"

Robyn bit her lip. "Yes. She says we have to stop Alix's plan to bomb the Heart. It could start a… a chain reaction?"

Jessa blanched. That would be bad. "What can I do?"

Quince pointed at the still-open gateway. "Take me back to the Heart and bring my carry sack."

The girl looked worried. "Quince, are you sure you can manage this?"

Quince nodded. "Have to."

"Okay." Jessa laid Morgan down, using her own carry sack to make a pillow for him, and helped Robyn get Quince to her feet.

Together, they helped her limp to the Heart.

Venin watched in shock as Jameson's self-assurance crumbled, and Xander's face turned from serene strength to abject fear.

"Venin, you have to get everyone out of there." Alix's voice rang through his head. "The carrier is inbound." His voice was calm, but there was an underlying tension that belied it.

Xander and Jameson both looked sick, really sick, yet somehow their wings continued to beat the air in a slow, steady rhythm. They looked like two flies trapped in amber.

"Venin?"

Jirron had gotten to them, somehow. "The Heart is mine."

The Heart is mine.

This was his moment. Suddenly it was all clear.

"Dani!" he shouted, and threw himself at her, his wings driving him into the ithani with the power of a freighter.

Jirron turned toward him and tried to spring away, but she was too slow.

Venin rammed into her, knocking her backward through the sky, and *reached* inside.

Jirron's mind was full of twisting currents, but there were whispers of Dani there. *Dani Black!* he shouted inside Jirron's mind.

Dani. I'm Dani. The voice was faint but unmistakable.

Jirron reacted furiously, trying to push Venin out.

Venin pushed back. *Dani!*

And suddenly she was *there.*

Jirron grinned. Zi'd taken back control of the Heart. Zis enemies were vanquished, and their plan, which had apparently been seeded by the traitor Erina a hundred thousand cycles before, had come to naught. "The Heart is mine."

Zi twisted the kings' minds and delighted in seeing the looks of pain on their faces. There was so much there to work with—betrayal, doubt, an old lover. Zi'd always enjoyed finding zis enemies' weaknesses and pushing them hard.

"Dani!"

Jirron turned in time to see one of the skythane hurling himself at zim— the one who had first challenged him. Zi tried to back away, but zi couldn't avoid the impact.

Blades slipped smoothly from between the knuckles of Jirron's hands—

Then the man was inside zis head.

Dani Black! The voice reverberated through zis mind.

Dani. I'm Dani.

No. Not now. Not when zi was so close. Zi pushed at the interloper, drawing on the Heart for strength.

Dani!

Zis mind was squeezed as Dani's personality reasserted itself with a vengeance.

Zi fought to retrench. *This isn't possible.* None of zis host minds had ever managed to come back to challenge zim.

None of them had been human.

Zi pushed back hard but was unprepared for the ferocity with which she attacked zim. She slashed at zim in her mind again and again, tearing at zim like an auxen's horns.

Meanwhile, the skythane man had zim locked in a death embrace as they plunged toward the ground.

Dani backed away and snarled at zim. *Get the fuck out of my head.*

Soon they'd hit the ground, and if zis host body died, zi would too.

With a snarl of zis own, Jirron gave up and left zis host, fleeing to the Heart.

Ze'd be safe there while ze plotted zis next step.

Quince showed Jessa and Robyn where to plant the nano traps she'd found in the OberCorp armory. They did so hurriedly.

She hoped they would work on the material of the Heart.

The weapons systems were banned across the Common Worlds because the underlying nanotech had the potential to get out of control, eating everything in sight if the shutoff protocol failed. It had happened on a small moon in the Eridinai system, and they'd had to bomb the whole place out of existence.

Using them was a great risk. Quince wondered where in the hell Ober-Corp had obtained them. Maybe they'd been in storage for a hundred years.

When you had a nail, whatever was at hand became your hammer.

She'd set them to self-destruct after two hours, long enough to devour the Heart. If they malfunctioned, things would get very interesting very fast.

While they were placing the traps, Quince took a deep breath and touched the Heart. It rippled under her hand.

The connection she'd found earlier was still there.

So were Jameson and Xander. She could still reach them, even if they were cut off from the Heart.

JIRRON WAS GONE.

Venin could *feel* the change.

He let go of Dani Black, his wings spreading to stop his fall fifty meters above the ground.

She did the same, and they circled each other warily. "You saved me."

He spat. "Not something I'm proud of. Call it collateral damage."

She was white as a sheet.

"What happened to Kadin?"

She turned away. "That monster. He killed him, once he sucked everything out of him."

"I'm… sorry."

"Thank you." She looked broken.

He almost felt sorry for her. What she must have endured, with Jirron rummaging around inside her head…. He shivered. She had done terrible things, but she'd also lived through something more horrible than he could imagine. A raping of the soul.

"So what happens now?" She watched him warily.

She had suffered enough. "We have a war to win. I wouldn't be surprised if a few of the enemy manage to slip through our grasp."

She stared at him for a moment, then nodded. "I won't forget this."

"I don't forgive you for what you did."

"Understood."

"Venin?" Alix's voice rang through his head.

"Good luck to you." He turned away, spreading his wings to catch an updraft to rejoin his friends in the skies.

When he looked back down a moment later, she was gone.

JAMESON BLINKED, looking around. "What the hell just happened?"

Xander shook his head. "Not sure. Jirron got to us through the Heart, I think. Then zi cut us off. Look!"

Jameson followed his gaze down. Venin and Jirron were plunging to the ground. Or Venin and Dani?

"Holy crap. We have to—"

Then the antagonists separated and leveled out.

"Jameson, what's going on out there?" Alix's voice shouted in his head.

Jameson ripped his gaze away from Venin and Dani to look around. "Jirron's gone, I think. Into the Heart."

"Then clear out. I have that Rentz Class Carrier coming in hot in about ninety seconds."

"Everyone, clear the scene! Bomber coming in hot!" He and Xander shot away from the Heart, toward the cloud wall.

The other skythane fled too.

Jameson.

Quince? She was in his head, but not like Alix. Her voice sounded weak. *Where are you?*

At the Heart. Tell Alix to call off the bombs. He'll set off a chain reaction that we won't be able to stop.

How—

No time.

"Angie, get me Alix."

"Connected."

"Alix, you have to abort the mission." *Thank the gods.*

"What?" Alix's voice was weak and tinny. "You're cutting out."

"Alix, abort!"

There was no reply.

The carrier burst through the cloud wall, hurtling toward the Heart.

"Angie, get Alix back. I need him now!"

ROBYN SET Quince down gently with her back against the wall in Daia's cavern.

Jessa shook Morgan awake. "Close the gateway, Morgan!"

The boy looked up, groggy, and then his eyes focused.

"You have to close the gateway."

Robyn looked back through it. There was a chuffing sound, and something black swarmed over the liquid surface of the Heart. It began to sag and collapse as the black wave spread over it like a dark tide.

Morgan twisted his hand, and the gateway snapped shut, locking the nanites on the far side.

"It's done." Robyn sank down next to Quince and took her in her arms.

The carrier would be diverted, or the end would come here soon. Either way, it was out of her hands.

She wrapped her arms around Quince and kissed her cheek. "I'll love you until the end of the world."

Quince smiled weakly. "Looking for a short-term commitment, huh?"

Robyn squeezed her tight.

"Venini!" Alix cursed. The communications out here were shit.

Jameson. He had a PA.

"Jameson, what's going on out there?" He waited breathlessly for a reply.

"Jirron's gone, I think. Into the Heart."

"Then clear out. I have that Rentz Class Carrier coming in hot in about ninety seconds."

"Everyone, clear the scene! Bomber coming in hot!"

Alix sighed and sat back. *Thank the Split, it's over.*

"Alix, you have to—" Jameson's voice dropped off.

Shit. "What? You're cutting out."

"…abort!"

"Jameson! I can't hear you!" Alix's mind raced. He checked the carrier's trajectory. Thirty seconds.

Abort.

If he was wrong… if he misheard….

The existence of Erro hung in the balance.

"Goddammit!"

Alia put a hand on his shoulder. "What?"

"We have to abort. Erissa, abort the mission."

"Authorization code?"

He entered his code.

"Authorization accepted."

"What happened?" Alia squeezed his arm.

"I honestly don't know. Jameson told me to abort the mission, but he was cut off before he could tell me why."

· · ·

Xander took Jameson's hand. "Erina couldn't foresee everything."

Jameson's face was glum. "I guess not."

"If it really is the end of the world, I'm glad I'm here with you." They'd come a long way together, crossing Erro twice. Crossing time too.

"Me too." Jameson squeezed his hand.

The carrier plunged toward the Heart.

"Maybe we'll see each other in the next life—"

"Look!"

The carrier had fired its jets at the last moment. It shot off away from the Heart, slamming into the ground ten kilometers east. There was a bright flash as the meso bombs went off, and the ground was fused in a wide circle.

Then the carrier was gone.

Below, the Heart collapsed, covered by a dark swarm.

Jirron slipped into the Heart. Zi was seething with anger. All zis hard work had come to nothing.

Still, zi wasn't finished. Zi had the Heart. Ze could regroup, strike out at them again. This was zis domain, not theirs. Zi owned the athrà. Zi could still—

It's over.

Zi spun to find a pair of ithani eyes staring at zim. *Who are you?*

Another pair of eyes appeared. Then another. *It's over.*

It's not over. This is my place.

More eyes. In chorus, they spoke to zim. *It's over.*

Soon they entirely surrounded zim.

The owner of the first pair stepped forward from the mist, zer golden carapace shining.

Erina.

Hello, Jirron.

Others appeared. Zi recognized each of zis former hosts, one after the other.

It wasn't possible.

The Heart is dying, and you're going to die with it. Erina shimmered with joy.

It can't be.

The athrà dissolved around zim. *What's happening?*

Then zis own spirit began to corrode.

Zi screamed as zis soul was torn into a million pieces.

"Venin, where are you?" Alix scanned the sky as the remaining ithani and skythane broke off from one another.

Alia looked over his shoulder. "Down there!"

A group of skythane had set down on a hillside.

"Take us down there."

The pilot nodded.

The ground came up quickly. He should be finding a way to talk to the ithani. He should be assessing the damage and figuring out next steps.

None of those things mattered.

The hoversport set down, and Alix was out of the hatch before it had finished opening. "Venin!"

All the skythane turned toward him.

Venin emerged from the crowd.

In three huge steps Alix was at his side, sweeping Venin into his arms.

Venin's wings enfolded him, and they kissed like lovers separated by a thousand years.

Morgan stared morosely at where the gateway had been. He'd failed his people.

They had destroyed the Heart, and the Thshnel'Jirron with it. They'd saved the ithani and nimfeach memories, but there was no seed.

Without the seed, there would be no new Heart. Without the Heart, there would be no more nimfeach, and the ithani would eventually die.

I failed. We saved the world, but at what cost?

Quince's hand touched his shoulder.

He looked up at her, and she held something up to him.

He took it and turned it over in his hands. It was about fifteen centemeters wide, a perfect sphere, with colors that swirled across its surface like a rainbow.

It was a seed for the Heart.

Morgan threw his arm around Quince and cried.

32

AFTERMATH

THE SURVIVORS gathered on a hillside overlooking the devastation.

Jameson, his arm around Xander, stared down on the sunken valley that had once been the heart of ithani culture. He'd seen it in its decline, but now it was nothing but a pit of despair. The cavern roof had sagged, the white towers were dead or dying, and the Heart itself had been reduced to a pile of slag by the nanites Quince had used against it. They had done their damage and had apparently expired on schedule.

He sighed. "What will the ithani do now, without a leader? Without a home?"

Xander turned to stare at him. "We just fought a war against them, and you're worried about what will happen to *them* next?"

Jameson nodded. "What will happen to us all. We have to learn to share this place, or none of us will survive."

Xander grunted. "I guess you're right." He stared at the ruin. "So many skythane and lander lives lost."

The efforts had begun to collect the dead. Alix had agreed to a mass ceremony, lander and skythane together. It was a small step toward unity.

Jameson separated from Xander, turning to look west. "We need to deal with Rogan."

"Yes. You haven't developed a soft spot for him too, have you?" Xander's tone was deceptively light, his look deadly serious.

"No. The man's a monster. More so than most of these ithani."

Xander scowled. "You'll get no argument from me."

"Do you think Jirron's really gone?" It had all happened so quickly.

"Quince says zi is. Destroyed along with the Heart."

A gateway split the air behind them.

Quince, Robyn, Jessa, and Morgan stepped through, and it snapped shut behind them.

Jameson grinned. "Well speak of the devil."

"Holy Split, you're here!" Quince ran up to Jameson, wrapping the two of them in her arms and wings. "I am so, so sorry about what I did to you. To both you and Xander. It was wrong. I see that now."

He held her out at arm's length. "It's okay, Quince. We worked it out. I forgive you."

Xander was silent.

Jameson nudged him. "Come on. You too."

"I do. Really I do. It's just going to take me some time to get past it. You really hurt us, Quince."

She looked down. "I know."

"I'll get there. Just give me some time."

"Okay." She kissed them both on the cheeks. Then the strongest woman Jameson knew began to cry. She hugged them again fiercely. "Where did you go? If you ever do that to me again…."

"It's a long story. Let's just say we went back to the beginning and leave it at that for now."

"Back to the beginning… by heaven and Erro, I'm going to get the whole story out of you soon."

Xander felt a hand on his shoulder.

He turned to find Robyn standing there.

They stared at each other for a moment. She was a proud woman, even now maintaining her regal bearing in the face of what must have been crushing exhaustion. "I'm glad you're safe."

Xander made the first move, pulling her close to him. She was stiff in his arms. "I love you," he whispered.

She melted, squeezing him tight. "I dreamed about you so many times, wondering if you were okay. What you were like. How your life was going."

"I dreamed about you too. I didn't know who you were. Just a beautiful angel." It was time for a new beginning between the two of them. He had to let go of his bitterness, toward Quince, toward life.

Robyn held him for a long time. "I thought I'd lost you." When they separated, her cheeks were wet, her composure lost.

Xander liked her better that way. She was human after all. "I'm okay. We both are. We'll tell you more later, when there's time."

She squeezed his hands in agreement.

Then he scooped up Morgan and laughed as he held the boy in the air. "Heaven and Erro, it's good to see you, little man."

Morgan felt uncomfortable, lifted into the air like a child.

Xander laughed, seeing his discomfort, and set him down.

Morgan nodded. "It's good to see you too, Xander."

Xander frowned.

Morgan wasn't giving Xander what he wanted, but he wasn't sure what to do.

"You *knew*, didn't you. When you gave Quince the key. You knew it would take us back to the ithani. To the first shift."

The first shift.

The last veil lifted from Morgan's memory.

A hundred thousand years ago or more, he'd been born into this world for the first time. In that first lifetime, he'd met two strangers—visitors from another time. Memories resurfaced, painful and joyful.

Losing his key when Jirron had stripped it from him.

Finding it again in the hands of a human stranger.

Stopping the shift and freezing his enemies in time.

And this one.

I am an old soul.

He reached out to touch Xander's face, because touch facilitated such sharing.

He closed his eyes and passed the memory to Xander.

Xander was looking at the Heart.

One of the amber chambers split open, and a nimfeach crawled out, wet with the chamber's fluids. It spread its wings tentatively and sniffed the air.

A golden ithani appeared in front of the nimfeach, holding out a milky-white key and a silver one that swirled like mercury. Ze knelt before him and handed him the silver one first. He touched it and it evaporated, drawn into the nimfeach just like the one Jameson had given Puck.

Xander's breath caught.

The second key vanished like the first, and the little nimfeach glowed, his wings radiant.

Erina touched his cheek. "Though your form is different now, little Puck, you still have a role to play." Zer golden fur shimmered. "He will call you *Morgan*. I have foreseen it. You will forget this now, but you will remember what you must do, when the time is right."

THE MEMORY DISSOLVED, and Xander opened his eyes, blinking back tears. "You… you're Puck?"

Morgan nodded. He threw his arms around Xander's neck and hugged him tightly. Xander held him for the longest time. Things had come full circle in a way he'd never expected. That day—so long ago, but just hours in his own past—he'd watched Puck vanish. It had cut him to the quick.

And now—

Jameson tapped him on the shoulder.

"Xander, look!" He held up a key—although it was far larger than any key Xander had ever seen.

"What is it?" He let go of Morgan and touched the surface. It was warm.

"It's a seed. For a new Heart."

Full circle. "Jameson, I want you to meet someone." He held his hand out to Morgan.

"I know Morgan already. You sure your head didn't get scrambled when we went through that last gateway?"

Xander shook his head. "Meet Puck."

QUINCE RETURNED with the remainder of the Hunters to Oberon City.

Morgan stayed behind to talk to the ithani. Now that Jirron was dead and gone, many of those who had opposed him silently were doing so openly. A new day was coming for the two intertwined races, and Quince was sure that Morgan would guide them there.

Alix provided the transportation, giving the weary fighters a chance to rest and swap stories. "Mylin is okay. She came through surgery well and is in recovery."

Quince sighed along with the rest of the cabin. The girl did good.

Jameson had been telling the story of what happened after he and Xander disappeared so abruptly from the conference room.

"We figured out that it was a gateway, but we wondered how far you'd gone." Quince was astonished at the tale Jameson and Xander spun. To finally answer the greatest question of the split worlds—not in her wildest dreams would she have imagined such a story.

Jameson nodded. "We weren't sure ourselves where we had landed, at first." His eyes narrowed. "You have a story to tell us too, don't you? What did you find under Oberon City?"

Quince laughed. It felt good. Sure, they still had troubles to face, but the immediate threat was behind them. "What I found will require a hell of a lot more showing than telling. Let's just say that while you were busy solving the mystery of the Split, we were off discovering the origin of the skythane."

Venin leaned forward. "On that note, I found this in one of the underground caverns." He held out a tarnished silver cross.

An electric jolt went through Quince. "Can I see it?"

"Of course." He took it off and handed it to her.

As she touched it, a memory flashed through her head. "It belonged to *her.*"

"Who?" Venin cocked his head.

"You look like an ithani." Jameson was grinning broadly.

"Ana. The woman who made the world minds." She held it reverently. This little symbol had come so far and had meant so many things to so many people.

Venin nodded. "I knew it had a history. Keep it. You seem to have a connection to it."

"Thanks." She squeezed it tight.

To her, it meant hope.

. . .

Xander watched as the med drone finished the installation of his bioware. It would be nice to have Ravi and his direct grid access again, especially with the plans to link the grid to Errian and Gaelan.

Jameson was off helping Alix's forces end Rogan's armed occupation of the city.

"Good morning, Xander." Ravi's voice sounded just like he remembered it.

"Hey there, old friend. It's been too long. I missed you."

His PA was silent for a moment. "I missed you too."

Xander smiled wryly. One day he would figure out just how much like people PAs really were. "Where's Jameson?"

"Wrapping up a cleanup operation in the Slander."

"Good." He had one outstanding item on his ledger. "Ravi, I need you to find Rogan for me."

"Priority?"

"Urgent."

"I will let you know when I find him."

It's time. Xander got up from the medical bench. He wandered down the hall of the OberCorp infirmary and poked his head into the room at the end.

Mylin lay there on her side, looking out the plas window at the new morning. It looked like it was going to be a glorious day.

"Hey."

She turned, wincing a little. "Xander!" She tried to get up.

"No, stay where you are!" She had a synth pack covering the right side of her abdomen. He pulled up a chair and leaned forward to kiss her forehead, then sat down at her bedside. "How are you feeling?"

"Okay. I'm sorry… I got myself shot. I wasn't careful enough."

"Hey, stop that." It came out harsher than he intended. "Mylin, you saved us all. You saved everything!"

"I did?" She smiled tentatively.

"Yes. Your warning came to us from Quince through the Heart, and not a second too soon. The carrier was just a few seconds away from impact."

She closed her eyes. "Thank the skies. I was so scared."

"Me too."

She looked up at him. "So *where* did you go? I've been dying to hear."

He grinned. "Do I have a story for you. We fell through the gateway and found ourselves on a strange new world in the middle of a sea of golden grass...."

He spun the story like a master storyteller, filling it with exclamations and gestures and lots of cliffhangers.

She made it through the part about the white city before she fell asleep.

He pulled the thin sheet over her and smiled at her. If Morgan was the closest thing he had to a son, Mylin was like a daughter.

Maybe it was time to settle down and start a family of his own.

There was a light tap at the door.

He turned to find the boy Mylin had been working with. Derrick? Aaron?

"Derren Sevvins. Nice to meet you." Derren held out his hand.

Ah, Derren. Yes. "We met, briefly." He shook Derren's hand.

"Yes, we did. I didn't think you'd remember me." Derren blushed.

Xander laughed. "Yes, I remember you. Here with a message? Or...?"

"I was here to... to see her, sir."

Ah. "Are your intentions honorable, Derren Sevvins?"

"Um, yes, sir. Entirely honorable."

"Carry on then."

He left them together, a grin on his face that he made sure the boy didn't see.

JAMESON SHOVED another one of the syndicate fighters through a gateway into the waiting arms of an Oberon enforcer. They were going to need a bigger jail when all this was done.

After a bit of sleep, some food, and a shower, he felt more human than he had in days. Ironic considering a decent chunk of him was decidedly inhuman. He'd have to work out how he really felt about that later.

"Xander wants to talk with you." Angie's voice was welcome in his ear. It was good to have her whole again.

"Put him through." Jameson closed the gateway, staring at the blasted street. The firefight had been about evenly matched until DOC had guided him to pick off the syndicate men one by one.

"It's time." Xander's voice sounded tight, restrained.

Jameson knew exactly what he meant. "Where is he?"

"At his estate. About to leave for parts unknown, according to DOC."

Jameson grinned. "Let's go finish our end of the bargain. Where are you?"

"On the roof of OberCorp."

"Don't even need a gateway for that one." He leapt into the air, winging toward the place that had once been home to his sworn enemies. Everything had flipped. Well, almost everything. "On my way."

The city below was a hive of activity. Alix and DOC had wasted no time tearing into the Slander. Drone construction machines were already ripping into the outlying buildings, knocking them down for scrap. In a month, the Slander would be no more.

OberCorp had opened a new subsidiary for human welfare on Erro, committed to building new housing in the outlying human cities along the coast of the Gildensea.

The Syndicate's days were numbered. Things were going to change, hopefully for the better.

Even Alix's mother was on board. She was still a little freaked out about the skythane, but she was working on it. Her words, not his. She was now in charge of the old business side of OberCorp again—under Alix's command.

Jameson snorted. He'd believe it when he saw it, but if there was a profit to be made....

Xander waved to him from atop OberCorp, the sun bright on his face.

After the Heart had melted down, the storm had dissipated, and they were anticipating a stretch of fair weather at last. That was fine with Jameson. If he never saw another day of rain in his life, it would be too soon.

He alighted next to Xander. "Ready?"

"I've been ready for this for ten years."

"Okay, here we go." He pulled out his key and opened a gateway to Rogan's estate. He wondered if the key belonged to one of the nimfeach. If so, he'd have to give it back one of these days, soon.

They stepped through to find a startled Rogan loading bags onto a small hoversport. He was all alone. *Guess the ship deserted the sinking rat.*

"Hey there. Where are you going? Extended vacation?"

Rogan was sweating profusely. "Just thought I'd get away for a bit." He glanced from one of them to the other, as if trying to judge their intentions. "And you two?"

"Oh, we had a bit of unfinished business to address with you."

Rogan threw himself at their feet. "I'm so sorry. I didn't mean for things to get out of hand. There were a few bad apples." He touched Xander's foot.

Xander pulled it away, a look of disgust on his face.

Jameson offered Rogan a hand. "We're not here to hurt you."

"You're not?"

"Of course not. We had a deal, remember?"

The heavyset man got up awkwardly and dusted himself off. "Thank you. You don't know how happy this makes me. Not everyone is so trustworthy in this town."

Xander snorted.

Jameson put on his most beneficent smile. "We promised you all the pith in our storage cave. I *never* go back on a promise."

"Really?" Jameson could practically see the gears turning in the man's mind. "But without a market…."

"Soon Oberon will be returned to its place among the Common Worlds. I assure you there will be a huge market for it."

Rogan laughed. It was an ugly sound, deep and guttural. "How… how do I get it?"

Jameson pulled out his key and opened a gateway to the cavern that held the stockpiles of pith Dani had collected in Gaelan. "Be my guest."

Rogan stared hungrily at the key, but then tore his gaze away from it to look Jameson in the face. "I want it legally recorded that all of that pith is mine, fair and square."

"I have a contract all drawn up. Angie, can you slit it to Mr. Horth for his signature?"

The man blinked twice at the mention of his last name. *That* had taken some digging to unearth. His eyes went blank as he scanned the contract in vir. "It all seems in order."

"If you would affix your v-sig…."

"Done."

Jameson checked the contract, then sent it off to be filed. "It's all yours."

Rogan all but ran into the cavern, picking up the first pack of pith to check it.

Jameson handed the key to Xander. "Want to do the honors? Just like I showed you?"

Xander nodded. "I hope the two of you share a happy eternity together," he called to his former tormentor.

Rogan's horrified face was the last they saw of him before the gateway snapped shut.

Xander kissed Jameson hard. "That was better than I even dared to hope."

Jameson took the key and put it away. "How long do you think it will take him to figure there's no way out?"

Xander flashed him a wicked grin.

QUINCE STOOD ALONE inside the cavern by the sea.

Above her, the world mind was dying.

Daia appeared to her, still young and beautiful, but faded somehow. Quince could see through her to the wood-covered cabin walls. Even in vee, she was a ghost, a spirit preparing to depart on a path Quince could never follow.

"Is it over?"

Quince nodded. "Jirron, the one who led the ithani astray, is gone."

"I'm glad. And the war?"

"Settled. Alix, Morgan, and the two kings are working out a truce now."

"A new world." Daia sighed. "I'm dying."

"I know." All that knowledge, human and ithani. It would be lost now, in spite of their best attempts to save it. "You waited for us for so long."

"I still remember."

"Remember what?" How she could choose among so many times, places, people… it boggled Quince's mind.

"What it felt like to walk barefoot on the sand, to feel the cool waves wash over my toes." She stepped outside the cavern, and the waves washed through her. She left no footprints.

The sun was setting over the Gildensea, and it bathed her in a golden glow.

Quince followed her outside, taking in a deep breath of the cool sea air. "I give you my blessing."

"Blessing?"

"To go. You've waited long enough. You don't need to stay any longer on my account. Or for any of us."

Daia's ghostly hand brushed Quince's cheek. "Thank you for that." She stared out at the sunset for a moment longer, and Quince wondered what thoughts or memories were passing through her head. At last, Daia turned and beckoned. "Come with me. I have something for you."

Curious, Quince followed her back into the cavern.

One of Daia's roots lowered to the ground, holding something.

It was oblong, bigger than Quince, covered in a dark husk.

A seed.

Quince recognized it from memory. The original Daia, the human Daia, had planted a seed just like it in this very place more than eight hundred years before. Well, maybe not just like it.

"When one of us produces a seed, it takes a lot out of us, but it's better this way." Daia placed her hand on it. "It carries everything you need, for you and for the ithani. Plant it in a good place, with room to grow."

Quince was speechless.

"Every tragedy holds the seeds of something new." Daia looked wistfully at the seed.

"Where will you go?" Quince managed at last.

Daia was transfixed by light. "I don't know. I think I'm going to join the others." Her face was radiant, actually glowing. "I'm glad I met you, Quince." The light grew and grew until it consumed her in a final burst of radiance.

"Me too."

Daia's last words were a breath on the ocean breeze. *Goodbye, Quince.*

XANDER, JAMESON, Morgan, Quince, Venin, Jessa, and Mylin sat on the hastily constructed stage.

Alix was at the podium, giving his prepared remarks, while nimfeach translators on either side repeated it in the ithani tongue.

Xander looked out at the assembled crowd on the shores of Lake Arliss. "Arliss" was the closest human approximation to the name of the ithani city that was being covered by its waters as the Demetrius and Theseus Rivers emptied into the former cavern. In the two months since the battle, it had filled up about halfway to the rim.

The ithani and the nimfeach had decided that their new city would rise on the shores of the wide circular lake. The lander cities already dotted the edge of the Gildensea, and the skythane had populated the far side of the planet, from the Argent Sea to the Mora Mountains. But the Outland was unpopulated and would give the ithani a place to call their own in the new world order.

Xander wished the ceremony wasn't necessary. He hated these things, but he understood the need to formally cement the ties between the three peoples. The nimfeach had been given back their hearts, which had been hidden in the great mountain Freyyr to the north. They had taken over the governance of the ithani, selecting a council to make the most important decisions.

He glanced over at Jameson. "We're kind of old hat at spinning worlds, aren't we?"

"Shush." Jameson stared straight ahead, but a smile played at the corner of his lips.

"… and we are ready for a new era of cooperation between lander and skythane, between human and ithani." Alix bowed, and the crowd cheered and clapped and shimmered their approval.

"He's good at this." The truce had called for the election of a governor, a real one, not the sham that OberCorp had perpetrated on the planet for hundreds of years. The last one had been little more than an OberCorp puppet.

Alix figured he had a good shot at snagging the post.

Venin got up and hugged Alix.

Xander hadn't seen that one coming. Venin and Alix? Nevertheless, he wholeheartedly approved of the match.

"Okay, you guys are on." Alix gave them the thumbs-up and kissed each of them on the cheek.

Xander followed the others down the stairs from the platform.

Alix's mother, Lena, was there. She gave him a hug, and Xander nodded at Alix. She had a lot to account for, but after learning what she'd been through, he thought he understood. He was glad to see Alix mending fences with his only family.

A wide circle had been cleared in the forest behind the platform. Eventually a new building would be grown from corrinder over the site, but for now, it was open to the air.

The sun was warm on his skin as he approached what they'd taken to calling "the garden." The two seeds lay there, side by side. One would become a new heart, and the other a new world mind. Like the two alien cultures that shared the planet, they would become intertwined, a hybrid creating something new.

"Are you ready?" He put a hand on Mylin's shoulder.

She shook her head. "I don't think I'm the right one for this."

Xander laughed. "You're the only one for this. The world mind is a repository of information unlike anything we've ever seen, short of maybe the original grid on old Earth. Who else better to organize it?" He squeezed her shoulder.

"Will it hurt?"

Quince took Mylin by the hand, giving Xander an *I'll take it from here* look. He nodded and backed away to stand with Jameson. "Daia assured me no. You'll come away entirely unharmed."

"Okay. If you think—"

"Come on." Quince pulled the girl close. "Everything will be fine." She led Mylin to the world mind seed.

The crowd followed, gathering around them.

Quince knelt, gently placing Mylin's hands on the rough husk. Then she put her own there as well.

Daia had shown her how to do this, as so many had done it before her. With her other hand, she pulled Mylin's black hair back behind her ears. "Ready?"

Mylin gulped and nodded. "I guess so."

"You'll do fine." Quince reached inside and found the seed's spark. She touched Mylin's cheek and the transfer began.

The girl's memories, dreams, and personality flowed through her into the seed.

Mylin had enjoyed a good childhood. She was smart and stable and beautiful, everything Quince thought a skythane should be.

Quince was humbled to be in this place, to help bring about a new order. *Thank you, Daia.*

They knelt as seconds stretched into minutes. All around, the crowd was hushed, watching the silent spectacle.

At last it was done.

They stood together, and Mylin looked up at her, an odd smile on her face. "It's weird."

"What is?" *Besides the entire situation?*

"I'm here, but I'm in there too."

Quince laughed. "Yeah, I suppose you'll get used to it eventually."

"Maybe in a hundred years."

They moved back with Jameson and Xander and watched as the nimfeach activated the other seed.

Then everyone waited.

The world mind seed moved first, its bark splitting with a loud *crack*, roots emerging to sink down into the ground below and questing around on the surface. They soon encountered the alien seed.

The sphere shimmered and melted, slipping over the questing root, running like quicksilver along the root to the other seed.

There, it spread over the rough husk and then seemed to burrow inside.

"Heart and mind in sync?" Xander whispered.

"Was that supposed to happen?" Mylin was staring at the strange scene, her brow furrowed.

"I don't know."

Then everything stopped.

Quince's heart dropped. Had she miscalculated? Had the two seeds killed each other?

Maybe they weren't as compatible as she'd hoped.

She held her breath.

Maybe we're stuck here.

Without the Heart, there was no way to return Erro to the Common Worlds.

Then the seed started to grow again. It had taken on a distinct silver cast.

The crowd let out a collective sigh.

"We've witnessed something historic here," Jameson whispered in her ear.

Quince nodded. That much was clear.

She just wished she knew what it meant.

Xander took Jameson's hand. It was time to finish what they had started.

The nimfeach ushered the ithani through gateways back to Freyyr, the mountain in the north. They went docilely enough, though Xander saw a few wistful gazes cast to the pink skies above. The last time they'd slept through a shift, the universe had changed around them.

It was for their own protection, Morgan had explained to him. Something about the energies released during the shift.

When the aliens were gone, the human crowd—skythane and lander— closed in around them. It seemed like half of Oberon City was here, though it couldn't have been anywhere near that many. Still, it was a substantial crowd that stood beneath the afternoon sky to watch the world spinners work their magic.

Xander and Jameson waited for the ithani to be safely tucked away as the sun dipped toward the western horizon. Finally they got the all clear.

Morgan took their hands.

He closed his eyes, and Xander felt both Jameson and Morgan through their bond.

Then they were in the athrà. The world of possibilities swirled in gray eddies all around them.

Someone stepped out of the mist. Two someones.

Mylin, or her virtual doppelganger. And Erina.

Xander smiled at the ithani, and ze rolled zer head on zer neck in zer equivalent of a grin.

"Ze's here." Jameson's stunned face was priceless. He turned to Xander. "You knew?"

"I guessed."

Morgan looked up at them. "Ready?"

Xander nodded. "Let's go home."

Morgan closed his eyes.

The athrà filled with energy, like static in the air.

Together the three of them opened the way.

Jessa stood apart from her friends, holding Dixon's hand. The pilot was strong and beautiful, but sweet and funny too, something she didn't expect from a military man.

Alia and Smythe had introduced them. If the pilot was a consolation prize, he wasn't half bad. In fact, she might even stop calling him that, one of these days.

He leaned over and kissed her on the cheek. "What a day, huh?"

She laughed. "Yeah, what a couple of months." Soon she'd be able to go home to Beta Tau, back to her safe life as news broadcaster.

Back to her parents' functions and money, and all that they implied.

Soon.

"I'm thinking I might hang around here a little while longer. If I had a good enough reason."

"This count?" Dixon took her in his arms and bent her back gently, kissing her on the lips. He smelled like sweetness and lust. And adventure.

As they kissed, the stars came out overhead.

When they separated, she looked up at the stars. Her old home was around one of those flickering lights. She didn't want to go back. "I think it's the perfect reason."

VENIN LAUGHED as the sky changed from day to night. "Holy Split, it worked!"

Alix grinned. "We're home." He kissed Venin, joining in the general air of celebration. When they separated, he looked his lover in the eyes. "Have you given any more thought to where you're going to live?"

Venin frowned. "I miss Gaelan, but I'm totally falling for this lander man in Oberon City."

Alix laughed. "I have a proposition."

"Tell me."

"Be my ambassador to the skythane. That way you can spend time with me, and we can go to Gaelan and Errian too."

Venin's face lit up. "That's a great idea. Where do I sign up? Is there an interview process?"

"I know a guy." He put his hands around Venin's ass and pulled him in close, whispering, "You've got the job."

THE SHIFT ENDED, and the weight of a world dropped off Jameson's shoulders. He opened his eyes, looking around.

They were back in "real" time, though the line between what was real and what was not had grown increasingly thin this last month.

Morgan looked up at them. "It's time for a new plan."

"I suppose it is." Xander laughed. "You have your people to look after."

"Yes." Morgan looked lost.

Jameson knelt next to him. "Tanner?"

Morgan looked up at him, his face suddenly that of a twelve-year-old boy. "Yeah?"

"Xander and I are here for you, whenever you need us."

The boy nodded and threw his arms around Jameson's neck. For all that the nimfeach part of him was an old soul, Tanner was still a child.

Tanner let go and grinned. "We're going to get our wings!"

"What?" Jameson looked up at Xander.

Xander shrugged. *I have no idea.*

Jameson *heard* his thoughts that way now sometimes. One more thing that had changed between them. "Wings?"

Tanner's face became more solemn. Jameson was getting used to these shifts of personality. "Tanner's mother was skythane. She lived in Egeus among the landers there. I didn't know until recently."

Jameson whistled. "Isn't that something."

Morgan hugged Xander. "I've got to see about waking the ithani."

Xander nodded. *They grow up so fast.*

Jameson laughed. It was a brave new society they'd created. A strange one, too, filled with humans and aliens and all kinds of things in between.

"It sure is."

Jameson grinned. That whole mind reading thing was going to take some getting used to.

He took Xander's hand and led him back to the others. To their friends.

They had a world to build together.

EPILOGUE

ALIX POKED his head into the construction zone. "How is it coming?"

Venin looked up and grinned. "Really well."

All around him, builder drones were busy creating his new *aerie*—that was Venin's word for it.

They'd purchased an entire floor of one of the arcos, not the top one, but high enough to have a good view. One of the sides, facing east, was being converted to a traditional apartment, albeit a huge one. The Governor of Erro needed to have a space commensurate with his position, after all, when wining and dining guests from the other planets.

Titan Station had been destroyed by the flare. Fortunately it had been empty by then.

The Common Worlds navy had been poking around Erro's star system trying to figure out how they'd lost half a planet when Erro had reappeared. It had given the top brass quite a fright, but they now had a temporary replacement station, and a new one was in the works.

He laughed at himself. The Split was gone. They were going to have to come up with some new epithets.

The legal pith trade had grown by leaps and bounds over the last six months since Erro had rejoined the human universe, but tourism was proving to be an even bigger draw. Everyone wanted to *meet the aliens*, so after he'd won the post in a landslide, Governor Preston had been forced to institute strict restrictions to keep the tourists from overrunning the planet.

He'd also severely restricted the mining of amalite at the request of the ithani, which had the related effect of driving the prices per kilo through the roof.

Venin's half of the apartment—well, technically it belonged to both of them—was open plan. Really open plan. Wide open to the outside air, with stunning views of the Gildensea and Erro's green sky. Windows could be closed as needed, but Venin enjoyed the fresh air and the smell of the sea.

"Let me see them." Venin's eyes twinkled.

Alix grinned and turned to display his new wings. They were still tiny. When Quince had brought him the ethilium to kick off the skythane half of his metabolism, she'd said they might take a bit to grow in because he was only half skythane, and they might never be as large as Jameson's or Xander's. He didn't care.

"Oooh, the feathers are coming in. They're red."

"What color did you think they'd be? They match the carpet."

Venin laughed. "When they finish growing, I'll take you out flying." He snuggled up behind Alix, nuzzling his neck.

"I can't wait." He'd finally be able to realize one of his dreams—to fly like the skythane.

"Are we still going to Errian next week?"

Alix nodded. "Trade meetings. Boring as hell, I know. But that's my life now."

Venin slapped him on the ass. "Don't give me that. You love it." He kissed Alix's cheek. "Come on! I have something to show you!"

He drew Alix across the apartment to a closed door. He palmed it open and pulled Alix through into another room. On the other side was a wide, round white bed and a replica of the gorgeous view from the main living quarters.

It made Alix lightheaded to be so close to the open air, but he decided he'd get used to it. "That's a strange bed."

Venin laughed. "You have no idea. I had it shipped in from the Outland." He sat on the edge of the bed and patted the mattress, sending ripples across the surface. "Come here. I've been waiting for you all day."

Alix complied, and Venin pulled him down on the bed and kissed him hard. "It's an ithani bed. Want to see what it can do?"

By the time night fell, Alix decided he was a huge fan of alien technology.

MYLIN WAS ONSITE IN ITHALIA, the new city of the ithani, overseeing the integration of the OberCorp core and grid and the world mind. It was strange, working with a virtual version of herself, but she was getting used to it. Soon they would be able to exchange data back and forth between the two systems, and then she hoped to extend that capability to Errian and Gaelan on the other side of the world.

Zim hovered before her in vir. "Derren would like to speak with you."

She nodded. "Tell him five minutes."

"I told him that five minutes ago."

"Tell him three minutes, then."

Zim zipped off, sounding miffed.

"That boy really likes you." Mylin's mirror inside the world mind grinned.

She grinned. "I think so. I'm still waiting for him to tell me."

"Maybe he wants to tell you now."

Startled, Mylin looked up at her counterpart. "You think so?"

The world mind winked at her. "Why don't you go see?"

The virtual Mylin knew her like she knew herself. "Okay, but we'll come back to this when I'm through."

"Deal."

Mylin slipped out of vir.

Derren was waiting for her, a bunch of wildflowers in his hand.

They were a sad bunch, for the most part, sagging and missing petals, but it was edging toward fall, and she imagined they had been hard to come by.

He gave her a tentative smile and held them out to her. "For you."

She accepted them gratefully. "They're beautiful."

"Mylin, would you have lunch with me?"

She grinned. Her other self had been right. "I'd love to."

She took his hand.

Together they walked out into the sunlight, surrounded by the growing towers of Ithalia—the white city of the ithani on Lake Arliss.

QUINCE LAID the shovel down in the long grass. Then she tilted the wheelbarrow up, pouring the wet plascrete into the hole she'd dug.

There was something tremendously satisfying about digging into the earth under your own power, turning it with a shovel and seeing all the life that lived within it.

She glanced up at the newly constructed cabin that backed onto the nascent forest that was growing up over the wreckage from the shift storm, as they'd taken to calling it.

They'd finally gotten their place away from it all. They'd chosen the once-beautiful valley below the mountain, where it had collapsed after the shift. The place Quince had finally found Robyn once again.

She'd borrowed a few builder drones from Alix after the initial cleanup of Oberon City had been completed. Morgan had obliged with a gateway to get them here in far less time and with much less expense than it would have taken to ship them. Now they labored, day and night, to clear away the forest debris near the house and to clean up the worst of the rubble in and around the lake.

It would take time, but one day this little valley would be a paradise once more.

"It's ready!" she called, sinking the shovel into the earth.

The cabin door opened and Alia leaned out. "We'll be right down."

Alia and Smythe had come to visit them for a couple days. It was nice to have company out here. It did get lonely, just the two of them so far from civilization, but the quiet was a balm to Quince's battered soul.

"Hurry—the plascrete is setting."

"Got it." The door slammed closed.

A minute later, the three of them—Alia, Smythe, and Robyn—came trotting down the hillside. Alia carried a big basket.

"I thought we'd make a celebration of it." She spread a hand-woven Erriani blanket out over the grass and set down the basket. It was full of fresh-baked bread, fruit, and meat from their stores. The aux herd was coming along nicely on the high pasture above the valley, and they'd traded another farmstead for the produce, though Quince had already planted a variety of fruit trees next to the cabin.

"Okay, let's do this while the plascrete is still wet." She lifted up the cross she'd made from the wood she'd taken from Daia's cave by the sea. She'd polished it and then lashed it together with aux leather. She pushed it into the plascrete as deep as it would go, and then used a trowel to smooth over the surface.

She stood back to look at it. The hand lettering carved across the front read "Daia." Not in perfect script, but it came from her heart.

Robyn put her arm around Quince. "I think she would have liked it."

"Me too. One more thing." She took off the necklace with the silver cross and laid the chain over the top of the wooden one.

"It's perfect." Alia nodded her approval. "Come on you two, let's eat. I'm hungry!" Alia gestured for them to join her and Smythe on the blanket.

"Thank you," Quince whispered, and then followed Robyn to the picnic.

She sat and took one more look around the wide valley.

This is where I belong.

Morgan perched at the top of the tower on Founder's Hill, watching the activity going on all around him.

Taylor came running up the stairs, out of breath. "You. Have. To. Wait. For. Me. Alia said so."

Morgan grinned, letting Tanner have his sway over their shared body. "You're too slow."

"I wish I had wings."

"Maybe your dads will buy you a pair of bi-wings when you're older." Alia was watching over the child who had been one of Rogan's slaves while Xander and Jameson were in Oberon City. They had taken him in when they'd been unable to find his mother.

Alia had given Morgan the responsibility for a couple days while she and Smythe were out at Quince's farm.

It was a task he'd been happy to take. Tanner needed friends.

"Yeah, maybe."

Together they looked out over Gaelan. The city was being rebuilt from the ground up, the aeries rising floor by floor. Soon it would be a bustling metropolis again.

Ithani mingled with skythane in the rebuilding process, as a way of atoning for what they'd done. Morgan was here to oversee the process.

He flexed his new bright blue skythane wings, nervously considering the ground far below. This was his first time.

Are we ready?

Can't we go already? I'm dying to fly.

Morgan grinned. His dual nature was confusing sometimes, but Tanner was unequivocally *ready*. *Now.*

"Wanna come?" he asked Taylor.

"Could I?"

"Climb on my back, and I'll fly us back down."

Taylor did as he was told. He was a skinny kid. Morgan could bear his weight easily.

He stood on the parapet and spread his wings. "Here we go!" Then he leapt into the air to fly.

Taylor laughed in delight all the way down to the ground.

Xander Kinnson lay on his bed, head thrown back, his heart racing.

Jameson's wings flared out above his body, sweat running down his bare chest as they both reached climax.

Jameson moaned and collapsed on top of him, kissing his neck gently.

Xander pulled Jameson to his lips, kissing him back.

He turned to look out the window, as he had all those months ago on the day they'd first met. Instead of rain, the sun was shining brightly.

Xander stared warily at Erro's sun. If past was prologue, they'd have to deal with it again in another seven hundred fifty or eight hundred years. *Not my problem.*

"Hey, where are you?"

He turned back to look up at Jameson. "Sorry. Just thinking about the day we met." He reached up to touch the golden sun sigil that Jameson still wore around his neck.

A slow smile stretched across Jameson's face. "I remember. You weren't so hot on me back then."

Xander sat up, laughing. "You were kind of a bastard."

"*I* was a bastard?" Jameson shoved him back onto the bed playfully and got up, heading for the ionic shower.

Xander watched him go, enjoying his perfect ass.

Jameson climbed into the shower. "We have to get one of these in Errian and Gaelan."

They'd decided to split their time between the two skythane capitals, meaning they no longer needed Xander's apartment.

"Sure. We'll see if we can figure that out." He looked around at the empty apartment. He'd lived here for ten years, but since Alix had left him, the apartment had never felt like home.

Jameson stepped out of the shower, and Xander took a moment to enjoy the frontal view.

Jameson grinned, flexing his golden wings. "Your turn?"

"Nah. I think I wanna smell you on me a little while longer."

"Your choice." Jameson kissed him and put on his shirt, lacing it up, and then pulled on his pants. "Come on. We need to be in Errian for the meeting by noon."

"Slave driver." Xander got dressed, taking one last walk around the place. Home or not, he was going to miss it.

He and Jameson had a new life to build, with Taylor. It was time to move forward.

Xander slipped into his riding chaps—it was good to have his own clothes again—and pulled on his black riding gloves.

He pressed his palm up against the clear plas of the window. It was warm to the touch. Twin doors slid aside in the floor, and his hoverbike raised into view. The doors sealed shut below it.

"You ready?"

"Thought you'd never ask." Jameson slipped onto the bike behind him.

"Ravi, open the doors."

"Acknowledged."

The plas window split apart, a straight hairline crack that spread from the base of the window up to six feet off the floor. Clear doors formed in the plas, and then they opened outward, letting in the warm summer air.

"Hold on."

Jameson's arms snaked around his waist, and his lover was warm against his back.

Xander palmed the ignition key and the machine roared to life underneath him. He powered up the bike's amalite drive and released the brake, soaring out of the arco into the open air.

"Woo-hoo!" Jameson's wings flew open behind him as the hoverbike veered around to head toward the Gildensea and Errian.

Xander looked back at Jameson. "We just need a sunset and this would be perfect."

Jameson grinned and kissed his cheek from behind. "Who needs a sunset?"

GLOSSARY

Amalite: Raw ore found only on Oberon that serves as Common Worlds power source. Called heartstone by the ithani

AmSplor: Exploration division of the Northern American Union

Andra Madainn: Queen of the House of the Sun, Jameson's mother

Anellia: Pop singer capable of singing in triple harmony

Angela Havercamp: Jameson's adopted mother

Annama: Soul mate

Arcatus: Interstellar ship Jameson came in on from Tander's World

Arco: Vast buildings where most of Oberon City's citizens are housed

Arctus: City on Beta Tau

Argent Sea: Titania's sea

Arliss: The capital city of the dhagani

Arracha Grain: Native grain grown as a staple on Oberon

Ashalla: The Titania universe

Athrà: The virtual or spirit world of the ithani

Auxen: Forest herbivores in the Riamhwood

Aux: Larger cousins of the auxen, they live on the northern plains

Avea (also Hermia): The ithani name for Hermia, Oberon's red moon.

Ballifor: Small Titania village where Quince is from

Bandia: Titania's golden moon

Banga Tree: Low, wide Titania jungle trees that resemble barrels

Beta Tau: Jameson's homeworld
Bi-Wings: Artificial wings used by the enforcers on Titania
Blackware: Illegal apps/software/code
Blade File: Electronic file format
Blevons: White birds that live in underground burrows near the south pole
Blueoak: Native Oberon tree
Bolcà Island: Island in the Argent Sea
Boxcorn: Genetically modified square corn ears used as base for foods/fuels on Oberon
Braid Seneford: One of the OberCorp board members
Breed Match: The merging of the three sexes of ithani to create offspring
Builder Drone: Drone used for construction and renovation purposes
Cafflite: Oberon equivalent of coffee
Camspecs: Eye glasses with a built-in tri-dee camera
Castain, the: The "castle" in Errian, also called the House of the Sun
Cattorah, the: A ritual removal of a skythane's wings, usually as punishment for a severe crime
Cheth: The ithani word for corrinder
Chit: Portable cash chip
Christianist: Throwback religious sect that hearkens back to conservative "Christian" values
Cirq: Bio-interface in the temple that allows users to access the grid
Citrone: Native yellow fruit that grows on vines on Oberon
Colifir Tree: Red native tree that grows by rivers
Common Worlds: Loose-knit government of human worlds
Conjunction: Alignment of one of the moons of Oberon with the planet and sun
Corrinder: The plants used as building stock in **Errian;** also the white material the plants are made from. See also cheth
Corybryte: A sharp white skythane cheese
Creach: Scavenger birds on Titania
Creeper Vines: Native silver ground vegetation on Oberon
Crits: Credit/money
Croyol: Fungus that burns without smoke
Daedus Madainn: Prior King of the House of the Sun
Damella Sléite: Prior Queen of the House of the Moon

Danner Black: A skythane pith trade runner who helped instigate civil war between the skythane

Dark Market: Black market on Oberon, run by the Syndicate

Daro: One of Dani's lander guards

Davos Madainn: Prior King of the House of the Sun

Dawson: Rogan's henchman

Dax: One of Rogan's enforcers

Deathhawk: Deadly bird of prey native to Titania

Deca: Oberon's tenth month

Deireadh an Domhain: The Mountain

Demetrius River: Southern tributary to the Theseus

Deterrent Field: Rope that is used to create a field to deter the local wildlife, especially wereveren

Dhagani: The enemies of the ithani

Dillan Farrai: Quince's brother

Distortion Field: Shield generated by a small device that blocks electronic surveillance

Distortion Zone: Zone of electronic interference at the edge of Oberon

Dixon: An OberCorp enforcer

Dorthia: Erriani woman who lives in Taycrob

Drimm the Dragon: One of Titania's constellations

Earth-Standard: Timekeeping based on Earth's clock/calendar

Egeus: City on Oberon

Elyra Sléite: Prior Queen of the House of the Moon

Enforcers: Men who work as the "muscle" of the Syndicate

Eraysses Sea: A sea on Beta Tau.

Errian: City of the Sun (as in House of the)

Erriani: Citizens of the House of the Sun

Erro: Sun God; also the ithani name for the whole world

Ethilium: Growth hormone that stimulates the development of wings in the skythane

Faery Caves: Caverns in Titania's mountains, often lit by glowing blue ponds

Faery Ponds: Blue glowing ponds in the caverns on Titania

Fizzpop: Carbonated sugar-alcohol drink popular on Beta Tau

Fynx: One of the Gaelani skythane at Torr Talam

Farris: Assistant to the Prison Master

Feather Trees: Trees native to Oberon

Fennow Root: Natural antiseptic
First Wave: First human colonists on Oberon, also called skythane
Freyyr: The mountain in the north; means "forge" in the ithani language
Fynx: Gaelani man in the war camp
Gael: Moon God
Gaelan: City of the House of the Moon
Gaelani: Citizens of the House of the Moon
Galaxion Hotel: Interstellar hotel chain
Gildensea: Oberon's sea
Glow Sphere: Portable light source
Governor: Governmental head of Oberon
Governor's Residence: Vast estate where the Factor lives
Granth: Feline equivalents from Pleiades Six, valued for their leather
Great Division: Period after skythane refugees were chased out of Oberon to Titania
Great Retreat: The flight of the skythane settlers before the landers and Ober Corp
Gregg: OberCorp Employee
Gresachh: An ithani word meaning disgraceful, dishonorable, unthinkable and perverse
Grid, The: Oberon's data and communications network
Gridcode: Programming code, etc.
GSN: Great Sky Network, one of the Common Worlds news services
Gumba Tree: Tall, leafy native tree often used as a windbreak for farms on Oberon
Hallerwood: Golden-leaved trees native to northern Titania
Hachmoss: Yellow moss native to Oberon
Harrol: One of Xander's companions on the way to Errian
Heart, The: The center of the ithani city
Heart Fungus: See Croyol
Heartbrier Bush: Titania bush with heart-shaped leaves and orange flowers
Heartstone: see amalite
Heartwood: Forest on Beta Tau
Hermia (also Avea): One of Oberon's two moons—red-colored
Hesies: Xander's past life
High Slopes: Northern district of Oberon City, where the Spaceport is
Hippolyta: City on Oberon

Hoarberries: Little blue berries covered in a sweet white "frost"

Hollyhock Trees: Trees found in the valley of The Mountain

Honey Ale: Titania alcoholic drink

Harsorch: The parasite that keeps the world mind quiescent

House of the Sky: Ruins in the center of Oberon

House of the Stars: Royal retreat in the center of Titania

Hover-Plat: Transportation platform used to move small amounts of goods

Hoverbike: One of the main methods of personal transport in Oberon City

Hoversport: Hover craft used for human transport

Hunters, The: The name for the group of allies fighting the ithani

Ice Rat: Native Oberon scavenger that lives near the southern pole.

Ice Pine: White tree native to the northern climes of Oberon—the Rim Forest

Imprean: Carrier-pigeon like bird used to carry messages

Ironwood: Tall trees in Titania that are impervious to flame

Ithalia: The new city of the ithani

Ithani: Original inhabitants of Oberon/Titania

Joseph Havercamp: Jameson's adoptive father

Keff: Titanian equivalent of coffee—tastes like herbal tea and coconut.

Knacks: Oberon insect pests

Landed: to be stripped of your wings, usually as punishment for a criminal act

Landers: Second wave human settlers

Lightdump: Long lasting light source

Lyda: Sculptor of the statue of Gael at the House of the Stars

Lydia Madainn: Prior Queen of the House of the Sun

Lysander: One of Oberon's two moons—golden color

Marli: One of the original skythane colonists

Martach: Six-legged jungle cat on Titania

Mattis Vinder: An OberCorp headquarters employee

Memfiles: Memory files stored in a cirq and/or the local grid

Meso Bomb (MB): Bomb that works by averaging out the molecular content of everything within its radius

Midcity: Heart of Oberon City

Mikelos: Miner on Tander's World

Morgan Kinnson: Xander's foster father

Mora Mountains (Sléibhte Mora): Titania's mountian chain

Mountain, The: Location of one of the gates between the two worlds, close to the House of the Moon

MRE: Meal Ready to Eat

Mugjuice: Oberon beverage made with pith

Neamiah: Erriani person trapped with Quince in the mines

New Davos: City on Beta Tau

Nerve Cuffs: Handcuffs that cut off the nervous system

Nim: An Erriani man at Torr Talam

Nimfeach: Butterfly-like creatures on Titania

Norcrest: Small purple bush found in the plains north of the Riamhwood

Northern Glacier: At the north pole on Oberon

Nutrisynth Bar: Nutritional bars Xander likes

OberCorp: Corporation that controls most of Oberon—The Oberon Mining Corporation

Oberon: Also known as Split—the half world where the story takes place

Oberon City: Capital of Oberon, with about two million residents, most living in arcos

Obieberry: Native red stippled fruit on Oberon

Orn: Main river on Titania

Outland: Desert and wilds beyond Oberon City

Paraba Bush: Titania shrub that has berries that can be ground for oil

Philo: City on Oberon

Pith: Psychoamoratic drug derived from the sap of the púca tree in Titania

Plas: Versatile artificial material with the hardness of diamond and the malleability of plastic

Pleiades Six: One of the worlds of the Common Worlds

Plascreet: Variation of plas used in heavy construction; a concrete analogue

Pocans: Edible white fungus that resembles a string of pearls and tastes like chocolate and bread

Pod-mates: The three "person" family common among the ithani.

Preachers, The: rough rock band

Psych: Therapist

Psych Guild: Association of Psychs

Psychoamoratic: A drug with aphrodisiac qualities

Púca Tree: Tree which pith comes form

Pulse Laser: High-powered blast-pulse weapon used on transport ships

Pulse Pistol: Small pulse weapon

Pulse Rifle: Large pulse weapon
Pyramus Mountains: Mountain range along the Eastern edge of Oberon
Rangers: OberCorp soldiers used in military campaigns
Ravi: Xander's PA
Ravier: Erriani man who lives in Taycrob
Red Sands: Desert covering the southern part of Oberon
Red Shanks: Big red-trunked trees with large heart-shaped purple leaves, native to the Titanian jungle
Redfruit: Fruit native to Titania
Redoak: Tree native to Titania
Rentz Class Cargo Carrier: Heavy lifter that carries amalite ore up from Oberon to interstellars
Rhyl: One of Mylin's non-binary friends
Riamhwood: Forest on Titania
Riding Armor: Body armor Xander wears when riding
Rift: The split that divides Oberon and Titania
Rim Forest: Forest on the northern half of Oberon
Rinroot: A natural antibiotic on Titania
Rix: One of Xander's companions on the way to Errian
River Apples: Native Oberon water fruit
River Cat: Small scavenger the size and temperament of a raccoon
Rocthane: Access key to bring the worlds together
Rohin the Explorer: One of the first skythane to find Titania
Sailfighter: Ithani war ship. See also "sleith"
Schracknell: Small winged creatures from the time of the ithani
Scurf: Domesticated, one horned herbivores on Titania
Second Wave: The second set of human colonists, also called landers
Semi-Autonomous Grid: A connected web of data run by a government entity or business, and connected to the main planetary grid
Sera Thorpe: OberCorp board member.
Seven Weeks War: War between the Erriani and Gaelani twenty-five years before
Sevyrn Triani: One of the Erriani skythane Jameson saved
Shift: Moving Oberon into Titania's space
Shift Storm: The great tempest that accompanied the shift of Oberon to Titania's universe.

Silverbark: Tall, thin tree with silver bark, leaves, and a dark stripe on the northern side, native to Oberon

Skythane: First wave of human colonists, who have wings

Slander, The: Slums of Oberon City

Sleeper: Sleep drug patch

Sleith: White sail ships of the ithani

Slit: Transfer funds or information electronically

Sneach: skythane term for orphan—mischievous spirits who cause trouble or death

Split: Nickname for Oberon; also used for its broken side.

Squamwat: A small domesticated animal that imprints on its human owner and shows absolute loyalty

Standing Stones: Guardian statues outside the faery caverns on Titania

Stendril: A sleek, fast fish in the lakes of the Mora Mountains

Stim: Stimulant

Stim Cuffs: Handcuffs that can deliver an electric shock

Swamp Bear: Harmless forest creature

Symbol of the Two Gods: Tapping your right fist against your chest twice

Syndicate: Crime ring that controls the Slander

Synth Meat: Meat grown in a vat from a cellular culture

Synth Pack: A device to help regrow lost skin and tissue

Synthglass: A more expensive form of plas that radiates light when touched

Tamara Fine: OberCorp's head of PR

Tander's World: Mining colony where Jameson was stationed

Tanner Michael Henshaw: Morgan's human half

Tartanga Tree: Oberon riverside trees with broad, tripartite silver leaves

Taslit: A rite of passage for skythane youth

Taycrob: Small Erriani village of tree houses

Tazim: Venin's lover, deceased

Teanna: Skythane woman in Gaelan

Teva Glynt, Dr.: Medic at OberCorp

Tevin: Erriani boy Jameson saves from the invaders

Tharsis: Home to one of the Tander's World miners, Mikelos

Thera: Prior Queen of the House of the Sun

Theron Sléite: King of the Gaelani, Xander's father

Theseus River: Main river in Oberon

Thousand Cycles War: War between the ithani and dhagani

Titan Station: Receiving space station for visitors to Oberon

Titania: Half of the planet on the other side of the rift

Tobin: Skythane man with Jameson in the mines

Toree: Erriani person trapped with Quince in the mines

Torr Talam: Tower in the time of Elyra and Daedus

Traxon: A smaller, light gravity Common Worlds planet

Tri-dee: 3-D video, video player

Tri-dee Table: the display device for holographic images and films

Toreor: Small Gaelani village where Dani Black was born.

Tubers: Native Oberon edible plant—can be eaten cooked or raw, like a jicama

Turbien: Plants used to grow the towers of Errian; another name for corrinder

Tweener: Someone who is nonbinary or gender fluid

Urshu: The human/ithani/Oberon universe

Vassir Honym: Prison master on the Split

Veril: a small rabbitlike creature that lives in the Riamhwood

Verrim: One of the ithani from Jameson's memory

Verthex: The Erro equivalent of cockroaches

Virgo Sléite: Prior King of the House of the Moon

Virtual Space ("vir"): full immersion in the grid

Water Cane: Native Oberon edible plant

Wayabout: Skythane manhood ritual journey

Wempole: Short, squat trees with wide purple leaves and fragrant white flowers the size of two hands that smell like vanilla and honey, found in the northern Riamhwood

Wereveren: Birds that transform at night into lethal pecking machines

Wetreeds: Native plant with numbing properties

Wetware: Bio implants that allow humans to interface with machines and the grid

Whipcat: Deadly feline equivalents in the mountains of Titania

Whirill: Titanian bird that lives in the Riamhwood

Wing Man: Slang for the skythane

Wrenwood: Tree from Titania whose wood burns without smoke

Xiini: One of the ithani from Jameson's memory

Z Pronouns: The Ithani have a complex (to us) system of pronouns and relationships. Three ithani are required to bear a child. These are ze / zer / zers (roughly analogous to she / her / hers – the one who provides the egg), zi /

zim / zis (he / him / his – the one who provides the sperm), and za / zaf / zas (no human equivalent – the one who provides the organs to carry the child to term). In addition, when pregnancy occurs, the three forms unite into one (zee / zeer / zeers) until the child comes to term.

Zain: Sculptor of the statue of Erro at the House of the Stars

Zakka: Poisonous reptile in the Red Sands

Zaxxim: One of the ithani from Jameson's memory

Zenia: One of Xander's companions on the way to **Errian**

Zenix: Lena Preston's house AI

ZephyrCorp: The company that first "discovered" Oberon and opened it for human colonization

Zimbee: Large, harmless pollinator on Titania

Zorin: One of the ithani settlers sent to the dhagani homeworld

ABOUT THE AUTHOR

I live with my husband of 28 years in a Sacramento, California suburb, in a little yellow house with a brick fireplace and a couple pink flamingoes.

As a writer, I've always lived between *here and now* and *what could be*. Indoctrinated into fantasy-sci fi by my mother at the tender age of nine, I devoured her library. But as I grew up and read the golden age classics and modern works, I began to wonder where the people like me were.

After I came out at twenty three, I decided it was time to create stories I couldn't find at Waldenbooks. If there weren't many gay characters in my favorite genres, I would reimagine them myself, populating them with men who loved men. I would subvert them and remake them to my own ends. And if I was lucky enough, someone else would want to read them.

My friends say my brain works a little differently - I sees relationships between things that others miss, and get more done in a day than most folks manage in a week. Although I was born an introvert, I learned to reach outside himself and connect with others like me.

I write stories that subvert expectations, and transform sci fi, fantasy, and contemporary worlds into something new and unexpected. I run both Queer Sci Fi and QueeRomance Ink with Mark, sites that bring people like us together to promote and celebrate fiction that reflects us.

I was recognized as one of the top new gay authors in the 2017 Rainbow Awards, and my debut novel "Skythane" received two awards. In 2019, I won Rainbow Awards for three other books, and became full member of the Science Fiction and Fantasy Writers of America in 2020.

My writing, whether queer romance or genre fiction (or a little bit of both) brings LGBTQ+ energy to my stories, infusing them with love, beauty and power and making them soar. I imagine a world that *could be*, and in the process, maybe changes the world that is just a little.

ALSO BY J. SCOTT COATSWORTH

Liminal Sky: Ariadne Cycle:

The Stark Divide | The Rising Tide | The Shoreless Sea

Liminal Sky: Oberon Cycle:

Skythane | Lander | Ithani

Liminal Sky: Redemption Cycle:

Dropnauts (May 2021)

Other Sci Fi/Fantasy:

The Autumn Lands | Cailleadhama | The Great North | Homecoming | The Last Run | Spells & Stardust Anthology | Wonderland

Contemporary/Magical Realism:

Between the Lines | I Only Want to Be With You | Flames (June 2021) | The River City Chronicles | Slow Thaw

99¢ Shorts:

Across the Transom | Tharassan Rain (March 2021)

Audio:

Cailleadhama (May 2021) | The Stark Divide (Summer 2021) | The River City Chronicles (Summer/Fall 2021)

FROM THE STARK DIVIDE
LIMINAL SKY: ARIADNE CYCLE BOOK ONE

Enjoy a little teaser for The Stark Divide - book one of Liminal Sky: The Ariadne Cycle.

Lex floated along with the ocean current. Her arms were spread out wide, her jet-black hair adrift on the surface of the water. For once, she felt at peace. Truly herself.

The sun shone above her, and she soaked up its rays, basking in its golden glow. Her blue eyes stared up at the equally blue sky, not a cloud in sight. Soon she'd be called back to duty. Soon she'd once again have to face her limited, jury-rigged day-to-day existence. For a few moments, she was free to just drift.

The *Dressler*, a Mission-class AmSplor ship, sailed toward a city-sized rock named 43 Ariadne, harvested from the asteroid belt and placed in trailing orbit behind Earth. The starfish-shaped ship flew on the solar wind, drinking in ionized hydrogen and other trace elements that allowed her to breathe and grow, coursing slowly through the dark reaches of space between Earth and the sun. The *Dressler* lived on solar wind and space dust, accumulating them with her web of gossamer sails between her arms, filtering them down into her compact body for processing.

The detritus flew out behind her, leaving a jet trail across the void to mark her passing, leading back to Earth. Somewhere out there, their destination awaited them, an asteroid floating on a sea of stars.

~

"*Dressler*, schematic," Colin McAvery, ship's captain and a third of the crew, called out to the ship-mind.

A three-dimensional image of the ship appeared above the smooth console. Her five living arms, reaching out from her central core, were lit with a golden glow, and the mechanical bits of instrumentation shone in red. In real life, she was almost two hundred meters from tip to tip.

Between those arms stretched her solar wings, a ghostly green film like the sails of the *Flying Dutchman*.

"You're a pretty thing," he said softly. He loved these ships, their delicate beauty as they floated through the starry void.

"Thank you, Captain." The ship-mind sounded happy with the compliment—his imagination running wild. Minds didn't have real emotions, though they sometimes approximated them.

He cross-checked the heading to be sure they remained on course to deliver their payload, the man-sized seed that was being dragged on a tether behind the ship. Humanity's ticket to the stars at a time when life on Earth was getting rapidly worse.

All of space was spread out before him, seen through the clear expanse of plasform set into the ship's living walls. His own face, trimmed blond hair, and deep brown eyes, stared back at him, superimposed over the vivid starscape.

At thirty, Colin was in the prime of his career. He was a starship captain, and yet sometimes he felt like little more than a bus driver. After this run… well, he'd have to see what other opportunities might be awaiting him. Maybe the doc was right, and this was the start of a whole new chapter for mankind. They might need a guy like him.

The walls of the bridge emitted a faint but healthy golden glow, providing light for his work at the curved mechanical console that filled half the room. He traced out the T-Line to their destination. "*Dressler*, we're looking a little wobbly." Colin frowned. Some irregularity in the course was common—the ship was constantly adjusting its trajectory—but she usually corrected it before he noticed.

"Affirmative, Captain." The ship-mind's miniature chosen likeness appeared above the touch board. She was all professional today, dressed in a standard AmSplor uniform, dark hair pulled back in a bun, and about a third life-sized.

The image was nothing more than a projection of the ship-mind, a fairy tale, but Colin appreciated the effort she took to humanize her appearance. Artificial mind or not, he always treated minds with respect.

"There's a blockage in arm four. I've sent out a scout to correct it."

The *Dressler* was well into slowdown now, her pre-arrival phase as she bled off her speed, and they expected to reach 43 Ariadne in another fifteen hours.

Pity no one had yet cracked the whole hyperspace thing. Colin chuckled. Asimov would be disappointed. "*Dressler*, show me Earth, please."

A small blue dot appeared in the middle of his screen.

"*Dressler*, three dimensions, a bit larger, please." The beautiful blue-green world spun before him in all its glory.

Appearances could be deceiving. Even with scrubbers working tirelessly night and day to clean the excess carbon dioxide from the air, the home world was still running dangerously warm.

He watched the image in front of him as the East Coast of the North American Union spun slowly into view. Florida was a sliver of its former self, and where New York City's lights had once shone, there was now only blue. If it *had* been night, Fargo, the capital of the Northern States, would have outshone most of the other cities below. The floods that had wiped out many of the world's coastal cities had also knocked down Earth's population, which was only now reaching the levels it had seen in the early twenty-first century.

All those new souls had been born into a warm, arid world.

We did it to ourselves. Colin, who had known nothing besides the hot planet he called home, wondered what it had been like those many years before *the Heat*.

Anastasia Anatov leafed through her father, Dimitri's, old paper journal. She liked to look through it once a day, to see his spidery handwriting and remember what he had been like. It was a bit old and dusty now, but it was one of her most cherished possessions.

She sighed and put it away in a storage nook in her lab.

She left the room and pulled herself gracefully along the runway, the central corridor of the ship, using the metal rungs embedded in the walls. She was much more comfortable in low or zero g than she was in Earth normal, where her tall, lanky form made her feel awkward around others. She was a loner at heart, and the emptiness of space appealed to her.

Her father had designed the Mission-class ships. It was something she rarely spoke of, but she was intensely proud of him. These ships were still imperfect, the combination of a hellishly complicated genetic code and after-the-fact fittings of mechanical parts, like the rungs she used now to move through the weightless environment.

Did it hurt when someone drilled into the living tissue to install mechanics, living quarters, and observation blisters? Her father had always maintained that the ship-minds felt no pain. She wasn't so sure. Men were often dismissive of the things they didn't understand.

Either way, she was stuck on the small ship for the duration with two men, neither of whom were interested in her. The captain was gay, and Jackson was married.

Too bad the ship roster hadn't included another woman or two.

She placed her hand on a hardened sensor callus next to the door valve and the ship obliged, recognizing her. The door spiraled open to show the viewport beyond.

She pulled herself into the room and floated before the wide expanse of transparent plasform, staring out at the seed being hauled behind them.

Nothing else mattered. Whatever she had to do to get this project launched, she would do it. She'd already made some morally questionable choices along the way—including looking the other way when a bundle of cash had changed hands at the Institute.

She was so close now, and she couldn't let anything get in the way.

Earth was a lost cause. It was only a matter of time before the world imploded. Only the seeds could give mankind a fighting chance to go on.

From the viewport, there was little to see. The seed was a two-meter-long brown ovoid, made of a hard, dark organic material, scarred and pitted by the continual abrasion of the dust that escaped the great sails. So cold out there, but the seed was dormant, unfeeling. The cold would keep it that way until the time came for its seedling stage.

She'd created three of the seeds with her funding. This one, bound for the asteroid 43 Ariadne, was the first. It was the next step in evolution beyond the *Dressler* and carried with it the hopes of all humankind.

It also represented ten years of her life and work.

Maybe, just maybe, we're ready for the next step.

THE CREW's third and final member, Jackson Hammond, hung upside down in the ship's hold, grunting as he refit one of the feed pipes that carried the ship's electronics through the bowels of this weird animal-mechanical hybrid. Although "up" and "down" were slight on a ship where the centrifugal force created a "gravity" only a fraction of what it was on Earth.

As the ship's engineer, Jackson was responsible for keeping the mechanics functioning—a challenge in a living organism like the *Dressler*.

With cold, hard metal, one dealt with the occasional metal fatigue, poor workmanship, and at times just ass-backward reality. But the parts didn't regularly grow or shrink, and it wasn't always necessary to rejigger the ones that had fit perfectly just the day before. Even after ten years in these things, he still found it a little creepy to be riding inside the belly of the beast. It was too Jonah and the Whale for his taste.

Jackson rubbed the sweat away from his eyes with the back of his arm. As he shaved down the end of a pipe to make it fit more snugly against the small orifice in the ship's wall, he touched the little silver cross that hung around his neck. It had been a present from his priest, Father Vincenzo, at his son Aaron's First Communion in the Reformed Catholic Evangelical Church.

The boy was seven years old now, with a shock of red hair and green eyes like his dad, and his mother's beautiful skin. He'd spent months preparing for his Communion Day, and Jackson remembered fondly the moment when his son had taken the Body and Blood of Christ for the first time, surprise registering on his little face at the strange taste of the wine.

Aaron's Communion Day had been a high point for Jackson, just a week before his current mission. He was so proud of his two boys. *Miss you guys. I'll be home soon.*

Lately he hadn't been sleeping well, his dreams filled with a dark-haired, blue-eyed vixen. He was happily married. He shouldn't be having such dreams.

Jackson shook his head. Being locked up in a tin can in space did strange things to a person sometimes. *I should be home with Glory and the boys.*

One way or another, this mission would be his last.

He'd been recruited as a teen.

AT THIRTEEN, Jackson had learned the basics of engineering doing black-tech work for the gangs that ran what was left of the Big Apple after the Rise—a warren of interconnected skyrises, linked mostly by boats and ropes and makeshift bridges.

Everything north of Twenty-Third was controlled by the Hex, a black-tech co-op that specialized in bootlegged dreamcasts, including modified versions that catered to some of the more questionable tastes of the North American States. South of Twenty-Third belonged to the Red Badge, a lawless group of technophiles involved in domestic espionage and wetware arts.

Jackson had grown up in the drowned city, abandoned by his mother and forced to rely on his own intelligence and instincts to survive in a rapidly changing world.

He'd found his way to the Red Badge and discovered a talent for ecosystem work, taking over and soon expanding one of the rooftop farms that supplied the drowned city with a subsistence diet. An illegal wetware upgrade let him tap directly into the systems he worked on, seeing the circuits and pathways in his head.

He increased the Badge's food production fivefold and branched out beyond the nearly tasteless molds and edible fungi that thrived in the warm, humid environment.

It was on one of his rooftop "gardens" that his life had changed one warm summer evening.

He was underneath one of the condenser units that pulled water from the air for irrigation. All of eighteen years old, he was responsible for the food production for the entire Red Badge.

He'd run through the unit's diagnostics app to no avail. Damned piece of shit couldn't find a thing wrong.

In the end, it had come down to something purely physical—tightening down a pipe bolt where the condenser interfaced with the irrigation system.

Satisfied with the work, he stood, wiping the sweat off his bare chest, and glared into the setting sun out over the East River. It was more an inland sea now, but the old names still stuck.

There was a faint whirring behind him, and he spun around. A bug drone hovered about a foot away, glistening in the sun. He stared at it for a moment, then reached out to swat it down. Probably from the Hex.

It evaded his grasp, and he felt a sharp pain in his neck.

He went limp, and everything turned black as he tumbled into one of his garden beds.

He awoke in Fargo, recruited by AmSplor to serve in the space agency's Frontier Station, his life changed irrevocably.

A STRANGE SENSATION brought him back to the present.

His right hand was wet. Startled, he looked down. It was covered with blood.

Dressler, *we have a problem,* he said through his private affinity-link with the ship-mind.